"WELL SIR..."

...he cleared his throat again and said, "We found her in the number eight compartment..."

—from "Stowaway"

ABOUT MACK REYNOLDS...

Mack Reynolds was one of the best-loved science fiction writers in the history of the entire genre. He started writing for the sci-fi pulp magazines back in the 1950s. His work appeared in all the leading science fiction magazines of his day. He also wrote dozens of well-received novels, including numerous entries in both his "United Planets" and "Joe Mauser" series. His first science fiction stories began appearing as early as 1950. Reynolds was born in Corcoran, California in 1917. He passed away in 1983. Here is a top-of-the-line collection of twenty-one of his most imaginative tales...

TABLE OF CONTENTS

MASTERS OF

SCIENCE FICTION

Volume 4

MACK REYNOLDS
Part one: "STOWAWAY"
and other stories

ARMCHAIR FICTION
PO Box 4369, Medford, Oregon 97504

The original text of these stories first appeared in *Science Fiction Quarterly, Imagination, IF, Amazing Stories, Planet Stories, Future Science Fiction, Fantastic Stories, Orbit, Other Worlds, Science Stories, Worlds Beyond, Universe Science Fiction, Super Science, and Fantastic Adventures.*

Cover suggests a scene from *Stowaway*

For more information about Armchair Books and products, visit our website at…

www.armchairfiction.com

Or email us at…

armchairfiction@yahoo.com

The Man in the Moon

Can man reach the moon today? Is it possible to cross the void? A story similar to the one you read here may be in tomorrow's paper!

"...to send an unmanned rocket to the moon and let it crash...is close enough to present technological accomplishments so that its design and construction are possible without any major inventions. Its realization is essentially a question of hard work and money.

"The manned moonship is a different story. The performance expected of it is, naturally, that it take off from earth, go to the moon, land, take off from the moon, and return to earth. And that...is beyond our present ability."

—from *Conquest of Space* by Willy Ley, published 1949

For military security reasons—Terra was still governed by numerous antagonistic, warlike nations—the first interplanetary travel was not disclosed to the public for approximately a year after it had been successfully accomplished. The first base on Luna was established by the United States, a capitalistic nation which existed on the North American continent during the 18th, 19th and 20th Centuries."

—from the *Encyclopedia Galactica*, published 2355 A. D.

THE THREE didn't have to be told this was it, but had they not already known, the general's mannerisms would have betrayed the importance of the occasion. He stood, West Point rigid, and cleared his throat characteristically before speaking.

"More than two years ago you gentlemen volunteered with some forty others for particularly hazardous duty. Only in the past six months have you learned what this duty was to be." He rumbled in his throat again. "Your names have been chosen by lot from among the thirty-two remaining of the original group. You still have the opportunity of withdrawing—your last opportunity."

Fred Gabowski and Jeff Stevens stirred in their chairs. Matt Evans sat impassively; nothing was said.

The general went on. "I should warn you that Stoddard, McCay and Bently didn't get through." He eyed them, one at a time. "All right," he rapped, as though irritated at their continued silence, "this is your final briefing. It is now X-20."

He handed them charts reproduced on tissue thin paper. "You should be as familiar with these by now, as with your own faces, however, it is unknown what mental strains you may be under, so you will each take a copy."

He shot a glance at his watch, cleared his throat and went on. "Briefly, the situation is this: We have fired almost one hundred rockets in all, directing them at Alphonsus Crater. Of these, nearly half reached Luna; only sixteen, however, landed in Alphonsus. Of the others, two or three are in Albategnius, six in Arzachel, five in Ptolemaeus. All should be recovered eventually but that does not concern us at present; we are interested in the sixteen in Alphonsus.

"Three types of rockets have been used. Neptune IX, the model that first crashed on Luna, is represented twice among the sixteen in Alphonsus. The payload was negligible and since they contained insufficient fuel for breaking it is to be assumed they have been completely shattered, landing as they did at the speed of over seven thousand miles an hour.

"The second type of rocket utilized, Neptune XII, is our freighter. In them we have attempted to carry a payload of as high as one ton. Fourteen of them, of eighty-three fired, landed in Alphonsus Crater; to what extent they were damaged we are uncertain.

"The final type, Neptune XIII, is designed to carry a payload of approximately three hundred pounds, and as you know, carries a pilot. Thus far, of the three fired, none made Alphonsus." He cleared his throat again, shot another glance at his wristwatch. "Any questions, thus far?"

Matt Evans asked softly, "What happened to McCay, Bently and Stoddard?" He'd been Dick McCay's roommate for almost a year.

THE GENERAL had relaxed somewhat as he talked, now he stiffened again. "Lieutenant McCay's rocket exploded at about two hundred and fifty miles, just as he was leaving earth's atmosphere. We don't know what happened to Captain Bently; our telescopes gave no indication that he reached Luna at all. Colonel Stoddard landed in Arzachel Crater, about fifty miles from his destination. At this time, we don't know whether or not he is alive." He anticipated the next question. "He had oxygen for eight days... Anything else?"

The general went on, "Colonel Stoddard was to be in command of the Luna base; Major Gabowski will now take his place." He rumbled in his throat. "Captain Evans will be second in command and in...er—emergency, will take over."

Jeff Stevens had barely heard the last. Inwardly he tingled. So Larry Stoddard was dead.

The general was still speaking, "*Brennschluss* will be reached on your booster after only three seconds. *Brennschluss* on your first step rocket will be reached at approximately fifty miles altitude; your second will see you well out of earth's atmosphere. You'll have about eight minutes of acceleration in all." He hesitated, then rapped, "We've been afraid you might not have quite sufficient fuel for a safe landing on Luna, consequently, we're giving you an acceleration of slightly more than four gravities, in an attempt to stretch out your supply.

"We're also cutting down on your oxygen supply to a total of six days. The others had eight. If you land in Alphonsus, six will be ample; if you don't, you'll probably be better off with the smaller amount. The extra capacity will be used for fuel."

The general's eyes flicked to his watch. "X-S gentlemen." They came to their feet hurriedly.

"One last word. We have just heard through Intelligence that our potential enemy has succeeded in establishing a Space Station. I'm not going to point out what this means; you know. The important thing is that we have less time than we thought. Either a Space Station or a Luna base completely dominates earth in the military sense; we must have one to counterbalance theirs." He snorted indignantly. "Every authority on the subject knew the Station in Space was the practical first step, but, no, we have to get our appropriations through men who are motivated by the fact that a base on Luna sounds more glamorous than a pseudo-satellite spinning around Terra at an altitude of approximately six hundred and fifty miles."

They filed out past him from the concrete blockhouse into the cold New Mexico dawn. He shook their hands and cleared his throat apologetically as they went. He didn't expect to see any of them again.

Captain Jeff Stevens knew it was deliberate, this waiting until the last moment before they were informed of the flight. The psycho-technicians had figured it that way; they didn't want you to have time to get your wind up. A red star shell blossomed over the blockhouse; two minutes to go.

They trotted to the concrete firing tables, each to his own ship. Stevens had only seconds to drink in the surroundings. Not that he wasn't already thoroughly familiar with them. It was just, well—

THE SMALL plateau, principally man-made, on the twelve thousand foot mountain. The fuel trucks, now empty and at a discreet distance from the heavy concrete aprons which supported the would-be spaceships. The almost indestructible blockhouse with its ten foot thick walls, its pyramidal roof, twenty-seven feet thick. The spaceships themselves, the three of them; massive, tremendous, with their boosters and two steps aggregating well over two hundred tons.

He scurried up the ladder to *Alice*, the name he'd inwardly chosen long ago for the Neptune XIII that would be assigned him. From the corner of his eye he could see Evans and Gabowski entering their craft.

Alice was almost lost in the bulks of *Step One* and *Step Two*. Her stubby wings were merged into the second step rocket, which in its turn was almost completely lost in the gigantic first step.

He was inside and lashing his slight body into the gimbals surrounded acceleration chair which would be his home for the next four days—if he was lucky. For the next four minutes, perhaps, if not.

It was seconds now. Suddenly his naturally nervous temperament boiled over, he wanted to scream, "NO!" He ran a thin hand over chin and mouth. He took it all back; his volunteering for this mad escapade was all a mistake; it was suicide!

He could sense, almost *feel*, valves opening, pumps beginning to stir; the liquid hydrogen and the ozone of the booster device beginning to gush into the booster motor. The initial ignition.

The roar began, audible, easily audible, even within his tiny compartment in the nose of *Alice*. It rose heavily, thunderously, penetratingly. This was it; there was nothing that could be done now. Outside, someone was yelling, "Rocket away!" But be was spared hearing that.

He could feel the chair give beneath him, gently. The booster was lifting the heavy mass from the firing table; in seconds *step one* would take over and the four gravities acceleration would begin. His eyes darted about the small cubicle, checking; as though there was anything he could do, even if something was wrong.

The acceleration chair sank deeply and the grip of the four gravities seized his small bulk as though to crush him. He felt darkness closing in. The general had said that in order to stretch fuel they were going to be given more than the four gravities for which they'd been trained; evidently, they were getting considerably more.

He could feel the *Alice* tilt sharply, roughly ninety degrees, and through the numbness momentarily felt another edge of fear; something had gone wrong. Then he realized the automatic tilting mechanism was in operation, directing the ship to the point Luna would occupy four days in the future, taking advantage of the velocity of the earth's rotation. Of necessity, the rocket had been fired vertically, but now it had assumed its true course.

He felt, as well as heard, the roar of the rockets diminish then swell again. He'd reached *Brennschluss* of *step one*, it had burned out and fallen away, leaving *Alice* and *step two* to go on by themselves. Shortly, *step two* would drop away as well and the comparatively small bulk of *Alice* would continue alone.

It occurred to him that the ship was already invisible from the base. Possibly they could still see the flame of his jets, but that too would be gone in seconds.

AND SUDDENLY it was over, unbelievably over. From the crush of more than four gravities he felt sudden relief. The acceleration was falling off, not all at once, but rapidly. His breathing, slightly labored before, now eased. He'd reached a speed of nearly seven miles per second, the escape velocity from Terra, and the integrating accelerometer had cut the motors.

The important phase of the trip was accomplished. He had the speed now to carry *Alice* to that point, about 215,600 miles from earth, where he would begin to fall moon ward. That would be the crisis. Would he have the fuel to brake his fall; to direct *Alice* to Alphonsus Crater? Any other point of landing would mean as certain death as though he had blown up in space.

The full effect of free flight was now upon him. Lashed as he was in the acceleration chair, he remained stationary, but he could *feel* the weightlessness that would be his until the motors cut in again. At the same time, his deep fears dropped away. The psycho-technicians had said they'd feel this way; it was principally the subsonic vibrations. The rocket motors had set up noise from all the registers of which sound is possible, and hadn't halted there; the human ear hadn't been able to pick up the subsonic notes, but the fear that accompanies them had been present.

It was quiet. After the roar of the motors, it was impossibly quiet. And that was the most startling feature of his experience; he hadn't thought of that—how still it would be.

He said experimentally, "Well, this is it," and felt foolish at the touch of braggadocio in his voice.

It came to him that he hadn't looked out as yet. He shot a hand over to the shutter, which covered the plastic window to his right, and swore when it flew up against the metal shutter. He hadn't corrected for the complete lack of gravity. He'd have to get used to this; he tried again and the shutter slid back easily.

Black, black space surrounded him. He peered behind for earth, a hollowness in his belly. There it was beneath him; he could see faint outlines on the massive ball; the Pacific, the Atlantic, most of North America. Extensive cloud formations looked like patches of snow on the ground.

His stare went out into space itself. Bright, and endlessly more numerous than he'd ever seen while earthbound, the stars filled the sky in all directions. Off to one side, the sun startled him with its appearance; a halo, a luminous crown, encircled its blinding brightness. He realized it was the corona, lying outside the chromosphere, or region of colored prominences, and visible on earth only during a total eclipse.

He could barely make out, near the sun, his destination. Luna! From here it looked small and inconsequential, with the tremendous bulk of Terra dwarfing it at one extent, the brilliant Sol on the other.

HE FELT, vaguely, that something was wrong with his sense of balance, and recalled that the medical authorities at the base had worried about that angle. They had been of the opinion that the one organ in the whole human organism that would be effected by the complete lack of gravity in space flight would be the organ of balance, those liquid filled tubes in the inner ear. They had been of the opinion, too, that other organs would quickly improvise means of circumventing the trouble. He shrugged; at least, he'd soon know.

Certainly, there was no reason to believe any other organs would refuse to operate. None of them, stomach, lungs, heart, kidneys, intestines, depended upon gravitation to function.

In some respects this first space flight was like the first airplane ride he had experienced as a child of twelve. It had seemed when he climbed into the plane, that the whole trip must be the most fascinating experience that could ever happen. But after watching the ground drop away, after looking down at the earth below and seeing it from the different perspective; after trying to spot roads, cars, hills, towns, the airplane ride became just a trifle boring. You quickly accepted the new things to be seen—and then there was nothing more.

So it was in space. After a comparatively short period of extreme interest in Terra's new appearance, as it slowly lessened in size, after the new aspect of the stars and of Sol and the destination, Luna, interest gave way to boredom, and he grunted inwardly at the prospect of being confined for four days to this tiny cubicle.

He checked the fuel gauges. They didn't tell him definitely if there was going to be enough or not; it would depend on just how much he was going to need for the unpredictable, the amount for corrections as he tried to settle in Alphonsus. Certainly he wouldn't have much to spare.

That brought Colonel Stoddard to mind. What had happened to Larry Stoddard? He'd made it safely away from Terra—while Dick McCay had blown up at the point of leaving earth's atmosphere. He'd even made it to Luna—while Bently became lost somewhere in-between. But he hadn't made the right point. He'd missed Alphonsus and landed fifty miles away in the neighboring crater of…what was it the general had said?…yeah, Arzachel.

He wondered if Alice Stoddard knew her husband had died trying to make the initial landing on Luna. No, of course not; she didn't even know to what service he belonged, thinking him an Air Forces officer. Jeff Stevens snorted in protest. Here Stoddard McCay, Bently, Evans, Gabowski and himself were—three of them already dead in the attempt—trying to establish an American base on Luna, and their countrymen weren't aware of the effort. Didn't even know there was a fledging Space Service in the armed forces of the nation.

He was trying to wrench his mind away from Alice Stoddard, but it wasn't working. There'd never been anyone for him but Alice. He made a wry face; now there probably never would be.

It had been Alice for months, for years. For one reason or another, they'd put off their marriage a half dozen times. It'd been bad for the morale of both, but there hadn't been any alternative. The last time had been a year ago; he'd received orders shifting him to New Mexico and again the wedding was *temporarily* postponed.

When next he saw Alice she was Mrs. Larry Stoddard.

JEFF STEVENS shook his head sharply. He wasn't going to be able to spend the next four days crying in his beer. That was behind now, the important things were ahead.

It wouldn't be a bad idea to check his supplies. The total payload of his Neptune XIII was three hundred pounds. He took up almost a hundred and twenty pounds of that, complete with clothes. It would have been a hundred and thirty once, but they'd starved him down to the lowest point consistent with health, before the blast-off. Every *ounce* counted here; he and Stoddard and the rest had been chosen for their size primarily.

He checked his water, finding two quarts of it. His eyes widened in disbelief; surely they didn't expect two quarts of water— He quickly investigated his food supply. There was none—not really; some chocolate, a few squares, a modicum of dried beef, a half dozen different types of pills. They were insane! How did they expect him to live...? He ran his hand nervously over his chin and mouth, pinched his lower lip.

Jeff Stevens drew up short, conquering the fright that had momentarily risen to the surface. The water and food here were enough to carry him to Luna; if he didn't make Luna, it didn't make any difference. If he did, every ounce that might have been expended on carrying water or food, was better used otherwise—for fuel. He stared at the pills and dried beef sourly. What had he expected, Turkey dinner?

Deliberately tearing his mind away from food and drink, he forced it to consider other aspects of his situation. It came to mind that he was traveling at the speed of twenty-five thousand miles an hour; except for the other five who were on this same mission, no man had ever reached that before. He felt no sensation of velocity whatsoever; they'd told him he wouldn't, that the human body senses *changes* in velocity, but has no way of detecting speed itself. He might as well be doing a hundred thousand miles an hour, or be stationary; there was no sensation.

Actually, of course, his speed was slowly falling off. After *Alice* had reached *Brennschluss*, at roughly seven miles per second speed, the motors were cut and now the earth's gravitational attraction was knocking off just short of thirty-two feet per second of velocity each second. The way it had been planned, he would be traveling at as low as a few feet a second by the time he reached the dividing line between the gravities of Terra and Luna.

HE SLID back the shutter on his left and looked out. The view was essentially the same. He remembered that there had been some debate about the advisability of the plastic windows, and shuddered at the thought of not having them. To be enclosed in this closet-sized cubicle without any way of seeing out, without reading material—the weight couldn't be afforded—without any manner of spending his time; without even a watch to check the passing of that time. He would have gone stark raving mad.

Perhaps he would yet; even with the windows. Perhaps that was what had happened to Colonel Stoddard. He tried to drive the thought from his mind. Why did he continually return to the man? Larry Stoddard, five feet four inches and one hundred and twenty pounds of Georgia born and bred, would-be aristocrat. Ever since they'd first met, Jeff Stevens' personality had clashed with the other's.

And it was one occasion in which the dislike couldn't be blamed on a subconscious antagonism brought about by his inferiority complex. Jeff Stevens was aware that he went through life like a nervous bantam rooster, trying to prove to the world and to himself that he was as big as the next man. Actually, his volunteering for this…

There he went again. He had four days and more of this time on his hands. If he couldn't keep his mind from doing cartwheels he was going to be loony by the time he reached Luna. He grinned sourly; he'd have to remember that pun in case he ever got the chance to tell the story of this trip.

There was no night and no day; there was no sound and there was nothing to do; there was practically no food to eat and little water to drink. And this lasted for four days.

There was nothing to do but sit and think.

Even the fraction of weight of a watch had been begrudged him. He slept fitfully a score of times, not knowing for how long; it might have been minutes or hours.

Luna was growing in the sky now; larger than earth. Jeff Stevens had no feeling of velocity, but he knew his speed must have fallen off tremendously. Somewhere in here he was going to touch that line of equality of gravitational attraction between Terra and its satellite, then he'd stop *rising* from earth and start *falling* toward its moon.

He checked carefully with the light, simple instruments they'd allowed him as part of the *Alice's* payload and estimated he was some four thousand miles off Luna now; too soon to start braking if he wanted to combine that operation with steering his craft toward Alphonsus Crater.

He watched now, excitedly. He could already pick out land-marks: Ptolemaeus, about ninety miles across; Albategnius, about eight miles in diameter; Arzachel, the crater in which Stoddard had crashed, some sixty miles. And Alphonsus, his target, sixty-five miles in diameter.

He ran his hand over his mouth and chin nervously, and felt warm sweat on his palms. The game was to wait but all his instincts were to try and do something, to try and guide the *Alice* toward its goal.

He must control himself. Fuel was life.

IT WAS TIME to turn the rocket about so that its rocket tube tail would point in the direction of Luna. A simple wheel, mounted universally and hand operated, accomplished this. His ship, its tanks still containing the fuel necessary for braking, weighed some five tons. The wheel weighed five pounds; by spinning it two thousand revolutions, the ship turned against the momentum until its direction was reversed.

The instruments which would control his landing were automatic; most of them, at least. His job, as pilot, was to so direct the firing of his remaining fuel that he set the *Alice* down in the designated area. He watched anxiously for any indication that additional directional firing at this altitude would be necessary; thus far it didn't seem to be.

He figured his best bet would be to wait until the last moment before braking, thus being able to check best on Alphonsus. Actually, all he'd need was a bit over two minutes, if he was willing to take the physical hardship of the higher acceleration.

This was it!

He touched the ignition switch, moved his hands desperately. The motors came to life, roaring, moaning, *howling!*

He was directly above Alphonsus; the original aim had been perfect. The four gravities hit him like a sledge; for a period of four days he'd lived in free space, weightless, now he was returning not merely to earth gravity but to four times it.

But he couldn't afford to black out! If ever, he had to remain conscious; the many months of training came to stand him in good stead now. He kept at his controls.

He was down! Unbelievably, he was down. The *Alice* was resting on her hydraulic stilts in Alphonsus Crater; he'd succeeded—thus far.

The four gravities were gone and in their place was Luna's normal gravity, approximately one sixth of Terra's. It didn't seem over strange, at that. His four days without gravity at all prepared him for the experience.

This was it then; and there was no time to sit and philosophize. He had only hours of time before his oxygen supply was gone; besides, he needed food and water—but quick. His inactive four days in the *Alice* had used little energy and he'd been able to get by with the chocolate, the pills and the pint of water per twenty-four hours. But it was different now.

He peered through his plastic windows. The view wasn't as strange as it might have been; there were portions of New Mexico and Arizona, which didn't look so very different. The ringwall surrounding the crater was high and spectacular, somewhat like the Sierra Nevada's seen from the east; the floor seemed to be covered with fine sand or pumice, perhaps dust would be the more accurate term. A supreme wasteland, beautiful in its desolation.

Man was on Luna at last, but he had no time for seeking the answers to the problems that had baffled the astronomers so long. No time to discover the true nature of the *rills* and *rays*. No time to explore the Crater Plato to find if there was moisture there; no time to discover the nature of the smooth floor of the ninety mile long Great Valley; no time for the snow storms on Mount Pico, nor the possible clouds or vegetation in Eratosthenes Crater. No time for any of the riddles of the moon.

Jeff Stevens was fighting desperately for life.

HE BROUGHT out the small, lightweight telescope and searched the floor of Alphonsus. The general had said fourteen of the freighter rockets had landed; where each had touched in relation to himself was another question. Gabowski's and Evans' rockets would bring the number up to sixteen—if they'd made it.

He was about twenty miles from the ringwall; roughly ten from the small central peak of the crater. It was about as good a position as he could have chosen. But now pure luck was involved.

He picked up one of the freighters almost immediately. It lay on its side not more than four or five miles away; a Neptune XII, painted blue; food, water, medical supplies, utensils. Relief flooded through him, but he withstood the urge to make for it immediately. Hungry and thirsty though he was, there were more pressing problems.

Continuing his search he located three more of the freighter rockets, varyingly colored and at varying distances, but he could find no trace of Gabowski and Evans. Fear was beginning to well up inside him, he brushed his hand over mouth and chin nervously, but then he picked up in the small scope that item which was most necessary to his survival, a checkerboard painted craft which lay about twelve or fifteen miles away.

Triumphant, he unlashed himself from the acceleration chair and stiffly climbed into the space suit. They'd had practice in the clumsy things as part of their training, but how they'd work on Luna was something else. He shrugged; no use worrying about it, he'd soon know.

As he dressed, his mind couldn't help turning to the others. Of course, they could well be out of range of vision; perhaps hid by the central peak, perhaps too far away on the other side of the crater for him to detect. It would have been better if all three of them could have gotten together immediately—but he could make out by himself.

He gobbled the last two bits of chocolate; hesitated, but forewent the remaining gill of water. Using the mechanical arms, he slipped the plastic helmet over his head, checked the valves and cogs, and opened the small circular door in *Alice's* side.

No time to stand and stare; no time for Columbus-like emotions; no time for some fitting words for future history books.

He began to work his way down the side of the hull, stepping clumsily in the indentations, which comprised the ladder arrangements for entry and exit from *Alice*. It was about forty-five feet to the ground.

It didn't make much difference what caused the slip; he didn't bother to investigate later; possibly one of the hydraulic stilts was emplaced in a spot less secure than the other three. At any rate, Jeff Stevens could feel it give way when he was about half down. He remembered, even as he fell, the negligible gravity, and knew there would be considerably less consequence than on Terra. He struck the ground and rolled desperately to avoid being struck by the collapsing *Alice*.

ALMOST, HE made it. A crumbling wing, caught his left arm immediately above the elbow and he felt the bone grate, then crush. His lips drew back and he gritted his teeth. The arm was broken.

He sat there for a long moment in the dust of Alphonsus Crater, pale-faced and shaken. Finally he came to his feet, still clumsily, and dragged his mind back to quiet contemplation of his situation; this was no time for panic. His first tendency was to make for the blue freighter, only four miles off. He could set his arm there, find food and water, rest for a few days, possibly the other two would be located by then.

The thought *rest a few days* cleared his mind of that possibility. The days were fourteen times the length of earth's. This was toward the end of the lunar day. The period had been chosen deliberately. In mid-day, the temperature on the satellite was well above the boiling point of water. By sunset, it cooled to the point of freezing and in the night the temperature drop was tremendous. He had only a short time to prepare—too short, even without a broken limb.

He gave up the thought of immediate care, immobilized his left arm to the extent possible within the spacesuit and began to make his way to the checkerboard rocket, a dozen miles away.

It had been expected when the suit was designed that the occupant would be able to travel rather rapidly on the face of Luna. Perhaps under ordinary circumstances that might have been true; the light gravity should have enabled him to have progressed by a series of jumps that would have eaten up miles. But only a few minutes of experimentation along this line taught him his broken arm wouldn't stand that treatment.

He finally worked out a method, which was a cross between skating, and a long stride that was somewhat faster and somewhat easier than walking on Terra, but was still considerably slower than he'd hoped.

The darkish dust through which he plowed had the consistency of the dry snow you find in the mountains of the Southwest. He started out doggedly; the arm throbbing protest.

Enough of the day's heat was still upon Luna to make him aware, painfully aware, of the fact that he'd only had half a gallon of water in the past four and a half days. His mouth was cloth-dry, and every step was taking him further from his nearest source of food and drink. The food he could forego for the time, although he felt pangs in his long empty stomach.

He fingered his chin nervously, inside the space suit. Suppose what he sought in the checkerboard rocket was damaged. Suppose it couldn't be utilized. He was afraid he'd never be able to make it back to the *Alice* and then on, another four miles, to the water supply in the blue rocket.

He walked for ages, stumbled, skated, slithered. His arm was shooting pains, burning, protesting. His half-stupefied mind wondered how long it would be before gangrene set in, before the tissues of his arm began to decay.

JEFF STEVENS had been trudging, plodding, over the crater floor for endless hours; he should be getting there; if he didn't soon— He climbed wearily up the ringwall of a *bead*, one of those miniature craters, only a few hundred yards across, within craters; when he made the top he was able to spot his goal, but there was something else that drew his attention. The tiny crater, upon whose ringwall he stood, was a newly created one. He could spot pieces of torn titanium alloy, the material of which the rockets had principally been built. The *bead* was man-made by the crash landing of one of the two Neptune IX models which had first successfully reached Luna, but without a payload and without braking fuel.

The extent of the *bead* was startling. He had a quick flash of what it would have meant to him if his motors had refused to ignite when he came in for his landing. Possibly this is what had happened to Larry Stoddard in Arzachel Crater.

For the first time, as he made his way back down the *bead's* ringwall, the full significance of Stoddard's death came to him. Alice was free! Alice Stoddard was a widow!

Her marriage hadn't been a successful one; the fact that she'd made a mistake must have been evident to her from the beginning. Swept by indignation and despair over the continual wedding postponements, she must have had long hours of wondering whether or not he was sincere, and must have accepted and married Larry Stoddard during such a period of doubt.

And Stoddard? Jeff wondered how much of his desire to marry Alice had been a matter of spite. Certainly, only weeks afterward it was obvious to both that the wedding had been foolish. But the Stoddards of Georgia, *suh*, never got divorces; and Alice was the kind that played the game, no matter how harsh the rules—so they remained in their caricature of marital bliss.

Did Alice still love him—Jeff Stevens?

He tried to tear his mind back to the present; this sort of thing could crack him. Had his own marriage to Alice gone through he might have never been here now; he might have been on Terra planning a home, children, security—looking forward to a long life.

He laughed bitterly, dryly, into his helmet. Here he was, instead, trying to prove that in spite of his size he was a man.

The arm had become almost unbearably painful. He was convinced he'd made a mistake in not going immediately to the other rocket; the arm should have been attended to first; he could have gotten codeine there, or morphine perhaps, anything to clear his mind of this pain.

The checkerboard rocket loomed before him now, laying there on its side. Twelve miles, it couldn't have been more; it felt like fifty.

As he plodded up to its side, he wondered dully if the contents had been damaged. This model rocket had some slight advantages over the *Alice*. The initial velocity hadn't been limited by the four gravities acceleration toadying to a human occupant; the fuel had been expended in a more efficient manner. But, on the other hand, the attempted payload was approximately a ton; considerably more than *Alice* had carried.

THE NEPTUNE XII didn't look particularly damaged. Mentally he crossed his fingers, hoping the release mechanism on the hatch at the nose wasn't jammed. It wasn't. Utilizing the thin metal arms that projected from the spacesuit, he threw the heavy snap that released it, and pulled the hatchcover off.

Inside, nestled in a spiderweb of shockproof rigging, was the tiny tractor.

He knew it well. Weighing approximately five hundred pounds, built principally of the titanium alloys used so widely in the rockets themselves, and powered by alcohol and liquid oxygen, the toy-like tractor was a miracle of engineering.

Jeff Stevens blessed the foresight of the men who'd planned the unloading of the freight rockets. Hadn't it all been made childishly simple, he'd never have managed with his one arm. As it was, it took more than an hour before the little tractor was standing, ready for operations, on the crater floor.

There was no seat and no instruments, they'd been sacrificed to lightweight and simplicity. He perched himself on the fuel tanks and checked the controls. This now was crucial. He flicked a switch, spun the miniature crank. The engine coughed stubbornly then caught; he could feel the vibration beneath him. Oddly, there was no sound, then he realized, all over again, that there would never be sound on Luna; there was no atmosphere.

He let in the clutch and the tractor chugged forward doggedly. Its motion sent new waves of agony from his crushed arm, but he could bear that now; he threw it into high which was slow enough but preferable to his staggering trip on foot.

Back at the *Alice* in a bit over an hour, he hesitated only long enough for the remaining gill of water and for a new oxygen container for his spacesuit, then proceeded to chug toward the blue rocket beyond. Fatigue was beginning to hit him hard now, but he could make it; the battle was too nearly won to lose by physical shortcomings.

When he reached it, he hesitated a long moment before deciding that he could wait for the food and water. He scooted his tiny vehicle to the nose of the Neptune XII, attached the tractor's thin cable to the ring in the prow, climbed aboard again and threw the gears into low. The tractor grunted, groaned, and began to lurch forward.

It took another hour to drag it back to the *Alice*.

He gave up then, almost collapsing; cut the engine of the tractor and broke into the nose compartment of the blue rocket for its water, its food, *its pain relieving drugs*. Things went blank then; later he didn't remember, but evidently he'd drank something, ate something, did up his arm as well as possible.

When he awoke, he was back in the acceleration chair of *Alice*, still wearing the spacesuit with the exception of the helmet. His slight body ached with physical exhaustion, it had never been meant to take this degree of punishment; the broken arm still throbbed agonizingly.

He forced himself to break out his telescope, and searched the crater for signs of Gabowski and Evans. He considered running up some sort of signal above his two rockets so that they could spot him, but gave it up. Had they been alive, they would already have contacted him, made their way to him. *If they were alive*—why pussyfoot—if they were incapacitated, hurt, he had no time for rescue operations. The truth was bitter, cold-blooded; the impassive Matt Evans, the easy going Major Gabowski, either might be out there somewhere, needing only a modicum of assistance to survive. But he had the work of at least three men to do; and only one arm with which to do it.

He searched again, this time for a green-painted Neptune XII, and found it, further away than he would have hoped for, but within possible distance.

JEFF STEVENS cranked up the tractor, mounted the fuel tanks again and started out. The sun was in the first stages of setting and wouldn't take long to go down entirely. Already the excessive heat of a few hours ago was changing to deep cold. Of course, earthlight would always be with him; some sixty times as bright as moonlight on Terra, earthlight would always give him sufficient illumination to even read in comfort. It was the cold that had to be fought.

Six or seven hours later he had managed to tow the new rocket to the side of the blue one. It might have been well at this point to look further, to bring up more of the freighters, but he wasn't sure just how long he could go on. He'd better make permanent camp here and now.

Engineering genius had gone into the contriving of the method for connecting the rockets. Even with the throbbing, agonizing arm he was able, by use of the tractor and the few tools provided him, to join them, to pull out the fuel tanks which had occupied most of their interiors, to remove and discard the turbines and pump assemblies; to make airtight the hulls.

The *Alice* he left intact. Later, much later, probably, she might be used for the return. First he would have to locate several of the red freighters with their cargoes of fuel; first he would have to do a good many things. There was no immediate reason for an attempt to return. Besides, as things were now, it would be extremely difficult for him to repair her stubby wing and her stilts and to get her upright again. Yes, preparation for the return to Terra would have to wait.

When the interiors of the two freighters were cleared he rearranged the payload of the green one. The quantities of pumpkin plants were placed in the sterns of the rocket hulls. There was enough potential oxygen here for a considerably larger number of colonists than Luna supported at present. Besides, there were at least two more of the plant-laden freighters in the crater. He could haul them in and attach them to the rest of the settlement at his leisure; at present, the acquisition of other supplements was more important.

A black freighter was only six or seven miles off. He refueled the tractor from the remnants of oxygen and alcohol in the tanks of the two freighters he'd already brought in, and made his way to the new one.

EIGHT HOURS later it was joined to the small group, connected with them so that the interiors of all, stripped of their tanks, motors, pumps and other accessories, were common. The new acquisition was filled with tools, refrigeration units, a heating system, two generating plants, one a solar plant that would have to be set up later when the sun arose again. Most immediately important was the equipment to make his rapidly growing establishment self-sufficient in regards to air and water.

The device drew the moisture thrown off from his body in breathing and perspiration from the air and condensed it, leaving pure distilled water, which, of course, could be used again and again. The carbon dioxide would be used by the pumpkin plants, which would, in their turn, throw off oxygen sufficient for breathing purposes. He arranged the light system over the plants so that they could continue their work.

He caught himself whistling, over and over, as he worked, some tune that had been popular ten or more years ago, and frowned trying to place it. At last it came to him: *Little Man You've Had A Busy Day.* He grinned. Always before he had avoided even to himself, the fact that he was little.

Exhaustion was on him again. He worked on the arm, trying to set it, bandaging it more securely, then fell asleep.

The cold awakened him. The setting sun had brought freezing temperatures and the work was going to be harder now.

He forced himself to eat a hearty meal of the concentrated and dehydrated food. Eventually, hydroponics would be utilized on Luna, but as long as all food had to come from Terra, concentrates were the order. Actually, the worst was over now. He was self-sufficient enough to carry on almost indefinitely. The immediate job was to drag in as many as possible of the remaining freighters but there wasn't any pressing hurry.

With his telescope he was able to spot three in all. One of them was red, fuel; one was green, another pumpkin plant load; the other was blue, food, water, medical supplies. He'd get the blue one first.

He'd arranged one freighter in such a manner that its nose compartment could be used as an airlock. Each time he left his base, he lost the air in that compartment; later, perhaps, some system of pumping could eliminate that loss, but for now he could get by.

His arm was less painful, but eventually he knew it would have to be re-broken and reset. There was nothing he could do about it for the present.

He refueled the tractor and made his way toward the blue rocket, some twenty miles off. It was going to be a long trip and a tiring one, and he settled himself stoically on the tiny vehicles fuel tanks for the ride.

Less than a half mile from camp, he came upon the crumpled body. Behind it, leading from the ringwall, was a ragged, all explaining trail. The sloughing footprints through the dust were interspaced with disturbed spots where the stumbling figure had fallen, raised himself, staggered on, to fall again.

Jeff Stevens swore, crushed to a halt, jumped from the tractor and skated his way to the fallen figure.

IT WAS Colonel Larry Stoddard, his helmet torn off, his face an agony of asphyxiation, his dead eyes staring up at Terra there in the sky above them. His face ashen and cold, Jeff Stevens bent over the frozen body.

Stoddard must have landed in Arzachel Crater ten days or so before and realized his only chance was to make it to Alphonsus on foot. He had probably had a small amount of liquid oxygen remaining in his fuel tanks after the crash; using it, he'd conserved his bottled oxygen for the spacesuit and remained in his rocket for a week, in hopes some of the others would make a successful landing in Alphonsus and prepare the base in time for his arrival.

He'd then plowed his way over the heights of the ringwall of Arzachel, then over the ringwall of Alphonsus by some superhuman effort, only to fail within sight of the base Stevens had established.

Larry Stoddard held something, a piece of paper, in one hand. Jeff Stevens worked one of the mechanical metal arms down into the suit and retrieved it. The paper read: "Suggestions for those that follow," and contained half a dozen items Stoddard had noted down as a result of his own experiences. It wound up, "Congrats to the spaceman who finds this, and so long.—L. S."

Jeff Stevens' face twitched uncontrollably. He stepped back and flicked the other as snappy a salute as was possible in the confining spacesuit.

"Last *Brennschluss*, spaceman," he whispered.

He stood there for a full five minutes, looking down at his rival. Larry Stoddard, when he realized he wasn't going to make it, had used his last efforts to make the way easier for those who followed. Deep within himself Jeff Stevens realized that even though he returned to Terra, Alice could never be anything to him except *Mrs. Stoddard*, widow of a fallen comrade.

He returned to the tractor, cranked it up again and made his way back to the base. He was unbearably tired; securing the other freight rockets could wait; there was no special hurry for them.

He cut the tractor's engine and reentered the base, stripped off the space suit and made his way to the small radar set. It was time to report.

He sat for a long time considering the message. It must contain a full report of the situation here; that he was established but that all the others were dead or missing.

Uncle Joe's intelligence boys must be aware that Uncle Sam was trying to reach Luna, but it was doubtful if they knew just how far Uncle had gotten. The important thing was to so disguise the message that the others would be misled, even if they managed to pick it up. Code was out, any code can be broken eventually. The thing was to word it in such a way that they couldn't get an accurate idea of the size of the establishment nor how long it had been in existence.

He looked about him. Here he was huddled within the confined space of several joined rockets, one arm broken and shaken and sick with fatigue. Colonel Stoddard, Major Gabowski, Captain Evans, each in turn who were to have commanded the expedition, were all dead. He was the only living person on Luna.

Jeff Stevens carefully tapped out:

SEVERAL CASUALTIES STOP REQUEST REPLACEMENTS STOP. SIGNED STEVENS, OFFICER COMMANDING, FORT LUNA, UNITED STATES SPACE SERVICE.

Please to Remember

Obviously, Uncle Manfred was off his rocker—imagine a person remembering what he was going to do years and years in the future!

IT WAS JIMMY, the whining brat, who started it off. Uncle Manfred had been quiet all evening, showing no signs at all of his—well, his peculiarity; and the rest of the family had been figuratively holding its breath in hope.

Jimmy must have read it in a comic book, or heard it on TV or something; he wasn't smart enough to have thought it up by himself.

He wrinkled his nose in disgust, pushed his potatoes—which had been cooked with their skins on—to the side of his plate and whined, "I hate potato skins, and I'm glad I hate 'em, because if I liked 'em I'd eat 'em—and I hate 'em."

Bertha screwed her plump face into what was meant to be a mildly reproving frown and said, *"Please,* dear, you have better manners than that." Which was a gross exaggeration.

Mike Wheaton, the guest, winked at Jimmy and said seriously, "I remember once when we were in Korea. All our fresh vegetables ran out and for a spell of nearly four months the nearest thing we had to fresh vegetables was the skin on our potatoes. We grew real fond of them."

Jimmy sneered, "You're kiddin'."

Mike shook his head seriously. "I mean it. You see, the vitamins and minerals in a potato are practically all in the skins; when you can't get your vitamins any other way then you…"

Uncle Manfred said thoughtfully, "I remember once on the Mars-Callisto run when we didn't have any Terran food but

29

dried chili-peppers for nigh onto a year. We'd crashed on Gany-mede and they took that long to rescue us."

There was a pregnant silence.

Finally Bertha cleared her throat and said hopefully, "There's peach cobbler for dessert."

It didn't work. Mike turned to Uncle Manfred and said, "The *what* run?"

Uncle Manfred took his time. He mashed his potato, poured on some gravy, stirred the two up until they were a satisfactorily homogeneous mess, then repeated, "The Mars-Callisto run. I was a jetman." He added, reminiscently, "It was a hell of a job."

Jimmy, whose recently acquired thirteenth year had put him among the ranks of those who have discovered that their elders aren't necessarily omnipotent, sneered, "I'll bet."

Bertha kicked him under the table, which was a mistake.

He yelped, then whined, "Aw maw, whatza difference? This new fella of Veronica's is gonna find out the old jerk is missin' half his marbles anyway. Whatza difference, huh? Whatcha wanta kick me for?"

Veronica maneuvered Mike Wheaton out of the dining room as quickly as possible and into the parlor, while Bertha went to work, as prearranged, at attempting to get Uncle Manfred to bed.

"I don't want to go to bed," he said irritably. "I'd like to talk to that young man. Most sensible youngster I've seen in some time. What war was he talking about, the scrap with Callisto?"

Bertha drew up her five feet two of plumpness and her face began to go scarlet with rage. She snapped, "Of course not, you stupid old fool. He's talking about Korea; Michael Wheaton's a veteran." She added, completely irrelevantly, "Besides that, he's Joseph Wheaton's son and will undoubtedly inherit the Wheaton Chemical Works. I'd think that with such an eligible young man, you'd watch the nonsense you…"

Uncle Manfred wasn't listening, "Korea," he said, in surprise. "Doesn't look old enough to have been in that." He shook his head. "Wonderful what cosmetic-surgery and those immortamines'll do these days." He scowled worriedly, "Or have I got my dates mixed up again? What year is this anyway, Bertha?"

The impossible fool! She just wished there was some way of…of knocking him over the head or something. He ruined everything, just *everything*; her bridge club, her social acquaintances—she *knew* she was the talk of the town. A psychopathic case in her home. And poor Veronica, how would the girl *ever* be able to hook…uh, that is, make a suitable match, with a notoriously crazy uncle to scare away the young men.

Finally she was able to wangle him up to his room.

BACK IN the parlor, Mike Wheaton was saying, "He wasn't kidding, was he?"

Veronica's usually washed out eyes began to flare, but she controlled herself. After all, she wasn't getting any younger and if she was ever going to get a husband and escape from this madhouse. Well—

She forced a smile, remembering to keep her lips down over her overly prominent teeth, and said in her shrill voice, "Oh, let's not talk about Uncle Manfred. Tell me more about your thesis; about the moddlecules and everything."

"Molecules," he corrected absently.

She clenched her teeth together and could feel her face going white. It was no use now. It would be better to tell the whole thing. "He was working, last year, at Los Alamos," she blurted, almost nastily. "There was an explosion or something—you know, you can never get the *details* of these things and everybody else on Uncle Manfred's project was killed. He was in the er…hospital for months but finally they released him and now he lives with us."

Veronica stopped, as though that explained everything.

Mike frowned. "But what's the matter with him?"

Lord! How she hated this subject. Everybody—but everybody!—learned about it sooner or later.

"He thinks he remembers living in the year 2050," she snapped.

"I beg your pardon?"

She repeated slowly, irritatedly, "He thinks he lived in the year 2050; that he was a member of the crew of a spaceship, and that he traveled between the stars. He's always talking about the cities of that time and the other planets and space and the other things he 'remembers' having seen."

Uncle Manfred had come back down from his room and entered the parlor unheard. He said mildly, "What a foolish thing to say, Veronica. I think no such thing."

She came hurriedly to her feet and spun around to face him. "You...you mean you've recovered," she shrilled. "You don't..."

He lit his pipe carefully. "I don't remember *having* done those things; I remember *going* to do them. After all, my dear, that's a hundred years in the future, and hasn't happened yet."

THEY HELD a tearful family conference afterwards. That is, it was tearful as far as Veronica and her mother were concerned. Uncle Manfred was more bewildered than anything else, and Jimmy, draped teenage-wise in a chair, stayed on the sidelines drinking it in with satisfaction.

"But, how can you?" Bertha wailed. "My own brother, making me the laughing stock of the town." Her various chins quivered.

Uncle Manfred puffed on his pipe and said mildly, "What's the matter now, Bertha?"

"That nice young man, that Michael Wheaton, he'll never want to see Veronica again." Her voice rose as she reached the end of the sentence. Had she only known it, young Wheaton was to remark later that old Uncle Manfred was the most likeable member of the family.

Veronica was in a screaming mood too, but she restrained herself, "Uncle," she said carefully, "don't you realize what people think when you start talking about spaceships and Mars and those other fantastic things? This is the year 1953—how could you possibly remember things that haven't happened yet?" Her voice began to go shrill, too. "And never will!"

Jimmy sneered, "He's missing his marbles," and earned a glare from his mother.

"I've gone through this before," Uncle Manfred sighed, "but I'll do it once more."

He took his pipe from his mouth and pointed the stem at his sister, "Bertha, most people have memories going only one way, into the past; mine—I don't know how or why—goes both ways, since my accident. I admit that sometimes it's confusing to me, but I'm quite lucid. I remember things that I will do as a young jetman in the space service a hundred years from now; I can…"

Bertha interrupted impatiently, "But don't you see how impossible that is?" she snapped, her face almost as red as the henna in her hair. "Even if you could 'remember' both ways, as you put it, how could you possibly remember being a young man a hundred years from now? You're fifty-five! A hundred years will see you dead and forgotten like all the rest of us."

He shook his head patiently, "You don't understand, Bertha. You see, the immortamines weren't discovered until 1960. When I say a 'young jetman,' it might be somewhat misleading; actually, of course, I just *looked* young." He added reminiscently, "Cosmetic surgery and the immortamines sure are going to make some big changes in the world. As a matter of fact, it was their discovery that drove man to the conquest of the other planets. The population increase after death was conquered was such that we *had* to find new worlds."

Jimmy shook his head. "Sometimes the old jerk gets me to thinking maybe *I'm* batty. First he says it's going to happen, then he says it has happened."

Uncle Manfred looked at him with mild reproof. "It amounts to the same thing, just about."

Bertha's lips were tight with peevishness, "*Please*, I refuse to argue further with you about this, Manfred; but I think it impossible of you not to do what the doctor has suggested. It would solve everything."

HIS EYEBROWS went up. "You mean for me to go to the sanitarium?" The oldster squirmed uncomfortably in his chair.

Her little eyes snapped, "Only for a year or so, perhaps."

He snorted. "Once they get me in there again, I'd never get out. They don't understand any more than you do." He knocked the ashes out of his pipe reflectively. "I remember once on the old *Venusian Princess*—what a rusty tub that was— we had a psycho-technician that had the whole ship on its ear. By the time we reached Luna, he had more than two thirds of the crew confined under guard to quarters; claimed they all had space cafard."

Jimmy asked, "So what happened? Sometimes you're better than TV." His ferret-like face held its petulant sneer.

Uncle Manfred said mildly, "When we got to Luna, it was found that the psycho-technician was the only mentally-upset case on board. It just goes to show—half the time the docs don't know what they're talking about."

Bertha glowered at Jimmy. *"Please,"* she snapped, "don't encourage your uncle, James."

"Whatza difference?" he whined. "He's around the corner, ain't he? He don't know the difference."

Veronica stopped her sobbing and said, desperation in her shrill voice, "Uncle Manfred, if we could prove you're wrong; that these insane stories you 'remember' aren't true, would you go willingly to the sanitarium and let the specialists try and cure you?"

He clicked the stem of his pipe on his teeth reflectively. Finally he sighed, "All right, Veronica; it's a deal. If you can prove, *to my satisfaction*, that I'm er…crazy, I'll go willingly."

The girl's eyes gleamed triumphantly. "Now don't forget!"

Uncle Manfred smiled ruefully, "You don't have to worry about my forgetting, my dear. My trouble is *remembering too much,* not too little."

ANOTHER family conference was held later that night, but this time between daughter and mother alone and in the secrecy of Veronica's room.

The girl explained carefully. "Don't you see? If we can get him to go on his own, we won't have criticism from our friends. After all, we could have him *sent*, but what would everyone say? Uncle Manfred is a hero, of sorts. We don't know just what happened at Los Alamos, but the government *did* decorate him; you can't just send a hero to an institution."

"But that's not all of it," her mother said petulantly. "If he goes to the institution, we'll probably be able to get his pension to keep the family going, but you know how little that is; we're also dependent upon his other income." She quivered heavily in exasperation. "If only we knew its source—just where he secures the rest of the money that he gives us; obviously, he doesn't work."

For a brief moment a qualm touched Veronica, "In a way, we sound cold-blooded, mother. After all, it's Uncle Manfred's money that supports us. And here we are…"

Her mother interrupted impatiently. *"Please*, darling; I think I'm better qualified than you to discuss my own brother's welfare. He'll be happier in a sanitarium where he can…well, where he'll be able to be with others like himself.

"Besides, I must think of you children. Young people today must have all the advantages if they are to keep up. Since your father's uh…disappearance, life has been a great burden to me, Veronica, a great burden. Now the problem, obviously, is to get your uncle to go willingly to the sanitarium, assigning, during his stay there, not only his pension but this other income of his— wherever it comes from.

"Of course, while your Uncle Manfred is in the institution we shall pray every night for his recovery."

"Of course," agreed Veronica earnestly.

Jimmy stuck his ferret-like head in the door. "You still talkin' about Uncle Manfred?" he whined. "He's screwy; everybody says so."

They glared him into silence.

Everything went quietly the next morning at breakfast, except for a mild protest from Uncle Manfred that the oatmeal hadn't been neo-vitaminized.

Veronica pounced on the statement. "There," she shrilled, "don't you see, Uncle? There is no such thing as neo-vitaminized. Doesn't that show that you're...well, unbalanced?"

His eyebrows went up in surprise. "There isn't?" He wrinkled his forehead. "Guess you're right at that; the process wasn't discovered until 1955. I always was bad at dates."

Bertha's chins trembled in exasperation.

Jimmy sneered, "The old jerk was tellin' me this morning that we wasn't going to have to brush our teeth after 1963. They'd just stick stuff in the drinkin' water that'd keep your teeth clean."

His mother scolded him absently and half-heartedly. *"Please*, dear, you mustn't talk that way; you might hurt your uncle's feelings."

"Not at all," Uncle Manfred said mildly.

But the campaign to put Uncle Manfred into a sanitarium where he'd be "happier with people like himself" didn't progress any too well during the next week. The theory was to convince the old boy that he was wrong but that didn't work out any too well either.

It was something like an argument between a Baptist and an atheist. Both *knew* they were correct, but neither's argument admitted of satisfactory proof to the other. Bertha and Veronica couldn't prove that Uncle Manfred hadn't memories of the future; but, on the other hand, he couldn't convince them that he had.

THE CLIMAX came as a result of an accident, since it was only an accident that Veronica stumbled upon the magazine in Jimmy's room. She'd called him twice in regard to mowing the lawn and finally came seeking the brat out.

He should have been in his room, but he didn't seem to be; the bed was mussed, as though someone had been sprawled upon it, but there was no sign of Jimmy. A magazine lay on the bedspread.

Veronica sighed with disgust. *"Dumfounding Stories*, indeed! No wonder he brings home such report cards," she shrilled.

That brought indignant response. "What'd'ya mean?" Jimmy whined, sticking his head out of the closet. "That mag is plenty educational."

She whirled, and he suddenly remembered that he'd just revealed himself, "Aw cripes," he mumbled. "I don't wanta do the grass. Why don't you get the old jerk to do it? He wouldn't know the difference."

Veronica took up the magazine and shuddered at the cover, but then her eyes narrowed. "'The Mars-Callisto Run', by Jets Larsen." Her forehead wrinkled. "That sounds familiar, somehow."

"It's a swell mag," Jimmy was whining. "I got to readin' it after listen in to all that hooey that Uncle Manfred gives out with."

Her eyes went wide. "Uncle Manfred!"

She flipped hurriedly through the pages, triumphantly opened to the story whose title had puzzled her, and let her eyes run through it rapidly.

"Jimmy," she shrilled, "go get your uncle and tell him that mother and I want to see him in the parlor."

Something in her voice called for obedience. He scooted out of the room, and she followed more slowly, her forehead still wrinkled with thought, but her eyes beaming satisfaction.

Uncle Manfred came in cheerfully; his foul briar making its presence known throughout the room in seconds. Both Bertha and Veronica sat primly, their hands in their laps, satisfaction oozing from them. The magazine lay face down on a coffee table.

"You wanted to talk to me?" he said easily.

Veronica leaned forward triumphantly. "Uncle Manfred, you remember the bargain we made, don't you? That you would agree to go to the sanitarium if we could prove your...well, your memories of the future aren't memories at all."

"I remember," he agreed, making himself comfortable in a chair, "but, of course; the bargain isn't exactly fair on my side."

"What do you mean," Bertha snapped, her chins quivering in agitation. "You promised..."

He waved his pipe stem at her negatively. "I'm willing to stick to it, but, you see, I know I'll never go to the sanitarium again."

"Please," she snapped, "why?"

He shrugged and put his pipe back in his mouth. "Because I can't remember doing it."

"Like a fruitcake," Jimmy sneered. "They don't come any nuttier."

VERONICA took a deep breath, "But you'll admit, Uncle Manfred, that if I can prove these memories of yours aren't memories of all, you should go to the sanitarium?"

He nodded agreeably.

She took up the magazine. "Uncle, I don't know why you've been reading these awful things, but, obviously, this is where you've been getting your impressions."

She turned to "The Mars-Callisto Run." "Now here's a story about a young jetman of the future whose ship crashes on Ganymede, and for nearly a year the only earth food they have is chili-peppers. *This is exactly the same nonsense you told Michael Wheaton the other night."*

Uncle Manfred looked embarrassed. "What's your point, Veronica?"

She shrilled excitedly, "Can't you see? The experience didn't happen at all. It's not a memory or your future; it's a story by,"—she glanced quickly down at the magazine again—"by Jets Larsen, and you must have read it somewhere."

He took his pipe from his mouth and ran a hand through his hair in irritation.

Bertha jumped into the breech, her chins quivering in excitement. "There's the proof, Manfred. Now will you do what we say?"

He got to his feet in disgust. "Proof, nonsense," he snorted. *"I'm Jets Larsen.* Just for something to do, I occasionally write up one of my experiences and sell the story to a science-fiction magazine. If you'll look in the back of the magazine at the fan letters, you'll find that I'm one of the most popular authors in the field. Why not? My stories all sound authentic, because they *are* authentic."

Veronica slumped back into her chair, reduced to shocked silence. Bertha said, "Then this proves nothing at all Manfred, nothing; I still say it's all your imagination, and if you really loved—"

"Cripes," Jimmy sneered. "I wouldn'ta thought the old crackpot was up to it."

"Please, James," Bertha reproved half-heartedly. "You mustn't talk like that to your dear uncle. Don't you realize that he might possibly resent it?"

Uncle Manfred took the pipe from his mouth and smiled at the two of them. "Don't bother, Bertha; you'd be surprised how little I mind. In fact, the frogs in my bed, the cut up rubber in my tobacco, the thumbtacks in my shoes, and even the occasional hotfoot, don't irritate me especially."

He returned the briar to its place between his teeth and puffed contentedly. "Ever since your husband ran off and left you—by the way, I never thought he had it in him—and I came to take care of you, I knew what it would be like. But, I thought it was more or less my duty; and, as I said, it doesn't irritate me especially.

"You see, a person who can remember the future as well as the past, has a considerable advantage; he can contemplate the fate of those around him."

Uncle Manfred smiled almost fondly at Jimmy, "You little will-be jailbird, you."

His smile turned forgivingly on his sister. "And stop worrying about your social position, Bertha; you'll be able to forget about it after Jimmy is sent up as a juvenile delinquent and after Veronica gets desperate and marries that fruit-peddler."

The three of them stared at him, speechless and unblinking.

"By the way," he said, "the whole routine around here seems upset since you've been trying to prove my insanity, and I notice that the mystery of my five hundred a month also agitates you. Possibly this will clear things up."

He took an envelope from an inner pocket and tossed it to Bertha's lap, then strolled leisurely from the room.

"He's crazy," Veronica sobbed, "he's *crazy,* mother."

"Brother, his roof *really* leaks," Jimmy sneered.

Martha took up the envelope and drew the letter from it, almost fearfully. She read, blinked, then reread.

"Well, what is it, mother?" Veronica shrilled. "More of his insanity?"

Martha said, "It's from the President of the New York Stock exchange. It says, *'Dear Sir: Please find enclosed your monthly five hundred dollars, which we pay you, as agreed in return for your abstaining from stock-market speculation. In view of your abilities, which could easily disrupt the entire financial system, let us again thank you for being so moderate in your demands.'"*

Tourists to Terra

They came from a far sun in a distant time, seeking thrills on alien planets.
Earth was their latest stop and its puny humans promised good sport!

DIOMED of Argos, son of Tydeus, drew his sword with a shout and rushed forward to finish off his Trojan opponent before help could arrive. Suddenly he stopped and threw up a shielding arm before his eyes. When he could see again, one who could only have been Aphrodite, Goddess of love and beauty stood between him and the unconscious enemy. She was dressed as though for the bridal room, her Goddess body, breathtakingly beautiful, revealed through the transparent robe she wore. She was attired for love, but held a short sword in her hand.

Aphrodite smiled at him in derision. "Now, then, Prince of Argos, would you fight the Gods?" She advanced the sword, half mockingly.

But the Greek was mad with bloodlust, half crazed with his day's victories; he snatched up his spear, muttering, "Pallas Athene aids me," and rushed her.

Her eyes widened, fear flashing in them, and she began to rise from the ground. The barbaric spear flashed out and ripped her arm; blood flowed and she dropped the sword, screaming.

Diomed heard a voice call urgently, "Go back! Go back immediately to—" And the Goddess Aphrodite disappeared.

He whirled to face the newcomer and saw another God confronting him. The extent of his action was beginning to be realized but Diomed had gone too far to turn back now; he charged his new opponent, shield held high and sword at the ready. The God lifted his hand, sending forth a bolt of power that brought the Greek to his knees.

Diomed's eyes were filled with sudden fear and despair, "Phoebus Apollo," he quavered.

The God was scornful. "Beware, Diomed," he said. "Do not think to fight with Gods."

The Greek cowered before him.

LATER, in the invisible space ship, hovering five hundred feet above the battle, Cajun faced her, his features impassive and his tone of voice faultless. He was boiling with rage beneath his courtesy.

"I will present your complaint to the Captain, but I would like to remind the Lady Jan that she has been warned repeatedly against appearing in the battle clothed as she is and without greater defenses. It was fortunate I was able to appear as soon as I did. If you'd been injured seriously, I hesitate to say what repercussions would've taken place on the home planet."

Her eyebrows went up. "Injured seriously! Just what do you mean by that? Do you realize this horrible wound will probably take half the night to heal? You saw that barbarian was insane, why didn't you come to my assistance sooner? You haven't heard the last of this, you inefficient nincompoop. When we return home I'll have you stripped of your rank!"

Cajun's face remained blank, "Yes, your ladyship," he said. "And, before I go, may I deliver a message from the Lady Marid? She said they await you in the salon."

She drew a cape about her and without speaking further, swept from the compartment.

A muscle twitched in his cheek. "Parasites," he muttered savagely, and turned to go to his own quarters where he could change from this ridiculous glittering armor, into his own uniform as ship's officer.

The Lady Jan stormed into the salon where the others had gathered to try the new concoction the steward had named ambrosia. Some of them still wore their costumes, others had changed into the more comfortable dress of their own world.

Her eyes blazed at them. "Who in the name of Makred told that Greek he would conquer anyone he fought today, even a God? The damned barbarian nearly killed me!"

The Lord Doren laughed gently. "It was Marid; she was playing the Goddess Athene. The sport was rather poor with that new bow of hers so she thought she'd inflame one of the Greeks and see just how berserk he would become if he thought he had the protection of a Goddess."

"He could have killed me!"

"Oh, come; now, Jan, you were barely scratched. Besides, Marid didn't know this Greek, Diomed, was going to run into you, or that he'd have the fantastic nerve to attack whom he thought one of his Gods."

She took up a goblet of the new drink, but she wasn't placated, "I'm of the opinion this stop shouldn't be made; it's too dangerous. I'm going to insist Captain Foren blast the city and obliterate both sides of this barbaric conflict."

THE Lady Marid, who was still dressed in her Pallas Athene armor, broke in. "Don't be so upset, Jan. We're sorry that brute hurt your arm, but what can you expect on this type of cruise? They guaranteed us thrills, didn't they? The very dangers we face are what we're paying so highly for." She laughed lightly. "Besides, that costume you wear as Aphrodite. Really! I don't know why you didn't get worse than a scratch on the arm. These Greeks aren't exactly civilized—nor exactly cold-blooded, either."

The other's face went red and she snatched another of the drinks from a tray. "Nevertheless, I'm going to complain. This war is absolutely too perilous to be part of the tour. And after all the trouble we went to in order to learn their fantastic languages and customs. Why I was under that damned Psycho-Study Impressor for nearly two hours!"

Captain Foren had entered behind her. "I agree with you Lady Jan, and can only apologize. I should've realized last week when Lord General Baris, fighting in the battle as the God Ares on the Trojan side, was speared by this same Greek. The company would never hear the end of it, if, on one of these cruises, a passenger was seriously injured."

The Lord General Baris shrugged. "It was wonderful sport. I killed a score of the beggars that day. I don't know how that one found a chink in my armor. I'll take measures against my costumer when we return home. " He grinned wryly. "I doubt if the Emperor would appreciate having one of his generals killed in a primitive war; while on leave."

"I think I'll have to take a crack at this Diomed, myself," Lord Doren said.

The Lady Marid laughed. "If I know you; you'll do it with a blaster from a hundred feet in the air above him."

Doren smiled in return. "Of course. Do you think I'd make a fool of myself by going down into their battle as Baris does? It's insane. This hand to hand conflict is much too risky."

The Captain changed the subject. "I'm sure you'll all appreciate our next stop," he said. "I plan to visit an even more astounding planet than this. We are to fight the swamp dragons of Venus."

"From what distance, Captain?" Lord Doren drawled.

The Captain smiled. "Their poisonous breath reaches half a mile, so it will be necessary to use long distance weapons."

Lord General Baris scowled. "It sounds too easy. I like to fight humanoids; there's more thrill in killing when your opponent looks like yourself, as do these earthlings."

The Lady Jan was nearing the nasty stage of intoxication. "It wouldn't be so thrilling if you weren't provided with defenses making it practically impossible to be hurt. You wouldn't enter these battles if you weren't sure you'd come out safely."

"I wouldn't deny it. Sport is sport; but I have no desire to be killed at it. At any rate, I'm opposed to killing these swamp dragons. It sounds as though it would be boring, and, Makred knows, we had enough boredom butchering those dwarfs at our last stop."

The Lady Marid backed him. She also thought Venus unattractive. If the Captain was of the opinion this war was too dangerous, wasn't there some other conflict on this planet?

The Captain told them he'd consult with his officers and let them know in the morning.

ONE thing was sure, Captain Foren thought, as he made his way toward the officer's mess. He'd have to get this group of thrill-crazy wastrels away from Troy. If one of them was hurt badly, he'd undoubtedly lose his lucrative position on the swank cruise ship.

The idea was his own, really, and a good one. In a luxury mad world the cry was for new titillations, new pleasures, new planets on which to play, new drugs to bring ever wilder dreams, new foods, new drinks, new loves; but, most of all, new thrills.

Yes, the idea of taking cruise ships of wealthy thrill seekers to the more backward planets and letting them join in primitive wars, had been his. It proved the thrill supreme. His cruises were the rage of half a dozen planets, and the company had increased his pay several times in the past few years. But he knew it could crumple like a house of cards, given one serious injury to a wealthy guest. The theory of the cruise was to let them kill without endangering themselves.

The stop at Troy, had, as a rule, been a successful one. The Greeks and their opponents were both highly superstitious and readily accepted the presence of the aliens from space as Gods taking place in the battle. Usually, they were too terrified to take measures against the strangers in their gleaming armor, but today had been the second occasion in which a tourist had been injured, in spite of scientific, protective armor.

His officers were awaiting him in the mess hall. They too had been conscious of the wounds suffered by the thrill-seeking guests, and hadn't liked it. Lady Jan was the daughter of a noble strong enough to have them all imprisoned, if the whim took him.

Captain Foren growled, "Have any of you an idea? I proposed the Venus trip, but, although they admit being leery about further risks here, they prefer fighting humanoids."

First Officer Cajun said, "Perhaps it would be better to head for the home planet, Captain."

Captain Foren shook his head. "We can't do that; the cruise has another week to go. If we went back now it would be obvious that something had happened and just bring matters to a head. If we can give them another week of thrills, possibly they'll have forgotten their wounds by the time we return."

The Chief Engineer turned to Cajun. "At what stage of development is this planet?"

"I believe it's at H-2. Why?"

"I was wondering at the possibility of going forward a few thousand years in time and participating in a war that dealt less in hand to hand conflict. They could have their fill of killing, with a minimum of danger—protected, of course, with suitable anti-projectile force fields."

CAJUN went over to the ship's Predictinformer and spoke into its mouthpiece. "What will be the military development of this planet in two or three thousand years; and would it be safe to take the ship into that period?"

They awaited the answer, which came approximately one minute later. "Probability shows the inhabitants of Terra will begin utilizing explosives for propelling missiles in two thousand years. About five hundred years later they will have developed this means of warfare to its ultimate. Safety for the ship is indicated."

Captain Foren mused, "That sounds practical. We could participate in some war in which our passengers could use such weapons as snipers, from a distance." Another thought struck him. "Besides, the Lord General Baris is quite intrigued with the possibilities involved in fighting the humanoids here. He had spoken of transporting large numbers of his troops to Terra and using the planet for a training ground in actual combat. Undoubtedly, the earthlings of the future would make better victims for his soldiers than these more primitive types. It might be well to look at the future of this planet."

The First Engineer said, "Such a step would wipe out the development of civilization on the planet."

Captain Foren shrugged impatiently. He ordered Cajun to make immediate preparations to take the ship forward twenty-five hundred years, and gave instructions to a sub-officer to locate a suitable conflict as soon as they arrived, so that the guests could begin their participation when they awoke in the morning.

The ship arrived effortlessly in its new location in time, but when the sub-officer returned from his patrol, First Officer Cajun took him to the Captain's quarters himself.

He saluted. "I don't believe this is quite it, Captain."

"Why not? Weren't there any wars in progress?"

Cajun said, "It wasn't that. There were several. They don't seem to have reached the development for which we were looking. For instance, in the region in which we've landed, the first stage of a conflict between two nations has begun. The countries are called Mexico and the United States and they're fighting over the northwestern possessions of the former; although, as always, both sides claim they are involved for idealistic reasons. However, the fighting still consists, to an extent, of hand to hand conflict. The soldiers carry explosive propelled missile weapons, but they're usually slow in loading and single shot in operation. Swords are carried at the ends of these weapons so that after it is fired the soldier may dash forward and engage his enemy personally."

The Captain was glum. "That's as bad as before, and I can't risk our passengers in any more hand to hand combat."

"Sir, these humanoids on Terra seem slow in progressing but I have an idea if we move forward another hundred years they will be using automatic weapons, and hand to hand combat will be antiquated. The calendar system they use calls this the year 1845. I suggest we travel forward to 1945.

Captain Foren made a snap decision. "All right, we'll go forward a century. As soon as we arrive, have a patrol go out again."

WHEN Captain Foren awoke in the morning, the hot desert sun was already well into the sky. The invisible spaceship had stationed itself a hundred feet off the ground in an area in which there were no signs of habitation and few of the works of man. He strode leisurely to the control room and returned the greetings of the morning watch.

"Any word from the patrol as yet?" he asked.

First Officer Cajun was worried; "No, sir, and he should've been back long before this."

"I trust nothing has happened to him. Has he reported at all?"

"Only once, several hours ago. Evidently there is a globewide war raging." Cajun ran his tongue over thin lips. "Our passengers should have excellent sport. In fact, Captain, if you can spare me, I would like to participate myself."

Captain Foren looked at him and laughed. "You, also? I'm afraid this must be a racial characteristic, this love of imposing death. I must confess, on my first trips, I too liked to join in the sport." He turned and glanced out an observation port. "What is that steel tower down there on the desert?"

"We couldn't decide, Captain, unless it's some structure for conducting tests of some sort or other. The surprising thing about it is that our instruments detect radioactivity…"

The Captain interrupted sharply, "Has anyone checked the ship's Predictinformer on whether or not this era is completely safe?"

Cajun said, "I assumed that you had, sir." He stepped to the instrument and spoke into its mouthpiece. "What is the military development of this planet? Is the ship safe ?"

The Predictinformer began its report. "In the past thirty-five years military science on Terra has developed tremendously under the impetus of two world-wide conflicts. At present the dominant power on this continent is experimenting with nuclear fission…"

Sudden fear came into the eyes of the captain of the thrill ship. "That radioactive steel tower! Blast off," he shrieked, "Blast off!"

The Predictinformer went on dispassionately, "…and is about to test an atomic bomb against which this ship's defenses would be…"

It got no further.

The Hatchetman

BY MACK REYNOLDS AND FREDRIC BROWN

When another world finds a way to turn one honest earthman into a dozen traitors—then it's time to call in the hatchetman...

CHAPTER I

MATT ANDERS, arrived at the New Albuquerque Spaceport on Venus in the early afternoon. His identification papers showed him to be one Harvey Giles: merchant, Philadelphia, Earth. Purpose of visit to Venus: purchase of precious stones. He was tall, but stooped with age; his gray hair and seamed face matched the photographs on his identification papers. Any resemblance to the real Matt Anders was impossible to detect.

He let the mechanics roll away the one-man Spacezephyr, while the two guards who had come to meet him escorted him to the administration building where his identification papers were checked and approved. After that, he was free to leave, carrying his briefcase containing—except for one secret pocket—only papers pertaining to his assumed identity.

A landcab swung in to pick him up. He hesitated momentarily and then waved the driver away. The residence of the Terran ambassador was less than half a mile distant, and a chance for exercise would be more than welcome after thirty-five hours in the tiny spacecraft. He took a deep breath of the exhilarating Venusian air and started down the street.

He felt no sense of danger. It was broad daylight and New Albuquerque is a safe, well-policed city. His disguise was impenetrable. Only a few people on Earth—and those were men in positions of high trust—knew of his presence here or the form of his disguise. The various unorganized crackpots and malcontents who hated him could not possibly know. And aggression on the part of the Martian Duplies, here on Venus, Anders didn't even consider. Mars was trying her best to keep Venus from taking sides in the strange cold war she was waging with Earth—a war in which neither side had made a direct move against the home planet of the other, although millions of men had died in space and in attacks on outposts. Certainly Mars would not risk antagonizing Venus by any overt act on the neutral planet.

So it was the very unexpectedness of the attack against him that enabled it to succeed. For a moment, except for him, the street was empty. Except for him and for the landcab that had offered to pick him up back at the spaceport. It must have followed him unobtrusively for some distance, and now it contained three men besides the driver. It swung up against the curb beside him and disgorged its occupants; two men tried to pinion his arms; the other swung an old-fashioned blackjack.

Matt Anders dropped his briefcase and tried to swing with his right at the Duplie holding his other arm. The blow was ineffectual, but it was the movement on his own part that caused the sap in the hands of the third man to accomplish less than had been intended. He was dazed by the blow, his knees buckled and he fell, but he didn't completely lose consciousness.

The Duplies who had hold of his arms lifted him and carried him to the landcab. The one who had used the blackjack took a quick look up and down the street, picked up the briefcase and followed them into the cab.

The whole thing had taken only seconds. And now he was between two of them in the rear seat and, leaning past the one to his right, the third man bent toward him. Now his hand held a hypodermic needle instead of the blackjack. Anders caught a fuzzy glimpse of it from a corner of his eye as the Duplie poised the needle to plunge it into his arm. He didn't know what it meant. Not death, most likely, because if they'd merely wanted

51

to kill him they could easily have finished him off back there on the street without taking the risk of carrying him into the cab.

THE LANDCAB swung sharply around a corner, and as it swerved Anders managed to press against the man on his right. He twisted his body so that the plunger of the small hypo was depressed. It lost a full half of its contents on his coat before he felt the prick of the needle. He jerked involuntarily at that and the wielder of the hypo laughed. "Coming out of the fog, huh? Well, that shot'll take you right back in again."

The driver spoke back over his shoulder. "He didn't come to, did he? We don't want him to remember anything beyond the blackjack."

"He wasn't awake; just jerked when he got the needle."

But he was awake, and stayed awake. He was dazed, sick, dull-minded, but still conscious and determined to stay that way. Fighting against giving in to the darkness to which his mind wanted to succumb as the contents of the hypo spread through his blood stream. He lay inert and motionless, deliberately breathing slowly and regularly, hiding every outward evidence of the fight his mind was putting up against unconsciousness.

It grew dark suddenly and he knew they had driven into a garage. The grip on his arms tightened again and he was half dragged, half carried, from the landcab. He allowed himself to open his eyes a mere slit, enough to make out his surroundings. Sure enough, they were in a garage and he was being hauled toward steps leading downward at the back of it.

"Shake it up," one of his captors said. "We're ten seconds behind schedule now. And don't worry about mussing the guy; he's supposed to be banged up plenty."

They hurried him down the cellar steps into a lighted room, a typical under-residence room that contained the standard heating apparatus and laundry equipment of the twenty-second century—and the typical trash and odds and ends that clutter a basement in any century whatever. But at the far end of the cellar, screened from view until they rounded a pile of packing crates, was an object that surprised Anders so much that he almost revealed his consciousness.

It was a Kingston Duplicator. An illegal, jerrybuilt one, here in New Albuquerque.

He knew all too well the character of the Duplies, products of the Duplicator. Their complete egotism, their utter lack of any moral sense whatsoever, their cold viciousness and inhumanity. But he was still amazed that they'd have the utter gall to construct an illegal machine of their own here on Venus.

Back of the Duplicator itself was a huge condenser of a type he'd never seen before, something the Duplies themselves must have developed for the purpose. They could load a condenser of that size with enough juice to operate the Duplicator once by feeding it current a little at a time over a period of weeks, so there would be no sudden great drain of power that would give away to the authorities the presence and use of a Duplicator. It was a clever idea Anders had to admit to himself. As far as he knew, nobody had used it before. Why, with the use of an attachment like that, there could be Duplicators in any city on Earth, undetected and undetectable.

He knew now all too well what they were going to do to him. If he'd had, the least bit of strength, he'd have tried a break then and there. But the combined effects of the blackjack and the drug had left him only an edge of consciousness. He couldn't have stood on his own feet and walked out, even if they'd let go of him. He'd have to wait for a later opportunity—not that he really expected to get one.

The machine, he'd seen at first glance, was adjusted for human duplication-transmission. They strapped him into the chair—for all the world like an old-fashioned electric chair except that it had no electrodes—that was bolted to the field platform.

When the switch was thrown there'd be a duplicate of him on Mars—except that duplicate would be a Duplie instead of a human being. It would be exactly like him in every way, except that it would lack that intangible ingredient "soul", that ingredient man had never been too sure he had until the Kingston Duplicator had proved it to him—and had created chaos in the process.

CHAPTER II
Trouble Comes Double

VENUS HAD been the first planet colonized. The first explorers to penetrate its eternal cloud envelope had found, to everyone's surprise, a breathable atmosphere. This had been hidden from the spectroscopes of Earth's astronomers by the peculiar constitution of that cloud envelope which hid Venus' surface from the observation of Earth.

The colonization of Mars had not been possible until almost a century later. There had been only experimental outposts there, under domes, until the technology of the late twenty-first century had provided the means of creating an artificial atmosphere. This was done by concentrating what oxygen there was in a narrow band close to the surface instead of letting it diffuse itself through the entire depth of atmosphere. Held close to the ground, it made Mars habitable, except for mountainous or plateau areas.

By that time, constant travel between Earth and Venus had caused interplanetary travel to develop to the point where it was easy and inexpensive, and the colonization of Mars had been very rapid. It had been a spontaneous emigration of the common people that had caused Mars, for a while, to suffer from a lack of trained scientists and statesmen—a lack of qualified leadership. Men who had achieved success and eminence on Earth did not care to emigrate.

That's where the Kingston Duplicator had come in; it had seemed to be a perfect answer to Mars' problem. It had enabled men like Duclos, Kingston himself, Barry, Wade and hundreds of others—the men who had contributed most to the science and political leadership of Earth—to remain at home on Earth, and to have duplicates of themselves sent to Mars. The Duplies were to contribute to the advancement of Mars what their originals had contributed and were contributing to the advancement of Earth.

There was a catch, but nobody knew about it until too late.

The Kingston Duplicator had been invented early in the twenty-second century. One Duplicator, adjustable either as transmitter or receiver, could send to another—at either close range or interplanetary distances—a duplicate of any object placed in the field of the transmitting machine. It did not involve, of course, any creation of matter. The receiving machine drew upon a hopper of anything at all, usually sand, which was transmuted electronically into whatever elements were needed for creation of the duplicate.

With respect to inanimate objects, the Kingston Duplicator had only one theoretical limitation; one that was learned the hard way. Fissionable material, even in less than critical quantities, could not be transmitted-duplicated without exploding in the sending machine.

The Duplicator had, of course, changed the economy of Earth (and of Venus and Mars) but not completely, not too greatly. The tremendous amount of power it required prevented its practical use for the reproduction of anything except expensive and valuable things. Of what benefit to reproduce a bushel of wheat or a chair at a cost of a thousand dollars worth of power when you can grow the wheat or make the chair much more cheaply? On the other hand, a five-thousand dollar mink coat becomes less of a luxury item when it can be duplicated for a fifth of that sum; small precision instruments, very valuable relative to weight, became cheaper in duplication; rare metals and elements (except the fissionable ones) became less prohibitively expensive and thereby opened new fields to technology.

The government had made one restriction to protect the investment of those who had money invested in precious stones: diamonds, except those necessary for industrial use, were restricted.

SO WERE human beings. Early experiments with lesser animals had shown that duplication of them was quite possible, without apparent harm to the animals—and also without commercial possibilites, since it remained cheaper to raise a pig than to duplicate it. But before a single human being had been duplicated by a Kingston Duplicator, governments acting in concert ruled against the attempt.

If for no other reason, there would be too many legal difficulties involved in the duplication of a human being. A wife could find herself with duplicate identical husbands; a job or a bank account or an insurance policy would find itself with duplicate identical claimants. And which was the original and what would be the rights of the duplicate? And, besides, there was no logical reason for permitting the duplication of a human being.

Until the lack of technicians and leaders in the new Martian colonies suggested an advantage to human duplication that seemed, if proper restrictions were observed, the perfect answer to the problem. Suppose Duclos, top electronics engineer of Earth—and electronics engineers were badly needed on Mars—agreed to have a duplicate of himself created on and for Mars. Duclos had nothing to lose—except that he signed a paper agreeing never to leave Earth, which he had no desire to do anyway. His duplicate would be required to agree never to leave Mars. The Martian government would give the Duplie an amount of money equal to whatever the original possessed. Only men with no close family ties could be chosen. As long as they remained as far apart as Earth and Mars, there could be no conflict of personal interests between them.

It seemed foolproof, and the experiment was permitted. Duclos was duplicated. His Duplie took over electronics development on Mars—and voiced no objection to his lot. Wade, top man in interplanetary economics. Kingston, inventor of the Duplicator, acquired a duplicate on Mars. Several hundred others, top men in every other important field.

Then the catch. The unsuspected missing ingredient.

The first of the Duplies had concealed, cleverly, their essential non-humanness, their plans, until the quota had been filled. Then—all of them—starting with those in positions of power at the top—they had taken over Mars. And few of the human people of Mars knew or even suspected that they had been taken over. There were top statesmen, top propagandists, among the Duplies.

And now Mars was at war with Earth. A peculiar war...

STRAPPED IN the chair, Matt Anders suddenly realized that he should have fought his captors, even without chance of winning, on the off chance that he might have been killed in the struggle. Until this moment he hadn't realized how much better it would have been to die rather than to be duplicated on Mars. For his duplicate would—at least after indoctrination—be on their side. And his duplicate would know every political and military secret of Earth known to him, Matt Anders, right-hand man, hatchetman extraordinary, of Dwight Morphy, President of the Council of Nations of Earth. The top secrets, just about all of them of Terran policy and planning. It wasn't only his ability, valuable as that alone would be to them that they were duplicating; it was his knowledge.

The instant he realized that, he would have rushed to commit suicide, had there been any possible way for him to do so before they threw the switch.

For a second, blinding light played around him, but he felt nothing. Except for the slight temporary pain in his eyes from the light—and that could have been avoided by a blindfold—duplication was painless, without sensation.

Then, the sudden aftereffect that had been noticed in every living thing, animal or human, who had been duplicated — temporary unconsciousness that would last a few minutes. He felt himself slipping into it and he knew, and was past caring, that in his case he'd never waken from it. Now that they'd duplicated him, they'd kill him quickly before he came out of the aftereffect, before they even unstrapped him from the chair.

The last thing he knew was that somebody was telling somebody else to hurry damn it hurry, and then the blackness and the blankness came...

SOMEONE WAS shaking his shoulder gently. Someone was saying, "Are you hurt badly? Was it a hit-and-run car? Should I call an ambulance?"

Matt Anders sat up groggily. He was at the point along the street where he had been attacked. He looked about him; his hat was lying in the gutter and his briefcase was where he had dropped it during the brief struggle. The landcab wasn't in sight.

There wasn't any evidence at all that he'd been kidnapped and then returned to the same spot where the assault had occurred. And they thought he'd been unconscious since that first blow with the blackjack; he wasn't supposed to know that anything besides the assault had happened; he wasn't supposed to know that he'd been duplicated.

And he hadn't any proof, except his own word that he had been. The Venusian authorities would tell him his story was fantastic—and it would sound that way. It was fantastic that there could be an illegal, private Duplicator, operated by Duplies, here in orderly and peaceful New Albuquerque. He himself could hardly believe what had happened. The Venusian authorities would accuse him of lying in order to create an interplanetary episode.

"Are you all right?" somebody said. "Shall I call an ambulance?"

He put his hand to the back of his head as he turned to look up. The man standing behind him was small, mild, inoffensive. A typical clerk or bookkeeper from one of the government offices.

"I'm all right," Anders said. "I'll be all right in a minute. Just a sore noggin from a sap."

"A sap? Oh, you mean a—a blunt weapon? Were you attacked and robbed?"

Had they been that thorough? He put his hand into the pocket where he'd carried money. It was gone. They'd been thorough enough to make it look like an assault and robbery. Not that the money mattered; once he was out of his disguise, his signature was good for any reasonable amount at any Venusian bank. But the valuable information in his briefcase— No, they wouldn't have bothered tampering with that. The papers in the secret compartment were valuable only for the information on them, and that information was in his head as well. It would also be in the head of his Duplie on Mars.

He got to his feet a little shakily and found that he was all right, except for the ache in the back of his head and the dustiness of his clothes. He said, "I'm all right, thanks."

"You're sure? You're sure you don't want—?"

"I'm sure," Anders said. "Thanks a lot, but I'm sure. I've got only a block to go, and I'll report this to the police from there." He knew it would seem strange to the little clerk if he didn't intend to report it.

He got his hat and briefcase and started off, a bit waveringly at first, but more firmly after he'd gone a few steps. After one try at putting the hat back on his head, he carried it in his hand. His head would be too sore for days to let him wear a hat. He grinned wryly as it came to him that his duplicate on Mars would have an equivalently sore head; the blow of the blackjack had fallen before the duplication.

HE WAS less than fifteen minutes late when he arrived at Ambassador Pearson's residence. He stopped outside the door long enough to brush most of the dust from his clothes and then rang the bell.

Pearson himself came to open the door. He looked blankly until Anders said, "Matt Anders, Mr. Ambassador. Please overlook the disguise—at least until I have a chance to remove it."

"Anders! But—" Pearson looked down at Anders' clothes. "—what on earth happened? Did you have an accident?" His eyes widened. "Or are you Matt Anders? That disguise—"

Anders grinned. "Is a good one. But if you'll suspend disbelief long enough to give me access to a lavatory for a few minutes, I think you'll recognize me. And after that I'll tell you what happened."

"Certainly. And while you're there, can I make you a drink? You look as though you could use one. Something Venusian, or—?"

"Whiskey," Anders said. "A big slug of it, straight, wouldn't hurt me a bit."

Pearson showed him a door. "That room will do. And your drink will be waiting, Matt."

In the lavatory, it took only a few minutes to remove the thin rubber mask, backed by sponge rubber in places, to change the shape of his features and to remove the gray wig that had helped cut down the force of the blackjack blow. There was a clothes brush and it removed the rest of the street dirt from his coat and trousers.

He looked at himself in the glass, and the face that looked back at him was a familiar one. A thin, angular face—vaguely Mephisphelean. Very Mephisphelean in the many caricatures of him that had been in the newspapers of three planets.

Not a popular face, even among people of his own planet. The face of a man reputed to wield too much power and to wield it ruthlessly—and a man whose face, particularly in caricature, looked the part. But a handsome face, an interesting one. A face all too easy to remember, which was why he wore such careful disguises when he traveled alone. How had the Duplies penetrated that disguise? His best friend—and that was probably President Morphy—couldn't have done so.

His drink, and a comfortable chair, was waiting for him when he rejoined Pearson. He sank into the chair and drank deeply and appreciatively. Then he put down his glass and said, "Mr. Ambassador, I believe I've learned the secret of the disasters we've had recently. I believe I know how the Duplies have been getting their information."

He frowned. "And it's about time if it isn't too late. It shouldn't be any secret that our morale has been on the skids for months. At this rate, in spite of the fact that we control space and have the Duplies pretty solidly blockaded, we'll lose the war due to apathy on Earth. Corruption, bribery, inability— let's face it—among our top military leaders. Our munitions industry breaking down—from the top. Our diplomats losing point in negotiations with Venus to come in on our side."

The ambassador winced at the last sentence. "That's rather a blow under the belt, isn't it, Matt? I've done my best."

"Sure. But you're bucking espionage beyond anything you've ever dreamed of. That's what I found out today. Mars knows already every detail of the information and instructions I've brought you—and I haven't even turned them over to you yet."

"Good God, Matt. Are you sure? How?"

Anders told him, briefly, the experience he'd just had—and wasn't supposed to remember.

Pearson's face was a pattern of dismay when he'd finished. He thought and then asked, "But why didn't they kill you? I don't understand that. Duplicated on Mars or not, you're still a valuable man to Earth."

"Two reasons, Sir. First, the information they'll get from my duplicate will be more valuable to them if, as they think, we don't know they have it. If I disappeared, or were found dead under whatever circumstances, there'd be at least a suspicion that they had the information I was carrying—a copy of it, even though the original was still in my briefcase. Second, what if they plan, later, to get my Duplie to Earth through the blockade—and they do get ships through it, either way—and then have me killed under circumstances where he can step into my shoes." He leaned forward earnestly. "And if that's happened already to some of our top men, it explains a lot. A hell of a lot."

"But if that's true—"

There was a knock on the door, a soft tap.

Pearson frowned. "Must be my daughter. Well—I won't let her interrupt us long." He raised his voice, "Come in."

THE DOOR opened and the girl who came through it was, Matt Anders thought, possibly the most striking girl he'd ever seen. There was something about the way she held herself, the way she walked... He remembered now having heard that Ambassador Pearson had a great grandparent who had been a full-blooded Sioux; it was obvious in his daughter. Her cheekbones were high, her complexion dark, her hair raven black and worn in braids across the top of her head. Tall, lithe, full breasted, calm-eyed, she carried herself with the pride and dignity of the Plains Indian. And although she was young — possibly ten years Anders' junior she had the poise and assurance of a woman who has been conscious of her beauty for years.

Matt Anders was on his feet before Pearson's murmured introduction. He swallowed, and immediately felt ridiculous at the reaction. But almost all the women he'd ever met had seemed weak and insipid to him. Marta Pearson was something else again. She was almost an atavism; she was as different from the modern woman of the twenty-second century as a tiger from its descendent, a tabby cat. And maybe that accounted, Anders thought, for his reaction. He had often suspected that he himself, emotionally, belonged in a different and earlier century.

She smiled distantly in acknowledgment of the introduction, but her smile didn't reach beyond her lips as she held out a cool hand to him. And her words were to her father. "I recognized Matt Anders immediately, Father. After all, one can hardly look at a periodical or tune in a visor without seeing the features of the famous alter ego of President Morphy. His *hatchetman*, I believe, is the commoner term."

Her father said sharply, "Marta!"

Matt Anders felt himself flush, the first time he'd done so, to his own recollection, since adolescence. But he made his voice calm. "It isn't always easy to serve your planet in the way your superiors direct, Miss Pearson. Especially when your position isn't an elective one from which you can be removed for unpopularity." He hesitated for a moment, then decided to continue: "Hasn't it occurred to you that, disliked as I am, President Morphy is the most respected and loved person on Earth? But if there wasn't a Matt Anders, a hatchetman, to do certain things for him, perhaps he could not even be re-elected. Right now, he's just about all that's holding Earth together and keeping the anti-war faction from letting the Duplies have their way on Mars."

He wondered, even as he talked, why he was bothering to justify himself. He was used to being hated by millions. Why worry about one more—except that the one more was suddenly important to him?

Marta Pearson still smiled coolly, "A convincing little speech, Mr. Anders. Unfortunately, it seems difficult for me to forget that it was you who ordered the Third Fleet to take the Martian base on Calypso at all costs. And all costs turned out to be the loss of three-fourths of the fleet. Oh, they took Calypso, yes. But where were you at the time, Mr. Anders?"

She had touched a raw spot. He paled, angry at her, angrier at himself for allowing her to put him on the defensive like this. "I was on Luna, Miss Pearson, when the Third Fleet left there on its mission. I did not accompany it, on strict and specific orders from President Morphy. He, not I, thought I was too valuable to risk, especially since I have no training in space combat and would have been of no special value to the fleet."

HER SMILE was openly sardonic now. "Yet you ordered them—and don't deny it was your order—to take Calypso at all costs. And they were obliged to obey that order even when it was found the satellite's defenses were far stronger than had been guessed."

"Marta!" her father said again.

"And they took it," she went on. "With losses of three ships out of four. My brother was on one of the ships that didn't make it; my fiancé on another."

She turned and walked from the room.

"I'm sorry, Matt," Pearson said. "I don't know what I can say or do…"

Anders grinned wryly. "You might get me another drink, Mr. Ambassador. If she'd waited, I could have told her my own brother happened to be with that fleet—and didn't come back."

"That I can tell her—and will, Matt. And I wish top secrecy didn't prevent my telling even my own daughter the reason that order was necessary, and would have been justified, even if it had meant complete loss of several fleets."

Matt Anders took the glass Pearson held out to him. "You know that?"

"Yes. Uranium on Calypso. None on Mars. Which is why that base was of vital importance to the Duplies and why it was equally vital to us to keep them away from it. If they once get quantities of uranium…"

Anders nodded gloomily. "If they do, then the war is no longer in space only. We'll have to destroy their cities to keep them from destroying ours—and it will end up with both being destroyed. As long as there's even a chance of the stalemate's continuing, anything would be better than that."

He flicked his hand in a characteristic gesture, brushing the subject aside. He downed his second drink before he picked up his briefcase and took papers from the secret compartment, which he handed to the ambassador. "Well, here's what I was to deliver to you, Sir, and now it's delivered. Only—and keep this between us—work on the certainty that the Duplies have this information, too. At least the general outlines of it. If I'd been able to memorize all the minor details and figures, of course, I wouldn't have carried the papers. But my Duplie will know all I knew about it—and that's enough to make it practically worthless."

Pearson looked puzzled. "But you said 'between us'. You mean you're not going to report what happened to you?"

"Not while I'm on Venus. I'm not to stay here long anyway. Just long enough, in fact, to get a night's sleep tonight. I'll leave in the morning. And what I've learned through my own kidnapping and duplication is so important I want to report it in person, direct to Morphy. I won't even trust the tightbeam; we're not sure the Duplies aren't tapping it."

"I see, Matt. Probably you're right. And I'm awfully sorry about Marta."

"It could have been worse. At least she didn't take a shot at me. And that's happened three times in three months back on Earth. Misguided people—and they weren't all Duplies, either—seemed to think killing me would solve all the problems of the solar system."

"Well—I'll talk to her before dinner. By the way, Matt, one thing I've wondered about. Not that it matters. Did you give that order to the Third Fleet? Or did you just transmit the President's order?"

"Oh, I gave it all right. It became a sudden emergency when we learned about the uranium angle on Calypso, and I couldn't reach Morphy immediately so I gave the order. Later, of course, he confirmed it. But the publicity went to my issuance of the order, not his confirmation of it." He shrugged. "Well, that's part of my job, to take the blame for nasty things off his shoulders. And that was a particularly nasty one from the outside—because we had to hold back, for security reasons, why Calypso was suddenly so vitally important."

Pearson nodded slowly. "I begin to see how tough a job you've got. Wish I could tell that to Marta. Suppose I can tell her that it was of vital importance, even if I don't tell her why. And that you lost your brother there, too."

Anders said, "Don't, please. It's part of my job to have people feel like that about me." But he knew, even as he said it that he didn't want Marta Pearson to feel that way. The girl attracted him as no woman ever had before.

THE AMBASSADOR cleared his throat. "Just the same, I'm going to talk to her. By the way, we dine early on Venus. If you wish, before dinner, to be shown to your room to bathe and…you didn't bring any luggage, so I presume you won't have to change—"

"The bath sounds good to me, but haven't you heard of washtex? I can wash these right under the shower with me and they'll dry, in the original folds, in three minutes. Luggage will be a thing of the past when these become common, unless one's taking a long enough trip to want variety in costume."

"Good. Then I'll show you to—"

"Wait, Mr. Ambassador. If we can spare a few minutes, I've just got an idea. Let me think it out a second, first."

Anders had stood up. Now, he sat down again in his chair, and the ambassador sat down again too. After a few seconds, Anders said, "I think it's a good idea. Listen, I know how we can put a crimp in whatever plans the Duplies may have for substituting my Duplie for me somewhere. They can't know how badly I was injured by that blackjack; they didn't have time to give me a medical examination. Suppose you put out a general story—give it to the newscast services —that, shortly after my arrival here, I died of a brain concussion. The Duplies will believe it."

"But—Good Lord, Matt—"

"Let me finish. You also send a tightbeam message to Morphy telling him that the newscast story is a phony; that I'll report to him as soon as possible and explain it. For him to arrange so I can land safely—in the same disguise and under the same name I used coming here—without being shot as a Duplie of myself. The Duplies know that disguise, but if they think I'm dead they won't be watching for me."

"But you yourself said we're not absolutely sure they don't intercept our tightbeam. What if they do?"

Anders' hand flipped the possibility aside. "Nothing's certain. If they do intercept it, we've lost nothing. If they don't, we're a jump up on them." He grinned. "And we can always announce that the report of my death was exaggerated—much as that will disappoint many people. You'll do it?"

"Of course, Matt."

"Let's see—Earth time—Morphy won't be getting up for a couple of hours yet. Get the telenews story out right away, if you will, but hold off until after dinner on the tightbeam correction; no use waking him up. His health's not been too good lately, and he's been working much too long hours."

Besides, he thought to himself, it wouldn't hurt Morphy to think for a few hours, if he got the telenews story first, that he'd lost himself a messenger boy. It might give him something to think about, before the secret correction came.

"If you want it that way, Matt—"

"I do. And now if I could go to my room—"

CHAPTER III
Death for a Duplie

HE STRIPPED and washed his clothes first, so they'd dry while he bathed himself. The bath felt wonderful, as did the few minutes he spent under the automatic masseur. By the time he was ready for it, his clothing was dry, unwrinkled, and looking as though it had just come from the factory. Washtex—this was the first time he'd tried it—was going to be popular indeed. He looked at the comfortable clean-sheeted bed yearningly and wished he could spend a few hours in it.

He knew perfectly well that Pearson would excuse him from dinner if he explained how tired he was after the trip from Earth. But—all right, admit it, he told himself—you want to see Marta again no matter how tired you are, and no matter what her attitude toward you may be this time.

Refilling his pockets with the sundry things he'd taken from them before washing the suit, he hesitated as he picked up the electrogun, which he always carried in an inside pocket. It was a neat and deadly little weapon, weighing only six ounces but packing the punch of an elephant gun and completely silent in its operation. He shrugged, checked the mechanism, and put it in his pocket.

He left his room and walked down the stairs, the neoplast soles of his shoes making no noise whatsoever. As he neared the door of the library where he'd had—his previous talk with the ambassador, and his embarrassing encounter with Marta, he heard both of their voices raised a little, he thought, above ordinary conversational level. Undoubtedly they were discussing him; probably Marta was being reprimanded for the things she had said—and was arguing back.

Curiosity got the better of him. Snooping or not, he wanted too badly to hear what Marta had to say about him to worry, just at that moment, about gentlemanly instincts. He took a few steps neared the door; he could hear clearly now what was being said, if there was a break in the conversation or if either voice approached nearer the doorway, he could start walking quickly and avoid the appearance of having, been standing there.

Marta seemed to be apologizing for the scene she had made. Matt Anders stood even more quietly; walking in now would be even more embarrassing than if he walked in on a quarrel.

AND THEN suddenly Marta's voice changed, became cold again. "But, Father, that isn't what I wanted to tell you. It is this: that information Matt Anders brought you—you mustn't present it at the conference tomorrow."

"I don't know what you're talking about, Marta. I can see, of course, how you could easily guess the reason for Matt's trip here. But why do you say—?"

"The Duplies have that information, yes. But hasn't it occurred to you that they won't have time, by tomorrow, to prepare a suitable rebuttal? That we can't let you present it?"

"I don't—what are you saying, Marta?"

"It's quite simple, Father. I mean—this."

Matt Anders had been slower than usual. He should have got it four sentences ago. He moved swiftly now to the doorway, and his electrogun was in his hand when he got there. Too late—just in time to see the purple arc of the electrogun in the hand of the Duplie of Marta Pearson leap from its muzzle to the chest of the ambassador. His own electrogun fired in almost the same instant.

He stepped quickly into the room, pulling the door shut behind him. There had been two thuds of falling bodies, but he doubted that the sound would have been heard in whatever quarter of the house servants were preparing dinner. Houses on Venus are made of thick concrete, and the sound of a jar does not carry easily even into the next room.

They were both dead, of course; he didn't have to verify that. An electrogun discharge doesn't mark a body, but no matter where it strikes, even a toe or finger, it is fully as deadly as a direct hit from a heavy space cannon.

His lips thinned back over his teeth as he stared down at the beautiful body that had been a Duplie of Marta Pearson. Had she been a Duplie that afternoon when he had first met her? Well, it didn't matter now.

But one thing did matter—and vitally. Had Pearson, before the start of the conversation with what he thought was his daughter, given out the news of Anders' death from brain concussion? If so, Anders was in a hell of a spot. Pearson was the only person who could send a convincing tightbeam message to Earth to contradict that report, and Pearson was dead. He didn't even know where Pearson's tightbeam transmitter was; it would be carefully concealed somewhere and would take hours, probably, to find. And he didn't have hours; the servants who were preparing dinner would be announcing it soon.

And here he was with two dead bodies on his hands—and nothing about Marta's body that would prove it was a Duplie of her instead of the original. And if his own death had already been announced, he was the one who would be taken for a Duplie and shot on sight by the Venusian police. Despite the fact that Venus maintained neutrality in the Earth-Mars war, they knew the character of Duplies and hated them as much as Earthmen did. No Duplies were tolerated on Venus; the members of the Martian consulate had to prove their origin and birth—had to be dupes of the Duplies, not Duplies themselves.

And damn vacillating Venus for that, for refusing to take active part in a war against inhuman things whom they recognized to be utterly evil.

But no time to think about that now. He'd have to act, and quickly. His eyes cast about and found the telenews set on a stand in the corner. He snapped it on, manipulated the dial until he found a station just starting on a news program.

A report or two on the war—news he already knew and to which he listened impatiently. Then: "It was announced half an hour ago by Terrestrial Ambassador Pearson that Matt Anders, personal aide to President Morphy of Earth, died this afternoon as a result of—"

He snapped it off; he didn't need to hear the rest. And Pearson would not yet have sent the tightbeam message of contradiction. He'd promised to wait until after dinner for that, and Pearson was a man of his word even in tiny things.

He went to the door and locked it; that would give him seconds of extra time if a servant came to announce dinner. Quickly, he dragged the two bodies out of sight behind a sofa; that would give him seconds more and a chance to talk his way out if he had to unlock the door.

He sat down in a chair to think.

It was fatal to stay on Venus. It would be fatal to go to Earth.

Suddenly he laughed. There was still Mars.

And why not? If he could get through the blockade—and others had done it—

I've got a Duplie on Mars, he thought viciously. He intended to replace me, if he could. Now the Duplies think I'm dead. *What if I can replace him?*

IT SOUNDED like a chance in a thousand. Maybe a million. Or maybe only a hundred, since the advantage of surprise would be completely in his favor, with the Duplies not even suspecting what he intended, since they would think—along with Earth and Venus—that Matt Anders was a dead duck.

Suddenly he was almost glad that tightbeam contradiction hadn't been sent.

Suddenly he was free.

Morphy, he thought, you've lost yourself a messenger boy.

How many minutes did he have? Enough to get back into his disguise as an elderly merchant of precious stones? He had to have enough minutes; otherwise he couldn't get his Spacezephyr at the spaceport.

He moved fast now. Telephone. The spaceport. His voice suddenly the voice of an old man. "Harvey Giles speaking. Owner of Spacezephyr SZ-1470. I learn I must return to Earth quickly; my son is seriously ill. Can you have the craft ready for me in ten minutes? Thank you. Thank you very much."

The bodies. A better job of concealment, so hidden that they wouldn't show unless someone deliberately looked under the sofa or over its back. Marta's body so beautiful. Damn Duplies. Was Marta alive somewhere? It was unlikely, almost impossible. Why would they have kept her alive after duplicating her? And after having her Duplie take her place. They'd kept him alive, but only because they had to wait until his Duplie had a chance to replace him. So forget Marta; she's dead. And luckily, her Duplie was dead now too.

He left the door of the library open behind him.

In his room, he jerked the briefcase open, took out the disguise, the rubber mask and wig. He got them on, not too good a job but it would pass casual inspection. Five minutes gone since he'd left the library. How many more before dinner? And for how many minutes thereafter would the servants look around the house before they called the police, or found the bodies and then called the police?

Down the stairs and his luck held. Outside, into the early evening. A landcab was going by and he hailed it. He'd take his chances on its being what it seemed; but his hand was on the butt of his electrogun as he got into it, and stayed there until it let him off at the spaceport.

The usual brief formalities, the casual glance at his identification and at himself. On Earth it would have been stricter. But then Earth was at war, and Venus wasn't.

His ship was ready, waiting.

Blastoff.

Straight up, of course, first; and when he moved the gyroturn handle, he turned the little ship toward Earth. Probably there'd be a routine radar check to see that he took the course he'd said he was taking; interceptors notified to challenge him if he didn't. Besides, eight or ten hours travel toward Earth would lose him only an hour or two. Luckily, Mars was in the same general direction across the ecliptic.

Luckily, too, he had benephrin tablets to keep him awake for the fifty-hour trip to Mars. One can't afford to doze on a one-man craft in space, which turned out to be far more crowded with meteors and planetoids than Earth-bound man had ever guessed. When he hit Mars, he'd need at least twenty-four hours sleep under another drug to counteract the benephrin binge, but he'd worry about that when he got there.

Forty-five hours later and a million miles out from Mars, he came to the blockade patrol. His receiver barked, "Identify yourself immediately or we open fire!"

THE WAR between Earth and Mars was a peculiar war. Earth could have destroyed Mars at any time—but didn't. Earth had atomic bombs; the hundred cities of Mars, which housed almost a billion people, could have been wiped out within a week. But those billion people were colonists from Earth, friends and relatives of almost every family on Earth.

The Duplies, of course, knew this emotional appeal and counted on it. They also pointed, propaganda-wise, to the fact that they had made no attack on the cities of Earth and did not intend to. Of course they did not intend to—without uranium to make bombs. Mars itself had no uranium, no fissionable matter of any kind. And it was fortunate for Earth that the Kingston Duplicator exploded on any attempt to duplicate a fissionable substance, else all the Duplies would have needed was one small piece of uranium, which they could have duplicated endlessly until they had enough to blow Earth out of the solar system. And no sense of morality to keep them from doing just that.

So the war had been in space, where Earth had the edge and had a blockade around Mars—although Martian blockade-runners frequently got through it. And the war, unknown to the citizens, was also a war on Earth—war of espionage, propaganda, sabotage of morale, conducted by a few well-placed Duplies.

And Martian propaganda didn't sound unreasonable, for it claimed it wanted only to be left alone. It would have been all too reasonable, except that the billion people of Mars were the dupes of the Duplies, under their absolute control.

Propagandizing the true Martian colonists about the real nature of the Duplies would have been the answer, but the Duplies controlled channels of communication. All Martian radios and televisors were tight-tuned to the big broadcasting station of Marsport; they could receive no messages from Earth or from ships in space. The Martians were completely shut off from the rest of the system—and had no choice but to believe the propaganda their leaders fed them. And their leaders were Duplies. The Martians thought they were fighting a War of Independence against Earth; they didn't even know that their independence had already been granted and that they were already a free planet and no longer a colony.

MATT ANDERS continued his course. The next challenge came only seconds later: "Identify yourself immediately or we fire."

He couldn't safely ignore that one. He pressed the two-way visiplate button so the flagship, which had done the challenging, was in visual as well as auditory communication. Lieutenant-Commander Gresham's heavy-jowled face appeared on the screen in the little Spacezephyr. Anders knew that, in the flagship, Gresham was seeing Anders' face with the disguise long since removed.

Anders said crisply, "You know me, Gresham. Confidential mission, highly important." If he could stall a few more seconds, he'd be through. Right now they probably couldn't fire at him because he was among them; thirty seconds more and he'd be out of range past them—if his bluff worked. If he could only make Gresham hesitate. If Gresham only hadn't heard the news that—

Gresham hesitated. His mouth opened a little, snapped shut, then opened again and he said, "But you're—"

He didn't finish, but Matt Anders knew that Gresham had heard the news Ambassador Pearson had given out to the newscasters.

Two more seconds passed, and then Anders knew that he was safe, for Gresham still stared at him. Then Gresham said, "But, Anders, we received no orders on this. I'm afraid I must ask you to report to me on the flagship for clearance."

And that had killed another dozen seconds. Gresham was stalling, letting him through. Gresham was a Duplie. Which accounted for the relative ease with which blockade-runners had been getting through. Now Gresham, having heard of his "death" on Venus, thought that he was one.

Deadpan, Anders helped with the stalling. "Afraid, Commander, that's impossible. Direct orders from President Morphy. Suggest you check with him." Gresham would check with him all right—to keep his own nose clean—but even if he got Morphy at once, enough minutes would have been wasted.

He was out of range now, already, and with a sigh of relief he clicked off the screen. He'd never thought, before, that he'd be glad to find out any highly placed Earth officer was a Duplie. If

Gresham hadn't been one he still might have bluffed his way through, but it would have been much tougher going.

He landed the Spacezephyr in a high valley between Martian mountains, about eighty miles from the main city of Marsport. A relatively safe place to laud the craft and to leave it; the valley was above the level of breathable atmosphere, so no Martian would come there for any ordinary reason. Anders would have to wear an oxygen mask to get down to breathable air, but the Spacezephyr carried one. His only danger of being spotted was from above, and he'd have to chance that.

He needed sleep; almost a hundred hours without it, even with benephrin to keep him going, had sapped his stamina so much that his physical and mental reactions were sluggish and he couldn't have walked half a mile, ever under Martin gravity, without keeling over. He needed at least twenty-four hours of sleep under the drug that was the counteractant to the benephrin. Here, before he left the little spaceship, in a spot no Martian would come to, was the best place to get it He took the counter-drug, made himself as comfortable as he could, and was asleep in less than a minute.

HE SLEPT longer than he'd intended, almost thirty hours. And when he awoke it was night. Deimos and Phobos, the two moons of Mars were in the sky, but gave little light. He'd have to use a hand flash and once he was in sight of the road over the top of the mountain, he would be conspicuous. He decided to wait until daylight for his trip over and down the mountain to the nearest road.

He waited until dawn before he left the Spacezephyr. The range he had to scale, up one side and down the other, would have been a day's work on Earth; on Mars, at .38 Earth gravity, he weighed less than sixty pounds so it was easy, if sometimes risky, climbing. He was over and down before the Martian noon. As soon as he was low enough for the air to be breathable, he hid his oxygen mask carefully in a place where he could find it again in case he lived long enough ever to want to make his way back to the spacecraft. Then he walked to the nearest road. He stood along the edge, waiting.

Luckily, it was a road used not too frequently. Landcars whizzed by at intervals of five or ten minutes, just about right for his purpose. He waited until a gray military one came along, with no other car in sight in either direction. He stood still until it was just past him, then drew his electrogun and fired at it. A purple flash darted from the muzzle of the gun to the speeding car. Possibly at that distance, and diffused by the body of the landcar, the shock of the bolt may not have been lethal. But it was enough of a shock to the driver to make him lose control. The car swerved, tires screamed. The car tipped, then rolled. Anders ran toward it. When he got there, its occupant was dead, his head a gory mess against the broken driving column. He wore a captain's uniform—or what was left of one.

Anders waited by the wrecked vehicle, knowing that the next military car wouldn't pass without investigating this one. Civilians would; hands off anything remotely resembling military affairs were their strict orders on Mars.

Several civilian cars went by in the next twenty minutes, slowing down out of curiosity—but pretending not to slow down—and their occupants looking curiously at the wrecked car and at Matt Anders, waiting there so calmly. But none of them stopped.

Then the jackpot he'd been waiting for. A gray car that stopped, brakes squealing, just beyond the wreck, and backed up. And the man in it wore the insignia of a lieutenant general; he might even be a Duplie. The captain had probably been only a dupe, and Anders had been sorry about that. But what was one life when billions were at stake?

The lieutenant general got out of the gray landcar and walked over scowling. "What's this? And what are you doing here? Who are—?"

Matt Anders shot from the electrogun got him. There was nothing to be gained by conversation. He pulled open the door of the wrecked car and shoved the body of the lieutenant general through it. That would stall investigation a little; whoever found the wreck next would assume the two had been riding together, with the captain acting as chauffeur. A missing military landcar wouldn't be looked for at once.

Just the same he got into the other landcar as quickly as he could and got away from there fast. He drove twenty miles before he found a side road; he turned into it, and as soon as he was out of sight of the main road he stopped and looked through the documents compartment of the car. He found what he wanted most, a road map of the area and a city map of Marsport. He also found enough identification to tell him it was the car of Lieutenant General MacWheeler. The name MacWheeler was recalled to him as being one of the original batch of Duplies sent to Mars. MacWheeler's original on Earth, he remembered, had been an expert in rocket technology.

One Duplie less now.

HE STUDIED the maps thoroughly; memorizing, so he wouldn't have to stop on a main road or in traffic, the route to Marsport; the simplest route through it which would take him to the domes, the Duplie headquarters. Here, if anywhere, he'd find his own Duplie. Beyond that, he couldn't plan.

As he neared Duplie headquarters, the insignia on the landcar he drove—fortunately for him indicating only the rank of its owner, not his identity—proved its value. Sentries snapped to attention, gates were opened. He parked the landcar and left it, tried to act casual as he strolled toward the domes.

Earth espionage on Mars by no means matched Martian—Duplie—espionage on Earth. He knew about the domes, but not much beyond the fact that they were Duplie headquarters, and that they were dozens of yards thick and proof against atomic bombing. Which meant that if Earth was ever forced to bomb Marsport they'd kill everyone except the Duplies, the only ones they'd want to kill.

There were half a dozen domes and he hadn't the slightest idea which one to head for. In which of them would new Duplies undergoing orientation and indoctrination be quartered?

He wasn't alone; there were other people on the walks to and around the various domes, and he started watching them, hoping for a clue. He'd have to keep watching until he got one. It could be a fatal error to try to enter the wrong dome, and all of them, he saw, were guarded by sentries at the single door of each.

He watched the people around him, studying them as carefully as he could without appearing to do so. Some of them, particularly those in uniform wearing high rank, were undoubtedly Duplies. The others were undoubtedly ordinary Martians, but those sufficiently indoctrinated by Duplie propaganda to be trusted by them beyond all doubt. Most of these were in civilian clothes. A few had Washtex suits like his own, a fact that encouraged him.

The number of women, in uniform or otherwise, surprised him. And some of them, he noticed, were dressed very seductively. Were they Duplie women—who would be, as were Duplie men, completely amoral? There had been fewer than a hundred women among the original three hundred and twenty first duplicated for Mars. But perhaps the Duplies had been willing to extend their quota when it came to acquiring women for themselves, women as amoral as they. He toyed with the thought, and a moment later was sure of it. He recognized one of the women—one of the scantily dressed ones—as Mona Wayne, the most beautiful telestar on Earth. Mona Wayne's Duplie, rather; and certainly she hadn't been duplicated to Mars because of her value in espionage.

Valuable in other ways, indubitably, although he himself preferred— He jerked his mind away from thinking about Marta Pearson. He'd thought about her plenty in those fifty-odd hours in space en route to Mars. But there'd been time enough to think then. Now, he had to concentrate on finding his own Duplie.

He tried to pull his mind away from the thought of her—and just then he saw her.

Or her Duplie. Another Duplie of her? It must be, because it was inconceivable that the original, the real Marta Pearson would have been brought to Mars. There was no reason for it, everything against it. Besides, she was dressed—one might even say undressed—in the fashion of the Duplie women. And the fashion became her; she had the body for it. Had she been duplicated for the same purpose for which Mona Wayne, the telestar, had undoubtedly been duplicated? He almost ground his teeth at the thought, and then remembered that this was a Duplie. He'd killed one Duplie of her just after it had killed her father; he could kill this one as readily.

Then they were abreast and she caught his eye. She said, "Hi, Matt," so casually that it startled him—until he remembered that there was a Duplie Matt Anders here, and she undoubtedly knew him and thought she was speaking to him. And that she took his presence so casually for granted proved that his Duplie really was here, and that he was close to his target.

He managed to wave and speak in reply with equal casualness, and forced himself to go to the next crosswalk without looking around. Only then did he turn and look back, lighting a cigarette to cover his standing there, and he let his eyes follow after her until she entered a dome.

He waited a few more minutes and then walked toward the dome into which she had entered.

CHAPTER IV
Two's a Crowd

TWO COLD-EYED guards stood, one on either side of the door. As he walked toward it, one—the one with sergeant's insignia—stepped forward and barred his way. He said, "The password, Sir." Courteously, but firmly.

Anders scowled and continued to advance up to the point where another step would have meant body contact with the man barring his way. He said, irritably, "Bother the password. I've forgotten it. You know me."

The guard stepped quickly back and there was an electrogun suddenly in his hand; one appeared also in the hand of the other guard. The first one said, "Our orders are to challenge three times. If the password is not forthcoming, we're to shoot."

The other one said, "That's right, Mr. Anders. Sorry, but this is the second challenge. The password, please."

Matt Anders knew he couldn't get his own gun out in time; he was just deciding the only possible course was to turn and stride away in simulated anger, hoping that they wouldn't shoot him in the back if he didn't wait for the third challenge.

A hand dropped on his shoulder. A voice said, "What's the matter, Matt?"

He turned his head, deciding in a split second that he wouldn't be surprised whoever stood there; the voice had been familiar although he couldn't place it. Sean Charlton, head of the W. B. I., the World Investigation Bureau, top man in counterespionage.

Despite his decision, for a second Anders' mind reeled. If Charlton, of all Terrestrials, was a Duplie… And then he realized that Charlton wasn't Charlton, the real Charlton, had been duplicated somehow and this was his Duplie. But the substitution still hadn't been made or the Duplie wouldn't be here; Charlton's Duplie must still be in the indoctrination period, as was his own.

He said, "I've forgotten the damn password, Sean."

Charlton laughed. He leaned forward and whispered in Anders' ear. Anders said, "Thanks, Sean." To the guards he said, "Hiroshima."

The nearest guard frowned. "That's irregular. He told you."

Anders grinned. "Nuts, Sergeant. You didn't hear him tell me; you're just guessing. Besides, it's okay—I just couldn't remember whether it was Hiroshima or Nagasaki, and I was afraid if I said the wrong one you'd shoot, so I was stalling. Now I just remembered which of the two it was."

It must have sounded reasonable; the sergeant shrugged. He stepped back and holstered his gun; the other guard holstered his.

Charlton's Duplie and Anders entered the dome side by side. The Duplie said, "Lucky Matt, lucky again that I came along just then. Lucky enough to be the last of the Duplies."

The last of the Duplies! What on three planets did Charlton mean by that?

HE DIDN'T dare ask, but he'd have to find out. They were walking past a building directory of the dome; Anders glanced at it out of the corner of his eye and tried to find his own name among the A's. He saw it, but they were walking too fast for him to catch the room number that followed it. Anyway, he did have a room here; he'd learned that much. And probably his Duplie was in it right now. Possibly with the Duplie of Marta Pearson? Had she been coming here, by any chance, to see him? It was possible, but only a possibility; as a relatively new Duplie she probably had quarters here too.

Anyway, he didn't want to go to his room right away now; first he wanted to find out, if he could, what Charlton had meant by that "last of the Duplies" business.

He said, "Let's go to your room, Sean. Like to talk a while."

"Okay, and we'll have a drink."

When they entered the elevator Anders saw that there were buttons for eight floors; the top few would be small in area because of the dome shape of the building. Charlton pressed the button for the fourth floor.

Charlton made drinks for them when they were in the room. "Ran into your friend Marta just outside the Communications Dome," he said. "Having trouble with her? She sure acts different since she got back this morning."

Anders wanted to ask where she got back from, but he couldn't risk questions to which he was probably supposed to know the answers—especially not after Charlton had given him the password he'd "forgotten." The Duplie might put two things together and come up with the right answer. He said casually, "Yeah, she does seem a little different. Don't know why."

"Guess it's a tough trip on the blockade-runners. Don't worry; she'll be all right when she's rested up. Well, a break for you things got fouled up there."

"I didn't get the details on that," Anders said. "Did you?"

"Not except that a wheel came off somewhere; she had to kill her original along with the old man, so she couldn't substitute. No chance to get rid of the body in time. So they brought her back."

A pulse was throbbing in Matt Anders' temple. He knew the Marta Pearson he'd killed was a Duplie. And this Marta, the one he'd seen enter the dome, had just arrived here, this morning, on a blockade-runner—not via duplication. Could it possibly be—

Charlton was saying, "Drink up, I'll make us another." He took Anders' glass. "Yes, you're a lucky guy, Matt. The last Duplie."

How could he fish for information about that, without asking? If the Duplies were stopping duplication of humans, stopping it completely, it meant something important, damned important. A change in plans? A showdown?

"Quite a plan, huh?" he said.

Charlton came back with the glass.

"It can't miss. They won't even be able to strike back, from Earth. Oh, the blockade fleet is probably carrying a few atomic bombs, but Gresham's in charge of the fleet—and, if nobody's mentioned it to you, he's one of us. If he can get away with it, he'll surrender without dropping a bomb, once Earth is kaput. If he can't—well, the fleet hasn't enough stuff to do more than ten percent damage to us, as against ninety-five percent to Earth." He laughed. "There isn't a town of less than five thousand there that hasn't got a Duplicator! And dozens of them in every big city. Imagine an A-bomb going off simultaneously in every Duplicator on Earth. What a bang that'll be. And enough radioactivity in the air to kill off everything that's left. That's the only bug in the plan: that it'll be so many years before, we can take over Earth. That radioactivity'll last a long time."

Anders stretched his lips over his teeth in what he hoped was a grin. The Duplies—probably the Duplie of Kingston himself—had figured some change in the transmitter end of the Kingston Duplicator that enabled an A-bomb to be sent from a transmitter without exploding. And if it exploded in the receiving end—well, that was what they wanted it to do anyway.

AND THAT would be the end of Earth. And what could he do here alone? Was there any way he could get more details without arousing— The hell with that, he thought suddenly. What did it matter if he aroused Charlton's suspicion, here alone with him in his room? Why not take the short cut? It meant he'd have to kill Charlton, but that would be a pleasure—next only to killing his own Duplie. Duplies weren't people.

He finished his drink and put the glass down carefully. Then suddenly the electrogun was in his hand, aimed at the Duplie. Anders said quietly, "Don't move."

Charlton didn't move, except that his eyes widened. He said, "What—" And then, in a different voice, "I get it. And I gave you the password."

"And now you're going to give me information. I haven't got time to fish for it. Give me the rest of the details of that plan."

"If I tell you, you'll kill me anyway."

"Maybe I won't. Maybe I'll knock you out and tie you up. I'll decide that later. But if you don't talk, I'll kill you right now. Want to talk?"

Charlton licked his lips. He said, "All right, you won't be able to do anything about it anyway. What do you want to know?"

"When?"

"Tonight, pal. Tonight. It's almost ready to go now. You won't be able to do a thing about it."

"How did Kingston—or whoever it was—fix the transmitters to send atomics?"

"I'm no technician. I don't know that. But I know they can do it—have done it. Where do you think we got the uranium? About a pound of it is all we got off Calypso before you got our base there. But Kingston and his gang got the bug out of his apparatus. There's an attachment they put on a machine that lets it transmit or receive radioactives. Touchy to operate, but it works. They duplicated that pound of uranium into enough for three juicy bombs. And they've got three transmitters, each being adjusted to duplicate simultaneously in all the Kingston Duplicators on Earth. They're setting the patterns now. Can I have a drink?"

Anders nodded; he wanted time to think what else to ask. He looked for flaws in what the Duplie had just told him—and watched carefully meanwhile as Charlton poured himself a straight drink and downed it quickly.

Anders said, "This isn't all of a sudden. Something like that takes time. And it eliminates need for espionage. So why, only a few days ago, did you Duplies take me on Venus? With a deal like that coming up, what's Matt Anders to you?"

"Three answers to that. One, although we've been working on this for months, final tests weren't positive until yesterday. Two, we've been keeping on with all espionage activities for the sweet reason that if we stopped them suddenly, something might be missed; we just carried on with all previous plans.

Three, and this is in your particular case only, the Chief wanted a Duplie of you—to serve him on Mars as you've been serving Morphy on Earth. You were to be—I mean, your Duplie was to be—*his* hatchetman. He isn't going to substitute for you; he's going to stay here and help hold Mars in line."

Anders swore. It made sense, all three reasons made sense. And explained a lot of things.

"Where are the three Duplicators that are going to send the bombs to Earth?"

"I don't know."

Anders raised the muzzle of the gun slightly.

CHARLTON said quickly, "I don't know, I tell you. Nobody knows, except a few of us assigned to operate them. And you know I wouldn't be one of them, not knowing one end of a duplicator from the other. You know I'm no technician."

He was right on that, but—maybe he was still lying.

Charlton said, "Listen, use your head. That information would be top secret—just in case of something like this happening. Why should anyone be told where the machines are? I doubt if anyone, from the Chief on down, knows where all three of them are located. They're in different places, hundreds of miles apart. Just in case there's a spy among us—as there damn well is, I just found out—so he can't possibly get a message to the blockade fleet and have those machines bombed before they're ready to go."

It made sense. Duplie sense. With three machines, widely separated, any one of them sufficient, with one A-bomb apiece, to be duplicated endlessly. And that was why Charlton had talked so readily, knowing he couldn't possibly give the final and most vital piece of information under any pressure.

Anders stood. Should he take time to knock out and tie up the Duplie? Or simply—

Charlton stood, too; he was a little drunk. He must have been drinking heavily before Matt had met him, or he would not have been so affected by the few drinks he'd had now, even though the last had been a long, straight one.

He said, "All right, Matt. It was a good gag; pays me off for the one I pulled on you yesterday. And I went along with it for you. Now, let's shake hands on it, huh?" He took a step forward, his hand out, and then the step turned into a sudden dive to get in under the gun—too late. The gun flashed, caught him on top of his head at one-foot range. He'd saved Matt Anders' deciding what to do with him; and in a way that met Anders fullest approval.

Anders went out quickly and back to the elevator. At the first floor, this time alone, he stopped to look at the directory. He picked his own name again and this time the room number too, 518. Marta Pearson, 310.

He punched the elevator bell for the third floor of the dome. He knocked on the door of 310.

He stepped in quickly as Marta opened the door, forcing her to take a backward step to avoid being run into.

He had to find out right away, and there was a short cut—crude though it would be. As he closed the door behind him he grinned at her and asked a question, a question that was deliberately so worded that only a harlot or a Duplie woman could fail to resent it. Color rose into Marta's face and her hand lashed out at him.

He caught the hand. He said, "Sorry, I had to do that. I apologize. But *you're no Duplie*. A Duplie woman wouldn't have blushed—even at that."

She jerked her wrist from his grasp and backed away.

He said, "Marta, I'm no Duplie either. We've got to work together, and fast. Something's going to happen to Earth tonight. If we pool what we know about this place, there's just a chance we can stop it."

She was breathing hard, her eyes wide. "All right, you trapped me. I'm not a Duplie, but you are. And—"

HE HADN'T been watching her hands, and he hadn't guessed that a garment as brief as the one she was wearing could have a pocket that could hold an electrogun—even one as tiny as the one she pointed at him. Only half the size of his own six-ounce one, it was fully as deadly, although one that size held only a dozen charges.

He was careful not to move forward now. He said, "Marta, you've got to believe me. Too much depends on it. If I were a Duplie, why would I have said I wasn't?"

Her voice was cold now, "I don't know. How can you prove you aren't? I still don't believe you."

He thought rapidly. "Call Room 518. You'll find my Duplie there—I hope. Get him down here." He had business with his Duplie anyway.

"Wait. Turn around." She walked up behind him when he'd turned; she held the muzzle of the gun against his back while she reached around and found the electrogun in his pocket. Then she stepped back again, "All right, I'll give you that chance. Walk over into the corner where I can watch you while I call."

He walked to the corner before he turned. She was standing by the speaker-receiver in the wall near the door; she'd already pressed the button and he heard her give the room number. He heard his own voice say, "Anders speaking," over the communicator.

"Marta Pearson. Could you come down to my room a moment?"

"Marta! Didn't know you were back. Sure I'll be down, but it'll be a few minutes. Making a report on Venus. I got to finish for the Chief, rush job. Be seeing you soon as I can get there."

She pushed the button again. But the gun hadn't wavered. She said, "All right, maybe Matt Anders had two Duplies. Or if there's only one, how do I know which—"

"You don't," he said. "But listen, time is valuable, and we've got a lot of notes to compare. I won't move and you've got a gun on me. But while we're waiting save some time by telling me what happened to you on Venus. Was it you who gave me a bad time about that Calypso battle—or was that your Duplie, whom I killed later just after she'd killed your father."

"That was I. Wait, why should I tell you anything until I know you're not—"

"Because there's nothing to lose. You can always shoot me after you've told me. And it'll save time. Besides, even if you think I'm a Duplie, you've already told me you're not one, so what would more details matter?"

SHE THOUGHT that over a few seconds, "All right. It was I who told you off. Then—I went outdoors for a walk. I stayed away until it was time for dinner, because I didn't want an argument with Dad over what I'd said to you. I was a little late coming back and I came in the back way, because it was the nearest, from my direction. I went into the library and was surprised to see no one there. I started to light a cigarette and dropped my lighter; it was a round one and rolled under the sofa and—"

"You found the bodies."

"Yes. Of course I knew mine was—a Duplie. I guess I panicked; I was afraid and wanted out of there, didn't even want to stay long enough to use the communicator. There's a security station two blocks away and I guess I decided to run there for help. Anyway, I ran out the front door. And a landcab that had been parked across the street U-turned and pulled up the second I was out of the door and someone said, 'Get in!' There were two Duplies in the car—a man and a woman. I knew they'd shoot me down if I ran, even if I tried to get back in the house. So I got in the back seat. Suddenly my scare was over and I was calm. I think I know, incidentally, when they duplicated me. I had an accident three weeks ago; I was bowled over by a hit-and-run landcab—I thought—and knocked unconscious. They must have taken me to a Duplicator then, while I was out."

Anders said, "Then they must have sent your Duplie in just as an assassin, with no intent to substitute her for you. I don't get that; any assassin would have done."

"No. From things that were said later, they did intend to substitute. The car had been waiting in front to intercept me on my way back to the house. If I'd come back the front way, instead of the back, they'd have kidnapped me and killed me, and my Duplie would have stayed—and never have been suspected of killing Dad, of course. But—you say—you killed my Duplie. And I'd come back the wrong way, so things had gone wrong for them. They drove to where they'd left their ship, a blockade-runner, and—well, we got here this morning. I'd managed to learn enough from them on the way here to—to get by until now."

"But why? I mean, didn't you try to escape from them before you took off from Venus?"

"I don't know, I might have been able to." Her eyes blazed. "I didn't try, I thought that here I might—"

"You might kill a few Duplies before they killed you. My idea, too, more or less. But there's something bigger at stake, Marta. Something that—"

He suddenly stopped and put his fingers to his lips; he'd heard the faint sound of footsteps outside in the corridor. Then there was a knock on the door. Anders stepped back farther into the corner and stood very quietly.

Marta Pearson slipped the gun back into the pocket from which she'd taken it, but kept her hand on it; she stood, as she opened the door, so she could still keep at least a corner of her eye on Matt Anders.

Matt Anders Duplie stepped in.

CHAPTER V
Decontaminated Vacation

HE SAID, "Marta darling!" as he closed the door behind him. "Wonderful to have you back." And then stepped forward to embrace her.

But Marta stepped back away from him, even more quickly, and the gun came out of her pocket and up. "Look behind you," she said. "And don't move, outside of that."

The Duplie turned his head and saw Matt Anders. His eyes widened and despite the threat of the gun in Marta's hand his own hand went to the inside pocket of his coat and brought out the electrogun whose mate Marta had just taken from Anders. He said, "Marta! This is no Duplie—this is *my original.* I'm going to—"

He was going to, but he didn't. The gun in Marta Pearson's hand flashed first.

It had been a close thing; there was sweat on Anders forehead as he stepped from where he'd been waiting in the corner. He said, "Sit down; we've got to talk fast, and then work fast—or try to. Listen, here's what I learned—from Sean Charlton's Duplie —since I got here." He told it quickly. "Can you confirm that—or add anything to it?"

Her voice was almost a whisper. "I —I guess it's right. I didn't know that much, but the few things I did hear fit into that story. That they now had three atomic bombs, and that something big is scheduled for tonight. That they had duplicators fixed so they could duplicate uranium. But I didn't know they could send the bombs to Earth and have them explode in— Oh, Matt, that's terrible."

He nodded grimly. "Anything else? Any details you can add?"

"Well—this, but I don't see how it helps. When human beings are sent through the Duplicators that are gadgeted to send uranium—they don't come out Duplies; the duplicates are human beings, too. Not amoral monsters."

"But how—? Why would that—?"

"They make this guess: in the human brain, in a certain part of it, there are submicroscopic particles of fissionable matter, just as there are minute quantities of so many other substances in the body. Too small to detect. And in duplicating a human being in an ordinary Kingston, those submicroscopic particles are exploded and injure a certain portion of the brain. The portion that houses—well, empathy, mercy, humanity—whatever you want to call the quality that makes people human instead of soulless monsters."

Anders nodded slowly. It seemed to explain something that had puzzled him—and everyone else, for that matter—for a long time. And it meant that if ever again a situation arose in which it would be legitimate and advantageous to duplicate human beings, it could be done without creating monsters.

But—for now—the knowledge didn't seem to help.

"Marta," he said, "do you know anything about the setup here? Which domes are which among the others besides this one? Where headquarters is?"

SHE SHOOK her head slowly. "Except the Communications Dome that's the small one, and I know they allow only Duplies in it and use only Duplies as the guards for it."

He leaned forward eagerly. "It's the source of the broadcasts that go out for Martians? The propaganda center from which they send all their programs for home consumption?"

"Yes. One of the two Duplies who brought me from Venus had worked there. He'd been a newscast announcer and—yes, that's where he broadcasts from. And I think it controls communications with Earth, too."

"Come on then. Let's go." He picked up his own electrogun where Marta had tossed it onto the bed and then picked up the duplicate of it, which his Duplie had dropped.

"You mean—"

"Yes, let's take over communications. Maybe we can get a message through to Earth. At least we can talk to the Martians—the real Martians. And tell them what the real score is."

"Oh, Matt, do you think we can—"

Suddenly she was trembling, and he put his arms around her to steady her. Then their lips were together and her arms were around him. Suddenly she pushed him away; there were tears in her eyes but she was laughing.

"All right—Hatchetman," she said. "Let's go. Business first—if we live through it."

"We'll live through it," he said, and wondered what the chances were. "Straighten your face. We're just taking a casual walk—till we get to the door of the Communications Dome."

They had the elevator to themselves. He asked, "How many Duplies will be in the building there? Any idea?"

"I've not been in it. At a guess, from what I heard, not over a dozen or so. It looks bigger from the outside than it really is. The walls of that one are nearly a hundred feet thick; it's the most bombproof of the lot, outside of headquarters."

They went along the walk to the smallest of the domes. The two guards at its door were in uniforms with high-ranking insignia, one a Colonel, the other a Major—both Duplies. No one else was near, and Matt Anders waited only until he was ten feet away, before there had been a challenge for the password. The hands of both rested on their weapons, but they hadn't drawn them—and never did. Anders' hand had entered his inner pocket with the deceptive casualness of one reaching for a cigarette—then the electrogun fired twice. The guards went down.

THEN MARTA and Anders were running through the door, along the long tunnel that led through the thick walls. The door at the inner end of the tunnel was a huge thing, beryllium steel and probably filled with lead to block radiation, eight feet thick. But it swung on its hinges lightly. "Keep your back to me.

Watch," he told Marta as he swung it shut, dogged it down. He played his electrogun over the inner surface of it—the tremendous voltage should short any mechanisms in the door that would permit it to be opened from the outside. Probably from the inside, too—in which case they were sealed in.

He turned back then. Marta's gun was flashing in her hand and he saw the figure of a Duplie who had stepped out of a doorway ahead suddenly fall.

"I don't think there's any alarm—yet," he whispered to her. "Kick off your shoes—I've got crepe rubber on mine—and here." He handed her the other electrogun, larger than her own. "We've got some hunting to do."

The hunting took fifteen minutes. The interior of the dome, relative to its outside size, was tiny, less than a dozen rooms; they found and killed seven Duplies and the place was theirs.

The main control room. Anders pointed to the huge bank of condensers—similar to the one, relatively tiny, which he had seen operate the Kingston Duplicator on Venus. "Power!" he said. "We're self-contained. They can't shut us off the air!"

He found the microphone—a Duplie newscaster who had been using it lay dead in front of it. It had been in operation and the newscaster's use of it had ended in the middle of a sentence.

"Citizens of Mars," he said. "Citizens of Mars who are not Duplies, this is Matt Anders speaking to you, speaking for President Morphy of Earth. Listen, this is of vital importance—"

He told them the story simply, everything their own newscasts and sources of information had denied them since the start of the war—and before. He told them the plans of the Duplies to destroy all of Earth, in one blow, that very night. "...No, I don't know where the three Kingstons are being readied for sending atomic bombs. Some of you probably do—that is, you know a new and ultra-powerful Duplicator has been set up and is being heavily guarded. Some of you know where another is, others will know the third. *Smash them* for the sake of

Earth, your mother planet. Kill the Duplies and take over. I've told you what they really are, how they've fooled you…"

And he told them again, and again. Not trying to be eloquent about it, just dishing out facts, straight facts that the Martian colonists had never been able to hear. Hammering those facts, over and over. Adding details, circumstantial details that would make them believable.

He was surrounded by panels of switches, but he didn't risk touching one. He knew that the mike into which he was talking was live and directed to all Martian private receivers—he didn't risk trying for more. Maybe he could have reached Earth with a message, maybe he could have reached the fleet and convinced them that their commander was a Duplie. But he didn't know one switch from another and didn't take a chance.

He talked, hammered facts. Maybe Earth or the blockade fleet would be monitoring the broadcast and get it anyway; if not, he wasn't going to take a chance on changing any settings. He talked to the people of Mars. Talked until he was hoarse, and then let Marta take over for a while, then talked himself hoarse again, repeating, hammering, arguing, pleading—

HE'D LOST all track of time when it happened—the thing he'd been hoping for, the thing that proved he was succeeding. There was a sound that was beyond sound, and the dome shook. He was knocked from his feet and so was Marta; he helped her up, his face shining with exultation, and was back at the mike.

"Thanks, citizens of Mars! I know now you're believing me, that you're doing something about it. The Duplies just dropped one of their three atomic bombs on the dome here. They'll drop the other two! They're losing Mars—now that you know the truth—and they've got to try to stop us. It's more important to them to hold Mars, right now, than to destroy Earth while you're destroying them. You know who most of them are. If you miss a few, they can be hunted down later.

There are only a few hundred of them, billions of you. You can—"

Again the dome shook. The second bomb. And they'd drop the third, too. They had to try; they had to see if three bombs in a row, in the same spot, would crack the defenses they themselves had made against atomic bombing. They couldn't let him keep talking to the people of Mars! The Duplies were realists; they'd know it would do them no good to destroy Earth, in revenge, if they were losing control over their own planet meanwhile. They had to stop him.

The third bomb, before he and Marta were on their feet from the impact of the second. Chunks of concrete fell near them, this time, but the dome held. And they'd won. The Duplies wouldn't have wasted one of the bombs on them unless his broadcast was going through; they wouldn't have spent all three of them unless their situation was desperate. The Martians were revolting against their Duplie masters.

But he didn't quit; there were obviously Martians who accepted the facts he'd been telling them, but maybe there were others who hadn't. The ones who had, since they'd acted so quickly, must already have suspected at least part of the truth despite the curtain of propaganda that had separated them from the outside, but the others— He went back to the mike; he kept at it.

Four more hours. Finally he said, "Marta, if that doesn't do it, it can't be done. Let's try to get something on what's going on. Anything around here that looks like a receiver to you? There must be other broadcasters, in other cities. If the colonists control them…"

He turned back to the mike and told what he was going to do. "I'll try to find a way to take an incoming message now." He found it.

"Anders, calling Matt Anders. If you hear me, pull over the mike and we can make it a two-way; I've still got you tuned in on a receiver."

"Anders speaking," he said into the mike. Marta was handling the receiver he'd found and tuned it loudly enough so he could hear. "I hear you. Come in. What's happening out there?"

"Revolt against the Duplies successful. Got all of them except some still holed up in the domes. Casualties light except in the dome area of Marsport; we were besieging the other domes when they dropped those bombs. But we've got cordons around the contaminated area; no Duplies will get out of there alive.

"Report from your blockade fleet; your broadcast was monitored there, heard by the Duplie of your commander as well as by others. He tried to order the fleet to add their bombs to the communications dome you're in, but was stopped; he's under arrest on his flagship. The fact that he gave the order to bomb the dome your broadcast was coming from convinced his under-officers that he was, as you claimed, a Duplie. The fleet has landed, in peace, outside Marsport and is now helping us with mopping up operations. There will be—there is—peace between Mars and Earth. Many of us had already suspected at least some of the things you told us about our own government. We rose quickly when we knew the truth. Are you hearing me okay?"

"I'm hearing you," Anders said. "I think we sealed ourselves in here. How soon can you get us out?"

"Don't even try to leave. There's food, water and liquor in the dome. The whole dome area—and especially, after three direct hits, your dome—is contaminated with radiation. We'll work at decontamination, but—I'm sorry about this—I'm afraid it'll be a week before it'll be safe to try to open the door of your dome, from either side."

Matt Anders grinned and turned to look at Marta Pearson. He said, "Don't let it worry you, don't even hurry. I think I've got a week's vacation coming—and I think I can find ways of spending the time."

Mercy Flight

*It was a lesson you learned in the Space-Forces, and you learned it good:
Out in the lonely void, when you get in a jam, you're on your own…it's you
against everything, and everybody. Anything goes…*

THE PHONE RANG AND ED Kerry wasn't doing
anything so he picked it up and said, "Yeah?"

He said yeah a few more times, his eyes widening
infinitesimally each time, and finally wound up with, "Okay,
Bunny."

He hung up and said, "That was Bunny, up in Oneonta. She
says a guy is coming in from Luna with a kid for emergency
hospitalization, radiation burns or something."

Jake was sitting back in his swivel chair, his feet on the desk
and his hands clasped behind his head. He growled, "That's the
trouble with women in this game; they've got no story sense.
She phones all the way from Oneonta on a story that's been run
a hundred times. Every time somebody gets good and sick up
on Luna they bring 'em to Earth for treatment." He shrugged.
"Okay, so it's a kid this time. Do up about a stick of it, Kerry,
and we'll put it on page three if you can work it into a tear-
jerker."

Ed Kerry said, "You didn't let me finish, Jake. Something's
wrong with this guy's radio."

Somebody on the rewrite desk said, "Something wrong with
his radio? He's gotta have his radio or he can't come in."

Jake took his feet from the desk and sat up. "What'd' ya
mean, something's wrong with his radio?"

"Bunny said he's calling for his landing instructions but they
can't get anything back to him. He's just reached *Brennschluss*

and he's in free fall now; it'll be four days before he gets here. That's the way they work it—he's supposed to get in touch with the spaceport he wants to land at, and…"

"I know how they work it," Jake growled. "See if there's anything on the last news wire from Luna about him."

Phil Mooney flicked his set on again and repeated carefully, "Calling Oneonta Spaceport. Phil Mooney Outbound Luna, Calling Oneonta Spaceport. Come in Oneonta."

Calling Phil Mooney. Calling Phil Mooney. Oneonta Spaceport Calling Phil Mooney. Come in Mooney.

He cast a quick glance back at the child, strapped carefully in the metal bunk. She was unconscious now, possibly as a result of the acceleration in leaving Luna. He'd had to reach a speed of approximately two miles per second to escape Earth's satellite, and that had called for more G's acceleration than Lillian's sick body could bear. His lips thinned back over his teeth; it would be even worse when they came in for landing and he had to brake against Earth's gravity.

He switched on the set again to give it another try. Instructions were to contact the spaceport at which you planned to land as soon as possible. There was plenty of time, of course, but the sooner the better.

He said, "Calling Oneonta Spaceport. This is Phil Mooney, Luna, Calling Oneonta. Come in Oneonta."

Calling Phil Mooney. Calling Phil Mooney. Oneonta Spaceport Calling Phil Mooney. Come in Mooney.

Ed Kerry came back to the city room with a sheet of yellow paper that he'd torn off the radiotype.

He said, "Here it is, Jake. This kid—her name is Lillian Marshall—is the only survivor of an explosion at that nuclear fission laboratory they had on the dark side. Her old man and her mother were working under this Professor Deems; both of them killed."

His eyes went on scanning the story.

"Evidently this Phil Mooney runs an unscheduled spaceline. Anyway, he blasted off to rush the kid to an earth hospital."

Jake took the dispatch and scowled at it. "Kerry," he growled, "see what we got on this Phil Mooney in the morgue." He rubbed the end of his nose thoughtfully. "They'll probably pick him up all right when he gets nearer."

Somebody on rewrite said, "It doesn't make any difference how far he is; they should be able to reach him even if he was halfway to Mars. Something's wrong with his set."

He decided to try one of the other spaceports. As a matter of fact, it made very little difference at which of them he landed. There'd be suitable hospital facilities within reasonable distance of any spaceport. He was three days out now, and, according to spaceways custom, had to let them know he was coming in. It wasn't like landing an airplane—they want plenty of time to prepare for a spacecraft's arrival.

He said, "Calling New Albuquerque Spaceport. Calling New Albuquerque Spaceport. Phil Mooney, Luna, Calling New Albuquerque. Please come in New Albuquerque."

Calling Phil Mooney, Calling Phil Mooney, New Albuquerque Spaceport Calling Phil Mooney. We are receiving you perfectly. Come in Mooney.

He tried once more.

"Calling New Albuquerque Spaceport. Calling New Albuquerque Spaceport. Please come in New Albuquerque. Emergency. Repeat Emergency. Please come in New Albuquerque."

Calling Phil Mooney. Calling Phil Mooney. We are receiving you perfectly, Mooney. Come in Mooney.

Kitty Kildare took up her notes and prepared to make her way back to her own tiny office.

"I've got it, Jake," she said breathlessly. Kitty was always breathless over any story carrying more pathos than a basketball score. "My column tomorrow'll have them melting. Actually, I mean."

Jake shuddered inwardly after she left.

Ed Kerry came up and drooped on the edge of the desk.

"Here's the dope on this Phil Mooney, Jake," he said. "He's about thirty. Was in the last war and saw action when we had our space-forces storming New Petrograd. Did some fighting around the satellites, too. Piloted a one seater, got a couple of medals, but never really made big news."

"Got any pix of him?"

Ed Kelly shook his head. "Like I said, he never really made the big news. Just one more of these young fellas that saw plenty of action and when the war was over was too keyed up to settle down to everyday life."

Jake picked up the thin folder and riffled through the few clippings there. "What's he doing now?" he growled.

"Evidently when the war ended he got one of these surplus freighters and converted it. Name of his company is Mooney Space Service; sounds impressive, but he's the only one in it. Probably going broke; most of those guys are—can't make the grade against the competition of Terra-Luna Spaceways and the other big boys with the scheduled flights."

The city editor scratched the end of his nose speculatively. "Maybe we ought to have Jim do up an editorial on these unscheduled spacelines. Something along the line of how heroic some of these guys are; that sort of stuff. Do up the idea that they're always ready, fair weather or foul, to make an emergency trip..."

Kerry said, "There isn't any weather, *fair* or *foul*, in space."

Jake scowled at him. "You know what I mean, wise guy. Meanwhile, get some statements from some authorities."

Ed Kerry said painfully, "What statements from what authorities?"

The city editor glared at him. "So help, me, Ed. I'm going to stick you on obituaries. *Any* statements from *any* authorities. You know damn well what I mean. Get some doctor to beef about the fact there aren't suitable hospitalization facilities on Luna. Get some president of one of these unscheduled spacelines to sound off about what a hero Mooney is and how much good these unscheduled spacelines are—and that reminds me of something—"

He yelled to a tall lanky reporter at the far end of the city room: "Hey, Ted. Get Bunny on the line up in Oneonta and tell her I said to look up some of these unscheduled spacelines guys and see if she can get a photograph of Phil Mooney from them. Maybe he's got some buddies in Oneonta."

There was one thing about being in free fall. You had lots of time to sit and think. Too much time, perhaps.

You had the time to think it *all* over. And over and over again.

There was the war which had torn you from the routine into which life had settled, from friends and relations and sweethearts, and thrown you into a one man space-fighter in which you sometimes stayed for weeks on end without communication with anyone, friend or foe.

There had probably been no equivalent situation in the history of past warfare to the one-man space-scouts. The nearest thing to them might have been the flyers of 1914, in the first World War—but, of course, they were up there alone only for hours at a time, not weeks.

"You develop self-reliance, men," was the way the colonel had put it. "You develop self-reliance, or you're sunk.

"You're in space by yourself, alone. You can't use your radio or they can locate you. If something happens, some emergency, or some contact with the enemy, you're on your own. *You* have to figure it out; there's no superior officer to do your thinking; you're the whole works."

And the colonel had been right, of course. It was a matter of using your own wits, your own ability. Fighting in a space-scout was the work of an *individual*, not of a team. Perhaps it would be different someday in the future when machines and instruments had been developed further; but now it was an individualistic game, each man for himself.

And probably it was because of this training that he, Phil Mooney, was unable to get back into the crowd after the war had ended. He was an individualist who rebelled against working not only *for* but even *with* someone else.

He should have known better. Industry had reached beyond the point where one man goes out by himself and makes a fortune—or even a living, he thought wryly. It's the day of the *big* concerns, of tremendous trusts and cartels, who didn't even have to bother with the task of squeezing out tiny competitors like himself. He was out before he started.

The *Mooney Space Service*. He snorted in self-deprecation.

Oh, well.

He pulled himself erect and made his way to the bunk. The kid was awake. He grinned down at her and said, "How's it going, Lillian?"

Her eyes seemed glazed, even worse than they'd been yesterday, but she tried to smile back at him. "All right," she whispered, her child's voice so low he could hardly make it out. "Where's mother…"

Phil Mooney held a finger to his lips. "Maybe you'd better not talk too much, Lillian. Your mother and father are…they're all right. The thing now is to get you to the hospital and make you well again. Understand?"

Kitty Kildare was saying indignantly, "What's this about no insurance on Luna?"

"Use your head, Kitty," Jake grunted. "What company'd be crazy enough to insure anybody working on Luna? By the way, that was a good piece on Mooney and the Marshall kid."

"Did you read it?" Kitty Kildare was pleased.

He shuddered. "No, but the letters have been pouring in. Maybe you ought to do another. Take it from some other angle this time."

"That's why I wanted to know about the insurance. Do you realize that this child, this *poor*, sick, defenseless child, is penniless? Actually, I mean. Bad enough that her parents have left her an orphan, but, Jake, that child is penniless."

"All right, all right," he told her, "work on that for tomorrow's column."

Ed came up with another radiotype report, just as Kitty was leaving. "This guy Mooney's calling all the other spaceports now, Jake. Evidently he's getting desperate; he's only two days out. And by the way, here's a new angle. This guy Harry Marshall, the kid's father, was a war-time buddy of Phil Mooney; they went to cadet school or something together."

Jake growled thoughtfully, "He hasn't got a chance, but it makes a tremendous story. Get somebody to rig up a set in the radiotype room, Ed, and we'll see if we can listen in."

There was a desperate, tense, taut inflection in his voice now.

"Calling New Albuquerque Spaceport or Oneonta Spaceport. Phil Mooney calling *any* Earth spaceport. Phil Mooney Calling Oneonta, New Albuquerque, Casablanca, Mukden, *any* Earth spaceport. Emergency. Emergency. Request landing instructions. Have Lillian Marshall, eight years old, needing immediate medical care, aboard. Please come in any Earth Spaceport."

Calling Phil Mooney. New Albuquerque calling Phil Mooney. Ambulance waiting on grounds. Receiving you perfectly. Come in...

Calling Phil Mooney. Casablanca Spaceport Calling Phil...

Calling Phil Mooney. Mukden Spaceport Calling...

Calling Phil Mooney. Oneonta Spaceport Calling Phil Mooney...

Ed Kerry looked up over the set in the radiotype room at the city editor. He wet his lips carefully and said, "He's only got one day now. They've got to pick him up in hours or he's sunk."

Jake said, "I never did understand how that works. Why can't he land himself? I know he can't, but why?"

The reporter shrugged. "I don't quite get it either, but evidently the whole operation is pretty delicate stuff. They bring him down with radar, somehow or other. It's not like landing an airplane. Landing a spacecraft is done from the ground up— not from the spacecraft down. The pilot has comparatively little to do about it. At least, that's the way it is with nine ships out of ten."

The set began to blare again, and they both listened tensely. It was Phil Mooney.

"Listen, you guys down there. If you're sitting around playing craps or something, I'm going to have a few necks to break when I get down."

The two newspapermen stared at each other over the set. Ed Kerry ran his tongue over his lips again.

The strained tone had gone from the voice of the spacepilot now and had been replaced by one of hopelessness. He said, "I don't know who I think I'm kidding. I know darn well that something's wrong with my receiver and I can't find out what it is. Maybe my sender is off too, for all I know. All I can pick up is some girl singing something about white roses. White roses, yet! I want landing instructions and I get white roses."

Ed Kerry jerked his head up and snapped, "Holy jumping hell, he's able to pick some commercial station!"

Jake came to his feet, stuck his neck out of the door and yelled at the top of his voice, "Phil Mooney is receiving some commercial station! Some dame singing something about white roses! Check every station in the city! Find out if any of them are broadcasting some dame singing about white roses."

Ladies and gentlemen, we interrupt this program for an emergency situation. Undoubtedly, you have heard on your newscasts and have read in your papers of the tragic case of Lillian Marshall, child victim of an atomic explosion on Luna, which orphaned her and necessitated her immediate flight to an Earth hospital.

For the past three days the spacecraft carrying her, piloted by war hero Philip Mooney, has been having trouble with its radio. Due to circumstances surrounding landing of spacecraft, the two have been given up as lost in spite of the fact that almost hourly it has been possible to receive messages from Mooney.

It is now revealed that he is able to pick up this program on the Interplanetary Broadcasting System network. We are not sure which of the nearly two thousand stations of our system he is receiving, but we will now attempt to reach Phillip Mooney with relayed messages from the Oneonta Spaceport where expert medical care is awaiting little Lillian Marshall.

Come in Oneonta.

Calling Phil Mooney. Calling Phil Mooney. Come in, Phil. This is Oneonta Spaceport, relaying through the Interplanetary Broadcasting System. Come in, Phil.

"Phil Mooney, calling Oneonta. I'm getting you, Oneonta. Come in, Oneonta. Over."

Okay, Phil. Now this is it. We should have had you two hours ago, but we'll make out all right. Your velocity is a little too high. Give it six more units on your Kingston valves. Get that? Over.

"Got it. Six more units on the Kingstons. Over."

All right now. Switch on your remote control, Phil. We'll take it from here. Stand by the coordinators…

IT WAS NIGHT, but a blaze of lights illuminated the Oneonta Spaceport. Hundreds of landcars stood on the parking lots, thousands of persons crowded the wire fence that kept all but port personnel from the field itself.

The old space-freighter sank easily to the apron and in seconds the rocket flames died. A surge of humanity ebbed over the field toward the craft.

Phil Mooney opened the pilot-compartment's hatch and stuck his head out, blinking in surprise at the mob beneath him.

"I don't know what this is all about," he began, "but I've got a sick kid aboard. There's supposed to be an ambulance…"

Police wedged through the crowd, convoying a white-haired, white-jacketed man. He called up to the spacepilot, "'We won't need an ambulance, Mr. Mooney. I've already made arrangements for facilities here at the airport for immediate treatment."

Phil Mooney made his way to the ground and scowled, still obviously startled by the swelling crowd.

"Who in *kert* are you?" he asked.

The other motioned for two assistants to enter the ship and bring out the child. "I'm Doctor Kern," he said. "I'll see…"

"Doctor Adrian Kern, the radiation expert?" The pilot frowned worriedly. "See here, doctor, the Marshalls were friends of mine, and I've taken over the care of little Lillian, but I'm—well, I'm afraid I couldn't afford to pay you…I mean…"

The famous doctor smiled at him. "I've been retained by the Interplanetary Golden Heart, Phil. You needn't worry about my fee. Besides," and he smiled easily, "I'm not going to accept any fee for this case. You see, I was listening to Marsha Malloy singing 'Love of White Roses' when your call came through, I believe it was the most poignant experience I have ever been through."

A girl next to the doctor gushed, "I'm Bunny Davis, Mr. Mooney. The managing editor of our newspaper chain has authorized me to buy your story for five thousand. If you'll just—"

Phil Mooney blinked, "I—I—"

A heavy-set man in a business suit grasped his hand and shook it with fervor, while flashbulbs went off blindingly. "Phil," he said huskily, as though moved by deep emotion, "as president of the board of directors of Terra-Luna Spaceways, I wish to take this opportunity to offer you a full—"

"Hey! Give us a smile, Phil," a man on top of a television truck yelled…

He was headed back for Luna the next day.

They'd been indignant, of course. There was Hollywood, and the television networks, and that Terra-Luna Spaceways guy who wanted to get in on all the publicity by offering him a vice-presidency. And the newspaper editors, and the magazine editors, and all the rest of them.

Approximately a billion persons had been tuned in to the Interplanetary network when the emergency landing instructions had been broadcast to him through that system. A billion persons had sat on the edge of their chairs, tensely, as his ship had been brought in.

He and little Lillian had received more publicity in the past twenty-four hours than anyone since Lindberg.

And the child would be all right now. Before he'd left, checks totaling over a quarter of a million had come in for her. Donations from all over the Earth and from Mars and Venus and even some from the Jupiter satellites.

And offers of adoption. Thousands of them, from rich and poor—even including Marsha Malloy, the video star who'd been singing that song, "Love of White Roses."

Yes, Lillian would be all right. He wouldn't have been able to pay for the medical care she'd needed; but now she had the most capable experts on Earth at her disposal.

They had been indignant when he blasted off again for Luna. They'd wanted to make a hero of him. This leaving on his part they interpreted as modesty—which, come to think of it, would make him all the more of a hero.

Phil Mooney slipped a hand down to his set and flicked it on. He dialed over a dozen different stations. The news programs were all full of him and of Lillian. You'd think, to hear them, that he was the noblest, the most daring, the greatest man since Alexander the Great.

He grinned wryly. One of the reasons he'd been so anxious to leave was to get away before somebody thought to check his set to see what was wrong with it. Why, if anybody had found that it was actually in perfect shape, they'd probably have lynched him.

Yeah. The colonel had been right. In the space-forces you learned to be self-reliant. When you got in a bad spot, you figured it out yourself. You're on your own; it's you against everything and everybody. Anything goes.

His grin broadened. Maybe he wasn't a hero—the way they were all painting him; but at least Lillian was all right now, and no longer penniless the way her parents' death had left her.

—And he wasn't doing so badly himself.

One of Our Planets is Missing!

If you find a missing planet let it alone. The reward will probably prove to be a one-way ticket to a psychiatric ward!

THE ASTRONOMER Royal, Sir Horace Peters, M. A. Sc. D., F. R. S., blinked his eyes in surprise and announced to his assistant, "Mars has disappeared."

"I beg your pardon, sir?"

The other glared at him. "Confound it, Feathers, didn't you hear me? I said that Mars has completely disappeared."

His assistant looked at him apologetically, wondering inwardly what was getting into the old boy. "Yes, sir, I heard you. Undoubtedly it will be visible again in a moment."

The glare intensified and its effect was increased by the appearance of a red flush creeping up Sir Horace's neck. Before saying anything further, however, the astronomer turned again and applied his eye to his telescope. He stood motionless for a full five minutes before confronting the other once more.

"Hah," he snapped triumphantly. "Just as I said. Mars has disappeared."

Feathers was beginning to get alarmed. This was unprecedented and Feathers didn't like things to be unprecedented. That was why he'd chosen astronomy as a vocation; he couldn't think of anything in the way of a livelihood that would face him with fewer precedents than astronomy.

"Are you ill, sir?" he asked, solicitously.

"Confound it, Feathers, will you stop being so dense? I announce to you the most startling fact to confront the science of astronomy since Galileo—and what do you say? You ask me if I'm ill."

"I don't understand, sir," Feathers said desperately. "You said that Mars had disappeared and I said undoubtedly it would be visible again in a moment."

The Astronomer Royal attempted to control himself. His face was red now, but he said softly, "I didn't say the skies were darkened by clouds; I didn't even say that atmospheric tremors were bothering my observations." His voice began to go high. *"I said that Mars has disappeared*, and, by Jove, I mean that MARS HAS DISAPPEARED!"

His assistant stared at him for a long moment. Finally he laid down his pencil and said timidly, "But, Sir Horace, Mars can't disappear. There must be some mistake."

The other took a handkerchief from his pocket and wiped his forehead. "Yes, yes," he said. "I must control myself. There must be some error. Forgive me, Feathers."

"Certainly, sir." Feathers picked up his pencil and went back to his notes.

Sir Horace reapplied himself to his telescope for another full ten minutes. Finally he straightened and turned back to the other again.

He said deliberately, "Feathers, I am using a telescope with a power of seventy-five. We are at a most favorable opposition. It should appear to be approximately as large as the moon is when seen by the naked eye. The sky is clear; the atmosphere is unusually free of tremors tonight. I tell you again, Feathers, *Mars has disappeared.*"

Feathers groaned inwardly. It was weeks like this that made him sorry he'd ever chosen astronomy. It was bad enough, the mobs of laymen who besieged the observatory these days and nights, hoping for some opportunity to view the rocket ship in which the three Americans had taken off in an attempt to circle Luna and return. Yes, that was bad enough, but now he had an obviously insane man on his hands.

"May I see, sir?" he said in what he hoped was a soothing tone. Weren't you supposed to humor a psychopathic case?

He bent down over the eyepiece.

Finally he straightened again, his face pale. "By Gad, Sir Horace, you're right. Mars *has* disappeared!"

ON THE other side of the globe, General McCall ran both his hands through his hair wearily then stuck them in his pockets and slumped to a stool in dejection. He was the youngest general in the army but he felt very old now.

"It's them, all right," he said. "They're coming back. I wonder what the hell it was this time."

The sergeant at the radio looked up at him. "Sorry, sir; still can't raise them. Haven't been able to get a thing since they left the atmosphere yesterday."

"It doesn't make much difference," the general said. "Once they get a couple of hundred miles off Earth everything seems to go to pot; radio, radar, everything. Maybe they'll have some answer to it."

The lieutenant at the radar said, "They're perfectly clear now, sir. Can't be more than a hundred miles up. They're braking, undoubtedly; soon they'll be able to use their retractable wings."

"Thanks, Lieutenant. I think I'll go out to the field."

The general came to his feet again and walked wearily to the door of the concrete blockhouse. This was the sixth failure in the past two years. Well, at least they were seemingly all right this time; maybe the *Neptune XIII* could be made ready for another try in the next few months. If another tragedy had occurred, such as the explosion of the *Neptune XI*, he doubted that further appropriations would have been forthcoming. People were getting jittery about these attempts to reach Earth's satellite.

He could see, now, the braking jets, high above the desert. Everything would seem to be in order; Captain Maddigan, Lieutenant Coty and Sergeant Evers would be telling him about it within half an hour.

The rocket craft was obviously undamaged. It came sweeping down toward the runway, firing minor rocket blasts intermittently. Its landing gear descended, and suddenly it was on the ground and taxiing toward them, looking surprisingly like a conventional airplane rather than a craft meant for the exploration of space.

The general ran out with the others as the *Neptune XIII* came to a halt. He stood impatiently while waiting for the occupants to open the hatch.

Finally, it swung free and a head and shoulders emerged. The man's face was pale and there was deep strain to be observed in it.

"Well, Maddigan, what went wrong?" the General snapped, then with concern in his voice, "You're all okay—aren't you?"

Captain Bill Maddigan said, "Yes, sir, but…"

"Then come on down. Don't be ashamed of your failure," the general said gruffly; "we'll start all over again tomorrow. Sooner or later we'll lick this thing and…"

Maddigan shook his head. "Sir, we didn't fail, not exactly." While those below stared up at him, trying to assimilate that, he paused, then added, "Sir, we've made some discoveries so shaking that we demand a hearing before a representative group of American scientists."

GENERAL McCALL glowered at him. "Are you completely around the corner, Captain? Come down here at once! What do you mean—you *demand?*"

Captain Maddigan's face was pale but he tightened his jaws stubbornly. "No, sir. We're afraid we'll be confined to an insane asylum if we give our report to army authorities alone. We've decided to stay in the ship, seal ourselves in, until we're guaranteed a hearing before a competent group of physicists and astronomers."

A figure next to the general whispered. "Humor him, sir; obviously something's happened. They're probably all out of their minds and not responsible."

The general shot a glance at the medical corp major. He ran a hand quickly through his hair. "You're undoubtedly right, Major Corcoran; you speak to them." His voice rose, to the scores of base personnel who'd surrounded the spacecraft. "All you other men clear out of here. Back to your quarters!"

The crowd scattered regretfully, all ranks from private to colonel, and as they went they gazed back over their shoulders, scowlingly, apprehensively. There was something definitely wrong here and everybody on the field knew it.

The doctor called up, "You'll be all right, Captain. Come on down, the three of you, and we'll take care…"

Two other heads made themselves visible next to Maddigan's. Lieutenant Mike Coty said, "You don't understand, Major. We're not crazy and we're not sick. We've just run into something that scares us and we're afraid that if you army medicos get your hands on us we'll wind up in a nut factory. We want some capable scientists to hear our story."

"That goes for me to," Sergeant Joe Evers gulped.

"Now see here, boys," the major began.

But it didn't do any good. They bolted the hatch again, threatening to take off and land in some remote spot from which they could escape, if attempts were made to get them out. They wanted some prominent scientists and nothing short of that.

"It's a matter of humoring them," the major told McCall in a low voice. "Flagstaff Observatory is only a few hundred miles and Los Alamos considerably nearer. We can have some physicists and astronomers here within hours."

General McCall snapped in irritation. "I'm getting to the point where I'm ready to blast them out."

"They're sick men, General," the major said softly. "Besides, the eyes of the world have been directed to the flight and not even army censorship could keep this from the papers. I suggest you handle the situation with care. Shall I give orders to assemble the specialists these men demand? That will, at least, give us the opportunity to get them out of there and—uh—get our hands on them."

"Go ahead," the general sighed.

THE HALF dozen physicists and astronomers from Los Alamos, and Flagstaff were seated in the officer's mess. Major Corcoran summed up the situation briefly.

"As you know, gentlemen, the army made its sixth attempt to reach the moon the day before yesterday. Three men, Captain Maddigan, Lieutenant Coty and Sergeant Evers made up the crew of the rocket craft. I won't go into the details of the *Neptune XIII*, but definite improvements had been made over the earlier ships and we had high hopes of the success of this try.

"It was expected that the trip would take approximately nine days in all; fours days to reach Luna, one to circle it, and four to return.

"Upon its leaving the atmosphere of earth, we lost radio contact with the *Neptune XIII* and, shortly afterwards, radar contact. Evidently, there are some factors at work with which we are as yet unfamiliar. However, we still had reason for elation; everything seemed to be going successfully."

The doctor paused momentarily before going on. "You can imagine our surprise, gentlemen, when the *Neptune XIII* returned yesterday after having been gone less than twenty-four hours. It landed successfully, and, from all indications, ship and crew were quite in order."

Professor Bryant, the noted physicist, said impatiently, "My dear Major, I can't see what this all has to do with us. The experiment is all very interesting but—"

General McCall held up a hand. "Please, Professor, let the major proceed. We aren't any happier about this than you are."

The doctor went on. "As I say, the men seemed to be all right except for one thing—they refused to leave the ship until an audience of American scientists was present to hear their story."

Felix Baumer of Flagstaff shifted his position uncomfortably and knit his heavy eyebrows. "I seem to have missed something there. What story?"

"That's the mystery, gentlemen. Beyond claiming that they'd made some discoveries so shaking they were afraid they'd be placed in a mental institution, they refused to say anything; that is, until competent physicists and astronomers were assembled."

"Preposterous!" Professor Bryant snorted. "Obviously, these unfortunate men have snapped under the strain. I can see—"

"'Professor, that is our own conclusion," General McCall said impatiently. "However, there is a good deal at stake. We seem to be on the verge of attaining to space travel, but the past five disastrous attempts have brought on considerable opposition. I am afraid a sixth—well, at any rate, we wish to give them every benefit of the doubt. Besides," he added with a grimace, "it was the only way we could get them out."

"Very well, General," one of the other physicists agreed, "where are they?"

McCall shot a glance at his wristwatch. "They should be here, momentarily. Maddigan went to the library for some book or other which he wanted before speaking to you."

THE DOOR opened and a lieutenant colonel entered followed by Captain Bill Maddigan, whose face was still pale and strained. Behind him, bearing a bulky tarpaulin wrapped object, staggered Coty and Evers. The lieutenant colonel stood aside and leaned against the door, while the three advanced until they faced the six experts, General McCall and Major Corcoran.

Bill Maddigan was obviously the spokesman; the other two stood behind him, near their burden and faced their audience half defiantly, half fearfully.

Major Corcoran made hasty introductions.

The captain of the *Neptune XIII* wet his lips carefully and said, "Gentlemen, I have no doubt that either General McCall or Major Corcoran has briefed you on the situation."

He attempted a wry grin, which looked nothing more than sickly. "I have no doubt, either, that they told you we were mentally upset and that this was an attempt to humor us and get us from our ship."

No one said anything. The major half lifted one hand as though in protest, but remained silent.

Maddigan went on, "Frankly, we're half inclined to agree with them. Hadn't it been for three or four books I'd read some years ago, undoubtedly our minds *would* have snapped."

He held up his right hand, which held a heavy volume. "My being familiar with this work saved us."

The pilot turned and faced Felix Baumer. "I understand, sir, that you are a well known astronomer. Please tell me how far the moon is from the Earth."

Baumer's heavy eyebrows went up. "I should think you would be perfectly familiar with that, Captain. It is approximately 239,000 miles away."

"How do you know?"

"I beg your pardon?"

"How do you know?" Maddigan repeated.

Felix Baumer looked from one to the other of his fellow scientists, raised his eyebrows again and said, "We compute the distance of heavenly bodies by use of triangulation. The moon, we have found, is 239,000 miles off."

"And the sun?"

"Roughly 93,000,000 miles."

"And Mars?"

"The planet Mars may be as near as 35,000,000 miles during a perihelion opposition; or it may be as far away as 63,000,000 miles at an aphelion opposition. Of course, when it isn't in opposition it is considerably further away than that."

"And how were these figures arrived at?" Maddigan went on.

General McCall interrupted. "Look here, Captain, you put our infant Space Service in a bad light. You are perfectly familiar with these things. The courses you've taken in preparation…"

For the first time, Lieutenant Mike Coty spoke up. "Sir," he said to General McCall, "that's why we wanted a group of scientists present when we made our report. Most of the courses we took are way off the beam."

"Way off," Sergeant Evers muttered.

Captain Maddigan said, "Please let me continue, sir."

The general snorted in disgust, but remained silent.

MADDIGAN OPENED his book at a page in which he'd been holding a finger. Before he read he looked up at the six specialists and said, "We use triangulation to determine the distance of heavenly bodies, but the method isn't even efficient for measuring things at comparatively short distances." His eyes went down to his volume and he continued, "According to the measurements made by Cook, the height of the mountain Mauna Loa is 18,410 feet; according to Marchand, it is 16,611 feet; according to Wilkes, it is only 13,761—all used the triangulation method."

He went on further. "In the 22-150 issue of the *Alpine Journal* there is a list of eight different measurements of the height of Mt. St. Elias. They vary from 12,672 to 19,500 feet—all used the triangulation method.

"An article in the *Scientific American* issue of 119-31 points out that there is always an error of at least ten percent in calculating the height of a mountain. The writer contends that Mt. Everest is somewhere between 26,100 and 31,900 feet."

Two or three of the assembled specialists began to protest; Felix Baumer even came to his feet.

Maddigan held up a hand. "Gentlemen, if we cannot measure accurately mountains right here on Earth by triangulation; how in the name of reason can we attempt to measure distances running into the millions of miles?"

Professor Bryant snapped. "Get to your point, young man. It would be very easy at this point for us simply to say, 'Do you think you can do better?' but obviously you are building up to some point you wish to make."

Captain Maddigan turned to him. "Yes, sir," he said, "my point is that our attempt to reach the moon the day before yesterday wasn't a failure."

General McCall gaped at him, then sputtered, "You were back in less that twenty-four hours. Are you—"

Bill Maddigan said wearily, "Gentlemen, the moon is considerably less in size than we have assumed and it is *less than four thousand miles away.*"

There was a long awkward silence. Maddigan took a step backward toward Coty and Evers as though seeking their support.

Finally, Major Corcoran said soothingly, "Then Captain, you claim that you actually circled the moon, in the short time you were gone, and returned?"

"Yes, sir. And while I'm at it, I might as well tell you that the sun isn't any ninety-three million miles away either. It's closer than that and not nearly so big as—"

Lieutenant Coty said tightly, "Give them the rest of it, Bill."

Professor Bryant snorted, "You mean there can be more?"

Bill Maddigan hurried on. "Yes, sir, there is more. All evidence in space indicates that we have been wrong is supposing that the earth circles the sun. Actually we're almost stationary. The sun, carrying Venus and Mercury with it, revolves at a distance of only a few tens of thousands of miles. The exterior planets which are, gentlemen, considerably smaller than we have thought, not only revolve about this central arrangement but approach and recede from us in loops."

THEY SAT staring at him, some in sympathy, some in disgust. Two essayed chuckles.

"I might as well wind it up," Maddigan concluded. "The earth isn't round, either; it's more top-shaped than spherical."

Major Corcoran laughed sympathetically. "Well, Captain, I think we should be off now. You wanted your story to be heard by a group of scientists and we gathered them for you. Now it will probably be best if we go on over to the hospital and make arrangements…"

"Wait a minute," Lieutenant Coty said. He turned to the six specialists, holding up one hand as though in supplication. "We knew we wouldn't have a chance with the army medicos, but we thought you'd be interested enough to at least check some of…"

Felix Baumer said, not without kindliness in his tone, "I am sorry, Lieutenant. We all sympathize with you deeply. I am sure that a very short stay in proper institutions will have you on your feet again."

The others nodded.

The lieutenant colonel, who had conducted the three spacemen to the meeting, got up from his chair and stuck his head out the door and called. Half a dozen medical corp men began to enter.

Sergeant Evers said desperately, "How about our proof, Captain?"

Captain Maddigan held up his hand. "One more thing," he said. "We were afraid of this so we brought something in the way of evidence."

"Possibly a piece of green cheese from the moon?" someone said.

The six medics continued to advance.

"Show 'em boys," Maddigan told Coty and Evers.

The lieutenant and the sergeant tore the tarpaulin from the bulky object they'd brought with them.

General McCall said, bitterness in his voice, "What the hell is that supposed to be?"

They all stared at the slightly luminous sphere.

"Why, why," Felix Baumer said, "it looks like a model of Mars."

Maddigan said hurriedly—the medics were almost to him— "When we got to Luna so quickly and saw some of the ramifications of these discoveries we've made, we knew we'd have to go on, to secure evidence. This is it, gentlemen."

McCall said, "What in the hell are you talking about?"

The medics had him by the arms now. Maddigan blurted, "We went over and picked up Mars and brought it back!" They began dragging him and the struggling Coty and Evers from the room.

"It's true," Evers yelled desperately. "It's Mars. That's the planet Mars!"

"Read the book," Maddigan shrilled, "the evidence is in the book!"

After the door was closed behind them, General McCall slumped back into his chair dejectedly. "This is the end," he muttered. "After this, there won't be another appropriation for the Space Service for *years!*"

Felix Baumer said idly, "You know, it's quite a coincidence. Something unexplained *has* happened to Mars. We haven't been able to pick it up at all in our telescopes at the observatory these past few nights." He yawned and shrugged. "Science is slow to arrive at conclusions; sometimes it takes generations to discover the why and wherefore of such things."

Professor Bryant went over and picked up the book from which Maddigan had been reading.

"The Books of Charles Fort," he snorted. "No wonder the poor fellows went mad, reading the works of that crackpot."

Final Appraisal

The answer was so simple they wondered why no one had hit upon it before. Then PropCorps made its suggestion and the fate of three planets rested on the white strip of paper in the MasterCyber.

THE assignment was a matter of talk, talk, talk, and talk, talk, talk. But that was Rand's strong point and he kept talking. He himself was thoroughly sold on the idea and that makes a difference; he *knew* how much depended upon him.

He cut red tape cleverly, expertly, rapidly; until he reached the offices of Harri Kristn, the CyberSupCom's right hand man. Kurt Rand spent a week in the anteroom of Kristn, charm, glibness, intensity and enterprise availing him nothing.

At least he was in New Washington and able to spend his nights at home. He and Nadine were infinitely fortunate, they had a mini-apt all to themselves. But, mini-apt or not, the nights were monotonously the same—although they thought of them as *deliciously* the same.

He'd come home, stand before the door and let the vizi-lock check him; enter the decontamination chamber and strip himself of clothes and helmet, stand patiently for the full five minutes, and finally enter.

It was a trifle larger than a medium sized trailer of the middle 20th Century. Everything was efficiently compact; the couch-bed, the bar-chair, the refresher, the folding servo-table, the televiz, and this-and-that the other things. So compact, so efficient, so complete—they knew nothing else, so they didn't realize—so cold.

But they were unbelievably fortunate; they had a mini-apt all of their own. There were a good many Space Commanders, a good many bird Colonels, that didn't have these comforts. Kurt Rand didn't deceive himself, it wasn't his influence that had managed to swing it, nor even the combined influence of he and Nadine. It was her's alone.

At night, he got there a half hour before her. From the decontaminator he'd go directly to the closet and bring out his terry cloth robe; two steps would take him to the refresher. He spent about ten minutes there, then came out and pulled the robe around his lanky form.

Habit made him shoot a quick glance at the chronom then, but it was only habit; the time was invariably 18:33. Only once or twice had he been more than half a minute off, Kurt Rand had this down pat.

He'd let the servo-table up and spend exactly three minutes in picking their menu for the night's meal. Nadine hated to have to choose her own dishes. It was the one unreasoning femininity she allowed herself—that is, except for Kurt.

He'd choose both their dishes, press the appropriate buttons, then go to the bar-chair and dial for Side-Cars. By that time he could hear the hum of the decontaminator. Nadine would hurry into the room, bird-like in her quick movements, without a glance at him, and dash to the refresher. While she was inside, he would get her robe and stand waiting at the door, eyeing with deep concentration the chronom.

She popped out at 18:51 and would slip her lithe form into the robe he held, but his mock scowl would remain on his face.

She would say, worriedly, "What time is it, darling?"

And he would answer, "You're three seconds late," or, "You're four seconds early," whatever it might be, and then would add, "You're much too early for dinner," or, "Dinner will be ruined."

Then they'd laugh and take the few steps to the servo-table arm in arm. It was the one light moment of the day allowed them; they'd made a ceremony of it.

Whatever he'd picked for her dinner was satisfactory. He should know, almost ten years of companionship had taught them to be thoroughly familiar with each other's wants, weaknesses, desires.

...If only things were such that a normal life could be theirs. But they never mentioned this. They had been born in war, their parents had been born in war, and their grandparents, and great-grandparents... And who, any longer, could tell what had been the original cause, the original spark that had lit the fuse, that had sterilized man's progress for a quarter of a millennium? Lost in history was the reason for it all, a history whose records were continually being changed by each generation to fit current needs, current propaganda.

ON the eighth day, Kurt Rand's name was called by the middle-aged WASC who presided at the portals leading to Harri Kristn's office and to the CyberChief beyond. She said wearily, "Lieutenant Kurt Rand."

He arose, slipped his pok-mag in a pocket and approached her desk.

Without looking up, she scanned her notes and said, "Mr. Kristn will be able to give you three minutes. If you are able to convince him of the importance of your project, he will let me know and I will contact you through PropCorps for a more lengthy interview."

His mind whirled. *Three minutes! He couldn't possibly...* He felt the old tic in his eye begin its clamor. *Three minutes!*

The door opened before him and he marched through woodenly.

This was it. This was the opportunity for which PropCorps—the least understood, the despised of all the service arms—had waited, had worked, for so long. This was why he, Kurt Rand, had been chosen to sell it. They had told him he had the silver tongue, the gift of gab, the old phony-baloney, as an earlier age had put it. Good old Kurt could convince them.

His eye ticked uncontrollably now. Three minutes was nothing.

Harri Kristn's face held the sallow paleness known to everyone equipped with a televiz set, or able to secure the newspapers issued by the PropCorps, or the pamphlets, or the PropCorps slanted novels. He didn't look like the unbelievably capable right hand man of the all-powerful CyberSupCom. He appeared a weary, ill man; and he was.

He didn't look up. He read from a sheet of paper before him. "Lieutenant Rand, Propaganda Corps. You have three minutes."

Kurt didn't salute. He took a deep breath and snapped, "Sir, I have been kept waiting for a full week in your outer office while the most important project ever hit upon by the PropCorps has languished. I *must* have the opportunity to speak to the CyberSupCom."

Harri Kristn looked up at him now, only mild interest in his colorless eyes. He said quietly, "I'm not distressed by your wait, Lieutenant; tell me, what could the PropCorps possibly hit upon which would be worth my time, not to speak of the CyberChief's?"

Kurt snapped, "An absolutely certain method of winning the war, sir." He spun on his heel and marched stiffly from the room.

The tired WASC at the desk looked up in surprise as he stalked by. "You used only one minute of your time," she said.

He didn't answer. He was in a hurry to get out of the building, before being called back. He wanted to give Kristn time to stew about it.

It wouldn't do to go back to the PropCorps offices now; and it wouldn't do to go home. Kristn would be able to locate him too easily.

He went to a sub-officer's bar; got himself a corner table and ordered a *woji*-flip. He would have preferred a Side-Car but he was quite sure the liquor here would be synthetic. Anything but *woji* would, at least. Not everybody could stand the fiery Martian drink so a good supply was more or less always on hand.

Ten minutes later, the Inter-Sectional Communicator speaker, above the bar, said, "Now hear this. Lieutenant Kurt Rand, PropCorps. Contact the office of Mr. Kristn immediately.

He sat tight and ordered another *woji*-flip.

The message was repeated after another ten minutes, more emphatically.

Fifteen minutes and two *wojis* later, a small detachment of SFPs came in the door and looked around. They approached the half dozen officers present one at a time, finally getting to Kurt.

The non-com in command of the squad saluted and said, "Sir, may I see your identification?"

Kurt handed it over. The sergeant flipped a quick look at the name and said, "Sir, you'll have to come with us. Mr. Kristn's orders." As an afterthought, he added, "Didn't you hear the call go over the communicator?"

Kurt said, "No," and reached for his helmet. He hadn't expected it this quickly. In fact, he was somewhat irritated, he'd wanted Kristn to stew for at least a couple of hours. "All right," he said, "let's go." The non-com marched ahead and his men followed along behind Rand. He wondered what kind of orders they had. The possibility seemed remote that he'd be disciplined because of the way he'd acted in Kristn's office, but you never knew. He could feel the tic in his eye again.

HIS escort left him at the desk of the WASC.

She said, "Mr. Kristn will see you immediately, Lieutenant."

He entered the sanctum again, marched up to the desk and came to attention, his face expressionless. This time Harri Kristn watched his progress across the room and nodded to him infinitesimally.

Kristn said quietly, "I assume your theatrical tactics are an indication that the PropCorps has come upon something they consider so important that it feels anything goes in order to achieve the ear of the CyberSupCom."

Kurt remained stiffly at attention keeping his face impassive. He said, "Sir, the PropCorps has discoverer a method of ending the war in a matter, probably, of months. It seems unbelievable that it is this difficult to reach the ear of the authorities necessary to put the plan into action."

Harri Kristn sighed deeply. "Lieutenant, in the past two centuries tens of thousands of persons have devised a method of ending the war in months. I myself, in the decade or so I have held this position, have had thousands approach me with this, that, or the other scheme." He toyed with a memo pad, reflectively. "Most never even actually get as far as this office, Lieutenant; practically none get past me to see the CyberChief. Those that have, somehow failed to end the war in a period of months."

Kurt remained silent, at attention, his eyes straight before him.

Harri Kristn said, "Tell me about it."

"No, sir."

The heavy eyebrows of the sick man went up. He showed no anger but there was surprise. "Why?" he asked. "How can you expect to get past my desk unless..."

Eyes still straight before him, Kurt Rand said, "Only three persons are aware of this project, sir. I won't even mention the names of the other two. Its success depends largely upon no one, not just the enemy, but *no one*, learning of it until the moment to strike."

Harri Kristn leaned back in his chair and regarded the other for a full thirty seconds. He said, as though to himself, "Obviously, you are not a crackpot, nor, I suppose, are the commanding officers of the PropCorps who sent you here." He sighed deeply, then, "The CyberSupCom isn't particularly partial to the Corps you represent, Lieutenant."

The statement called for no answer. Kurt Rand knew it was true; he didn't say anything.

Harri Kristn shifted in his chair. He took a small box from the top drawer of his desk and brought a pill from it. Pouring a glass of water from a desk carafe, he took the pill expressionlessly.

"I assume your project involves the use of the MasterCyber."

"Of course it does," Kristn went on reasonably, "or you wouldn't be here. Your own corps has the use of minor cybernetics machines, although I would imagine there is little use for them in propaganda."

Neither of them spoke for a moment. Finally Kristn sighed deeply again. "Very well, Lieutenant. Tomorrow morning you may have fifteen minutes with the CyberChief. I will arrange matters that if he cares to allow you additional time, there will be a half-hour following your period into which he can run over. Be here at—" he checked his memo pad "—be here at 0805." He smiled wanly and added, "Good luck, Lieutenant, and I hope you're right."

"Thank you, sir," Kurt said. He swung on his heel and marched toward the door, his stomach empty in the fear that the other would call him back and change his mind.

THAT night at the mini-apt he varied things. For one, the almost fantastically rare bottle of earth-side champagne, awarded him by Doctr Gail and the Commodore as a result of the wager they'd made on his being able to get the interview, decorated the servo-table instead of the usual Side-Cars. For another, the dinner hadn't come from the community kitchen. A roast chicken, which had cost him a half month's pay, graced the table.

The decontaminator hummed. He waited, dead panned, in his usual position.

Nadine entered in her bird-like, darting manner, and headed for the refresher. She shot a glance at the table, continued on her way, then shot it another unbelieving look, then one at him.

"Kurt!" she squealed.

He grinned at her as she spun around and hurried to the table.

"Chicken! Real chicken! And—and champagne. Oh, Kurt, you made it. You're going to see the CyberChief."

He still grinned.

"Oh, Kurt, you've won. This'll mean promotion for you." She came into his arms. Then, looking up worriedly, "If this project you speak of will be as successful as you say."

He said softly, "More than an ordinary promotion, darling. I'll be *promoted* to civilian clothes."

She looked at him, surprise and questioning in her eyes. "What do you mean, Kurt?"

He hesitated. "I shouldn't have said that, Nadine. Not even to you. Let's forget it and enjoy our celebration. Tomorrow you'll probably know all about it."

THE office of the CyberSupCom lay beyond that of Harri Kristn. In distance, his desk was approximately a hundred feet from that of the WASC who sat outside the office of Kristn. It was a hundred feet in distance, it had taken Kurt more than a month to make it. He was sitting in the reception hall before 0730 the following morning trying to control the tic in his eye.

At 0803 the WASC said, "Lieutenant Rand."

He came to his feet and hurried toward the door.

Harri Kristn looked up only briefly from the papers he was studying. He nodded, then gestured with his head at an inner door. Rand crossed the room briskly—every second counted— and twisted the knob.

He came to attention within the other office, and snapped a salute to the heavy-set man at the desk. The other looked up at him, scowled peevishly, and said to his secretary. "Who in *kert* is this, Captain?" His voice held a petulant growl.

His secretary said, "Lieutenant Kurt Rand, sir. PropCorps. According to Mr. Kristn, the PropCorps claims to have developed a secret method—"

"I know, I know," he snorted, "a secret method of ending the war in—how long, Lieutenant?—three weeks, a month?" He made no effort to disguise the insulting tone.

Kurt Rand said, "A period of several months, sir. Certainly less than a year."

"The Propaganda Corps, eh? I've become used to using the MasterCyber for finding the holes in fantastic schemes concocted by the BacterCorps, the RadCorps, and especially the FissCorps; but now we get the PropCorps. What in the name of *Wodo* did Kristn mean by letting you in here to take up my time?"

His secretary said easily, "Sir, although we don't know *why* Harri Kristn has thought it worth your while for you to spend fifteen minutes with the Lieutenant, you've trusted Mr. Kristn's judgment for a long time."

He turned and glared at her. "Captain," he snapped. "*I* shall decide—" His eyes softened, and some of the characteristic peevishness went away from his mouth, and he said, "Very well, Nadine; you are quite correct." He cleared his throat heavily. "I note, by the way, that the Lieutenant's name is Kurt Rand. Is there any relationship here, Captain?"

Nadine's little chin came up infinitesimally, "He is my husband, sir."

"Oh?" The CyberChief's eyes went from one to the other. "And you've made no effort to help him through your connections with me?" There was no answer. He seemed impressed. "All right, Lieutenant, let's have your story. Tell me why the PropCorps thinks it should have access to the MasterCyber. I warn you in advance that there is less than one chance in a thousand; as always we are months behind in our work."

Kurt Rand stepped forward earnestly, dropping his military pose. He took a chair across the desk from the CyberChief and leaned forward, "Sir, for background, let me do a brief review of the situation that applies today."

The CyberSupCom looked at his desk chronom even as he shrugged his beefy shoulders, "You have thirteen more minutes, use them as you will, Lieutenant."

"Sir, the Two Hundred Years War, as they are already beginning to call it, was a cold war, at first. Neither Mars nor our own planet were able to do much in the way of attacking each other. But, as the decades went by, inter-planetary warfare developed. During the same period all the planets and satellites of the Solar System were drawn into the conflict on one side or the other—Venus, of course, excepted. Only Venus of all the settled planets and satellites has remained completely aloof."

The CyberChief growled petulantly, "The cowardly *makrons*—if they would only come in on our side, as they should, this stalemate could be broken and the war would be over."

"Exactly, sir," Kurt told him with satisfaction.

The other stared at him, belligerently. "You mean the PropCorps claims to have worked out a method of bringing Venus into the war on our side?"

"Yes, sir."

"Well, don't sit there holding it, you fool! What is it?"

"A little more background first, sir, if you don't mind. One of the factors which has contributed most strongly to the balance of power between Mars and her allies and Earth and hers; has been the fact that we've both utilized a MasterCyber, the super-brain. Both sides submit their important problems to the MasterCyber and receive correct replies. It is impossible for the MasterCyber to make a mistake. And, of course, that is what makes your position, as CyberSupCom, the most important in Earth's forces."

"What in *kert* are you trying to do, young man, tell me about my own job? Get to the point! I know all there is to know about the MasterCyber and its importance."

"Yes, sir," Rand said doggedly, and ignoring the other. "To go on, the MasterCyber has every bit of human knowledge ever accumulated. It can draw upon this endless knowledge to—"

The CyberChief gritted his teeth. "Yes, yes—and the Martian MasterCyber has it all too. We are perfectly counterbalanced, so the war drags on. What *is* your point, Lieutenant?"

Kurt Rand let his eyes go from the CyberChief to Nadine, and then back again. This was it. "Sir, the MasterCyber is incapable of error. We of the PropCorps suggest that the following problem be fed into it: WHAT WOULD BE THE IDEAL PROPAGANDA TO CONVINCE THE VENUSIANS THAT OUR SIDE IS IN THE RIGHT AND TO PERSUADE THEM TO ENTER THE WAR IN OUR SUPPORT?"

The CyberChief slumped back into his swivel chair, his eyes wide. He said nothing for a full five minutes.

Rand broke in finally. "It is common knowledge that with the forces of Venus aligned with ours, the war would be terminated in months. In fact, the Martians and their allies would probably surrender upon the entry of the Venusians to our ranks."

The other growled hesitantly, "But we've never put that type of problem into the MasterCyber. It—"

Rand insisted, leaning forward excitedly in his chair. "But why not? Why is its ability limited to devising new weapons, new bacteriological warfare methods, new gases, faster space-drives? Remember, sir, that it has *all* of the knowledge of the human race; it is incapable of making error."

The CyberChief had not reached his position of authority by accident. He snapped to Nadine, "Captain, have Major Waltrs and Colonel Crewsn up immediately. Have the machine cleared of whatever problem it presently contains within the half hour."

As Nadine flicked to work, he turned back to Kurt. "To what extent is this restricted? How many of the PropCorps are—"

"There are three of us, sir—only three, Doctor Gail, Commodore McComas and myself."

The CyberChief's eyes, hard now and infinitely alert, went back to Nadine. "Have them placed in immediate seclusion, Captain. Under no circumstances are they to have any conversation whatsoever with *anyone* except myself. Captain, Lieutenant, you two are not to leave these offices until further instructions. We have quarters we can provide for you. There must be no leak on this."

THEY stood before the typer of the MasterCyber; the CyberSupCom, Colonel Crewsn, the binary authority, Major Waltrs, cybernetics engineer, Captain Nadine Rand, secretary of the CyberSupCom, and Lieutenant Kurt Rand of the Prop-Corps. The last two stood closely together, their hands clasped unobtrusively.

"Darling," she breathed to him. "If it works, if it *only* works."

He said softly, grimly, "It *has* to. It's the end of the war, Nadine. A return to real life; to homes, to children, to ambitions and goals…"

Colonel Crewsn had punched up the cards himself—all other personnel had been cleared from the large, ultra-fortified underground building, which housed the most important weapon in the arsenal of Earth and its allies. Crewsn, his face as tense as those of the others, placed the cards in the machine's hopper.

The CyberChief touched the start button with a heavy, trembling finger and the cards fed rapidly into the maw of the MasterCyber.

"It shouldn't take too long," the engineer muttered.

It didn't. The typer reset, spaced up two spaces on the endless roll of white paper which fed into it, and began to stutter.

They watched it, white faced and tense.

It typed:

QUESTION: WHAT WOULD BE THE IDEAL PROPAGANDA TO CONVINCE THE VENUSIANS THAT OUR SIDE IS IN THE RIGHT AND TO PER-SUADE THEM TO ENTER THE WAR IN OUR SUPPORT?"

ANSWER: NO ANSWER POSSIBLE.

Rand's eye ticked uncontrollably. The CyberSupCom snapped his teeth together.

Major Waltrs said unbelievingly, "But that's impossible. Such an answer is impossible."

Colonel Crewsn growled some profanity and returned to his key punch. He began punching up more cards angrily.

Kurt Rand hadn't moved. He stared down at the words on the white paper as though they held some deep meaning but as though he lacked the ability to read.

The others remained silent, too, until Crewsn's return.

The binary expert put his new cards in the MasterCyber's hopper and jabbed the start button viciously. "This is the best chance I've ever seen for ending this damned war," he growled. "There's no reason why this super-brain can't do it."

The typer reset, spaced up two more spaces and began to type. It wrote:

QUESTION: WHY IS NO ANSWER POSSIBLE TO THE QUESTION: WHAT WOULD BE THE IDEAL PROPAGANDA TO CONVINCE THE VENUSIANS THAT OUR SIDE IS IN THE RIGHT AND TO PERSUADE THEM TO ENTER THE WAR IN OUR SUPPORT?

ANSWER: YOUR SIDE IS NOT IN THE RIGHT.

Six-legged Svengali

BY MACK REYNOLDS AND FREDRIC BROWN

All the explorer had to do was prove he was smarter than a mud turtle—but on Venus that's not so easy!

BASE CAMP certainly looked good to me after hours of wandering alone through the eternal thick fog and thin drizzle that is Venus. You can never see more than a few yards ahead of you, but that's all right; there's nothing worth seeing on Venus anyway.

Except, while our expedition was there, Dixie Everton. It was strictly on account of Dixie that I'd joined the Everton Zoological Expedition, led by her father, Dr. Everton of the Extra-Terrestrial Zoo at New Albuquerque. I was paying my own expenses, too; Dr. Everton didn't think I'd be a worthwhile addition to the party. What was worse, he didn't think I'd be a worthwhile husband for Dixie. And there I disagreed with him, but definitely.

Somehow or other it was up to me, on this small expedition, to prove to him that I wasn't quite as *non compos mentos* as he thought. Maybe that sounds kind of corny, but that's the way it was. And judging by my luck thus far, I had about the chance of a popsicle on the sunward side of Mercury of convincing him.

Actually, I had little real sympathy for the expedition. I've never thought much of people penning animals in cages to be gawked at. Already, of the sparse animal life on Venus, two species had become extinct: the beautiful Venusian egret, to supply plumes for hats in a ridiculous revival of the millinery styles of the 19th century, and the kieter, whose meat was delicious beyond belief, to adorn the tables of wealthy gourmets.

Dixie heard me come into camp. She stuck her beautiful head through the flaps of her tent and smiled at me. That helped considerably. She asked, "Get anything, Rod?"

I said, "Only this. Is it any good?" I opened the moss-lined box I used as a game carrier and took out the only animal I'd caught, if it *was* an animal. It had gills like a fish, eight legs, a comb like a rooster's, only larger, and blue fur.

Dixie looked it over. "It's a weezen, Rod. We have two back at the zoo, so it's not a new variety." She must have seen the disappointment on my face because she added quickly, "But this is a good specimen, Rod. Don't let it go yet; Daddy will probably want to study it when he has time."

That's my Dixie.

Dr. Everton came out of the main tent and looked at me distastefully. "Hello, Spenser. I'll shut off the signal now, Crane's back, too."

He walked over and shut off the radio-like gadget that had been broadcasting a directional click signal to enable Crane and me to get back to camp. On Venus without that transmitter and a matching pocket receiver, you'd be hopelessly lost a few dozen yards from your base.

"Crane get anything?" I asked.

"No specimens," Dr. Everton said, "but something well worth eating. He got a swamp-hen, and he's cooking it for us now."

"Wouldn't let me touch it," Dixie said. "Says women can't cook. It must be about ready; he's been working an hour. Hungry, Rod?"

"Almost hungry enough to eat *this*," I told her, looking at the weezen I was still holding. Dixie laughed and took it from me to put in one of the hold boxes.

We went into the main tent. The swamp-hen was ready and Crane served it proudly. He'd done a good job on it and had a right to be proud. A Venusian swamp-hen, properly cooked, is as much better than fried chicken as fried chicken is better than boiled buzzard. It's out of this world, or any world.

And it has four legs instead of two, so there was a drumstick for each of us.

There wasn't much talk while we ate. But over coffee, Dixie said something to me that didn't make any sense at all—something about a turtle.

"Huh?" I said. "What turtle?"

Dixie looked at me as though to see whether I was kidding or not and then she looked from her father to John Crane, and then there was an awkward silence.

I frowned and asked what went.

Crane sighed. He said, "A Venusian mud turtle, Rod. What this expedition came for, primarily. And apparently you found one this morning."

"I don't know what you're talking about," I said patiently. "I not only didn't find one, but I never even *heard* of one. What kind of a gag is this?"

Dr. Everton shook his head sadly. "Spenser, we let you come along only because you swore you knew how to capture one."

"*I* said that?" I looked at Dixie pleadingly. "Is this a conspiracy to kid me, or what?"

Dixie looked down at her plate unhappily.

Dr. Everton said, "Yes, definitely you found one of the turtles, or were near one. I'll explain.

"You see, Spenser, many creatures have amazing protective mechanisms for use against their enemies. There are the insects that survive by resembling twigs—the harmless snakes that have the markings of deadly vipers—the small fish that can puff itself up so large that it cannot be swallowed—the chameleon that—"

I interrupted him, "I'll concede protective mechanisms, Dr. Everton. But what's that got to do with whatever we're talking about?"

He waggled a finger at me. "All right, you concede protective mechanisms. Now we come to the protective mechanism of the Venusian mud turtle. Like all other forms of life on Venus, it has limited telepathic powers. In its case, a special adaptation of telepathy. It can induce temporary amnesia concerning itself—its very existence—in the mind of any creature coming within a certain range of it.

"In other words, if anyone goes out hunting a Venusian mud turtle and finds one—he not only forgets he was hunting it but that he saw it or ever heard of it!"

Probably my mouth dropped open a little. I said, "You mean that *I was out hunting a*—"

"Exactly," said Dr. Everton, a bit smugly.

I looked at Dixie and this time her eyes met mine. She said, "That's right, Rod. Finding a way to capture one of the turtles was the main purpose of this expedition. And part of the reason Dad let you come along was the fact that you swore you knew how to do it."

"*I* did?"

"Just a minute, Rod; I'll show you. I know you're finding it hard to believe, when you don't remember." She left the tent a minute and came back with a letter; I could see that it was in my handwriting. She gave it to me and I read it and my ears began to burn.

I handed it back to Dixie and there was a long silence.

Finally I broke it. "And I didn't even give any of you a clue," I asked, "as to how I was going to go about being smarter than a mud turtle?"

Dr. Everton spread his hands. "You wouldn't tell us."

"How long will this amnesia last? Is it permanent?"

"No, it will run its course in a few hours—five or six, perhaps. But after that, if you encounter another of the beasts, it'll happen all over again."

I thought that over and it didn't help any way that I could see. But I suddenly wondered about something. I asked, "If everyone who sees one forgets about it, how is it known to exist?"

"It's been photographed several times—but by explorers who didn't remember taking the photographs until after they were developed hours later. It looks considerably like a terrestrial turtle; has six legs instead of four and is round rather than oval. You studied pictures of it quite closely."

Crane had arisen from the table and secured half a dozen photographs from a small portable desk that sat in one corner. "Here's your object of search, Rod." There was amusement in his eyes.

I stared at them, still unbelievingly. "They're cute little fellows," I muttered. "Big eyes. Look kind of wistful."

"Rather rare, even as Venusian life forms go," Crane told me. "This area of twenty or thirty square miles is the only spot they've been reported."

"Rare is correct," Dr. Everton grunted. "And at the rate things are going they'll be extinct before we ever secure a specimen."

I frowned at that. "What do you mean?"

Crane shrugged. "Some of the attempts to catch them have been rather disastrous to the mud turtles. One biological expedition tried a poison gas, thinking to kill a few and at least have some dead specimens. However, what obviously happened was that upon death they sank deep into the mud. Another expedition used a narcotic in hopes of rendering some unconscious. They—"

Dr. Everton put in, "Well, be that as it may, if this expedition fails, it will probably be the last. The attempts to capture the mud turtle are proving much too expensive."

I rubbed a hand across my face. This was like having a hangover after a six-day binge. If it hadn't been for that letter in my own handwriting I might still have suspected that they'd conspired to play a joke on me.

I said ruefully, "Whatever idea I had, it must have been wrong. I have met the enemy and I am its. If you'll excuse me—"

"What are you going to do, Rod?" Dixie asked.

"Going off to think awhile." I turned to Dr. Everton. "Unless you want me for something."

"No, go ahead, Spenser. We're going out hunting again, possibly our last trip before we leave. But—" He didn't exactly say that I wasn't going to be a very valuable addition to the hunting party, but he meant it all right. And I didn't blame him.

I went back to my own tent—each of the four of us had a small private tent outside the big one—and sat down on the cot. I tried to remember something, anything, about turtles or a turtle. But aside from what they'd just told me, I couldn't dredge up a thing.

What idea had I had? Well, whatever it was, it hadn't been very good. I felt like ripping my hair out.

There was a cough at the tent entrance. "May I come in?" It was Dr. Everton's voice.

"Sure," I said.

He came in and I motioned him to sit down, but he shook his head. He said, "I'm sorry I have to remind you of this, Spenser—while you're down, as it were—but it wouldn't be fair to me if I didn't. And you've indubitably forgotten it along with everything else concerning the turtle."

I looked up at him, puzzled.

He said, "You don't remember our agreement?"

I shook my head.

"It was simply this: I told you that if you could do what you said you could, I'd withdraw my objections to your marrying Dixie. In return, you agreed that if you failed—"

"Oh, *no.*"

"You did, Spenser. You were so sure of yourself that you seemed to think you weren't taking any chance at all. But you *did* promise that if you failed, you'd accept my verdict and not continue to see Dixie."

It seemed impossible that I'd have said that—but I knew Dr. Everton was an honest man. I had to believe him.

He said, "I'm sorry to have to remind you of it. And frankly, I've come to rather like you somewhat, personally. But I still don't think you'd be a good husband for my daughter. She is a brilliant girl. She is entitled to someone who—uh—"

"Who's smarter than a mud turtle," I supplied glumly.

He said, "Well—" and went on kindly to try to make me feel a bit better about it, but it didn't help. Pretty soon he left and I sat there.

And sat there.

I must have had an idea that I'd been pretty confident of, I knew, if I'd made a deal like that with Dr. Everton. But *what* had the idea been? What good is an idea if you don't remember? *Or could I possibly have been smart enough to have left a message for myself?*

I went quickly to the footlocker that held my clothes and equipment and lifted the lid. There was a message chalked on the inside of the lid, all right, and it was in my own lettering. Three sentences. I stared at them. "TURNABOUT IS FAIR PLAY. CAN A PERSON WITH AMNESIA GET AMNESIA? PHASE IS THE ANSWER."

I stared at the message and groaned. I'd had to be cryptic, yet. I couldn't have put it in plain English so I'd know what I was talking about. Probably I'd figured that if I put it plainly Crane or Everton might see it and steal my idea. But what had I *meant?*

TURNABOUT IS FAIR PLAY. CAN A PERSON WITH AMNESIA GET AMNESIA? PHASE IS THE ANSWER.

Nuts. It must have meant something to me when I chalked it there, but it meant absolutely nothing now.

TURNABOUT IS FAIR PLAY. Did that mean that I'd deliberately let myself get caught by a turtle first *so I could turn the tables and then catch it?* Can a person with amnesia get amnesia? Wasn't I immune now? Maybe, but what did I mean by *phase* being the answer?

I heard sounds of the others leaving camp and I grabbed my equipment quickly, including the moss-lined specimen box, and hurried out. They were out of sight—from the sound of their voices, about twenty yards away—but they answered when I called out, and waited while I slogged through the mud after them.

Dr. Everton was last, and I fell in beside him. I said, "Listen, Doctor, I'm almost getting a glimmer of what my idea was. I think I let that turtle get me on purpose. I think I went out alone on purpose so I'd come near one."

"Yes? Why?" He sounded interested.

"Because you see that, having been caught, I'm going to be subject to that amnesia for another four hours or so. And while I am, I think I'm immune. I think that if I see a turtle *now*, I won't forget what it is and that I want to capture it."

He turned and stared at me. "Spenser, maybe you've got something there. But it's a slim chance."

"Why?"

"This visibility—or lack of it. According to those pictures it blends in pretty well with the mud. It crawls along on top of the mud, but it's the same color. You wouldn't find one unless you happened almost to step on it."

I looked around and mentally agreed with him.

I thought, *phase is the answer*, and then tried to figure out what I meant. It made nuts.

We slogged along, with me concentrating so hard that I was afraid of spraining a convolution. What had I meant by *phase*? Why had I had to be so cryptic? And this was going to be my last chance...

I strained my eyes into the fog as I walked.

"How large would you say the turtles were, Doctor?"

"About six inches in diameter, I'd say from the photographs."

Not that it mattered much. At six yards, in this fog, you couldn't have seen an elephant. Dixie and Crane were only two steps ahead of us and I could barely see them.

"And it's exactly the color of mud?"

"Beg pardon?"

"The turtles," I said. "Are they the same color as this mud?"

He turned and looked at me. "Turtles? Are you crazy, Spenser? There aren't any turtles on Venus."

I stopped walking so suddenly I skidded in the mud and almost fell. Dr. Everton looked back at me. "Something wrong, Spenser?"

"Go on," I said. "I'll catch up with you in a minute, I'll explain later."

He hesitated, as though he wanted to ask me more questions, and then, obviously realizing he'd lose sight of Crane and Dixie unless he hurried, he said, "All right, see you at the camp if we get separated."

The minute he vanished into the mists I put down my specimen box as a landmark on the exact spot where I stood. I started walking in a spiral around it.

Phase is the answer! It wasn't cryptic after all. I'd merely let myself get caught—alone—by one of the turtles so I'd be out of phase with the others. I was immune, for this short period, and they weren't. So the turtle had "got" Everton and that was my clue.

I was making my fifth circle of the specimen box, about six or seven feet away from it, when I almost stepped on something that was motionless and almost invisible on top of the mud. It was a six-legged turtle. I picked it up and said, "Aha, my beauty. Turnabout is fair play, and phase was the answer!"

It looked at me with a pair of big, soulful eyes and said sorrowfully, "Yeep?" I felt a twinge of conscience. I knew good and well that now a method had been found, other zoos, other museums, would want specimens and—

I suppressed that line of thought and put the turtle firmly into my box. This meant Dixie, and Dixie meant everything. Using the directional click signal as a guide, I slopped back to camp.

I was chuckling to myself when they got back a few hours later. It was turnabout again, but I was ready to convince them. I'd dug into my footlocker and found all the ammunition I needed—scientific periodicals with articles about the Venusian mud turtle, newspaper accounts of the departure of the zoological expedition and its primary purpose. And, of course, Exhibit A, one Venusian mud turtle in excellent condition and alive.

I got Dr. Everton aside and, as diplomatically as he had reminded me of the deal between us, I reminded him.

He sighed. "All right, Rod," he said. "I don't remember it but I'll take your word. I think that—right now—I'd say yes anyway, regardless of whether there's a wager covering the matter."

We shook hands, and he smiled suddenly. "Have you and Dixie set the date?"

"I'll have to check with Dixie," I told him, "but I know what day *I'd* choose. And you're technically captain of a spaceship and can perform the ceremony before we leave." I grinned at him. "In fact, I'd better cash in before I get amnesia again and forget what the deal was."

"Get amnesia again? You think you will?"

"Unless this is the same turtle I came near the first time, I think I will, yes. As soon as the period of immunity from the first turtle wears off, this one will get me and I'll forget things again for a few hours. And that's about due to happen, if it's going to."

I found Dixie in the main tent and the exact words of what I said and what she said are none of your business. Half an hour later, Dr. Everton married us and then, because we wanted to do our packing and take off before the approaching end of the Venusian day, we pitched in.

I did most of the work inside the ship, getting it ready, so I was the last to pack my own duffel and bring it abroad. Naturally I threw away everything I didn't need—one always does before a trip in space—including emptying the moss out of my specimen box and releasing an odd turtle-like creature that couldn't have any value as a specimen; it must have got the catch open and crawled in by itself because it was, nothing I'd ever caught. An appealing little creature, somehow; I was glad I didn't have any reason to keep it a prisoner.

Maybe I should have asked Dr. Everton about it, but I was in a hurry to start the trip back to earth—and my honeymoon.

Troubador

His primitive music was a threat to civilization's perfection. He could not be granted immortality! No jury would disagree...

"WHAT is your name, please?"

Willie actually had to think for an instant. It had been so long since he'd used it, or heard it used. "William Dennison, 14K-49R-3rd."

"I understand you have a pseudonym, er...nickname. Please tell the court what it is."

The defense specialist supplied by the Solar System League for Civil Rights raised his head as though to protest, but then said nothing.

Willie answered so softly that the video-technician had to ask him to raise his voice, "Willie," he repeated.

"Is it Weary Willie?"

Willie said, "Sometimes; usually just Willie."

The presidor allowed himself a smile, to the prosecutor's satisfaction. Possibly this was going to be easier than he'd thought. "Would you explain the significance of the name, please?"

Willie cleared his throat. "It's a joke. Long ago a fictional character possessed that name."

"What was the nature of this fictional character?" the prosecutor pursued.

"He was a wanderer...a vagabond."

"A vagrant?"

Willie didn't answer.

"Is it true," the prosecutor smiled tolerantly, "Weary Willie, that you are also called the last of the hobos?"

Willie stirred uneasily, he was unable to make himself comfortable in the witness chair. He said, "I've preferred the title, last of the troubadours."

The prosecutor remembered and softened his scowl. "I'm sure you do," he said, "but we'll come to that later. Is it true you are more often called the last of the hobos?"

"I...I suppose so."

"Please describe to the court the meaning of the word hobo."

Willie hesitated.

Turning to the presidor's bench, the prosecutor said, "With your permission, I'll read this extract from the *Grosset Glossary of Ancient Colloquialisms*. Under the heading *hobo*: United States, circa 1875 A. D.-1975 A. D., A vagrant; a migrant worker of the lowest class; sometimes a petty criminal. The hobo was the 20th Century equivalent of the gypsy, using the railroads and the highways to replace the caravans of the latter."

The prosecutor asked his next question. "Do you think the estate of hobo is an honorable one, Weary Willie?"

The defense specialist made a wry face and said, "I demur."

The presidor motioned to the video-technician. The vote of the audience-jury was taken and the panel above the presidor's bench flashed red indicating the question was to be answered.

Willie said, "Yes. I think..."

The prosecutor held up a hand and beamed at him. "Never mind, please, you have answered my question. Now then, you said earlier that you would prefer to be named the last of the troubadours. Explain that."

Willie stirred again; he still couldn't find comfort in his chair. "The troubadour was an ancient musician who wandered about the countryside entertaining people with his songs, usually his own compositions."

The prosecutor snapped, "Then you claim to be a musician?"

Willie hesitated, "In a manner of speaking."

"What musical universities did you attend?"

Softly, "None."

"Then of just what does your musical specialization consist?"

"I play a guitar and sing, sometimes my own compositions, sometimes ancient folk music." For the first time there was an edge of defiance in Willie's tone.

The prosecutor smiled tolerantly. "My dear Weary Willie," he said, "surely you are aware of the fact that we have equipment far superior to man in creating music. For half a millennium the human voice hasn't been used for vocalization; for thrice that time instruments have been played by efficient machines; for a thousand years composition has been done by mathematical formula, you say that you compose your own music. Didn't you know that musical composition technicians are divided into forty-seven divisions, each with their own score or so of sub-specialization's?"

"Forty-nine," the presidor interjected needlessly.

The prosecutor thanked him. Actually, he'd known it was the higher number but he knew the correction would amplify his point.

Willie said, "I compose a different type of music."

The prosecutor beamed at him. "I'm sure you do," he said, "however, the authorities on musical science don't consider your efforts as exactly coming under that category. But to get back to the question, Weary Willie, just what is your profession?"

"I am a troubadour," Willie said stubbornly. His mind went back to Kraus...

HE had met the old man—old in the former sense of the word—surprisingly enough, on one of his few incursions into the larger population centers. He was one of the few persons Willie ever met who refused the rejuvenation process needed every half century to insure immortality. The old man never explained why and it was possibly three hundred years after his death before Willie knew.

Kraus was the last man in the system to practice handicrafts, specializing in musical instruments that for centuries had been discarded in favor of the more practical, ultra efficient, ultra varied machine played devices of the new civilization. Most of his products went to museums. Few were ever utilized.

He taught Willie the guitar and when he had no more to teach, sent him to the other side of Terra where there existed an obscure musical museum containing the last wire recordings of ancient folk music.

It was through Kraus and through those recordings that Willie found himself. Through them he became, in his own mind, the last of the troubadours...

The prosecutor was saying, "Weary Willie, do you believe in the destiny of the human race?"

He brought his thoughts back to the present, but the sense of the question eluded him. The prosecutor said again, "Do you believe that man is destined to develop, expand, to one day dominate the universe?"

Willie shifted his position uncomfortably. It wasn't the way he would express it, but he said, "Yes."

There was more triumph than kindliness in the prosecutor's smile now. "Do you believe that to accomplish this the misfits of society must be eliminated?"

The defense specialist said, "I demur. I can see no connection with the purpose of the trial."

The presidor motioned impatiently to the video technician who put the question to a vote. Throughout the system, the audience-jury considered, then pressed the suitable key. The majority found for the prosecution and the panel flashed red.

Willie asked cautiously, "What do you mean by misfit and what by eliminated?"

The presidor said, "The question is quite clear. Answer it."

Willie twisted in his chair. "I...I suppose...yes, but I would..."

"The prosecution retires," said the prosecutor, beaming at the defense specialist from the Solar System League for Civil Rights.

THE defense specialist arose and approached Willie. He was far more perturbed than he had been at the beginning of the trial.

He began, "The degree of true democracy to be found in any social system in any age is to be measured by the extent to which it protects its minorities. No matter how small, that minority which is..."

The presidor shook his head impatiently. "The defense will remember that a summation period follows." He allowed himself a slight smile. "Even slogans of the League for Civil Rights can wait until that time. Please examine the respondent."

The defense specialist took a deep breath and asked Willie, "Do you consider yourself a misfit in society?"

Willie straightened in his chair and said firmly, "No."

"You call yourself a troubadour but the prosecutor has pointed out that there is no such specialization in musical science. Please tell us why you disagree with either the prosecutor or the present heads of musical art."

This was better. Willie began, "I believe that the soul has gone out of music, and not only music but of all society. I believe that if we are to…"

"I demur," interrupted the prosecutor. "An attack upon musical science by an admittedly unschooled person is obviously beside the point."

The presidor said, "Take the vote, please."

The panel turned green.

The defense specialist tried to reword it. "Please tell the court why you believe yourself suitable for rejuvenation."

The presidor raised a protesting hand. "You have already been warned that such material belongs in your summation period."

The defense specialist's lips thinned and whitened. He said, a tone of desperation in his voice, "William Dennison, it has been pointed out that you are sometimes known as the last of the hobos and the term hobo is defined partially as a sometimes petty criminal. Have you ever committed a crime of any type?"

Willie stirred. "Of course not."

"Of what have your activities consisted in your approximate eight hundred years of life?"

Willie smiled, "Of trying to bring a little music into the hearts of…"

The prosecutor rapped, "I demur. Never before in the history of the race has there been more universal recourse to the best music produced by musical science. There is no need in society for vagrants playing before tiny audiences; video is available to all."

The panel flashed green when the question was put.

The defense specialist stood silent for a long moment. His eyes flashed from prosecutor to presidor, then to the video panel. Twice he began to speak, but restrained himself.

The presidor asked, "Does the respondent's defense specialist have further questions?"

The League for Civil Rights man turned to Willie and said, "Do you have anything else to say, short of our five minute summation?"

IT had slowly come to Willie why he was in revolt against things as they were. It finally became clear and he knew why Kraus, the old man who had so carefully made his ancient instruments of music by hand, had refused renewal of life.

Man was becoming stratified, stereotyped. He had solved his problems of the production and distribution of an abundance of the necessities and even the luxuries of life. He had built himself a social system that guaranteed the freedom, for which he had so long striven. In short, man had reached what had always been thought the millennium—Utopia!

And then the question—never really expressed, of course, but there—arose, "Where do we go from here?"

Nobody answered.

Hundreds of thousands of years before, an early man-form had used a stone or a piece of wood to knock some fruit from a tree. That had started the progress of the tool, and man's attempt to free himself from the tyranny of nature. For countless centuries he improved his tools until finally they became machines, and super-machines, and ultra-super-machines. And as they developed man had to change his ways to fit his new environment.

Nature was conquered, but somewhere along the line man had become a slave to the machines he had created to free himself from nature's oppression. Progress continued and with it came the ultra-specialization of Willie's time.

"We are becoming like ants, like bees," was the way Willie put it.

Of course his efforts were less than a tiny meteorite flashing in the endless blackness of space, but, he fought on. Here and there he found a convert, a kindred spirit, another who fought against man's trend to the anthill. There hadn't been many; for one thing he was kept from reaching the masses of mankind by his lack of a means of spreading his philosophy other than by word of mouth...

The presidor was saying, "The prosecutor will address his summation to the audience-jury."

The prosecutor spoke easily. The trial had gone even better than he had hoped. His sponsors of the Eugenics Society and the Association for Development of the race would be pleased.

"I shall not need my full five minutes," he said. "The case is a simple one. Weary Willie," he smiled when he used the nickname, "has proven by his testimony to be a misfit, a throwback, an atavism. His presence amidst mankind as unfortunate. Possible offspring could well inherit his tendencies; those who come in contact with him might well be, er...corrupted.

"We do not claim that Weary Willie is a criminal, certainly not in the ordinary sense of the word, since crime has for all practical purposes been eliminated. We do claim, however, that he is a public enemy.

"Obviously, we do not ask punishment, the world has progressed beyond the point where its misfits are punished as they were in ancient times. We do ask, however, that society protect itself. The protective device is an obvious one; the prosecution demands that Weary Willie not be granted rejuvenation, and that his life end when it has run its natural course.

"I would also like to point out that this case has drawn interplanetary interest due to the fact that the decision here will set a precedent for future cases of this category. The question the audience-jury will vote upon today is not just whether or not William Dennison, 14K-49R-3rd, or Weary Willie, shall be refused further rejuvenation but whether man will protect himself from the atavisms who would destroy, were they able, man's progress."

THE prosecutor resumed his seat and congratulated himself inwardly. He thought it had gone very well.

The presidor nodded approvingly and said, "The respondent's defense specialist will address his summation to the audience-jury."

The defense specialist cleared his throat. "Against my advice, the respondent has decided to make his own summation."

The presidor nodded and said, "That is unusual, but permissible."

Willie asked, "May I have my guitar?"

It was brought from the corridor outside, where his other few possessions were also awaiting him.

He cleared his throat and looked into the video device and tried a wry grin. He said shyly, "I've always wanted a larger audience than I've ever had as a…a troubadour."

As he went on he unconsciously stroked the dark wood of the ancient instrument, as a man would caress something he loved deeply. "It seems to me that everything hinges upon whether or not the troubadours in life are necessary to man's progress. I think they are."

He ran a gentle finger over the strings of his guitar. "I'm going to play and sing. The prosecutor said that because I failed to study musical science in some gigantic musical university and to learn a specialization in the art, I cannot make music. I guess it's up to you to decide. This song is not one of my own, but one of those simple tunes that was sung long, long ago—when man still had a soul and a love of real music which came from the heart, not from mechanical instruments played by robots. It's called *'Blue Tail Fly.'*"

His fingers began to strum and he sang softly, shyly:

When I was young I used to wait,
On my master and serve him his plate,
And pass the bottle when he got dry,
And brush away the blue tailed fly.
Jimmy Crack Corn and I don't care,
Jimmy Crack Corn and I don't care,
Jimmy Crack Corn and I don't care,
My master's gone away.
One day we rode around the farm,
The flies so numerous they did swarm.
One bit the pony in the thigh
The devil take the blue tail fly.
Jimmy Crack Corn and I don't care,
Jimmy Crack Corn and I don't care,
Jimmy Crack Corn and I don't care,
My master's gone away.
The pony run, he jump, he pitch,
He throw my master in the ditch,
He died, the jury wondered why,
The verdict was, the blue tail fly.
Jimmy Crack… "

The prosecutor came to his feet hotly. "I demur. The respondent is mocking the court. Instead of allowing his council to present what little defense possible, he makes a spectacle of himself and…"

The presidor scowled. "The prosecutor will please refrain from interruption while the respondent is utilizing his summation period in the manner he thinks best."

The other flushed. "I demur."

The presidor's scowl deepened but he motioned to the video-technician who put the question to the vote. The panel went red.

The presidor said, "The prosecution will refrain from further interruption of the respondent's summation."

But Willie shook his head. "No," he said. "He's right; it was ridiculous. I suppose I have too much of what they used to call the *ham* in me. I couldn't resist the opportunity of having such a large audience. Undoubtedly, it will give them the chance to decide even more easily that I am what the prosecutor has said, a misfit." He took up his guitar and began to return to his chair.

The prosecutor said with satisfaction, "I call for the decision of the audience-jury."

A muscle worked in the cheek of the presidor, but he raised his hand in signal and the video-technician touched switches and buttons.

The panel flashed green.

PRESIDOR, and prosecutor, defense specialist and respondent, and even the video-technician, stared at it unbelievingly.

The prosecutor was on his feet again. "I demand an actual count," he sputtered. "The video equipment is obviously out of order. There is…"

The presidor silenced him with a glare, but turned to the video man. "A count," he requested.

More switches and other buttons. The figures flashed on the panel. Acquittal—12,654,302,917; Guilty—235,104.

The prosecutor's eyes bugged out in disbelief. He sputtered, "That's fantastic, obviously those figures mean that the video-computer is in error."

The defense specialist smiled broadly at him. "To the contrary, it means that over 200,000 members of the audience-jury must be tone deaf. Also that for the first time in centuries man has heard music." The defense specialist realized that this moment was historical and that he was playing a major part in it. He added, somewhat ostentatiously, "Possibly man is taking his first step toward regaining his soul."

Willie's grin matched that of his defense specialist—and, to his surprise, that of the presidor and the video-technician. He ran his fingers over the guitar strings. "Maybe they'd like to hear the rest of *Blue Tail Fly*," said the last of the old troubadours, the first of the new.

The Word from the Void

Tyrant of Mars...undying king of space—all roads were open to Camp—save Man's immortal right to be—himself!

I SHOOK my head again in an attempt to clear it of the woji *fumes. It did little good. The ultra-sights of my silogun were hazy, indistinct. I cursed the Venusian Gadaboot who'd kept me up half the preceding night buying me drinks.*

I tried to concentrate, to steady my shaking hand. It was no good; I couldn't risk the shot in my present condition.

In the valley below, the Saturnian Slaber bent over Deema Tas, the Martian desert princess. Three of his eyes gloated over her delectable beauty, while the other three kept a cautious watch for enemies. Thus far, I was sure, he hadn't spotted me.

I knew his awful desire; to intensify her terror to the point where her mind was on the verge of snapping, and then to consume her life forces. In all the system—nay, in all the universe, there was no more horrible, monstrous creature than the Slaber. My own mind reeled at the danger with which my betrothed was faced.

Could I cover the half-mile distance to them in time! I doubted it. I felt despair. And then, suddenly,

And then, suddenly, what? Ray Camp leaned back in his chair and stared at the yellow sheet of paper in his typewriter for long moments.

And then, suddenly, nothing. No more would come.

He reread the last two hundred words and grimaced. It was lousy. He looked through the empty pack absently for the tenth time, and threw it back on the desk. He patted his

157

clothes for a stray cigarette, gave up, and finally resorted to locating the largest butt in the ashtray.

He read the two hundred words again and snorted with disgust. I was worse than lousy.

He took two quick puffs on the cigarette and ground it out again in the ashtray; tore the paper from the typewriter and threw it into an already overflowing wastepaper basket. Then he reached into an open drawer of the desk for another sheet. He rolled it quickly into the machine.

Ray Camp stared at the yellow sheet for a long time. The thought came to his mind that he was lucky it wasn't white. He remembered the old gag about the writer who got snow-blindness from staring at a blank sheet of white paper.

Finally he said aloud, "Maybe I should take it from the girl's angle."

The typewriter started to clatter again.

Slowly I came out of the faint, merciful unconsciousness, which had overwhelmed me, when I first glimpsed the Saturnian Slaber. My brain reeled, but I fought to control it. I knew that I could not afford weakness now. My chances of escape were too slim; too fearfully, desperately slim.

And, too, I must remember my pride of race. For more than forty decals, the equivalent of sixty Terran millennia, the proud Deema Clan had ruled the Zeizz tribes of the Martian deserts.

In me, the Princess Deema Tas, was the last hope of the dying Zeizz. If my marriage to the Terran hero, Hari Brun, was the success our witch-scientists predicted, perhaps a new life would flow into the bloodstream of the desert tribesmen.

The Slaber crouched above me, drooling. Three of his eyes ran over my body, noting the torn madlerobe, symbol of Zeizz nobility, noting the scratches I'd suffered in my escape from the Mercurian Bouncer a scant hour ago. I knew what was in his evil mind. When my terror had grown to the ultimate, he would drain the life forces from my brain, leaving my body a mindless hulk.

Oh, where was Hari Brun?

YEAH. Where was Hari? Hari was up on the hill squinting drunkenly through the sights of his silogun, so bleary-eyed that he had a hard time making out which was Deema Tas and which was the Slaber.

Ray Camp leaned back again and grunted. He picked up the empty cigarette pack and felt around in it hopefully. He stared at it somewhat in surprise; he thought he'd just bought a new pack an hour or so ago. A little fishing around in the ashtray brought to light a longish butt.

He read what he had just written and groaned. The more he looked at this story, the sorrier he was he'd ever started it. For the ten thousandth time, he wondered who in the world bought the magazines for which he was trying to write.

The stale cigarette bit his tongue; he ground it out in the tray and tore the sheet from the typewriter with his left hand. He sighed and reached for another with his right.

The typewriter started to stutter again.

I bent over the Martian female. From deep inside, I could feel wave after wave of flooding desire for her life forces. It had been many koorls since my mairdeen buds had feasted. I was weak from lack of life.

But not so weak that I was unable to detect the presence of another life upon the hill behind us. I reached out with my thirteenth sense to scan it.

A Terran! Curse of the Slabers! The only life form in the system with which we were unable to cope. I muttered a quick prayer to Wodo, pledging a new altar to his sacred name if I were but successful today.

As I contemplated the fullness of the life forces in the Martian princess sprawled before me, I scanned the brain of the Terran.

159

Ah! Praise be to Wodo! His brain was befouled with woji. *He was attempting to slay me with one of the deadly Terran siloguns, but the effects of the narcotic-alcoholic drinks were preventing him from using his sight-organs properly. Once again I praised the Gods of Saturn that we of the Slaber race needed neither food nor drink.*

Almost maddening glee welled up within me. I had the time to drink of the priceless life of the princess. In mere moments, her life forces would be part of mine.

I bent over and gazed deep into her eyes. She was terrified,

Ray Camp stopped again and regarded the typewriter with disgust.

"That does it. The more I write, the lousier it gets."

He reached for his cigarette pack and noted with surprise that it was empty.

He kicked his chair back and reached for his hat. It wasn't necessary to think about it. He knew where he was going.

Ray slammed the door behind him and walked down two flights to the street. It was a beautiful day, but he didn't bother to notice. He made a beeline for the corner bar.

When he entered, the bartender, a Venusian Gadaboot, looked up from the *bourl* he was mixing. "Hello, Ray," it shrilled. "How are you?"

"Sober," Ray Camp grunted.

The bartender finished the drink, slid it over to the Mercurian Bouncer who had ordered it, and rang up the two credits on the cash register. He came over and leaned on the bar before the writer. "What'll it be, Ray?"

"Might as well make it *woji*. I've given up trying to do any work today."

The Venusian bartender mixed the drink expertly, getting in the exact three drops of Plutonian absinthe.

"You still trying to make your living writing for the magazines, Ray?" he whistled.

"Yeah."

The bartender slid the drink over to him and leaned on the bar again. "You still trying to crash those confession magazines?"

Ray Camp sipped the drink appreciatively. "Yeah. I've been trying to write a confession story all morning. If I don't make some money soon, I'm going to have to leave Mars and go back to Terra and get a job."

Your Soul Comes C. O. D.

Norman knew just what he wanted from life. Except whom to call on for help in collecting the payoff.

IN VIEW of the trouble to which he had gone in order to acquire such out of the way items as a piece of unicorn horn and three drops of blood from a virgin, it was rather disconcerting to have the spirit appear even before the prescribed routine. In fact, he hadn't even got his protective pentacle drawn when he looked up to find the entity materialized in his rickety easy chair.

The spirit said, "You don't really need that, you know."

Norman Wallace stared at his visitor, even after all these months of research, unbelievingly. The other was far from what the young man expected. Somehow, he was reminded of Lincoln, his face almost beautiful in its infinite sadness.

The spirit nodded at the pentacle. "Mere superstition. It couldn't protect you if my purpose was to do you harm. But, more important still, I am quite incapable of such aggression. Man has freedom of choice, free will; we of the other worlds can only help him destroy—or elevate—himself, we cannot initiate."

Norman was shaken, but not quite to the point of speechlessness. He pointed to his assembled drugs, charms, potions and incenses and said, almost indignantly, "But I haven't performed the rite, as yet."

The other nodded and shrugged. "What's the difference? You wished to summon a spirit. Very well, here I am. The desire is of more importance than the act of combining those rather silly items. But, to get to the point, just what is it you desire?"

Norman Wallace took a deep breath and got down to business. He indicated his shabby quarters. "I can bear this no longer," he said. "I want a few years of decency in living, a few years of the good things of life that others enjoy. So—"

"So in your desperation you wish to sell your soul in return for help."

"That's right."

The spirit considered momentarily. "Suppose I give you my support for forty years? Suppose I guarantee you love, wealth, power, to the degree you desire them? At the end of that time your soul is mine?"

Norman Wallace's mouth tightened, but he said, "That's agreeable."

The spirit came to its feet. "Very well, the pact is made."

The other frowned. "Don't we make out a contract or something? Don't I have to sign in blood?"

The faintest of smiles came to the melancholy face of the spirit. "That won't be necessary. The pact has been made, neither of us will nor can break it."

Suddenly he had disappeared.

And almost simultaneously came a knock at the door. Dazed, Norman came to his feet and opened it.

Harriet was there and immediately in his, arms. "Oh, darling, darling, I was so wrong."

He held her back, at arm's length, in amazement. "You mean that you've changed your mind, you'll marry me?"

"Oh, darling, yes. I thought going away from you, spending a few months in Florida, would let me forget. I was so wrong."

Frowning worriedly, he indicated the poverty of his room. "But Harriet, we'd still—"

She smiled now, and laughed up at him. "Remember that little farm I told you my aunt left me? The one in Louisiana?"

He nodded, uncomprehending.

"Oil, darling," she bubbled over.

"Enough to give you the start you need."

AND so it went for forty years. Wealth to the modest extent he desired it; prestige to the small degree his ambition demanded; but, most important of all, love that ripened and ever grew as the years went by. And a home rich with children, and the respect and affection of his neighbors and his associates.

Not that he had ever seen the spirit again, not in all those years. Almost, it was possible for him to look back at his life and think it was all of his own doing. Each success had seemingly been not unordinary good luck, or a result of his own efforts. Sometimes he had even tried to convince himself that the pact he'd made was a figment of his imagination, that the demon he had thought he had summoned was a result of too much worry, too much work, too little food and recreation back in those days of his poverty stricken youth.

But subconsciously he knew. He *knew!*

And so it was that after his forty years he sat alone in his study and waited. Harriet had gone on to bed; the children, of course, had long since been married themselves and were living their own peaceful, happy lives.

He wondered now, as he looked back over the years, at the use to which he had put the demon's assistance. He had been promised love, wealth, and power to the extent he desired them. But, somehow, he had wanted no more than sufficient for himself and his family. He had made no attempt to accumulate the fortune of a Midas; nor, for that matter, had he attained his possessions by recourse to the racetrack or stockmarket. He had worked hard during those forty years.

He had been promised power, too. Why had he taken so little? He had been content to assume a position in society that coincided with his natural abilities. He could have been president or, for that matter, dictator of the world. Why hadn't he?

Ah, but he had taken his full measure of the other. His cup had overflowed with love. In all the years, the romance between Harriet and him had never waned. And the children? Well, for instance, the way they had returned to the old home from all over the nation this last Christmas had proven their affection.

AND NOW suddenly he thought he knew his motivation. Somewhere, beneath it all, he had been attempting to forestall the fate awaiting him. Subconsciously he had told himself that if he were moderate, if he led the good life, if he abstained from demanding the ultimate, his reckoning with the demon would be the easier.

He laughed abruptly, bitterly.

And suddenly fear washed over him. The reckoning was now.

No matter what he had done with the demonic powers awarded him. No matter how he had loved and been loved. No matter how much he repented now.

His soul was the spirit's.

He clasped his hands tightly to the arms of his chair.

Run! *Hide!* ESCAPE!

But he sank back again. There was no place to run. No place to hide. No way of escape.

The spirit materialized on the couch across from him.

Norman Wallace nodded his gray head in submission. "I was expecting you."

"Your forty years are up," the spirit told him.

"Yes, I know." Hopelessness had replaced fear now.

"Is there any reason why our pact should not be fulfilled? You are satisfied that I have suitably kept my part of the bargain?"

The old man hesitated, then nodded again. "I am satisfied."

"Then you are ready to go? You have taken farewell of those you love, made what arrangements you thought necessary?"

"Yes. Yes, I am ready." His voice was firm now. "I suppose it will be hard on Harriet for a time, but then, we must all face the end sooner or later, and only recently my doctor warned me of my heart. Harriet always said she wanted me to go first, that she would hate to think of me alone in life after we have been so close."

The spirit came to its feet. "Very well, let us be on our way."

Norman Wallace arose too and the shock was not so great as he might have expected when he was able to look back and see himself sitting there in the easy chair, his face pale and his eyes staring unseeingly.

"Then I am dead already?"

"Yes," the spirit told him. "Your doctor's diagnosis was quite accurate. Come."

And suddenly they were in another place and Norman Wallace stared about uncomprehendingly.

He said, "It seems that in all my relations with you I have been continually surprised at the inaccuracy of the legends and myths."

"Oh?" the spirit said.

"Yes. When you first appeared you didn't look like my life-long conception of a demon. Nor in my dealings with you have you acted the way I supposed you would. Now, this place has none of the attributes I had expected of hell."

The spirit smiled. "My dear Norman, why is it that so many suppose that souls are of less interest to us than to our adversaries? Why should not one side strive for a worthy one as well as the other? I am not a demon, nor is this hell."

Desperate Remedy
Novelette of Souls Aspace

Space cafard had a formula: monotony, times boredom, times confined space times time! After twelve months aspace, man would crack—and the madness would spread like uncontrolled plague. And this expedition was on a two-year mission!

FIRST OFFICER Johnny Norsen, his lanky body sprawled awkwardly in the acceleration chair in the wardroom of the *New Taos*, grunted his disgust. "Listen," he said; "listen to this. One of these ancient books of the Doc's. It says nothing is more interesting and broadening than travel. Says no one's education is complete without travel."

Dick Roland, ship's navigator, didn't look up from his game of solitaire. He said, "Maybe that's the way it was in the old days when they traveled in chariots—or whatever it was they used in those days. What *did* they travel in back in ancient times?"

The third occupant of the tiny wardroom, chubby Ensign Mart Bakr who had vacantly been contemplating the overhead stirred in his chair and said listlessly, "It's all according to what period your talking about. Back in United States days they went overland in hot rods—vehicles propelled by internal combustion engines. Had simple aircraft for longer trips. Or did they come later?"

"Anyway," Dick Roland insisted, "possibly traveling was more interesting in those days. More broadening, like Johnny's book says."

Johnny Norsen threw the book to the table emphasizing his disgust. "Naw," he said. "Listen, traveling is never anything but monotony. Reaching your destination might be interesting, but travel itself—I don't care what the medium is—is just plain boredom."

Mart Bakr said, "Sure, and the more advanced it gets, the more boring. Maybe walking has a certain amount of interest, but as soon as you devise a vehicle you get through the country quicker and see it less. Speed it up to the airplane and after a few interesting seconds of takeoff there's nothing at all to do but sit, and the longer the trip lasts the worse it gets. And take us, now, Space travel. Forty-five men cramped in a little sliver of metal. Are we being broadened? Are we completing our education? Hell no, we're about to go stark raving mad with space cafard."

A voice from the door said, "What's this about cafard?"

Norsen looked up. "Hi, Doc. We were just talking about the boredom of traveling. I think it compounds when you don't know where you're going. When's the skipper going to break down? We've been out almost a full year, and nobody knows where we are or where we're going—except him."

Dick Roland said, "Not even me, the ship's navigator. Trip ought to be over by now. Never heard of any crew being asked to stay out more than one year. Not even on bigger ships than this."

"As a matter of fact," Doctor Thorndon said, "it was at my suggestion that the ship's destination be kept secret." The doctor was a small, easy going, roly-poly man, his cheeks still pink but his hair thinning and graying. He looked about forty-five—old for space service—and was the most popular man aboard.

All eyes were on him in surprise.

"Well…*why*, Doc?"

"The Captain will be in shortly. He told me, just now, to round you all up; he's going to give us the word on the significance of this expedition."

"About time," Norsen grumbled. "We've seen all the film, read all the books six times over, played all the games until we can't stand the sight of them." He paused and grinned at his shipmates. "Nor of each other, for that matter."

"You ain't just a whistlin' *Terra Forever,*" Bakr agreed. "I'm sure glad this trip is about over; another few weeks and we'd all be down with cafard."

COMMANDER Mike Gurloff entered the wardroom in time to hear the last of the third officer's words. He scowled down at Bakr, then looked around at the rest of them, "Keep your seats, gentlemen," he growled. Then to the pudgy Mart Bakr, "The trip is only half completed, Mr. Bakr."

They stared at him in disbelief. Johnny Norsen was on his feet, incredulous. "Half through! Listen, skipper, you're kidding; no ship in the service has ever been out for longer than a year. It... Why, hell, skipper, no crew could take it."

Mike Gurloff ran a weary hand back over his shaven head and sank into an acceleration chair himself. "That's why the *New Taos* was chosen, gentlemen. The moral of the story is never to become the pride of the fleet—the one ship that always comes through on a tough assignment."

"*Tough* assignment?" Dick Roland blurted bitterly. "*Suicide* assignment is more like it."

Johnny Norsen, still on his feet, demanded, "What's this about the Doc, here, advising you not to tell us our destination?"

Thorndon said, "We knew the expedition would take less than two years. I was afraid if it became known throughout the crew that they were scheduled for that long a period in space the predilection to space cafard would increase. As it is, most are of the opinion that the whole thing has been very mysterious, but that we are now nearly home; thus far, there have been no signs of cafard whatsoever."

Mart Bakr stuttered indignantly, "Sure, fine. But what's going to happen *now*, when they do find out?"

The doctor rubbed the tip of his nose and screwed up his cherubic face. "We'll see," he said. "The danger of cafard is always less on the way back; every day that passes brings us that much the nearer home."

Dick Roland, still bitter, said, "Yeah. But it's one thing when it's three or four months; we're a whole year out." His saying it brought the significance of his statement home to the navigator. "Where are we?"

Commander Mike Gurloff had been following the conversation, noting the reactions of his officers, in silence. Now he said, "Yes, gentlemen, we come to the *raison d'être* of the whole thing."

They became quiet, looked at him.

He said, "Gentlemen, just before this trip came up, for what were we scheduled?"

Johnny Norsen replied. "The expedition against those Deneb rebels." His usually boyish face hardened. "That expedition I would have enjoyed."

Mike Gurloff nodded. "We all would have. How the religio-political movement that has swept the Deneb planets ever got started in this age is a mystery; but there it is."

Dick Roland slapped a palm on the wardroom table. "And there it should have been squelched, immediately, before it spread any further. Now the threat of losing everything the race has accomplished in millennia. A return to industrial feudalism, wars, race and religious hatreds, class divisions, an economy of want depressions and un-employment. That's where *we* belong—with the rest of the fleet, suppressing the Deneb rebellion."

Mike Gurloff said, "The rest of the fleet isn't suppressing the Deneb rebels, Mr. Roland."

Another bombshell. They gaped at him.

"The rest of the fleet is awaiting our return."

"All right," Johnny Norsen said finally. "Why?"

Mike Gurloff said, "Because, gentlemen, on the results of this expedition the Solar System High Command will determine whether or not to recognize the new Denebian government and come to peace with the rebels."

THEY HAD been struck with too many bombshells to be further shocked. They sat numbly, waiting for him to explain.

"Gentlemen," Gurloff went on, "there is only one thing that could move our government to such a step, recognizing the rebels. Only one thing."

"*Nothing!*" Mart Bakr blurted, clenching a chubby fist emphatically.

"One thing," Mike Gurloff insisted. "The Denebians are human. They are colonists from the solar system, whose inhabitants in turn all stemmed in antiquity from Terra. All intelligent life, in our galaxy, is originally native to Earth; we've sent our colonists to a thousand other stars, which boasted planets suitable for man-life. Deneb is just one of them—one that went sour; one that needs correction before the souring spreads."

Their expressions tightened, but they didn't interrupt.

"Gentlemen, there is only one thing that *must* unite all humans, regardless of internal difficulties."

"Aliens," Dick Roland said. "Intelligent alien life!"

The commander nodded, seriously. "In all our history, man has never found an intelligent life-form with which he could deal peacefully. The answer, I suppose, is obvious. Any intelligent life-form will eventually dominate the universe—that is, if it has no opposition. And the opposition can only be another intelligent life-form."

"Like the Kradens," the Doctor murmured.

"Like the Kradens," Gurloff agreed. "We fought them only after decades of trying to meet them on a peaceful level; but they knew from the beginning what we learned only through our experience with them. The instinct of all life is to perpetuate itself, to increase itself. The instinct is so fundamental that it is impossible to rise above it. Any other intelligent life-form stands in the way of our journey to domination of the universe. It is a potential enemy—and a potential enemy, gentlemen, is an enemy in fact."

"This is elementary, Skipper," Norsen told him; "you realize what we want to know."

"Very well. Shortly before the Solar System fleet was to blast off for Deneb to suppress the revolt there, our posts on the outer-most inhabitable planets in our galactic system, recorded an immense explosion in deep space. An explosion, gentlemen, that could only have been set off by an intelligent life-form, and one that indicated a knowledge of neo-nuclear fission."

"That eliminates the Kradens," Doc Thorndon pointed out; "their science hasn't progressed that far."

"Well, what kind of an explosion? You mean right out in inter-galactical space?" Norsen queried. "I don't quite get it."

Mike Gurloff shook his massive head. "We don't know; we don't know the reason, or anything else. All we know is that some intelligent life-form set off an explosion of fantastic magnitude. The *New Taos* is now in the vicinity of that explosion's origin. Upon our reports will depend whether or not the Solar System will recognize the Deneb rebels, so that man can draw close his ranks for a battle with an alien foe."

It was all out now and they considered it.

Finally Dick Roland said, "You haven't picked up any evidence as yet?"

Gurloff shook his head, "None."

"What did they expect us to find?"

Gurloff shrugged burly shoulders. "Don't know; it's just a matter of cruising around. Looking for wreckage, perhaps, or an alien ship. If we don't find anything, we'll shortly head back." He came to his feet. "Frankly, I think it's a wild goose chase, but it wasn't up to me to decide."

There was an indistinct babble from the corridor, which grew in magnitude until it reached an echoing roar. They spun and faced the door at the clatter of approaching feet.

A messman, his eyes wide and disbelieving, scurried up and ripped off a fast salute.

"Well, Spillane?" Gurloff growled.

"Captain," the boy shrilled. "Captain, we found Corcoran, sir. Dead. Down in compartment eight."

"Dead!" Doc Thorndon snapped. "Why the man wasn't even ill. I'd examined him less than two hours ago." He came quickly to his feet.

Spillane collected himself, lowered his voice an octave or so. "Sir, he wasn't sick. He was killed, sir. A knife sticking in his back. He was murdered, Corcoran was."

TWO

THEY scrambled down the companionway, unheeding of their supposed dignity of rank; Commander Gurloff and Doctor Thorndon took the lead, followed by the three ship's officers and with Spillane, still sputtering, bringing up the rear.

"Murder!" Mike Gurloff bit out. "Ridiculous! Hasn't been a case of murder in the history of the space service."

They hurried their way down to compartment eight, which was crowded with crewmembers staring and milling about the crumpled body.

"Mr. Bakr," the Commander snapped, "clear this compartment of personnel. Doctor?"

The ship's doctor was already bent over the corpse, his fingers deftly prodding for pulse. He was silent only for a few moments, then he looked up at them. "He's gone, all right. By the condition of his body, I would say that he's been dead for approximately fifteen minutes, not longer." He indicated the knife still hilt-deep in the victim's back. "Cause of death, obviously."

For a lengthy moment, even Mike Gurloff was speechless. Then he muttered, "Cafard. Only could have been committed by somebody completely mad."

Doc Thorndon came to his feet, eyed his commander thoughtfully. "No, Mike, I stake my reputation as a physician that there is no cafard on this ship—certainly not advanced enough a case to call for this." He indicated the corpse.

Muscles worked in Gurloff's face. "Mr. Roland," he snapped, "bring me an inter-compartmental communication mike."

The ship's navigator drew his fascinated eyes from the deceased, and hurried to a small compartment set into the ship's wall to return immediately with a microphone.

"Here you are, sir."

Mike Gurloff took the device, cleared his throat, and said into the mouthpiece, "Now hear this. Signalman Corcoran has been found...uh, slain. Anyone—including the man or men responsible—knowing anything of this affair will immediately report to me in compartment eight."

He flicked off the switch and tossed the mike back to Dick Roland.

They stood about indecisively for a period of fifteen minutes or more, ample time for anyone on the ship to have made his way to them.

No one appeared.

"This is incredible," Doc Thorndon protested. "What could anyone expect to achieve by silence?"

"Doctor," Mike Gurloff said, "please take the measures necessary to preserve Signalman Corcoran's body for decent burial upon our arrival at New Albuquerque." He turned to the others, Norsen, Roland and Bakr. "The rest of you gentlemen come with me to my quarters and we shall begin arrangements to have each member of the crew subjected to questioning under narco-scop."

AN HOUR later, the crewmembers began filing into the captain's quarters one by one to be received identically by Gurloff and Thorndon. The doctor quickly injected each with five units of narco-scop, and the commander waited a full minute for it to take effect before asking his questions.

"Did you murder Signalman Corcoran? Do you know anything which might aid in the apprehension of his killer?"

Spillane: "No, sir," in surprise.

Woodford: "Who, me? No, *sir*," indignantly.

Taylor: "No sir, I been in my bunk for the past six hours, Captain. I didn't even know nothing about it until Ensign Bakr woke me up."

Heming: "I'm a cook, sir; I never been down in number eight since I been on this ship, sir."

Rosen: "No, sir, I didn't," emphatically.

Forty men came and went and with slight variations answered the questions identically. No, they had not murdered Corcoran; no, they knew nothing about his death.

When all had finished, Mike Gurloff looked at the doctor for long moments. He said, finally, "Any chance that the stuff isn't working?"

Doc Thorndon shook his head, "Narco-scop is the most efficient truth serum of all time. There has never been a case in medical history where a person under its influence was capable of telling an untruth."

The skipper motioned with his head at the container from which the doctor had been filling his hypodermic needle. "It could have been tampered with."

"No, Mike." The doctor was emphatic. "It was sealed; you just saw me open it. And, besides, it was locked in my medical chest. I'd take my oath that it couldn't have been tampered with."

Mike Gurloff slumped back into his swivel chair and stared at the other. Meanwhile, his three officers finished with their tasks of rounding up the men and ushering them periodically into the room, gathered at the doorway.

Gurloff finally said, "Did I understand you to say that Corcoran had been dead for approximately fifteen minutes when we arrived?"

Doc Thorndon nodded. His kindly face was expressing as much disbelief as was his commander's.

"Then," Mike Gurloff pointed out needlessly, "it would have been impossible for one of us five to have done it. For at least twenty minutes preceding the discovery of the body we were all together in the wardroom. How *sure* are you of that fifteen minute period?"

The doctor frowned back at him. "Pretty sure, Mike. In fact, I went over the body more thoroughly after you had left. I am quite certain that the death took place approximately fifteen minutes before the time I made my first examination. Most certainly not more than twenty minutes.

The skipper banged a beefy fist down on his desk. "Mr. Norsen," he snapped, "take three men, armed with stun-guns, and make a thorough search of the ship!"

"Yes, sir." The lanky first officer spun about and hurried away.

"Captain," Dick Roland protested. "There can't be anybody hiding away on this ship; we've been in space for almost a full year. Where would he hide? How would he eat?"

"Mr. Roland," the Captain growled at him, "have you any alternative suggestions? We have just seen that it couldn't have been any member of the crew, and we know it wasn't one of ourselves. Do you suggest that Corcoran committed suicide?"

The doctor shook his head emphatically. "Impossible. No one—not even an accomplished contortionist—could have placed that knife at exactly that angle in his own back." He added wryly, "And Corcoran was not double-jointed."

COMMANDER Mike Gurloff was winding up an address to the ship's crew. He had chosen the officer's wardroom and was speaking into an inter-compartmental communications mike which sat on the table before him. Dick Roland and Doctor Thorndon were present.

"To sum it up, then: we have been sent on one of the most important and most difficult scouting expeditions in the history of the space-service, and thus far we have handled it with success. Never before has the service asked of a ship and crew that it spend a period of more than twelve Terran months in space. This has been asked of the *New Taos*, and, I repeat, thus far we are succeeding.

"We have reached our destination, made our examination, and find nothing to indicate the presence of alien life-forms. We have now begun our return and upon arrival at New Albuquerque will be able to give the reassuring word which will free the High Command of indecision, and send the fleet on its way to the destruction of the Deneb Rebels and their fanatical regime."

"Good," Dick Roland said softly.

"There is, one more matter," Mike Gurloff went on. "When it was first decided to send the *New Taos* upon this expedition, it was realized that only the most experienced and the most balanced of personnel could possibly be used. No one ever touched with cafard, no matter how slightly, could be considered; no man whose health was not at the peak. It was for this reason that some half of the original crew of the *New Taos* was replaced from other elements in the fleet.

"Of these new men, Signalman Franz Corcoran has come to a tragic end, as you all know. In spite of our attempts to find his brutal murderer, we have as yet met with no success. A complete search of the ship reveals no stowaways; a questioning of the crew under the influence of narco-scop brought forth no knowledge of the affair.

"We have not solved this crime. But I pledge this: we shall solve it and that as soon as humanly possible. Lieutenant Norsen has been placed in charge of the investigation. I suggest that each of us rack his brain for information about Signalman Corcoran that might give us a clue to his murderer and bring him to justice.

"That is all."

MIKE GURLOFF threw the switch on the mike and pushed the instrument away from him. He looked up at the ship's doctor. "What do you think, Doc?"

Doctor Thorndon pursed his lips. "You mean about our chances or getting back? You want it straight?"

"Don't pull your punches with me, Doc; I'm the skipper, you know."

The ship's doctor rubbed the end of his nose with a thoughtful forefinger. "They aren't any too good, Mike. The crew is in fine shape right now; the excitement of the past few days has swept away any cafard-indications that I'd noted. The revelation of the purpose of the cruise; the

179

inability to locate any signs of aliens; the fact that we've turned and are heading home; above all, the murder and its investigation—all have had an invigorating effect." He shrugged slightly before going on. "But a week from now, these diversions will be forgotten and we'll be face to face with the realization of almost another year in space."

Dick Roland spoke up bitterly. "Yeah, and this time, because of the longer trip we had a smaller than usual weight-allowance for books and films and games. Every time-killing activity we have has become so stale with use that it's almost preferable to sit and stare. I still think the High Command was slipping its clutch when it sent us off on a trip of this duration."

"Somebody had to go," Gurloff growled.

Dot Thorndon said wearily, "We'll see, Mike. But there's never been a case of a ship in space for more than a year without space-cafard setting in. And you know cafard; let one good raving case of it break out and it'll sweep through the ship like fire." He grunted in self-deprecation. "And I'd probably be right in the middle of it, as raving as anybody."

Roland shivered, "Let's talk about something else."

Mike Gurloff looked at him. "How are you making out on that Corcoran assignment I gave you, Mr. Roland?"

The navigator's face was puzzled. "I was going to bring that up, Captain. It seems to me that possibly I ought to spend some more time on it."

Mike Gurloff scowled at his second officer. "What do you mean? It was a simple enough matter. I wanted you to check among the crew, find out who Corcoran's closest friends were, see if you can get anything on his background. Personally, now that I think back, I hardly remember the man. Of course, there's practically no use for a signalman on a scouting expedition in deep space, and I wasn't in contact with him to any degree."

"That's it," Dick Roland told him. "*Nobody* seems to know much more than that about the man. Captain, he *had* no friends."

Doc Thorndon was interested. "What do you mean, Dick? How about his bunkmates, his messmates?"

"Sure, he had bunkmates and messmates but none of them were really friends of his. You know, they didn't know him back on Terra; didn't know his family—if he had one. Nobody had ever been on leave with him; nobody seems to know where he used to live."

Mike Gurloff looked at him strangely, then came to his feet. "Come on, Mr. Roland," he growled. "Let's take another look at the files on Franz Corcoran; we'll see you later, Doc."

The doctor yawned and turned to a shelf of the ever-present onion skinned, paperback novels of the ship's library and selected one he had read no more than five or six times.

THE COMMANDER led the way down the companionway to his nearby combination living quarters and office, Dick Roland following along behind.

He opened a metal file, built compactly into the wall, and thumbed through an index. "Here we are," he grunted, "folder on Franz Corcoran, Signalman Second Class."

He drew it forth and turned to sit in the swivel chair at his desk. "Most of the new crew members, as I recall, came from the *Pendleton;* but one or two, including Corcoran, came from battlewagons. Seems to me I recall that Corcoran was formerly on the *Serpedon.*"

He opened the folder and his back stiffened.

Mike Gurloff turned and faced his second officer. "In checking on Corcoran's background, Mr. Roland, did you come in here and look up his file?"

"Why, no sir; I wouldn't come into your office without permission."

Gurloff opened the file envelope wide for the other's inspection. "It's empty, not a scrap of paper in it."

The navigator was incredulous. "But *why*. What would be the point, Captain? Anybody on board could sneak in here and get into your files; they aren't locked. But *why*. For that matter, you went through those papers shortly after we found Corcoran. There wasn't much of interest, from what you said afterwards, but you read through them."

Gurloff was scowling his own puzzlement. "Rather hurriedly. But, as you say, there didn't seem to be anything of interest in them. I agree with you; I can't think of any reason for their theft." He grunted his disgust. "I guess it's a matter of using Doc's narco-scop again—and I wonder just how much good that will do."

There was a polite knock at the open door and the two officers turned. Three of the ship's non-coms stood there awkwardly, truculence in their faces.

Gurloff scowled at them. "Well, Brown, Woodford, Levy?"

Woodford was the spokesman. "Sir, we've been elected a delegation from the crew."

"Delegation?"

"Yes, sir. Sir, the crew is just as upset about this killing as you are. We figure that unless the murderer is caught maybe someone else'll get it before we finish the trip. Maybe the killer is off his rocker and might try to blow up the whole ship."

"Get to the point, Woodford," Gurloff growled. "What do you want?"

"Sir, the other day we were all given narco-scop and questioned, and there weren't any results; none at all."

The commander was impatient. "We know that."

"Yes, but sir, only the men were given narco-scop; you four officers and Doctor Thorndon weren't."

Mike Gurloff's face hardened. "Are you suggesting…?"

Chief Gunner Brown spoke up. "Yes, sir, we are, sir. If it wasn't one of the men, it has to have been one of the officers. It's too important, Captain to let go by; all our lives are in danger."

Dick Roland said, "Men, it couldn't have been one of us; we were all five in conference at the time of Corcoran's death."

"How do we know?" Woodford said stubbornly.

The navigator explained. "Doctor Thorndon says that Corcoran's death took place about fifteen minutes before his body was discovered; for more than twenty minutes before that we all five were in the officer's wardroom."

"Listen, sir," Brown said, "that's what the Doc says. Sure, I'm as fond of the Doc as the next guy; he's pulled us out of plenty of spots. But it's just as easy for him to crack as anybody else. How do *we* know that Corcoran was dead only fifteen minutes before his body was found? Sir, the ship's crew respectfully petitions the Captain under Article 16G of Space Service Articles, to treat every ship's officer with narco-scop, and question them on the death of Signalman Corcoran."

There was a wry chuckle behind them and Doc Thorndon wedged his way into the small office.

"They're right, you know, Mike," he said. "It's unfair to the crew not to take the stuff ourselves."

THREE

THE delegation from the crew, grim faced, watched in the tiny ship's hospital as Doc Thorndon loaded his hypodermic and one by one, injected the Captain and his three officers.

"Commander Gurloff, did you kill Franz Corcoran, or do you have any information which would lead to the apprehension of the killer?"

"Absolutely not."

"Lieutenant Norsen…?"

"No."

"Lieutenant Roland…?"

"No, to both questions."

"Ensign Bakr…?"

The chubby third officer shook his head emphatically. "Not me."

"Now you, Doc," Woodford said, his face worried.

The ship's doctor handed the hypodermic needle to his captain and bared his arm. "You want to do this, Mike?"

Mike Gurloff made the injection and stood back for a moment for the narco-scop to take effect. Then, "Doctor Thorndon did you kill Franz Corcoran or do you have any information which would lead to the apprehension of the killer?"

"No," the doctor said readily. "No, I did not; and no, I have not."

Chief Gunner Brown's sigh came from deep within him. "Then that's that," he breathed.

"Return to your posts, men," Gurloff growled, again the commander.

"Yes, sir." The three crewmembers turned and left.

Mike Gurloff looked at his officers, "You too, gentlemen. This, of course, changes nothing; we already knew that it was impossible for one of us to be the culprit."

"Just a minute," Mart Bakr said, "I've got something, sir."

All eyes went to him.

He held up a small object, a spindle-like device that would have weighed no more than two or three ounces.

"What is it?" Johnny Norsen asked him. "Where'd you get it?"

Mike Gurloff's eyes narrowed. "Where *did* you get it, Mr. Bakr? It looks like one of those experimental, ultra-miniature neo-fission bombs."

"Yes, sir. I think that's what it is." The third officer made no attempt to conceal his excitement. "Sir, I found it hidden in the mattress in Corcoran's bunk."

"In his mattress!" Roland blurted. "Lord, whoever did him in couldn't have been planning to do it with a thing like that. Why, it'd blow up this ship and half of this part of space."

"Just a moment, let me think." Mike Gurloff's eyes went flat. He said slowly, "Yes, there *is* somebody that'd pull a stunt like that—a Denebian spy."

"And kill himself at the same time?" Norsen protested.

Commander Mike Gurloff took him in, nodded his head affirmatively. "Those Rebels are fanatical Mr. Norsen. They're as bad or worse as the old Nazis or Stalinists back in primitive times."

HE CAME to his feet, began pacing up and down the ship's hospital to the extent the tiny room allowed. "How about this? The Denebians learn about the explosion in space and smuggled one of their crackpots aboard. He has orders to blow up the *New Taos*. Okay, he loses his guts and doesn't do it but somehow Franz Corcoran finds out about it; so he kills Corcoran."

"Why would the Denebians want to blow up the *New Taos* rather than any other ship in the fleet?" Mart Bah said.

"That's obvious," his commander growled. "If the *New Taos* explodes out here, rather than returning, the Solar System High Command will think it an act of hostile aliens and make peace with the Deneb rebels."

185

"How did this spy of yours get around the narco-scop?" Doc Thorndon asked quietly.

"I don't know."

"Listen, I just thought of something," Dick Roland broke in. "Possibly Franz Corcoran was tailing this spy; possibly Corcoran was a member of the Solar System Bureau of Investigation. An S.S.B.I man."

"Could be," Norsen said. "Anyway, if you're right, skipper, we have a spy aboard. A spy that was sent to blow up the ship but has—temporarily, at least—lost his guts."

Mart Bakr whistled through his teeth. "Temporarily is right. If the reb gets just a touch of cafard it'll probably depress him to the point where he'll go ahead and end it all. And us with him."

They stood about silently for a time, thinking it over.

Gurloff growled finally, "We have no way of telling who this Denebian might be."

"Well, at least he's not one of our old crew," Roland said. "We've been together for years; we know each man like we know the members of our own families. That narrows it down to the new men."

"Wrong," Gurloff bit out. "Seemingly nobody is immune to the religio-political madness that has sprung out of Deneb; they're acquiring converts all over the inhabited systems. I make no attempt to explain it, but the fanaticism is spreading everywhere." His eyes went over them. "I've known all of you gentlemen for more than five years, but I would take no bets that one of you hasn't succumbed."

Doc Thorndon nodded. "The skipper is right. The thing is like a virus. Unbelievable. Anyone of us might have become a convert."

Gurloff turned to his first officer. "Mr. Norsen, I want you to go through this ship with a fine toothed comb. I want every explosive aboard jettisoned. Empty the tractorpedos; flush overboard every spacerifle shell."

"How about handweapons, sir?" Norsen asked.

"Overboard with them—any weapon we have is capable of melting a hole in our hull." He paused. "And, Mr. Bakr, give instructions to the crew that all watches are to be stood in duplicate. No man is to be alone on the bridge, in the engineroom, or even in the galley."

"But, sir—we don't have the manpower for a step like that."

"Lengthen the watch hours. Mr. Bakr, and *make* more manpower available. Signalmen and gunners are worthless to us now; put them to work standing watch on bridge or in the engineroom. Switch the messmen over. We can make our own beds, serve ourselves."

Norsen and Bakr saluted and were off.

"I guess I'll have to address the crew on this," Gurloff growled. "I'm beginning to feel like a politician with all my talking."

Doc Thorndon pursed his lips. "Good idea, though, Mike; makes them feel like they're part of the team." He got up to leave. "Well, I guess I won't be worrying about cafard for a week or so. This'll stir up excitement enough to last them for awhile."

IT WAS A month later that Lieutenant Johnny Norsen, sprawled in his usual ungainly manner in the wardroom and ignoring in boredom the three dimensional film being thrown in a wardroom corner—a film he had seen a hundred times over—blinked his protest as someone flicked on the lights.

"Hey, I'm watching a show," he protested, then recognized the other. "Oh, it's you, skipper."

Mike Gurloff snapped a switch to kill the projector. "You weren't looking at the thing anyway."

"I guess I wasn't at that, skipper. I've just been wondering what there was about some of these films when we first got them aboard that was so funny, or heartrending, or interesting, or whatever we thought they were at the time."

He indicated the one he had just been viewing. "If I ever see that comedian in person, when we get back to Terra, I'll strangle him with my own hands."

Mike Gurloff managed to get off a sour grin. "You'll have to stand in line, Mr. Norsen; every member of the crew feels the same way." He sank into an acceleration chair opposite his first officer. "Anything new in the investigation?"

Johnny Norsen shook his head. "Men are beginning to grumble about this watch in duplicate thing."

"They are, eh? Let them grumble."

"They've split themselves up into two factions; that's beginning to cause friction."

"Two factions?"

"Ummm. Divided almost equally, about twenty men to the faction. The original *New Taos* crewmen say that they knew each other so well, that they're positive the killer couldn't be one of them; consequently, it must be one of the new men. The fellows from the *Pendleton* and the other ships claim that before they got assigned to this job they went through a security check so strict that any Denebian, or any crackpot, would have been weeded out. *They* figure it must be a crewmember or officer of the original ship's complement."

Mike Gurloff growled, "Both factions just loaded with good sense, eh? What do they do about it?"

"They just watch each other, so far. I think they've elected committees and each faction member reports daily to his committee. I don't know what they expect to accomplish." Norsen yawned deeply. "Think we should put an end to it, skipper?"

The ship's commander had lowered himself wearily into a chair. "Put an end to it? No! Gives them something to be worked up about, excited about. I don't care if they break out into open fist fights—there's nothing else left on board for them to fight with—just so it doesn't hinder the efficient operation of the ship." He ended bitterly, "As a matter of fact, another murder just about now would be just what the doctor ordered."

Johnny Norsen sat upright in his chair. "What!"

The captain waved a hand negatively, impatiently. "Exaggerating, of course, but the theory is correct." He gestured at the film projector. "How'd you like the show you were running off?"

The first officer grunted his disgust. "I put it on and then forgot to look at it."

"Exactly. There isn't a form of entertainment left on the *New Taos* with which we're all not bored stiff. No entertainment, that is, except *Murderer, Murderer, Who'll Catch the Murderer;* it's the only thing that's keeping us all from cafard."

THE OTHER squirmed uncomfortably at the mention of the dread illness: "Do you think we'll make it skipper? Do you think we'll get back to the Solar System before cafard hits?"

Mike Gurloff shook his head. "No, frankly; I didn't when we were sent off on this wild goose chase, and I don't now."

"We've got to get back," Norsen blurted. "We've got to report this alien threat a false alarm so the fleet can take on the Denebians. We've given them too much time to spread, too much time to prepare, as it is."

"I'm no doctor," Mike Gurloff said sourly, "but I have a working knowledge of space cafard; I've seen enough of it. It's nothing more than monotony and boredom and claustrophobia all blended. Combined, they add up to stark raving madness of a type that tends to spread—wildfire fashion. No man cooped up in a spaceship, averaging only a few cubic feet of space he can call his own, can see another driven mad by boredom and confining walls without blowing his own gaskets. If I was a mathematician the formula would go something like this: monotony *times* boredom *times* confined space *times* time equals cafard. Time has always been the crucial factor and I have never heard of an authority who claimed a man, any man, no matter how balanced, could spend more than twelve months in space without contracting cafard."

There was a knock at the door and the two officers looked up. Four crewmen stood there, sullenness predominating over respect in their facial expressions.

"Another committee," Johnny Norsen sighed.

"What is it, men?" Commander Gurloff growled. "What is it this time? Your committee seems to have grown—four of you now instead of three."

Woodford said, an element of defiance in his voice, "This is really two committees, sir. Levy and me, we represent the original crewmembers of the *New Taos*. Brown and Harkness represent the newcomers."

"Well, what's the reason for this delegation? I suppose the *New Taos* crewmen want the more recent additions to our happy family jettisoned and vice versa."

Chief Gunner Brown flushed resentfully. "No, sir; we're in agreement on this particular matter."

"Well, what is it man? What is it? I don't have forever."

Johnny Norsen had to chuckle inwardly at that. Maybe the skipper didn't have *quite* forever, but he almost did.

Woodford said, "Sir, a month ago Mr. Norsen came through and gathered up all the explosives aboard and flushed them out into space." He squared his shoulders.

"Not that we didn't think it was a good idea, under the circumstances, sir."

"Oh, fine," Gurloff growled.

Woodford went on doggedly. "He flushed out all the spacerifle shells, the tractorpedo warheads, even the small arms. Everything some damn Denebian spy might be able to use to blow up the ship."

"Get to the point, confound it, Woodford!"

"Sir, he didn't flush overboard *your* sidearms; you four ship's officers still got your guns."

MIKE GURLOFF was on his feet, his heavy face flushed with anger. "Do you men mean to say you have the mutinous gall to approach me and demand that I—the commanding officer of this vessel—surrender my sidearm's to you?"

Brown said doggedly. "There's been no proof, sir, that the Denebian spy ain't one of the officers. There's been no proof. But even supposin' it ain't, it don't mean that the spy couldn't conk one of the officers over the head and get his gun away from him. Sir, the ship's crew unanimously petitions the Captain, under Article 16G of Space Service Articles, to jettison the four sidearms in the possession of the ship's officers."

The other three nodded their heads definitely.

"It's unanimous, sir," Woodford repeated.

They stood silently for a full five minutes facing each other, glaring.

Suddenly, Mike Gurloff's hands dropped to his belt. "Mr. Norsen," he said harshly, "here is my sidearm. With your own and those of Mr. Bakr and Mr. Roland, flush it overboard."

"Yes, sir," Johnny Norsen said wearily.

There was commotion in the hall, an elbowing and a thrusting aside of the committeemen.

"Probably another delegation," Johnny Norsen grunted.

It was Messman Spillane, as usual, breathless.

"Captain Gurloff!" he shrilled. "It's the Doc... Doc Thorndon, he's been killed too."

They stood, stunned.

Johnny Norsen said, "Here's your second killing, Skipper—the one you said was just what the doctor ordered."

FOUR

DOC THORNDON was sprawled on the floor of the tiny ship's hospital. The room was about the size of a bedroom of a Pullman of the Twentieth Century. It had two bunks, a tiny folding table, a medicine chest built into the titanium alloy wall, a lavatory. The hospital also doubled as the doctor's quarters; if he had two patients at once he had to leave his place and bunk with the third officer—but that was seldom.

Ensign Mart Bakr, his plump face screwed up as though in effort to prevent tears from flowing, was standing guard at the door. When he saw the ship's commander approaching he stuttered, "I've kept everybody out, sir. I didn't...I didn't know what you might want to do in the way of investigation."

Mike Gurloff brushed his way past his third officer and surveyed the room quickly. The story was obvious. The bottom bunk was rumpled; a pocketbook lay on its back on the floor. Doc Thorndon's body was near the medicine chest, one arm extended as though in last effort to reach the drugs it contained. He had undoubtedly been stretched out on his back in the bunk reading when something warned him of disaster. He tried to get to the medicine chest—and hadn't made it.

Commander Mike Gurloff wasn't a particularly compatible man, but Doc Thorndon had been his closest friend for half a dozen years on the *New Taos*. His face entirely expressionless, he sank to his knees beside the other.

"Who discovered him?" he asked.

"I did," Mart Bakr said. "Spillane and I were coming along the corridor. The door was opened and I glanced in; there he was. I rushed Spillane to get you."

Mike Gurloff scowled and reached for the doctor's pulse. "You didn't check the body…? …*He's not dead!*"

"What!" Bakr blinked. "But…"

"Here dammit, help me get him onto the bunk. What's that on the floor?" They struggled to get the roly-poly doctor's form stretched out on his bunk.

"What's what on the floor, sir?" Bakr puffed.

"He's scribbled something on the floor with his stylus. Damn it, can you see it? I can't make it out."

Dick Roland had entered behind them, took in the situation at a glance, got down on his hands and knees beside his commander. "It's the name of some drug," he said. "He's written out the name of some drug. It's *unidote.*" He looked up at the other two. "What's going on? What's wrong with Doc?"

Bakr said, "We found him on the floor here; thought he was dead. I guess he must've written that before he passed out."

"He's hardly breathing," Gurloff snapped. "Where is the key for that medical chest? He's been poisoned."

Mart Bakr, perspiration running down his chubby face, was fumbling through the stricken doctor's pockets. "Here they are."

IN MOMENTS they had the chest open and were searching through the multitude of drugs.

"Here it is," Roland blurted. "*Unidote*. There's no directions on it. Let's see. No, here it is. Just one capsule with water."

"All right," Gurloff barked, "get it into him. Bakr, hand me that medical guide there." He began leafing rapidly through the thin pages while Roland lifted the unconscious doctor's head under one arm and forced the pill between his lips. Bakr hustled over with a water carafe.

"Not that water," Roland told him. "Go get some from the wardroom; maybe the poison, whatever it was, is in that carafe."

The water was quickly forthcoming and the pill washed down through reluctant lips. The water dribbled over bunk, patient and first aid administer unheeded.

Gurloff, his eyes on the medical guide, growled, "Here it is. *Unidote*. The stuff's an almost universal antidote for poisons administered through the stomach. If he's been poisoned, it should bring him out of it."

Johnny Norsen, a pack of crewmembers behind him, was at the door now. "What's going on," he rapped out; "what's the matter with the Doc?"

Mike Gurloff snapped the book closed and faced them, his face granite hard. "Doc Thorndon has just been poisoned. We don't know if he'll come through this or not; he's still alive, and we've got the antidote into him."

The murmur went back through the crewmembers. "It's the doc; somebody's tried to kill the doc."

Johnny Norsen scowled his incredulity. "But who'd want to kill Doc Thorndon? There's not a man on board who doesn't love old Doc."

Mike Gurloff growled viciously, "All weapons have been flushed overboard, but there is one weapon the spy still has at his disposal—and one that can destroy the ship without his revealing himself. Space cafard. With Doc Thorndon dead, cafard would soon hit the ship and we'd have a crew of raging, maniacs."

He took in his three officers. "My orders regarding watches in duplicate will continue in force. In addition, gentlemen, will be this: no man of this ship's complement will ever be alone until completion of the cruise. Each man will be assigned a companion from whom he shall never be separated. Under no circumstances shall any crewman or officer ever be out of the sight of his companion. As soon as such a separation does take place, if it does, the companion will immediately report to me.

"Do you understand, gentlemen? From this day, no man in this crew is ever to be alone. Mr. Norsen, you will never be out of the sight of Mr. Roland, and vice versa. Mr. Bakr, you will never be out of sight of Chief Gunner Brown; make arrangements for him to bunk with you. Divide the rest of the crew likewise, each man to have a companion."

From the corridor someone said softly, "It's a good idea, but how about you, Captain?"

Gurloff's face hardened but he snapped back, "The point is well taken; as soon as Doc Thorndon has recovered he and I will be a pair, always within sight of each other."

ON THE bunk behind him, the doctor stirred and they spun to face him. He shifted in his bed, shook his head weakly. *"Unidote"* he mumbled. "Been poisoned. *Unidote."*

Mike Gurloff was at his side.

"Doc," he said. "Doc, are you all right?"

The doctor's eyes opened. "Mike," he said weakly. "Poison. Didn't even think about it. Check all water aboard. All food; my medicine chest. Throw overboard all bottles with red labels." His eyes closed again.

"What's the matter?" Dick Roland demanded.

"Nothing. Nothing's the matter, he's sleeping. I think he'll be all right." Mike Gurloff got to his feet. "You heard his suggestions, gentlemen. They're good. Begin an immediate check of all food, water, oxygen supplies."

"Yes, sir," Johnny Norsen spun to be off.

"Just a minute, Mr. Norsen," Gurloff growled. "Mr. Roland goes with you. My order is to be obeyed; from this time onward, no man is to be alone on this ship. Not even for a moment."

Johnny Norsen's angular face was sheepish. "Yes, sir," he said. "Come on Dick."

They left and Mike Gurloff turned to his third officer. "Mr. Bakr, you and your companion, Chief Brown, will begin assigning the crewmembers their associates. I want you to take particular pains in assigning men to a person they *do not* personally like. I do not want *friends* to be linked as companions. Each newcomer to the crew of the *New Taos* will be assigned to an old-timer; I want men who will watch each other, understand?"

"Yes, sir!"

"Very well, and as soon as you have completed this measure and impressed its significance on the crew, report to me here. I have a few other measures in mind."

The few other measures included such items as every member of the crew exchanging his clothing and bedding. Mike Gurloff was taking no chances that the spy might be equipped with espionage devices concealed in buttons or textile materials. Nor did any crewmember know who was wearing his former garments. All clothing on the ship was gathered, laundered and redistributed under the supervision of the ship's officers.

Nor did Mike Gurloff stop there. The personal belongings of every man aboard were gathered and jettisoned.

No secret source of poison or explosives was to be left aboard.

There were no complaints at the measures.

EVERY DAY that passed saw Doc Thorndon visited in the hospital by every member of the crew—coming in pairs, of course, since from that time on no man on the *New Taos* was ever alone. But, in spite of all the attention that could be showered upon him, his recovery seemed slow. He admitted that he didn't know what poison had been used on him, nor how it had been administered. As best he could remember, it was intuition more than anything else which had brought him suddenly from his bunk, and sent him to his medicine chest for antidote.

It was about a week after the poisoning that Commander Mike Gurloff entered the ship's hospital and closed the heavy door behind him.

Doc Thorndon looked up from his book. "Hi, Mike," he said. "You look tired; drag up a bunk and lie down."

The ship's commander hoisted himself into the upper bunk, put his hands under his head and stared up at the overhead above him.

Doc marked his place in the book with a finger and said, "You've got something on your mind, Mike."

Mike Gurloff growled softly. "And it's about time; you see, Thorndon, I've been thinking."

It was the first time in the doctor's memory that the other had addressed him by his last name alone. He closed the book and slipped it beneath his pillow and waited for the other to go on.

Mike Gurloff said, "I kept on thinking until I figured out who killed Franz Corcoran."

"Oh. Who?"

"You did, Thorndon; you're the only man on board who could possibly have killed him."

"Not exactly killed him, Mike. I executed him."

Mike Gurloff stiffened and began to come to one elbow. But then he sank back again.

"How did you find out?" Doc Thorndon asked softly.

"I don't know. It wasn't one thing, and it didn't come all at once; it was just little things piling up. I couldn't accept it at first, so I kept refusing to realize that you alone could be our killer, our spy. How could you do it, Doc?" For the first time, the captain's voice was bitter.

"It was easy," Doc Thorndon said, still softly. "I'm a physician Mike. It isn't hard for me to cut out a tumor, to amputate a gangrenous limb; nor was it hard for me to execute a Denebian spy."

"What!"

"Of course, Mike. But I'm interested. *How* did you figure it out? I'd rather hoped that nobody would. We still have eight months to go; tell me what you know, and I'll tell you the rest."

"Well, first of all it was you that told us Corcoran had been dead for fifteen minutes. None of the rest of us had the medical background to check on that; it gave you an alibi."

"That's true. Corcoran was dead at least a half hour at the time he was discovered."

MIKE GURLOFF went on. "Second, narco-scop *always* works. It was working when we tried it on the crew. As you pointed out, it couldn't have been tampered with, because its container was sealed. But when we questioned the officers, including yourself, a week later, it was no longer sealed and *had* been tampered with—and you're the only one who could have done it. Actually, we were probably injected with water, or some such, instead of narco-scop."

"That's a good guess," the doctor admitted freely. "I knew it would only be a matter of time before someone insisted that the officers be subjected to narco-scop as well, so I substituted water. What else, Mike?"

"When I thought back about it, you being *poisoned* the way you were seemed doubtful. Your scribbled note giving the antidote was just too *pat* to be believable."

"I had taken a couple of sleeping pills," Thorndon said, a trace of disappointment in his voice. "I thought I'd put it over fairly well. Of course, if you hadn't found the antidote message I'd scribbled, I would have come out of it in a few hours anyway. I would have still claimed to have been poisoned."

Mike Gurloff's voice had deepened to a harsh growl now. "All right, Thorndon, so you admit it; now explain why."

The doctor rubbed the tip of his nose reflectively. "Well," he said, "it was as I said. Franz Corcoran was a Denebian spy. I believe I told you that I'd examined him a few hours before his death. The examination was a psychological one rather than physical; I was giving him a routine check for cafard. Some of my questions must have inadvertently stepped on his ideological toes. Before I knew it, I had a wild eyed fanatic on my hands, roaring his accusations against the Solar System League and his boasts of what he was going to do about it."

Mike Gurloff remained silent but his facial expression was changing.

The doctor went on. "You see, Mike, that mysterious explosion out in space wasn't such a mystery, after all. Evidently, the Denebians—in an attempt to gain time and to prevent our fleet from attacking them—sent a robot ship out into inter-galactical space with a large neo-fission warhead. It went beyond the point ever reached by a crewed ship, and then automatically exploded.

"But that was only part of their plan. They correctly assumed that a Solar System ship would be sent out to investigate, and made all efforts to smuggle a fanatical spy aboard. The spy's job was to destroy the *New Taos* upon reaching the vicinity of the mysterious explosion—committing suicide himself, of course, when he did it. Very well. Do you realize what that would have meant to our High Command?"

"Ummm," Mike Gurloff growled. "They'd assume we were lost in a fight with hostile aliens, and come to a truce with the Denebian rebels."

"Quite correct; happily, I stumbled upon the spy before he was able to use his explosive."

Mike Gurloff bit out, "Doc, you had no right to take the matter into your hands. Assuming that I accept your story, your duty was still to report to me, to turn Corcoran over to me."

"Oh?" Doc Thorndon said easily. "And just how were we going to get the *New Taos* back to the Solar System, Mike? What was going to keep the crew from cafard during that year period?"

"What'd'ya mean?"

"I mean that the only thing that has kept this crew sane is the interest and stimulation brought on by this mystery. The killing itself; the stolen papers on Corcoran from your files; the arguments between crew members and the various committees they formed; my being poisoned; the orders to jettison everything a spy could use to destroy the ship; the more recent orders that every watch be stood in duplicate, that no man ever be left alone. All these things, Mike, have kept the ship in a continual dither—and has kept cafard from taking over."

Mike Gurloff snorted his disgust. "You're right, damn it, Doc."

"Of course, I'm right," Doc Thorndon said with satisfaction. "And now that I think about it, I'm glad you found out; now, at least, there'll be two of us."

The captain didn't get that. He peered down over the edge of the bunk at the other, his face scowling. "What do you mean by that?"

The ship's doctor was bland. "When you were assigning everyone on board a constant companion, didn't you team yourself and me? We're the only two aboard who know that I destroyed Corcoran. We'll have to keep the mystery alive, keep things hopping. Good grief, Mike, we've got another eight months more in space. If cafard is to be staved off we've got to play this game to the hilt."

Mike Gurloff groaned and lay back on the bed again. "For instance, like what?"

There was a shrug in Doc's voice. "Oh, I don't know. Maybe a month or so from now we'll bean you over the head with a wrench or something, and let them find you unconscious somewhere. Then later you can have all the ship's tools except those continually under guard, jettisoned."

Doc Thorndon's voice went thoughtful now. "Maybe later on we can start a fire…"

Commander Mike Gurloff growled disgustedly. "I should have become a salesman like my poor old mother wanted. When I entered the Space Academy I never figured I'd wind up sabotaging my own ship for a period of eight months—in order to get it back home."

After Some Tomorrow

Alan's plan might save the race from extinction—but he was the clan's only husband and had to be protected from his own folly...

BEFORE THE first shots rang out, Alan was sitting with twenty young people of the Wolf clan in a grove of aspen approximately halfway between the fields and the citadel on the hilltop. He was teaching myth-legend and, as usual, the girls were bored and unbelieving, the boys open mouthed.

He realized, even as he spoke, that the telling had changed even since his youth. As a boy of ten, before it was definitely known whether or not he was a sterilie, he had sat at the feet of the Turtle clan's husband as open mouthed as those who sat at his feet now. But the telling was different. Now, had he spoken openly of when men bore weapons and women lived at home with the children, he would have crossed the boundaries of decency. It hadn't been so in his own youth, but then, when he was a boy, they had been one generation nearer to the old days, which weren't so far back after all.

Helen complained, "It's so silly, Alan. Why don't you tell us something about...well, about hunting, or true fighting?"

He looked at her. Could this be a daughter of his? Tall for her fourteen years and straight, clear of eye, aggressive and brooking of no nonsense. The old books told of the femininity of women, but...

The shots went *bang, bang, bang*, from below, faint in the half mile or more of distance. And then *bang, bang* again and several *booms* from the new muzzle loading muskets.

Helen was on her feet first, her eyes flashing. Instantly she was in command. "Alan," she snapped. "Quick, to the citadel. All of you boys, hurry! To the citadel!"

She whirled to her older classmates. "Ruth, Margo, Jenny, Paula. Get stones, sharp stones. You younger girls go with Alan. See if you can help at the citadel. We'll come last. Hurry Alan."

Alan was already off, herding the boys before him. Possibly all of them were steriles and so wouldn't count. But you never knew.

As they climbed the hill, he looked back over his shoulder. Down in the fields he could see the workers scattering for their weapons and for cover. One stumbled and was down. In the distance he couldn't make out whether she had fallen accidentally or been wounded. Further beyond the fields he could see the smoke from a half dozen or more places where the shots had originated. It didn't seem to be an attack in force.

Not far up the hill from the field workers, on an overhanging boulder in a lookout position, he could make out Vivian, the scout chief. She sat, seemingly in unconcerned ease, one elbow supported on a knee as her telescoped rifle went *crack, crack, crack*. If he knew Vivian there was more than one casualty among the raiders.

Who could it be this time? Deer from the south, Coyote or Horse from the east? Possibly Eagles, Crows or Dogs from Denver way. The clan couldn't stand much more of this pressure. It was the third raid in six months. They couldn't stand it and put in a crop, nor could the drain on the arsenal be maintained. He had heard that the Turtle clan, near Colorado Springs, the clan of his birth, had got to the point where they were using bows and arrows even for defense. If so, it wouldn't be long before they would be losing their husband.

He was puffing somewhat by the time they reached the citadel. Helen and her four girls were coming much more slowly, watching the progress of the fight below them, keeping their eyes peeled for a possible break through of individual enemies. The stones in their hands were pathetically brave.

The rounded citadel building, stone built, loopholed for rifles, loomed before them. He swung open the door and hurried inside.

"Hello, honey," a strange voice said pseudo-pleasantly. "Hey, you're kind of cute."

Alan's eyes went from the two figures before him, automatic rifles cuddled under their arms, to the two Wolf clan sentries collapsed in their own blood on the floor. They had paid for lack of vigilance with their lives.

He could see that the strangers were of different clans by their kilts, one a Horse the other a Crow. This would mean two clans had united in order to raid the Wolves and that, in turn, would mean the Wolves were outnumbered as much as two to one.

"Relax, darling," the second one said, a lewd quality in her voice, "Nothing's going to happen to *you.*" Her eyes took in the dozen boys ranging in age from five to twelve. "Look like a bunch of steriles to me," she sneered. "Get them up above, and those girls too. You stay here where we can watch you, honey."

The Crow went to a small window, stared down below. "Wanda is holding them pretty well but they're beginning to work their way back in this direction." She laughed harshly. "These Wolves never could fight."

Her companion fingered the Bren gun that lay on the heavy tabletop in the round room's center. Aside from four equally heavily constructed chairs the table was the large room's sole furniture. While Alan was ushering the boys and younger girls up to the second floor where they would be safe, the Horse said musingly, "We could turn this loose on them even at this distance."

The crow shook her head. "No. It'll be better to wait until they're closer. Besides, by that time Peggy and her group'll be coming up from the arroyo. There won't be a Wolf left half an hour from now."

Alan, his stomach empty, stared out the loophole nearest him.

One of the women said, grinning, "You better get away from there, honey. Make you sick. That's a mighty pretty suit you've got on. Make it yourself?"

"No," Alan said. As a matter of fact one of the sterilies had made it.

She laughed. "Well, don't be so uppity. You're going to have to learn how to be nice to me, you know."

Both of them laughed, but Alan said nothing. He wondered how long the women of these clans had been without a husband.

Down below he could make out the progress of the fighting and then realized the battle plan of the aggressors. They must have planned it for months, waiting until the season was such that practically the whole Wolf clan, and particularly the fighters, would be at work in the fields. They'd sent these two scouts, probably their best warriors, to take the citadel by stealth. Only two of them, more would have been conspicuous.

They had then, with a limited force, opened fire on the field workers, pinning them down temporarily.

Meanwhile, the main body was ascending the arroyo to the left, completely hidden from the defending forces although they would have been in open sight from above had the citadel remained uncaptured.

Alan could see plainly what the next fifteen minutes would mean. The Wolf clan would draw back on the citadel, Vivian and her younger warriors bringing up the rear. When they broke into the clear and started the last dash for the safety of their fortress, they would be in the open and at the mercy of the crossfire from arroyo and citadel.

If only these two had failed in their attempt to…

The Crow woman said, "Look at this. Five young brats with stones in their hands. What do you say?"

It was Helen and her four girls.

Alan said, "They're only children! You can't…"

"You be quiet, sweetie. We can't be bothered with you."

The Horse said, "Two years from now they'll all be warriors. Here, let me turn this on them."

Alan closed his eyes and he wanted to retch as he heard the automatic rifle speak out in five short bursts. In spite of himself he opened them again. Helen, his first born, Paula, his second. Ruth, Margo and Jenny, all his children. They were crumbled like rag dolls, fifty feet from the citadel door.

Now he was able to tell himself that he should have called out a warning. One or two of them, at least, might have escaped. Might have escaped to warn the approaching fighters of the trap behind them. Tradition had been too strong within him, the tradition that a man did not interfere in the business of the warriors, that war was a thing apart.

Jenny's body moved, stirred again, and she tried to drag herself away. Little Jenny, twelve years old. The rifle spat just once again and she slumped forward and remained quiet.

"Little bitch," the Crow woman said.

The heavy chair was in his hands and high above his head, he had brought it down on her before the rage of his hate had allowed him to think of what he was doing. The chair splintered but there was still a good half of it in his hands when he spun on the Horse woman. She stepped back, her eyes wide in disbelief. As her companion went down, the side of her face and her scalp welling blood, the Horse at first brought up her rifle and then, in despair, tried to reverse it to use its butt as a club.

She was stumbling backward, trying to get out of the way of his improvised weapon, when her heel caught on the body of one of the fallen Wolf sentries. She tried to catch herself, her eyes still staring horrified disbelief, even as he caught her over the head, and then once again. He beat her, beat her hysterically, until he knew she must be dead.

He worked now in a mental vacuum, all but unconsciously. He ran to the stair bottom and called, "Come down," his voice was shrill. "Alice, Tommy, all of you."

THEY CAME, hesitantly, and when they saw the shambles of the room stared at him with as much disbelief as had the enemy women. He pointed a finger at the oldest of the girls. "Alice," he said, "you've been given instruction by the warriors. How is the Bren gun fired?"

The eleven-year-old bug eyed at him. "But you're a husband, Alan…"

"How is it fired?" he shrilled. "Unless you tell me, there will be no Wolf clan left!"

He lugged the heavy gun to the window, mounted it there as he had seen the women do in practice.

"Tommy," he said to a thirteen-year-old boy. "Quick, get me a pan of ammunition."

"I can't," Tommy all but wailed.

"Get it!"

"I can't. It's…it's *unmanly!*"

Tommy melted into a sea of tears, utterly confused.

"Maureen," Alan snapped, cooler now. "Get me a pan of ammunition for the Bren gun. Quickly. Alice, show me how the gun is charged."

Alice was at his side, trying to explain. He would have let her take over had she been larger, but he knew she couldn't handle the bucking of the weapon. Maureen had returned with the ammunition, slipped it expertly into place. She too had had instructions in the gun's operation.

Alan ran his eyes down the arroyo. There were possibly forty of them, Horses and Crows—well armed, he could see. Less than a quarter of them had the new muzzle loaders being resorted to by many, as ammunition stocks for the old arms became increasingly rare. The others had ancient arms, rifles, both military and sport, one or two tommy guns.

He waited another three or four minutes, one eye cocked on the progress of the running battle below. Vivian, the scout chief, had dropped back to take over command of the younger warriors. She was probably beginning to smell a rat. The intensity of fire wasn't such as to suggest a large body of enemy.

The women in the arroyo were placed now, as he wanted them. He forced himself to keep his eyes open as he pressed the trigger.

Blat, blat, blat.

The gun spoke, kicking high the dust and gravel before the Horse and Crow warriors advancing up the arroyo.

They stopped, startled. The citadel was supposedly in their hands.

They reversed themselves and scurried back to get out of their exposed position.

He touched the trigger again. *Blat, blat, blat.* The heavy slugs tore up the arroyo wall behind them; they could retreat no further without running into his fire.

They stopped, confused.

Alan said, "Maureen, get another pan of ammunition. I'll have to hold them there until Vivian comes up. Alice, run down to the matriarch and tell her about the warriors in the arroyo. Quickly, now."

Little Alice said sourly, "A husband shouldn't interfere in warrior affairs," but she went.

When Vivian strode into the citadel she had her sniper rifle slung over her back and was admiring a tommy gun she had taken from one of the captured Horses. "Perfect," she said, stroking the stock. "Perfect shape. And they seem to have worlds of ammunition too. Must have made some kind of deal with the Denver clans."

Her eyes swept the room and her mouth turned down in sour amusement. The Horse woman was dead and the Crow had by now been marched off to take her place with the other prisoners who were being held in the stone corral.

"What warriors," she said contemptuously. "A *man* overcomes two of them. *Two* of them, mind you." She looked at Alan, the reaction was upon him now and he was white faced and couldn't keep his hands from trembling. "What a cutie you turned out to be. Who ever heard of such a thing?"

Alan said, defensively, "They didn't expect it. I took them unawares."

Vivian laughed aloud, her even white teeth sparkling in the redness of her lips. She was tall, shapely, a twenty-five year old goddess in her Wolf clan kilts. "I'll bet you did, sweetie."

One of the other warriors entered from behind Vivian, looked at the dead Horse woman and shuddered. "What a way to die, not even able to defend yourself." She said to Vivian worriedly, "They've got an awful lot of equipment, chief."

Vivian said, "Well, what're you worrying about, Jean? *We* have it now."

The girl said, "They have three tommy guns, four automatic rifles, twenty grenades and forty sticks of dynamite."

Vivian was impatient. "They had them, now they're ours. It's good, not bad."

Jean said doggedly, "These raids are coming more and more often. We've lost ten fighters in less than a year. And each time they come at us they're better equipped and there're more of them." She looked over at Alan. "If it hadn't been for this...this queer way things worked out, they'd have our husband now and we'd be done for."

"Well, it didn't happen that way," Vivian said abruptly, "and we still have our husband and we're going to keep him. This wasn't a bad action at all. They killed three of us; we've got more than forty of them."

"Not three, eight," Jean said. "You forget the five girls. In another couple of years they'd have been warriors. And besides, what difference does it make if we've got forty of them? There're always more of them where they came from. There must be a thousand women toward Denver without a husband between them."

Vivian quieted. "Let's hope they don't all decide on Alan at once," she said. "I wonder if the Turtles are having the same trouble."

"They're having more," Alan said. He had lowered himself wearily into one of the chairs.

The two warriors looked at him.

"How do you know, sweetie?" Vivian asked him.

"I was talking to Warren, a few weeks ago. He's husband of the Turtle clan now, they traded him from the Foxes. Both, clans were getting too interbred..."

"Get to the point, honey," Jean said, embarrassed at this man talk.

"The Turtles are having more trouble than we are. They have a stronger natural fortress at the center of their farm lands, but they've had so many raids that their arsenal is depleted and half their warriors dead or wounded. They're getting desperate."

"That's too bad," Vivian muttered. "They make good neighbors."

Jean said, "The matriarch told me to let you know there'd be a meeting this afternoon in the assembly hall. Clan meeting, all present."

"What about?" Vivian said, her attention going back to the beauty of her captured weapon again.

"About the prisoners. We've got to decide what to do with them."

"Do with them? We'll push them over the side of the canyon. Nobody thought we'd waste bullets on them did they?"

Alan said, mildly, "The question has come up whether we ought to destroy them at all."

Vivian looked at him in gentle annoyance. "Sweetie," she said, "don't bother your handsome head with these things. You've had enough excitement to last a nice looking fellow like you a lifetime."

Jean said, echoing her chief's disgust, "Anyway, that's what the meeting is about. Alan, here, has been talking to the matriarch and she's agreed to bring it up for discussion."

Vivian said nastily, "Sally is beginning to lose her grip. If there's anything a clan needs it's a strong matriarch."

"A wise matriarch," Alan amended, knowing he shouldn't.

Vivian stared at him for a moment, then threw her head back and laughed. "I'm going to have to spank your bottom one of these days," she told him. "You get awfully sassy for a man."

AS CHAIRMAN, Alan had a voice but not a vote in the meetings of the Wolf clan. He sometimes wondered at the institution, which had came down from pre-bomb days. Why was it necessary to have a chair*man*. Of course, myth-legend had it that men were once just as numerous and active in society's economic (and even martial!) life as were women. But that was myth-legend. It all had a *basis* in reality, perhaps, but some of it was undoubtedly stretched all but to the breaking point.

Of course if all men *had* been fertile in the old days. But if you started with *if*, as a beginning point, you could go as far as you wished in any direction.

He called the meeting to order in the assembly hall which stood possibly a hundred feet below the citadel in one direction, another hundred from the stone corral which housed their prisoners, in the other. The Wolf clan was present in its entirety with the exception of children under ten and except for four scouts who were holding the prisoners. As chairman, Alan sat on the dais flanked by Sally, the matriarch, 35 years of age, tall, Junoesque, on one side and by Vivian the scout chief, on the other.

Before them sat, first, the active warrior-workers, some thirty-five of them. Second, the older women, less than a score. Further back were the steriles, possibly twenty of these and quite young, only within recent memory had they been allowed to become part of the clan, in the past they had been driven away or killed. Further back still were the children above ten but too young to join the ranks of either warrior-workers or steriles.

Alan called the meeting to order, quieted them somewhat and then invited the matriarch to take the floor.

Sally stood and looked out over her clan, the dignity of her presence silencing them where Alan's plea had not.

She said, "We have two matters to bring to our attention. First, I believe the clan should make it clear to Alan, our husband that such interference in the affairs of women is utterly out of the question. I am speaking of his unmanly activities in the raid this morning."

There were mumblings of approval throughout the hall.

Alan came to his feet, his face bewildered. "But, Sally, what else could I do? If I hadn't overcome the enemy warriors and turned the Bren gun on the others you would all be gone now. Possibly none of you would have survived."

Sally quieted him with a chill look. "Let me repeat what is well known to every member of the clan. We consist of less than sixty women, a few more than thirty-five of whom are active. There are twenty steriles and twenty-five or so children. And one husband. A few more than one hundred in all."

Her voice slowed and lowered for the sake of emphasis. "All of our women—except for two or three—might die and the clan would live on. The steriles certainly might all die, and the clan live on. Even the children could all die and the clan live on. *But if our husband dies, the clan dies.* The greatest responsibility of every member of any clan is to protect the husband. Under no circumstances is he to be endangered. You know this; it should not have to be brought to your attention."

There was a strong murmur of assent from those seated before them.

Alan said, "But, Sally, I saved your lives! And if I hadn't, I would have been captured by the Crows and Horses and you would have lost me at any rate."

This was hard for Sally Wolf, but she said, "Then, at least, *they* would have had you. If you had died, in your foolhardiness, you would have been gone for all of us. Alan, two clans, husbandless clans, united in this attempt to capture you from us. While we fought to protect our husband, the life of our clan, we hold no rancor against them. In their position, we would have done the same. Much rather would we see you taken by them, than to see you dead. Even though the Wolf clan might die, the race must go on." She added, but not very believably, "If they had captured you, perhaps we could have, in our turn, captured a husband from some other clan."

"The reason we probably couldn't," Vivian said mildly, "is that since we've turned to agriculture and settled, our numbers have dropped off by half. We had more than sixty warriors while we were hunter-foragers."

"That's enough, Vivian," Sally snapped. "The question isn't being discussed this afternoon."

"Ought to be," somebody whispered down in front.

"Order," Alan said. He knew it was a growing belief in the clan that giving up the nomadic life had been a mistake. From raiders, they had become the raided.

Sally said, "The second order of business is the disposal of the Horse and Crow prisoners captured in the action today."

Vivian said, "We can't afford to waste valuable ammunition. I say shove them into the canyon."

Most of those seated in the hall approved of that. Some were puzzled of face, wondering why the matter hadn't been left simply in the scout chief's hands.

Sally said, dryly, "I haven't formed an opinion myself. However, our chairman has some words to say."

Vivian looked at Alan as though he was a precocious child. She shook her head. "You cutie, you. You're getting bigger and bigger for your britches every day."

Two or three of the warriors echoed her by chuckling fondly.

Alan said nothing to that, needing to maintain what dignity and prestige he could muster.

He stood and faced them and waited for their silence before saying, "You feminine members of the clan are too busy with work and with defense to pursue some of the studies for which we men find time."

Vivian murmured, "You ain't just a whistlin', honey. But we don't mind. You do what you want with your time, honey."

He tried to smile politely, but went on. "It has come to the point where few women read to any extent and most learning has fallen into the hands of the men—few as we are."

Sally said impatiently, "What has this got to do with the prisoners, Alan dear?"

It would seem that he had ignored her when he said, "I have been discussing the matter with Warren of the Turtle clan and two or three other men with whom I occasionally come in contact. At the rate the race is going, there will be no men left at all in another few generations."

There was quiet in the long hall. Deathly quiet.

Sally said, "How…how do you mean, dear?"

"I mean our present system can't go on. It isn't working."

"Of course it's working," Vivian snapped. "Here we are aren't we? It's always worked—always will. Here's the clan. You're our husband. After we've had you for twenty years, we'll trade you to another clan for their husband—prevents interbreeding. If you have a fertile son, the clan will either split, each half taking one husband, or we'll trade him off for land, guns, or whatever else is valuable. Of course, it works."

He shook his head, stubbornly. "Things are changing. For a generation or two after bomb day, we were in chaos. By the time things cleared we were divided as we are now, in clans. However, we were still largely able to exist on the canned goods, the animals, left over from the old days. There was food and guns for all and only a few of the men were sterilies."

Vivian began to say something again, but he shook a hand negatively at her, pleading for silence. "No, I'm not talking about myth-legend now. Warren's great-grandfather, whom

215

he knew as a boy, remembers when there were four times or more the number of men we have today and when the steriles were very few."

Vivian said impatiently, "What's this got to do with the prisoners? There they are. We can kill them or let them go. If we let them go, they'll be coming back, six months from now, to take another crack at us. Alan is cute as a button, but I don't think he should meddle in women's affairs."

But most of them were silent. They looked up at him, waiting for him to go on.

"I suppose," Sally said, "that you're coming to a point, dear?"

He nodded, his face tight. "I'm coming to the point. The point is that we've got to change the basis of clan society. This isn't working any more—if it ever did. There's such a thing as planned breeding…" it had been hard to say this, and the younger women in the audience, in particular, tittered "…and we're going to have to think in terms of it."

Sally had flushed. She said now, "A certain dignity is expected at a clan meeting, Alan dear. But just what did you mean?"

Vivian said, "This is nonsense, I'm leaving," and she was up from the speaker's table and away. Two or three of her younger girls looked after, scowling, but they didn't follow her out of the hall.

"I mean," Alan said doggedly, "that one of those Crow women has been the mother of two fertile men. To my knowledge she is the only woman within hundreds of miles this can be said about. We men have been keeping records of such things."

Sally was as mystified as the rest of the clan.

Alan said, "I say bring these women into the clan. Unite with the Turtles and the Burros so that we'll have three clans, five counting the Horses and Crows. Then we'll have enough strength to fight off the forager-hunters, and we'll have enough men to experiment in selective breeding."

Half of the hall was on its feet in a roar.

"Share you with these…these desert rats who just raided us, who killed eight of our clan?" Sally snapped, flabbergasted.

He stood his ground. "Yes. I'll repeat, one of those Crow women has borne two fertile men children. We can't afford to kill her. For all we know, she might have a dozen more. This haphazard method of a single husband for a whole clan must be replaced…"

The hall broke down into chaos again.

Sally held up a commanding hand for silence. She said, "And if we share you with another forty or fifty women, to what extent will the rest of us have any husband at all?"

He pointed out the steriles, seated silently in the back. "It would be healthier if you gave up some of this superior contempt you hold for sterile males and accept their companionship. Although they cannot be fathers, they can be mates otherwise. As it is, how much true companionship do you secure from me—any of you? Less than once a month do you see me more than from a distance."

"Mate with steriles?" someone gasped from the front row.

"Yes," Alan snapped back. "And let fertile men be used expressly for attempting to produce additional fertile men. Confound it, can't you warriors realize what I'm saying? I have reports that there is a woman among the Crows who has borne two fertile male children. Have you ever heard of any such phenomenon before? Do you realize that in the fifteen years I have been the husband of this clan, we have not had even one fertile man child born? Do you realize that in the past twenty years there has been born not one fertile man child in the Turtle clan? Only one in the Burro clan?"

He had them in the palm of his hand now.

"What—what does the Turtle clan think of this plan of yours?" Sally said.

"I was talking to Warren just the other day. He thinks he can win their approval. We can also probably talk the Burros into it. They're growing desperate. Their husband is nearly sixty years old and has produced only one fertile male child, which was later captured in a raid by the Denver foragers."

Sally said, "And we'd have to share you with all these, and with our prisoners as well?"

"Yes, in an attempt to breed fertile men back into the race."

Sally turned to the assembled clan.

A heavy explosion, room-shaking in its violence, all but threw them to the floor. Half a dozen of the younger warriors scurried to the windows, guns at the ready.

In the distance, from the outside, there was the chatter of a machine gun, then individual pistol shots.

"The corral," Jean the scout said, her lips going back over her teeth.

Vivian came sauntering back into the assembly hall, patting the stock of her new tommy gun appreciatively. "Works like a charm," she said. "That dynamite we captured was fresh too. Blew 'em to smithereens. Only had to finish off half a dozen."

Alan said, agonizingly, "Vivian! You didn't...the prisoners?"

She grinned at him. "Alan, you're as cute as a button, but you don't know anything about women's affairs. Now you be a honey and go back to taking care of the children."

Off Course

Shure and begorra, it was a great day for the earth! The first envoy from another world was about to speak—that is, if he could forget that horse for a minute...

FIRST ON the scene were Larry Dermott and Tim Casey of the State Highway Patrol. They assumed they were witnessing the crash of a new type of Air Force plane and slipped and skidded desperately across the field to within thirty feet of the strange craft, only to discover that the landing had been made without accident.

Patrolman Dermott shook his head. "They're gettin' queerer looking every year. Get a load of it—no wheels, no propeller, no cockpit."

They left the car and made their way toward the strange egg-shaped vessel.

Tim Casey loosened his .38 in its holster and said, "Sure and I'm beginning to wonder if it's one of ours. No insignia and—"

A circular door slid open at that point and Dameri Tass stepped out, yawning. He spotted them, smiled and said, "Glork."

They gaped at him.

"Glork is right," Dermott swallowed.

Tim Casey closed his mouth with an effort. "Do you mind the color of his face?" he blurted.

"How could I help it?"

Dameri Tass rubbed a blue-nailed pink hand down his purplish countenance and yawned again. "Gorra manigan horp soratium," he said.

Patrolman Dermott and Patrolman Casey shot stares at each other. "Tis double talk he's after givin' us," Casey said.

Dameri Tass frowned. "Harama?" he asked.

Larry Dermott pushed his cap to the back of his head. "That doesn't sound like any language I've even *heard* about."

Dameri Tass grimaced, turned and reentered his spacecraft to emerge in half a minute with his hands full of contraption. He held a box-like arrangement under his left arm; in his right hand were two metal caps connected to the box by wires.

While the patrolmen watched him, he set the box on the ground, twirled two dials and put one of the caps on his head. He offered the other to Larry Dermot; his desire was obvious.

Trained to grasp a situation and immediately respond in manner best suited to protect the welfare of the people of New York State, Dermott cleared his throat and said, "Tim, take over while I report."

"Hey!" Casey protested, but his fellow minion had left.

"Mandaia," Dameri Tass told Casey, holding out the metal cap.

"Faith, an' do I look balmy?" Casey told him. "I wouldn't be puttin' that dingus on my head for all the colleens in Ireland."

"Mandaia," the stranger said impatiently.

"Bejasus," Casey snorted, "ye can't—"

Dermott called from the car, "Tim, the captain says to humor this guy. We're to keep him here until the officials arrive."

Tim Casey closed his eyes and groaned. "Humor him, he's after sayin'. Orders it is." He shouted back, "Sure an' did ye tell 'em he's in Technicolor? Begorra, he looks like a man from Mars."

"That's what they think," Larry yelled, "and the governor is on his way. We're to do everything possible short of violence to keep this character here. Humor him, Tim!"

"Mandaia," Dameri Tass snapped, pushing the cap into Casey's reluctant hands.

Muttering his protests, Casey lifted it gingerly and placed it on his head. Not feeling any immediate effect, he said, "There, 'tis satisfied ye are now, I'm supposin'."

The alien stooped down and flicked a switch on the little box. It hummed gently. Tim Casey suddenly shrieked and sat down on the stubble and grass of the field. "Begorra," he yelped, "I've been murthered!" He tore the cap from his head.

His companion came running, "What's the matter, Tim?" he shouted.

Dameri Tass removed the metal cap from his own head. "Sure, an' nothin' is after bein' the matter with him," he said. "Evidently the bhoy has niver been a-wearin' of a kerit helmet afore. 'Twill hurt him not at all."

"YOU CAN talk!" Dermott blurted, skidding to a stop.

Dameri Tass shrugged. "Faith an' why not? As I was after sayin', I shared the kerit helmet with Tim Casey."

Patrolman Dermott glared at him unbelievingly. "You learned the language just by sticking that Rube Goldberg deal on Tim's head?"

"Sure, an' why not?"

Dermott muttered, "And with it he has to pick up the corniest brogue west of Dublin."

Tim Casey got to his feet indignantly. "I'm after resentin' that, Larry Dermott. Sure, an' the way we talk in Ireland is—"

Dameri Tass interrupted, pointing to a bedraggled horse that had made its way to within fifty feet of the vessel. "Now what could that be after bein'?"

The patrolmen followed his stare. "It's a horse. What else?"

"A horse?"

Larry Dermott looked again, just to make sure. "Yeah— not much of a horse, but a horse."

Dameri Tass sighed ecstatically "And jist what is a horse, if I may be so bold as to be askin'?"

"It's an animal you ride on."

The alien tore his gaze from the animal to look his disbelief at the other. "Are you after meanin' that you climb upon the crature's back and ride him? Faith now, quit your blarney."

He looked at the horse again, then down at his equipment. "Begorra," he muttered, "I'll share the kerit helmet with the crature."

"Hey, hold it," Dermot said anxiously. He was beginning to feel like a character in a shaggy dog story.

Interest in the horse was ended with the sudden arrival of a helicopter. It swooped down on the field and settled within twenty feet of the alien craft. Almost before it had touched, the door was flung open and the flying windmill disgorged two bestarred and efficient-looking Army officers.

Casey and Dermott snapped them a salute.

The senior general didn't take his eyes from the alien and the spacecraft as he spoke, and they bugged quite as effectively as had those of the patrolmen when they'd first arrived on the scene.

"I'm Major General Browning," he rapped. "I want a police cordon thrown up around this, er, vessel. No newsmen, no sightseers, nobody without my permission. As soon as Army personnel arrives, we'll take over completely."

"Yes, sir," Larry Dermott said. "I just got a report on the radio that the governor is on his way, sir. How about him?"

The general muttered something under his breath. Then, "When the governor arrives, let me know; otherwise, nobody gets through!"

Dameri Tass said, "Faith, and what goes on?"

The general's eyes bugged still further. *"He talks!"* he accused.

"Yes, sir," Dermott said. "He had some kind of a machine. He put it over Tim's head and seconds later he could talk."

"Nonsense!" the general snapped.

Further discussion was interrupted by the screaming arrival of several motorcycle patrolmen followed by three heavily laden patrol cars. Overhead, pursuit planes zoomed in and began darting about nervously above the field.

"Sure, and it's quite a reception I'm after gettin'," Dameri Tass said. He yawned. "But what I'm wantin' is a chance to get some sleep. Faith, an' I've been awake for almost a *decal.*"

DAMERI TASS was hurried, via helicopter, to Washington. There he disappeared for several days, being held incommunicado while White House, Pentagon, State Department and Congress tried to figure out just what to do with him.

Never in the history of the planet had such a furor arisen. Thus far, no newspapermen had been allowed within speaking distance. Administration higher-ups were being subjected to a volcano of editorial heat but the longer the space alien was discussed the more they viewed with alarm the situation his arrival had precipitated. There were angles that hadn't at first been evident.

Obviously he was from some civilization far beyond that of Earth. That was the rub. No matter what he said, it would shake governments, possibly overthrow social systems, perhaps even destroy established religious concepts.

But they couldn't keep him under wraps indefinitely.

It was the United Nations that cracked the iron curtain. Their demands that the alien be heard before their body were too strong and had too much public opinion behind them to be ignored. The White House yielded and the date was set for the visitor to speak before the Assembly.

Excitement, anticipation, blanketed the world. Shepherds in Sinkiang, multi-millionaires in Switzerland, fakirs in Pakistan, gauchos in the Argentine were raised to a zenith of expectation. Panhandlers debated the message to come with pedestrians; jinrikisha men argued it with their passengers; miners discussed it deep beneath the surface; pilots argued with their co-pilots thousands of feet above.

It was the most universally awaited event of the ages.

By the time the delegates from every nation, tribe, religion, class, color, and race had gathered in New York to receive the message from the stars, the majority of Earth had decided that Dameri Tass was the plenipotentiary of a super-civilization which had been viewing developments on this planet with misgivings. It was thought this other civilization had advanced greatly beyond Earth's and that the problems besetting us—social, economic, scientific—had been solved by the super-civilization. Obviously, then, Dameri Tass had come, an advisor from a benevolent and friendly people, to guide the world aright.

And nine-tenths of the population of Earth stood ready and willing to be guided. The other tenth liked things as they were and were quite convinced that the space envoy would upset their applecarts.

VILJALMAR Andersen, Secretary-General of the U. N., was to introduce the space emissary. "Can you give me an idea at all of what he is like?" he asked nervously.

President McCord was as upset as the Dane. He shrugged in agitation. "I know almost as little as you do."

Sir Alfred Oxford protested, "But my dear chap, you've had him for almost two weeks. Certainly in that time—"

The President snapped back, "You probably won't believe this, but he's been asleep until yesterday. When he first arrived he told us he hadn't slept for a *decal*, whatever that is; so we held off our discussion with him until morning. Well—he didn't awaken in the morning, nor the next. Six days later, fearing something was wrong we woke him."

"What happened?" Sir Alfred asked.

The President showed embarrassment. "He used some rather ripe Irish profanity on us, rolled over, and went back to sleep."

Viljalmar Andersen asked, "Well, what happened yesterday?"

"We actually haven't had time to question him. Among other things, there's been some controversy about whose jurisdiction he comes under. The State Department claims the Army shouldn't—"

The Secretary General sighed deeply. "Just what *did* he do?"

"The Secret Service reports he spent the day whistling Mother Machree and playing with his dog, cat and mouse."

"Dog, cat and mouse? I say!" blurted Sir Alfred.

The President was defensive. "He had to have some occupation, and he seems to be particularly interested in our animal life. He wanted a horse but compromised for the others. I understand he insists all three of them come with him wherever he goes."

"I wish we knew what he was going to say," Andersen worried.

"Here he comes," said Sir Alfred.

Surrounded by F. B. I. men, Dameri Tass was ushered to the speaker's stand. He had a kitten in his arms; a Scotty followed him.

The alien frowned worriedly. "Sure," he said, "and what kin all this be? Is it some ordinance I've been after breakin'?"

McCord, Sir Alfred and Andersen hastened to reassure him and made him comfortable in a chair.

Viljalmar Andersen faced the thousands in the audience and held up his hands, but it was ten minutes before he was able to quiet the cheering, stamping delegates from all Earth.

Finally: "Fellow Terrans, I shall not take your time for a lengthy introduction of the envoy from the stars. I will only say that, without doubt, this is the most important moment in the history of the human race. We will now hear from the first being to come to Earth from another world."

He turned and gestured to Dameri Tass who hadn't been paying over much attention to the chairman in view of some dog and cat hostilities that had been developing about his feet.

But now the alien's purplish face faded to a light blue. He stood and said hoarsely, "Faith, an' what was that last you said?"

Viljalmar Andersen repeated, "We will now hear from the first being ever to come to Earth from another world."

The face of the alien went a lighter blue. "Sure, and ye wouldn't jist be frightenin' a body, would ye? You don't mean to tell me this planet isn't after bein' a member of the Galactic League?"

Andersen's face was blank. "Galactic League?"

"Cushlamachree," Dameri Tass moaned. "I've gone and put me foot in it again. I'll be after getting *kert* for this."

Sir Alfred was on his feet. "I don't understand! Do you mean you aren't an envoy from another planet?"

Dameri Tass held his head is his bands and groaned. "An envoy, he's sayin', and meself only a second rate collector of specimens for the Carthis zoo."

He straightened and started off the speaker's stand. "Sure, an' I must blast off immediately."

Things were moving fast for President McCord but already an edge of relief was manifesting itself. Taking the initiative, he said, "Of course, of course, if that is your desire." He signaled to the bodyguard who had accompanied the alien to the assemblage.

A dull roar was beginning to emanate from the thousands gathered in the tremendous hall, murmuring, questioning, disbelieving.

VILJALMAR Andersen felt that he must say something. He extended a detaining hand. "Now you are here," he said urgently, "even though by mistake, before you go can't you give us some brief word? Our world is in chaos. Many of us have lost faith. Perhaps..."

Dameri Tass shook off the restraining hand. "Do I look daft? Begorry, I should have been a-knowin' something was queer. All your weapons and your strange ideas. Faith, I wouldn't be surprised if ye hadn't yet established a planet-wide government. Sure, an' I'll go still further. Ye probably still have wars on this benighted world. No wonder it is ye haven't been invited to join the Galactic League an' take your place among the civilized planets."

He hustled from the rostrum and made his way, still surrounded by guards, to the door by which he had entered. The dog and the cat trotted after, undismayed by the furor about them.

They arrived about four hours later at the field on which he'd landed, and the alien from space hurried toward his craft, still muttering. He'd been accompanied by a general and by the President, but all the way he had refrained from speaking.

He scurried from the car and toward the spacecraft.

President McCord said, "You've forgotten your pets. We would be glad if you would accept them as—"

The alien's face faded a light blue again. "Faith, an' I'd almost forgotten," he said. "If I'd taken a crature from this quarantined planet, my name'd be *nork*. Keep your dog and your kitty." He shook his head sadly and extracted a mouse from a pocket. "An' this amazin' little crature as well."

They followed him to the spacecraft. Just before entering, he spotted the bedraggled horse that had been present on his landing.

A longing expression came over his highly colored face. "Jist one thing," he said. "Faith now, were they pullin' my leg when they said you were after ridin' on the back of those things?"

The President looked at the woebegone nag. "It's a horse," he said, surprised. "Man has been riding them for centuries."

Dameri Tass shook his head. "Sure an' 'twould've been my makin' if I could've taken one back to Carthis." He entered his vessel.

The others drew back, out of range of the expected blast, and watched, each with his own thoughts, as the first visitor from space hurriedly left Earth.

United We Stand

To save the peoples of Earth, a young man prepared to die a hero's death in the toughest way of all—without appreciation!

IT WAS something like sitting in a closet, a small closet, for days on end. And only the chronometer kept him from feeling it was weeks, months.

The psycho-technicians had been correct in insisting on the chronometer over the protests of the weight conscious, space conscious, engineers. Hadn't it been for the chronometer he would have been convinced that he'd already been weeks in his cubicle and that he'd missed his goal.

They had insisted, too, on the books—specially printed for him, agate type, tissue thin paper, coverless—and the tiny phonograph. The engineers had gone wild in protest over the books and the phonograph, but the docs had been right. Without them he would nave been raving mad by now. As it was, he had something to break the monotony of just sitting and waiting and thinking of the world he had left behind and the one he was approaching.

* * *

Excerpt from announcement by Arch Donelly at Madison Square Garden, July 8: "Ladees and Gennulmun, before we bring you the principal bout of the evening, the contest for the Heavyweight Championship of the World, I would like to remind you that alone in space tonight, more than thirty-five million miles from the home he loves, Lieutenant Philip Albright is attempting the first flight from Luna to Mars.

"Ladees and Gennulmun, I am going to request that this here audience stand and hold a moment of silence in honor of an American hero who is carrying the stars and stripes to…"

* * *

From Associated Press: Moscow, July 8. — Commissar of Defense Andri Goroloff, in a statement today, accused the Western Alliance of taking steps that would inevitably lead to war. He contended that the establishment of bases upon Luna, and the further exploration of space toward Mars, were motivated solely by military expediency.

"Such bases," Commissar Goroloff is quoted as having said, "have no possible use save as launching points for guided missiles directed against the peace, loving nations of the Eastern Confederation. They are a dagger directed against our hearts."

He warned, further, that the Eastern Confederation would not long stand for such preparations for aggression against it. "If to survive we must take countermeasures," he warned, "we will not hesitate to…"

* * *

From the Washington World: Washington, D.C., July 9. — In calling for increased military appropriations, Senator Warren Miles scoffed today at Eastern Confederation claims that the Western Alliance was planning aggression. "To their twisted minds, preparations for defense are an attack," he said. "Actually, they would have the world confused on the point of just who are the wolves and who the lambs. It has been done before and we do not propose to…"

* * *

From Station KIO: We interrupt this program to bring you a bulletin from New Albuquerque, Luna, takeoff point for Lieutenant Philip Albright in his attempt to reach Mars. General Arnold Dwight, commandant of the Luna base, has just announced that a radar message has been received from Lieutenant Albright reading: LANDED SAFELY MARS. Stay tuned to this station for further news of…

* * *

From New York Telegraph: Washington, D.C., July 10. — Sources close to the White House made known today that appropriations for further enlargement of the Western Alliance military base on Luna would undoubtedly be doubled within the week. The rapidly developing possibilities of space travel, emphasized by the report of Lieutenant Philip Albright's successful landing on Mars, and the military advantages of the Luna base, are generally believed to be the principal reasons for the step.

The steadily darkening international outlook has spurred defense measures…

* * *

Excerpt from broadcast of Commentator Roy George: "There is both good and bad news tonight, radio friends. And here it is!

"First, we have just been handed a bulletin from New Albuquerque, American base on the moon. A further report has been received from Lieutenant Philip Albright, who landed a few hours ago on the planet Mars. You will recall that Lieutenant Albright is restricted in sending, due to the necessity of conserving power, but that he is able to receive communications from Luna at all times. His message is brief but startling, friends. It reads simply: SIGNS OF INTELLIGENT LIFE. No more than that, but how much it says.

"Our second bulletin comes from Long Island where the United Nations Assembly is in session and making desperate last moment efforts to avoid the outbreak of hostilities which seem, at times, only hours away. Secretary of State Fuller Martin, in a strong verbal attack upon the warlike moves of the Eastern Confederation, stated that under no circumstances would this nation accept a situation in which…"

* * *

From Station KIO: Station KIO brings you the latest news flashes every hour on the hour... New Albuquerque, Luna. Nothing further has been heard from Lieutenant Philip Albright who landed on Mars yesterday. It has been ten hours since his last message, which reported briefly that he had discovered signs of intelligent life on what was supposed to be a dead planet. Meanwhile, here on earth, a storm of conjecture in scientific circles has been raised by his disclosure... London, England, Prime Minister Winston Clement, in a press conference today, revealed that the full strength of the British army and navy would be thrown into the conflict immediately, if and when hostilities come. He stressed that the colonies and dominions of the British Commonwealth are in complete accord with the...

* * *

From Station WBCD: We interrupt this program to bring you another flash from New Albuquerque, Luna. Lieutenant Philip Albright, first human to land upon another planet, has been heard from again. The message began, MARTIANS ARE TAK...and broke off in the middle of the third word. It is unknown what caused the break in communication. Stay tuned to this station for...

* * *

From the Associated Press: Sofia, Bulgaria, July 11. — Premier Josep Kosloff, in a speech to cheering thousands gathered in a mass meeting in the city square today, announced that he has ordered the immediate mobilization of all Bulgarian forces.

* * *

From the United Press: Peiping, China, July 11. — Chu Mao, Commissioner of Defense, declared today that in the eventuality of hostilities between the Western Alliance and the Eastern Confederation, China would immediately march on all

Southeastern Asia, "…as a measure of defense against the imperialistic powers of the West."

It is understood that the full military strength of Chu's armies has not been diminished since the recent termination of the civil war and that…

* * *

From Station KIO: Here's a news bulletin. President James Harford has just ordered that all stored elements of the American fleet be taken from "mothballs" and restored to active duty.

* * *

From the International News Services: Stockholm, Sweden, July 11. — It was reliably reported today in diplomatic circles of this neutral capitol that Poland and Czechoslovakia have both secretly ordered mobilization of their forces to full war strength. There have also been rumors of divisions mobilizing upon the borders of Finland and Hungary, and large scale troop movements on the…

* * *

From the New York Telegraph: New Albuquerque, Luna, July 12. — There is still no further word from Lieutenant Philip Albright, whose last message from Mars was cut off after the words MARTIANS ARE. It is assumed here that Albright's radar set, used for communications with his Luna base, has failed. In such case it is unknown whether or not he will be able to repair it before his return since neither tools nor spare parts were included in his equipment.

General Arnold Dwight, New Albuquerque commandant, has revealed that a twenty-four hour watch is kept listening for further messages from the hero of the first Mars flight. The general also stated that failure of the radar set will not hinder the return flight of Lieutenant Albright to his Luna base. Although optimism is high, Dwight refuses to minimize possibilities of…

* * *

From the Associated Press: Ankara, Turkey, July 13. — Military circles here have reported Eastern Confederation army leaders expect World War III to last less than three days. Present weapons they claim to possess, will mean complete destruction of all Western Alliance forces in that period.

* * *

From the United Press: Paris, France, July 13. — Marshal Henri Dumar, hero of Sedan in World War I, predicted today that if hostilities broke out, the Eastern Confederation would be destroyed within forty-eight hours under the impact of secret super-weapons developed by the Western nations. Calling upon his experiences of the first World War, the Marshal said...

* * *

From the International News Service: Washington, D.C., July 13. — It was revealed unofficially today that American military heads do not expect the pending war, if it develops, to last more than a matter of hours.

"Our defenses will hold until we have completely destroyed their military and industrial potential," one source close to the Pentagon is alleged to have stated. "Progress in the development of new and better..."

* * *

From the New York Telegraph: New Albuquerque, Luna, July 12. — There is still no further word from Lieutenant Philip Albright, pilot of the first rocket to reach Mars. More than forty-eight hours have elapsed since his radar equipment failed in the middle of a report to his Luna base.

General Dwight has revealed that Lieutenant Albright was scheduled to blast off for his return flight four hours ago. It is possible that…

* * *

From Station KIO: Ladies and gentlemen, in common with every radio and TV station in North America, we interrupt our program to bring you a message direct from General Arnold Dwight, Commander of New Albuquerque, our Luna base.

Come in, General Dwight—

"Hello, Americans. I can't over-emphasize the importance of the report I am about to make. I will state the facts barely and leave to my listeners the conclusions to be drawn.

"We have again, and for the last time, heard from Lt. Philip Albright. It would be impossible to convey to you just how much it means to me to reveal that it is now the *late* Lieutenant Albright, for we can only suppose that he has perished.

"The omissions in the following message are his own; obviously he was hurried in getting the communication through. His last message reads:

"HAVE ESCAPED MARTIANS TEMPORARILY STOP STARTLED AT TERRA CONQUEST OF SPACE STOP HAVE DISASSEMBLED SHIP AND LEARNED SECRET OF SPACE TRAVEL STOP ARE PREPARING BUILD SPACE FLEET ATTACK TERRA STOP BEWARE OF…"

"Fellow Americans, that is all of the message. I need not point out to you the almost insurmountable difficulties Lieutenant Albright must have met with in his struggle to escape his captors and warn the human race of threatening disaster.

"I propose the following slogan to be used in man's struggle against these inhuman beasts from Mars.

"We Shall Come Again!"

* * *

Excerpt from the book "Inside Terra": President James Harford, of the United States, was about to make the shortest and the most effective speech of his career; a speech that would go down in the annals of oratory with the Gettysburg address, inspirational words of another president who fought for unity.

He stood before the assembled delegates of the United Nations. There was complete silence. He ran his eyes over them slowly, seriously. Then he spoke.

"Fellow Terrans," he said quietly, without inflection in his voice, "you are all familiar with the message received yesterday from the first human being to reach the planet Mars.

"I shall call Philip Albright, the man who sent that message, the first *Terran* hero. Not an *American* hero, fellow Terrans; Philip Albright is not of one nation, one race, one color, or one religion. In his valiant and successful effort to warn earth, he represented *all* Terra. He belongs to all Terra.

"Fellow Terrans," President Harford paused for a long pregnant moment. "Fellow Terrans. United we stand..."

The rest of the sentence was drowned in the hysterical roar of cheers from the assemblage.

PHILIP Albright flicked his cigarette away. The things were too hard to smoke here anyway. If he smoked in the ship, he soon had the confined space reeking with stale smoke. If he smoked outside, without his helmet on, of course, the thin air had him gasping for breath after one or two puffs.

He looked out over the desolate waste that was Mars and grunted. What a planet! Not even the lowly lichens that the scientists had been quite sure would be found. Actually, Mars looked amazingly similar to Luna.

He glanced up into the sky and sought out Terra, and allowed himself a wisp of a smile. He didn't mind sitting out the rest of his life here on this barren waste, that part of it was all right; but he would have liked to have known whether or not he'd succeeded. After he'd sent that last lulu of a message, they'd cut off all radar sending.

He figured roughly it'd be ten years before Terra even tried to send another rocket here. Next time it would be a fleet, loaded for action.

And by that time earth would be welded into one, united against a non-existent foe. United to an extent that world government and peace would continue even after it was found that Philip Albright's message was a hoax.

Optical Illusion

If aliens from another world are among us, how would we detect them if their disguise is perfect? Well, perhaps some of us are not perfect humans, and therefore…

MOLLY brought my plate, silver and side dishes and placed them before me without fuss or comment. I was an old customer and one of the things I liked about Molly was that she never fussed over me.

I usually make a practice of eating after the rush hour but today I was early and the restaurant crowded. It was only a matter of time before someone would want to share my table.

I didn't look up when he asked, "Is this seat taken?" His voice was high, almost to the point of shrillness in spite of his attempt to control it.

"No," I told him, "go right ahead."

He hung his cane, or umbrella, whatever it was, over the back of his chair and fumbled his hat underneath it before climbing to his seat. Then he picked up the menu from where it stood between the catsup and napkins.

"Nothing fit to eat," he muttered finally.

I said, "The pot pie is quite good today."

Molly came up and he said to her, "I'll have the swiss steak, Miss. Green peas, french fries. I'll decide on the dessert later."

"Coffee?"

"Milk."

I don't know what it was that first gave me the idea that the person seated across the table from me wasn't a midget at all. Not a midget or dwarf, but a child pretending adulthood and doing a fantastically good job of it. As I say, I don't know what it was that gave me the hint, possibly I'm more susceptible to such intuitiveness than the next man.

But whatever it was, he knew almost as soon as I did.

That is, he knew that I'd caught on to him and somehow it frightened me. The whole idea was so bizarre—a child, not yet in his teens, passing himself off for some reason of his own as a mature, if stunted, adult.

"So," he said, his shrill voice almost a hiss. He put down his fork. "So…"

How can I describe that cold voice? The voice of a child…but not a child. Not a child as we know one.

I reached for the sugar, which was there where it always is at the end of the table next to the salt and pepper and the mustard jar. I measured out a spoonful very carefully without looking up at him. As I have said, somehow I was afraid.

He said, still softly, "So at last a stupid human has penetrated my disguise."

A *human*, he had said.

His voice was a child's but his words dug into me viciously. "Ah, so that surprises you, my curious friend. You wonder, eh?" There was a sneering quality now, a contemptuous overtone.

I cleared my throat, tried to cover my confusion by taking a gulp of the coffee. "I don't know what you mean…sir."

He chuckled and mimicked, "I don't know what you mean…sir." Then his voice snapped over at me, even as he kept his tone low. "Why did you hesitate before adding the sir, eh? Why?" He didn't wait for an answer. "I'll tell you why. Because somehow you've discovered that my age is less than I would have it known."

He was boiling with rage and in spite of his size and the public nature of our whereabouts. I was afraid of him. Why, I didn't know. Somehow I sensed that—impossibly—he could destroy me at will.

238

I fumbled my cup back into its saucer, kept my face averted.

"You're terrified," he snapped again. "You recognize your master even as you wonder about him."

"My master?" I said. Who did he think…

"Your master," he repeated. "Mankind's master. The new race. The super race, *Homo Superior*, if you will. He is here, my snooping friend and you, you and your stupid nation-divided, race-divided, class-divided, religion-divided humanity will never stand before him."

It was hard for me to assimilate. I had come into my favorite restaurant for my mid-day meal. It had been a routine day and I had expected it to continue as one. Now, I had been startled so many times in the past few minutes that I felt I was in a state of shock.

"Oh, it's been suggested before," he went on, seemingly welcoming this opportunity to explain to me, to gloat over me. "The possibility that mutations would develop, a super-race, a super-humanity as far above man as man is above the ape."

"How…what…"

He cut me off. "What difference if it was the atomic bomb, laboratory experiments, or only nature's continual plodding advance? The fact remains, we are here, a considerable number of us and in a few years, when we have developed our full capacities, man will hear from us. Ah, how he will hear!"

Long ago an icy hand had gripped my heart. Now it squeezed.

"Why," I stumbled. "Why tell me all this? Surely you wouldn't disguise yourself if you didn't wish to keep it all a secret."

He laughed mockingly. There was still much of the immature in him, super-race or nay.

"Because it doesn't make any difference," he whispered. "None at all. Ten minutes from now, you will remember nothing of this conversation. Hypnotism, my stupid *homo sapiens*, can be a developed art when practiced on the lower orders."

His voice went hard and incisive, "Look up into my eyes," he ordered.

I had no power to resist. Slowly my face came up. I could feel his eyes drill into mine.

"This you will forget," he ordered. "All of this conversation, all of this experience, you will forget."

He came to his feet, took his time about securing his things, and then left.

Molly came over later. "Gee," she said, "that little midget that was just here, he sure tips good."

"I would imagine," I told her. I was still shaken. "He probably has a substantial source of income."

"Oh," Molly said, making conversation as she cleaned up. "You been talking to him?"

"Yes," I told her, "we had quite a discussion." I added thoughtfully, "and as a result I have duties to perform."

I came to my own feet and reached up for my hat and cane where they hung on their usual hook.

I thought: *possibly man has more of a chance than these hidden enemies realize. Mental powers beyond us they may have, although they would seem lacking in the more kindly qualities. But this one hadn't been as sharp as he liked to think himself. Hypnotic powers he might possess beyond our understanding, but that didn't prevent him from making a very foolish error. He hadn't caught on to the fact that I'm blind.*

I. Q.

*In a time when teaching machines and batteries of educational tests seem
to be determining the intellectual nobility of the next generation,
this story has meaning for all of us...*

ON the way over to the Administration offices Professor
Roy Thomas McCord was stopped several times by students and
colleagues offering congratulations. He tried to protest their
prematureness but they brushed his objections aside. They all
knew he'd come through.

He'd expected in the period it would take to stroll to
Peterson's office to find time to read a few pages of the book of
verse he'd brought along, but he was interrupted often enough
that he gave up.

A youngster named Doolittle, an earnest chap in Physics
who probably was going to flunk out this term, took off his hat
and said breathlessly, "Everybody says you've made it, sir."

"Thanks," Roy said. "Everybody seems to think so but me.
Quite the most difficult tests I've ever seen. It should give the I.
B. M.'s quite a mechanical headache grading them. Good heav-
ens, Doolittle, put your hat back on. Do you think I'm a lady?"
He laughed in embarrassment.

Doolittle said earnestly, "Academician. Only the third one
this school has produced. And you're hardly more than thirty,
sir."

"Well, that's no reason to take your hat off."

"It is for me, sir."

"Oh, get along with you, Doolittle. But thanks, again."

In Peterson's anteroom, Nadine looked up from her desk
and beamed at him. "It's all over that you took highest awards,
Professor McCord. Or should I say, Academician McCord?"

Roy tried to keep from flushing. "I haven't heard officially, Nadine. But anyway, the name is Roy, if you'll recall."

"Hardly," she grinned back at him. "We can hardly call the school's only living Academician by his first name."

His smile was a bit on the wan side. "I'm not sure I'm going to like it then." She was speaking in jest but there was all too much truth in what she said.

Nadine said, "Superintendent Peterson is waiting for you. Just go right in." She chuckled her soft Nadine laugh. "In fact, sir, I doubt if you'll ever be waiting in this office for an appointment ever, ever, again. Not even a Superintendent of Deans allows an Academician to wait on him."

"Go on with you," Roy said uncomfortably. "And don't call me sir. You make me feel old."

"Your mother called," Nadine said after him. "Said to be sure you didn't forget this afternoon."

"All right," he said over his shoulder. "Thanks, Nadine."

Adam Peterson wasn't ordinarily the type to gush, but today he was absolutely overflowing. Of course, it didn't hurt the school's reputation, nor his, to have produced a scholar of Roy Thomas McCord's aptitudes.

He shook hands drastically.

Roy said, "Well, I suppose your enthusiasm indicates it's official. All the way over here I've been getting congratulations."

"It's official all right, all right," Peterson glowed. "Sit down, Roy. Here, this chair Great Scott, man. I suppose I should really call you *sir.*"

Roy laughed uncomfortably.

"At any rate, the examinations put you twelfth in the nation. Twelfth! And at the age of…"

"Thirty-two," Roy supplied.

"Such a short time!"

Roy took the heavy leathern chair. "Such a long time," he said.

Peterson had hustled over to his small, portable bar and was examining his stock. "A drink, of course. This calls for celebration!"

"Sherry would be fine," Roy said.

Peterson came back with the drinks and handed the new Academician his Spanish wine. The usually glum faced Superintendent of Deans was the one expressing the elation he evidently expected in the other. He took his own chair and beamed. *"Salud!"* he said.

Roy muttered a standard response and sipped at the wine.

Peterson said, "What do you mean, such a long time?"

Roy made a wry face, in self-deprecation. "Twenty-five years," he said. And then, with seeming non-relevancy, "Youth."

The older man frowned at him. "Great Scott, man, you've reached one of the highest points possible in the Educational Sequence."

Roy looked down into his glass of wine. "Would you believe me if I told you that I wish I'd dropped out somewhere back along the line?"

"Dropped out?" Peterson didn't understand.

The new Academician seemed to change subjects. He said, "By the way, how did I do in Creative Ability?"

Peterson scowled. "Well, you know, Roy, not even an Academician is free to check the exact result of tests. Not unless, of course, it's his task-field. It might give him an unfair advantage in further examinations."

"I know," Roy said wearily. "I just meant broadly. In relation to my other ratings."

Peterson said uncomfortably, "Actually, it was your weakest, Roy..."

The Academician winced.

"...with Mathematical Aptitude strongest. Somewhat to my surprise, your M. A. was the nation's highest."

"Why surprise?" Roy said, depressed.

The older man shifted bulky shoulders. "Well, your work here while adequate, of course—always adequate, of course—has never shown the absolute genius in the field that your aptitude would indicate."

It was Roy's turn to shrug. "Well, as you know, aptitude doesn't mean that you will ever use it. Frankly, mathematics bore me."

"And me," Peterson chuckled. "But, to get on to business, I suppose we shall have to provide you with a larger suite of offices. You'll be able to take over some of the social duties of the faculty officers, Roy. In fact, there's a delegation from…"

Roy interrupted, "I don't suppose there's any manner in which I could drop away." His tone indicated that he didn't expect an affirmative answer.

Peterson's enthusiasm fell off in one split second. He all but gaped. "Drop away!" he blurted. "You mean leave the university? Drop away! You're considering deserting us for another school? Great Scott, Roy…"

Roy McCord was shaking his head. "Not just this school, Adam, education as a field. My rank entitles me to retirement at my own discretion."

"Retirement! You're not even forty years of age! Roy, the strain has been too much. You need a vacation. Retirement! Great Scott…" The Superintendent was on his feet again. He grabbed the sherry bottle from the bar, hurriedly refilled the other's glass. "A vacation! Perhaps to Common Europe. You'll be feted in every university on the continent. An Academician at the age of thirty-two. The Education Sequence of Europe will be at your feet."

"That's what I'm afraid of," Roy said bitterly. "I'd never see anything except the insides of schools, never talk to anybody but a bunch of doddering old scholars."

PETERSON sank back into his chair again, aghast. "Roy! What are you saying? You sound as though you have no affection for your Sequence."

Roy McCord snorted. "Frankly, I haven't. Is that unknown?"

The Superintendent collected himself. "Not unknown, of course, but certainly rare. From your earliest youth you've been carefully tested, rated, channeled in the direction your aptitudes indicated. Had you been mechanically inclined, you would have eventually wound up in a Sequence where your abilities would have best suited you and the nation. Had you shown aptitude for medicine you would have eventually been channeled into that Sequence, finally gaining the level your competence permitted."

Roy said bitterly, "And had my Creative Ability so indicated, I might have wound up a poet."

Peterson said uncomfortably, "Actually, your Creative Ability is high, not fantastically so, but quite high. It's just that it is so eclipsed by your other aptitudes, Roy. But, I don't understand. You've reached the heights in our Sequence, in the field of education. What would you rather do?"

"I think I would rather be a poet than the world's most celebrated scholar, Adam."

"A poet!" The other grunted skeptically. "Your aptitudes indicate that even had you gone into the artistic field, your work would hardly startle the world."

"Nor would I expect it to, or necessarily want it to. Why must the greatest painters work in oil; what is wrong with the sketch, the watercolor? Listen." He took up the book he had been carrying under his arm and read,

> *"Jenny kissed me when we met,*
> *Jumping from the chair she sat in.*
> *Fate, you thief, who loves to get*
> *Sweets into your list, put that in.*
> *Say I'm weary, say I'm sad,*
> *Say that health and*
> *wealth have missed me.*
> *Say I'm growing old, but add,*
> *Jenny kissed me."*

"Very sweet," Peterson nodded. "Seems to me I recall it from my own student days, but I forget the poet."

"Leigh Hunt," Roy said. "A little poet, eclipsed by his contemporaries, Keats, Shelley, Byron. But, frankly, I prefer the little poets." He added softly, "I would prefer to be an Emily Dickinson, a Stephen Crane, a Thomas Hood."

"Look here," Adam Peterson said. "Let's face reality. All of us have hobbies, methods of relaxing from our work. Write your *little* poems in your leisure hours. Why not? But your *field* is education, and you are a phenomenon in it."

Roy McCord was shaking his head. "You can't. Or, at least, I can't. You need relaxation. Your mind free of all except your creative urge. You need to be able to spend long hours in the shade of a tree, or on a shell strewn beach, or perhaps in watching without distraction of any sort the twig of a maple, ridged inch deep in the pearl of snow. If I were to be a poet, I would have to be *all* poet. Just as today I am all scholar."

Peterson was on his feet and pacing. "See here, Academician McCord. You can't drop out of this Sequence at your age. You owe it to your fellows, to society, to continue."

Roy looked at him flatly. "I do?"

Peterson said, "I'm going to reiterate some truths which you already know, but which perhaps need repeating. For the first time in the history of civilization, man has achieved a society in which he assumes his place according to his ability and by no other means. There is no ruling property class, no priesthood, no militaristic state to arbitrarily decide our status. It makes no difference who your parents were, nor how much treasure you might have accumulated by whatever means; you take your position in our culture according to your aptitudes."

"No test is perfect," Roy muttered.

"Of course, and that is why we continually work to improve them. Actually, they have reached a high level of competence. The tests are compiled by men but are given and evaluated by machine, and there have been no known cases of mistakes within recent memory. Roy, this system works, and it's good. In the past, a man had status in his culture based on the most fantastic of reasons. Prime among them was the possession of money, possibly the greatest status symbol of all. Also ranking high was the position in society of your parents and relatives. The extreme example of this, of course, was the feudalistic nobilities in Europe and elsewhere, but it also existed in the United States especially in New England and the South.

"Today? Today, Roy, you achieve status by your own abilities. Long ago man solved the problem of the production of abundance. There is no poverty, everyone possesses all he needs. We can no longer award our geniuses, our heroes, with wealth—since there is wealth for all. We honor them, instead, with rank. Each man contributes to society what he can and those who can contribute more, through their greater abilities, their genius, are awarded with such titles as Doctor, Supervisor, Superintendent, or, in our own Educational Sequence, Academician."

The Supervisor of Deans went on. "You have been so highly honored, Roy McCord, because our tests indicate your aptitudes as high as any. But for you now, after twenty-five years of continual studies, to drop away and not utilize your abilities would be a betrayal of the hundreds of thousands, the millions of our citizens who, because their aptitudes were less than your own, work in the mines, in the mills, and in the fields. They contribute their share to society so that persons such as you and me, in a different and possibly gentler Sequence, may eat, be clothed and sheltered."

Peterson summed it up. "You have the *right* to retire on your rank at this stage, Academician Roy McCord. But I don't think you will be able to do so."

Roy stood up wearily. "No, I suppose you're right," he said. He looked down at the book of verse and said, irrelevantly, "I've often wondered what the Acropolis looked like by moonlight."

I. Q.

As he left the Superintendent's office, Nadine said to him, "Your mother called again, Roy…ah, Academician McCord. She said to remind you that…"

"I know, I know," Roy said almost tartly. "She's having in all her friends and neighbors for a celebration."

Nadine looked up at him. "Well, I'm not surprised. How many of her friends have a son who has won your honors?"

Roy sighed. "Yes, and how she revels in it. It was bad enough with my Doctor's degree. But now!"

Nadine laughed at him. "Go and take your medicine, Hero."

He grinned ruefully in response and left.

His father met him at the door of their suburban house. Actually, as a Senior Technician Warren McCord wouldn't ordinarily have resided in this part of the city. Even in this advanced society, rank had its prerogatives; perhaps few, compared to cultures of the past, but still prerogatives. One of them was to segregate itself, and that, of course, was understandable. An artist who had reached the heights found his most compatible companionship among doctors, scientists, educators who had achieved the equivalent in their own fields.

This was a neighborhood that reeked with prestige, and the McCord family resided here as a result of Roy's fantastic progress in the Educational Sequence.

Actually, Roy McCord would have preferred to have lived in a more Bohemian quarter where he might have found time occasionally to associate with the off-trail artists who were his envy. Each culture, and each generation of that culture, has its equivalent of a Lost Generation, a *beatnik* element, or its Angry Young Men. Within himself, Roy didn't find it difficult to identify with them. Whenever he paused in his work to realize this, he had to smile in deprecation. What would Peterson think if he knew it; and, above all, what would Dora McCord, Roy's mother, think?

Warren McCord, a man of not quite sixty, looked an older version of his son. There was the same weary, rueful—perhaps wistful—expression that so easily broke into a smile for another's sake, but failed to indicate happiness within.

He grinned sourly at Roy now.

"You're in for it," he said. "Every biddy your mother has known for the past thirty years—ever since you were born—is in the garden."

"Good Lord," Roy muttered. His father looked at him oddly. "Congratulations, son." He held out a hand to shake. "You don't seem overly pleased by your accomplishment."

Roy said irritably, "Accomplishment? What accomplishment? The only thing that's happened is that the grading computers have informed the Educational Sequence that I have one of the highest aptitudes in the field. That doesn't mean I've accomplished anything."

His father looked away, as though embarrassed. He cleared his throat and said, "No one in your family, on either side, has ever attained such an honor."

Roy felt contrition, although he didn't exactly know why. "Well," he said, "I hope that I'm able to deliver something in keeping with what those damn testing machines seem to think I'm capable of."

Warren McCord said, "You don't really have to worry about that, you know. Not really. The computers might indicate a man has great aptitude for scientific research and he might be placed in a position to utilize his abilities—but that doesn't necessarily mean he'll come up with some startling new discovery. It an works on percentages."

"I suppose so," Roy sighed. "Well, Dad, let's go face the celebrity hunters."

IN the garden, Dora McCord was beaming with a radiance that almost made up to Roy for the grind of the afternoon. Long years ago he'd explained to himself that she was a status seeker of a type that should have become extinct a century or so earlier. All her life she'd been depressed by the lack of her husband's ability to rise above the rank of Senior Technician. Actually, Roy suspected his father had gone further than his real abilities in achieving even that rank. Only by exertion far beyond the call of duty, and far beyond that of his fellows, had the elder McCord achieved to Senior Technician. He was proud of the attainment, small as it was.

But not Dora McCord. Roy's frenetic and lovable mother was a worshipper of the prestiged. She never made a mistake in calling a man by his correct title, never failed to attend local ceremonies honoring an attainment, and most of her reading was confined to contemporary biography. It had been a cruel blow to her that the man she loved was simply not cut out to reach the highest positions of the nation. A cruel blow.

Now she hustled Roy around like a destroyer convoying a carrier. Her introduction varied little. "My son, the Academician Roy Thomas McCord," or "May I present our family's new Academician…" As though, Roy told himself wryly, family members of that rank were a common occurrence. Actually, of course, there weren't another half dozen men of his status, in whatever field, in this city of millions.

After an hour or two of this battering, his father got him to one side long enough for a glass of sparkling wine.

Warren McCord said, "Your mother is a remarkable woman, Roy."

Roy swallowed the wine, put the glass down and wiped his forehead with a handkerchief. "Thank heavens there's no further for me to go," he growled.

"No," his father said thoughtfully. "Academician is about it, unless you went into national administration."

"Um-m-m," Roy said. He looked at his father and frowned. "Dad, when are you going to knock off?"

"Knock off?"

Roy said, "You're pushing sixty. You could have retired ten years ago. Could have moved to a gentler climate than this."

His father shifted his eyes, poured them both another glass of the cold, sparkling wine. "I suppose I should. In the past, well, I think your mother would have hated not to be here as you continued your advances in your Sequence, Roy. And although I was never able to meet the grade, in your mother's eyes, I've certainly not begrudged her the glory of seeing you do it."

Roy looked at him. "You love her, don't you Dad?"

Warren McCord laughed with characteristic wryness. "Yes. She's a vain little thing, a pusher. An earlier and less kindly era would have labeled her a social climber. But, to answer your question—yes, son, as far back as I can remember, I have loved your mother."

He switched subjects. "With this new rank, what will your duties be, Roy?"

Roy McCord shrugged distastefully. "Showing off for the university, for the most part, I suppose. Attending an endless number of banquets, conferences, congresses and what not. Heavens knows, my field is one where you're not hard pushed to prove the aptitudes the grading computers rate you." He snorted. "Now you're different. As a Senior Technician, the only possible way you could attain your rank is by having it on the ball, right on the job. You can't fake there, surrounded by your fellows."

His father said uncomfortably, "It's not a very high rank." He scowled, then added, "You don't seem very happy about this new position, Roy."

"Why should I be?" the other grunted. "Lots of prestige, which turns out to be something that doesn't particularly interest me, but little, if any, satisfaction in the work."

His father was still scowling. "But what would you rather do?"

Roy shrugged it off. "I don't know. I suppose I'd like to take a hiking tour of the wine provinces of France and Spain." He looked down into his glass. "See where this product comes from. The vineyards, the bodegas. Perhaps write about it a little."

His father was staring at him. "You know, I'm not sure we've ever really gotten to know each other very well, son. I…I never went very high in my Sequence, but I've always liked the work. You've climbed right to the top, but you evidently hate it. Somehow, I never really realized that."

He was obviously depressed.

Roy chuckled ruefully. "Well, there's nothing you could do about it, Dad. I have a confession to make to you. All my life I've wanted to be a writer. Not a big name, not a high prestige author of the type we've got in this neighborhood, but an easy going, you might even say lazy, poet observing the remnants of nature that man has still left on this globe of ours and trying to get the feeling of it down on paper."

His father was staring at him, with sadness in his eyes.

Roy laughed again, to cover. "I suppose I've had too much of this wine. At any rate, to get back to you. So you think you might retire at last? Those IBM, machines can do without you, Dad. Nobody is indispensable."

"Yes, I suppose you're right," his father said, something still wrong with his voice and his eyes.

Dora McCord came sweeping up with one of the neighbors in tow. "Roy, dear," she said fondly, "Mrs. Worthington, you know, her husband is Doctor Worthington, wants to congratulate you."

Roy muttered banalities in answer to those he heard.

Mrs. Worthington said smilingly, "Isn't it amazing what genetics will do? Here we have a simple mechanic and his son achieves to one of the highest ranks in the field of education."

Roy saw his father wince, and his mother bridle.

Roy said flatly, "Being a Senior Technician in charge of repair of some of the most complicated computing machines in the country is hardly the work of a simple mechanic, Mrs. Worthington. I doubt very much whether either your husband or I could do more than make fools of ourselves were we exposed to the tasks involved in repairing such equipment."

"Please don't misunderstand," she stammered uneasily.

"We didn't misunderstand," Dora McCord said.

It was at that split second that the realization came to Roy Thomas McCord.

IN the morning he gave Nadine a ring and when her face lit up the screen he said to her, "Nadine, I don't want to talk to him myself—he probably has a dozen things for me today ranging from talks with the TV press to lectures to students and faculty on the necessity of buckling down and raising the standards of the university—but I want you to tell Superintendent Peterson I won't be in today."

"Won't be in!" Nadine wailed. "But, Academician McCord, we're already swamped. The Civil-Mayor has a luncheon…"

"Call me Roy," Roy said, "and look here, I'm going to phone you again later in the day and ask you one of two questions."

"One of two questions?" she said vaguely.

"Yes. It will either be, how about having dinner with me to-night? Or, will you marry me?"

She blinked at him.

She said finally, "I don't think that's funny, Roy. Any woman in the country would be proud to have dinner with you—or marry you. On the face of it, I'm only a Senior Effective."

"An impressive rank, considering your youth," Roy said definitely. "I'll be calling you later." He broke the connection.

At the Bureau of Records, Academician Roy Thomas Mc-Cord was received with a flutter. The secretary of Superintendent Frol Plovdiv hastened to explain that her superior was in conference but that it wasn't important and she'd immediately inform him of the Academician's presence.

Roy said mildly that he could wait.

She wouldn't hear of it. The Superintendent would be indignant.

He was in the other's office within minutes.

Superintendent Plovdiv was a man in his early middle years and reminded Roy of Adam Peterson. Was there something in these administrative positions that called for such types? He looked like a man who would be difficult to work under but who'd be the height of cooperativeness with his equals in rank, and almost, not quite, subservient to his superiors.

He congratulated Roy with booming sincerity.

Roy came directly to the point as soon as they were both seated. He said, "I've developed an interest in the nation's aptitude tests and although I am not yet too clear in my own mind just what my possible investigations will consist of, I'd like to ask your cooperation."

"Our facilities are all yours," Plovdiv gushed. "Could I assign you an assistant? Someone to devote full time to your needs for as long as you require."

"Perhaps that would be a good idea," Roy said. "However, would you have the time, right now, for some preliminary questions I'd like to ask?"

"I'll be honored to make time, sir."

Roy continued thoughtfully. "Of course, in my field we are already acquainted with the nature of the aptitude tests. In fact, the Educational Sequence composes many of these. However, it has not been my own particular specialization and I would like to go further into the matter. Since at this time I am rather full of my own recent examinations, I think that might be a good point at which to begin."

Plovdiv pursed his lips. "Of course."

"Now I understand," Roy said, "the security involved in the Bureau of Records. Your discretion is justly famed."

Frol Plovdiv was expansive. "In your case, my dear Academician, ordinary precautions obviously won't apply, especially since you are aiming your researches in this direction."

Roy nodded his thanks. "Then I wonder if I could ask some questions about my own record?"

Plovdiv was already flicking a switch. "Ruth. A precis of Academician McCord's aptitude records. Immediately, Ruth."

The communicator said, "Immediately, Superintendent."

While they waited, Frol Plovdiv leaned back in his chair. "It's quite an honor to have an Academician in our city," he said.

Roy smiled wryly. "What is there to say to that? In the old days, to obtain the respect of his fellows, a man achieved something in whatever his field might be. Today, he periodically takes machine given tests and is acclaimed according to how some highly intricate computers grade him."

The Superintendent smiled. "The way you put it, the old system seems more reasonable."

"Of course, there are ramifications," Roy admitted. "In the old days, many a genius must have lived out his life in squalor, never to come in contact with the particular field in which his aptitudes lay." He added, musingly, "I wonder how many potential poets died in the textile slums of Birmingham while *Lord* Byron and *Baron* Shelley were able to pursue their art in security and even luxury."

"That's the point," Plovdiv nodded. "In the past, you might become a monarch of an Empire as large as England's simply because your father before you held the position. You might become a general, or an admiral, because your family wielded enough influence to send you to the nation's military academy. You might become head of a great industry, because you inherited wealth. You might attend one of the world's great universities simply because your family was born into a high status group."

Ruth entered at that point with a bound file and handed it to the Superintendent. She smiled awkwardly at Roy McCord, did everything short of dropping a curtsey, and returned to her own office.

Plovdiv laughed tolerantly. "I'm afraid you're quite the highest ranking citizen Ruth has ever seen, Academician. She'll probably ask for your autograph as you leave." He looked down at the papers before him. "Now then, what did you wish to know?"

Roy pursed his lips. "For instance, my Creative Ability records."

Plovdiv flicked pages. "Possibly you know, Creative Ability is rated on one of the older systems. Average is 100; 100 to 110 is Good; 110 to 120 is Very Good; 120 to 130 is Superior; 130 to 140 is Very Superior; and above 140 is Gifted. We don't particularly like the term genius, it has been widely misused."

"Um-m-m," Roy said. "And my rating?"

Plovdiv cleared his throat. "Theoretically, of course, this information shouldn't be available to you."

"Of course."

Plovdiv said, "It's your lowest rating, Academician McCord. You have a Creative Ability aptitude of 124."

"I see," Roy said. "And, ordinarily, suppose as a youth I had decided to go into the arts? To study, say, writing? Perhaps verse."

"With that aptitude, my dear sir, you would have had no difficulty whatsoever in beginning as an Apprentice Effective in the arts." He laughed sourly. "I would say that our aptitude tests are least accurate in this field. We do what we can, but we are continually betrayed when a great composition is written by someone with supposedly little aptitude for music, or a whole new school of painting developed by someone who our machines would contend should be putting second coats on barns."

Roy said slowly, "And my other grades?"

The Superintendent shrugged hugely. "My dear Academician, you are gifted in every other test we have devised."

"*Every* one?" Roy McCord was somewhat taken aback.

"You are quite a phenomenon," the other nodded.

"And how far back do the records you have there go?"

"Certainly you must know that your tests are from earliest childhood."

"And even then?"

"By your fourth year it was definitely seen that your case was quite unique and you ultimately due for the nation's highest honors."

"I see," Roy said. "Ah, I'd like to think further about this before going on. I wonder if I could take advantage of your earlier offer and have assigned to me a guide to take me about the establishment?"

"Immediately," Superintendent Plovdiv said. He flicked a switch again.

HE let the bright young Junior Supervisor give him the complete treatment. Up one corridor, down another. Through this department, through that. Down long banks of impressive, unbelievable looking machinery. Long files of punched cards, endless cans of tapes. Chattering automatic typers. Endless rows of Effective and Junior Effectives manually punching cards, reproducing them, interpreting them, sorting and collating them.

Roy McCord allowed himself the comments he assumed were standard. In fact, after an hour or two his guide had run the gauntlet from awe at the other's standing, to a slightly tolerant superiority. Each man to his own field, Roy thought wryly.

Finally, the new Academician said to the other, "I wonder if it would be possible for you to leave me on my own for a time?"

"On your own?" the Junior Supervisor said blankly.

Roy smiled at him. "I'd like to observe the Electives at work without them being so self-conscious. When they see you conducting me they freeze up. Obviously, I'm a—what was the old term?—VIP, being given the royal treatment!"

"I see what you mean," the guide said. "Well, let's see, the Superintendent said to treat anything you request as an order from him. I'll be in the cafeteria when you need me again."

"Fine," Roy said. "And thanks."

The other went off and Roy McCord took up his wanderings again. From time to time he made an inquiry from one of the Effectives.

Finally he found him.

"Hello, Dad," Roy said.

Warren McCord looked up from his work, startled. "Why, Roy. What are you doing here?

Roy said, "No use fencing around at this late date, Dad. I've discovered why you failed to retire almost ten years ago, when you were first eligible."

His father came to his feet, from the machine he'd been dabbling with, and cleaned his hands with a bit of waste. He looked at Roy warily.

"Oh?" he said.

Roy said, "I'm not going to ask you *how*, I assume I wouldn't understand even if you told me. I've seen enough here to realize that probably not one citizen in a thousand has even the faintest idea of the complexity of it all. But I would like to be sure I know *why.*"

Warren McCord said wearily, "I suppose I could say something stupid such as I don't know what you're talking about, but as you say, it's rather late in the game to fence around."

"But *why*? I think I know, I just want to be sure."

His father said, "I suppose I could blame it all on your mother, Son. Say that I did it all for her so that she'd enjoy the prestige I wasn't ever able to bring the family." The older man hesitated. "But that's not all. It was for me too. I worked hard to get no further than I am. But what was it Mrs. Worthington called me? A simple mechanic."

Roy said bitterly, "At least you deserve your rank, Senior Technician. It's not to be scorned. What do I really deserve, Dad?"

His father looked miserable. His eyes went to the floor. "Actually, your aptitudes are quite high, Roy. I wouldn't have dared to tinker, otherwise you would have been shown up."

Roy McCord took a deep breath and said tightly. "Just one thing. My Creative Aptitude. How do I rate there—really?"

His father scowled at him, his eyes still wary. "Actually, that's the one test I never messed with, Son. It's your highest. I figured if I made you a genius in *everything* it might look suspicious."

Roy McCord's face broke into a bloom of pleasure. "That's fine," he said, "that's just fine."

His father looked at him astonished.

Warren McCord began to gush an incoherent apology, but his boy took him firmly by the arm. "Listen, Dad, any confessions to the authorities at this point wouldn't accomplish anything, and might do a great deal of harm to innocent people—including mother. Now listen to me.

"Tomorrow I want you to apply for retirement. What you do then is up to you. You've really always wanted to spend your final years in the South. Possibly that's what you'll do."

"And you?" his father said anxiously.

"I'm going to drop out of the Education Sequence. Drop all my academic honors and make a new start. I'll tell you about it later." He grinned again at the old man. "Don't worry about it. I'm certainly not."

He started down the line of chattering I. B. M. machines, saying happily over his shoulder, "See you later, Dad. I've got some business."

NADINE looked up from her auto-typer and smiled her Nadine smile at him. "You were tight this morning, Academician McCord," she accused. "You didn't know what you were saying. Your mother must have had quite a celebration for you last night."

He said, "Not as big as the one you and I are going to have tonight, and the name is Roy."

"Ah, ha," she said, keeping it light. "So that's the question you decided to ask—have dinner with you. You can hardly expect a Senior Effective to be gallivanting around with an

Academician. What would people say? You'd be accused of pulling your rank to overwhelm a poor…"

Roy said, grinning mockingly at her, "That's why I'm resigning my Educational Sequence prerogatives. Tonight, at dinner, under the proper romantic setting, I'm going to propose to you. But I'm giving you fair warning, it's going to be a step-down for you. By that time, I'll be a lowly Apprentice Effective in the Creative Arts Sequence."

She blinked at him.

His face went thoughtful.

"We'll have to think about the honeymoon. What do you say the South Seas, or perhaps Greece? You know, I always wanted to see the Acropolis by moonlight."

Stowaway

The New Taos was headed into space for a year when the stowaway was discovered. As Lt. Norsen said, "Forty-five men and one woman—oh, no!"

LIEUTENANT Johnny Norsen, his lanky body sprawled uncomfortably in an acceleration chair, was playing Spartan rules with the darts, and paused only momentarily before each shot. Spartan rules were pretty Spartan, but in spite of the handicaps he hit the bull's eye six times out of six and grunted in disgust.

He complained, to no one in particular, "A swell game when we first brought it aboard. Now everybody is as good as it's possible to get. We might as well flush it overboard."

No one in particular happened to be Dick Roland, ship's navigator. He looked up from the onionskin, paper bound history he was reading. "Umm," he said vaguely. "Maybe we could toughen up the rules."

"How?" Norsen grumbled. "They're as tough already as it's possible to get them. We'd have to close both eyes, or something." He shifted in his chair, yawned and recrossed his legs. "What in the *kert* are you reading?"

"Decline and Fall of the United States. Ancient history. What do you think of it?" The navigator was young, rather handsome in an easy-going sort of way, but almost colorless in his lack of aggressiveness.

Norsen yawned again. "I don't like history, so I've only read the book four or five times." He looked up at the earth time chrono on the wall. "Let's crack today's video-news."

Dick Roland followed his eyes. "We've still got five minutes to go," he protested mildly.

The other was irritated. "Five minutes, ten minutes, what's the difference? Today is today. It's not as though we were cracking next week's news. Besides, I think Doc Thorndon's crazier than a *makron*. What difference does it make when we show a news wire?"

He knew the answer to his own question as well as anyone else in the *New Taos*, but it was something to talk about.

Dick Roland said, "I think it's a good idea. Keeps us interested in things. Every day we can look forward to getting the news. Sure, it's a full year old, but that doesn't make any difference to us. *We* haven't heard it yet. Doc Thorndon says it's one way of keeping space cafard from hitting the crew—something new every day, something to look forward to."

Norsen screwed up his angular face. "Where'd Doc get the idea, anyway? We never did it before."

Dick closed his history and tossed it to the wardroom table. He'd read it half a dozen times already, himself. He said, "You know Doc. Always reading those old books. From what he says, back in ancient times they used to pull the same idea—weather station men who were stuck up in the Artic and snowed in for maybe six months at a crack. They'd have a file of newspapers on hand, and each day they'd take one off the top. The news was exactly one year old, but it didn't make any difference to them. They hadn't read it before and so it was as fresh as though it'd just happened. When their supplies came in, in the Spring, they'd get another batch of papers."

Lieutenant Norsen looked up at the chrono again. "Well, it's time now. Let's crack today's. I want to see if there's anything on Jackie Black. It's about time for him to pull one of his jobs again. That little makron is sure giving the S. S. B. I. a run for their credits."

Dick Roland was on his feet and getting the video-news wire from its built-in file. "Umm," he said. "Most effective criminal for the past century. If he keeps on making haul after haul, he ought to be set for life pretty soon."

Ensign Mart Bakr, his chubby face questioning, and his mouth still working on some tidbit or other, hurried through the wardroom door. "Haven't started the video-wire yet have—" He saw they were about to run it and interrupted himself. "Good," he said, and slumped into a chair.

"Be ready in a second," Dick Roland told him.

"Good. By the way, you fellows hear the news?"

They weren't particularly interested. There *wasn't* any news that could develop on a space cruiser on a year long trip.

He said, nonchalantly, "Commander Gurloff thinks he'll turn around and head back home."

They spun on him. *"What!"*

He grinned at their excitement. "April Fool!"

They stared at him, then their eyes went to each other, questioningly.

Doctr Thorndon entered the tiny officer's mess and wardroom just in time to pick up the end of the conversation. He said soothingly, "Never mind, boys, he's not down with cafard. It's a joke."

"A joke?" Johnny Norsen grumbled. "Why the fat little *makron* had Dick and me believing him for a minute. What's this about April something or other?"

Doc Thorndon settled into a chair. He was a cheerful, roly-poly man, his cheeks still pink but his hair thinning and graying. He was about forty-five—old for the space service.

"April Fool," he said. "It's a time-honored jest. By the ancient calendar there was a day in the Terran year during which persons played practical jokes on each other. When the victim became indignant, the perpetrator merely called out *April Fool!* and the other was forced to admit himself duped."

They still didn't quite get it. Doc Thorndon added, patiently, "If we were still following the old calendar, this would be April 1st. All Fool's Day, as they called it."

Dick Roland said, "Well, anyway, here's the video-news for *last* April Fool's Day." He dimmed the room's lights and flashed the video wire on the wall so that everyone could read.

Over an hour later, he said, "Should we run it again now, or should we wait another couple of hours."

"Three times is enough," Johnny Norsen said. "We'll get tired of it, otherwise. Remember, it's another twenty-four hours until we get another one. Let's sit around and discuss it for awhile."

"Yeah," Mart Bakr said. The chubby third officer shook his head in reluctant admiration. "Did you see that item about Jackie Black? They almost got him there on Calypso, but he's too slick for them."

Johnny Norsen grunted contemptuously. "I don't think that was him at all. Too big, for one thing. I wouldn't be surprised if Black was still on Earth. They've been reporting him on every planet and satellite in the system, but I'll bet he never left Neuve Los Angeles, where he pulled his last—"

"Caper," Doc Thorndon said.

The other three looked at him. "His what?" Bakr asked.

"His caper," the doctr repeated, pleased with himself. "It's a new word I ran into today. Criminals used to call a crime a *caper.*"

Dick Roland shook his head and grinned. "What a hobby. Prehistoric slang."

There was a gentle knock at the wardroom door and the four of them looked up at the messman who stood there, somewhat nervous at being in officer's country.

"Yes, Spillane?" Johnny Norsen said.

The messman cleared his throat. "Could you tell me where the skipper is, sir?"

"I think he's sleeping, Spillane. What is it?"

"Well, sir. Well...there's a stowaway on board." He cleared his throat again and said, "We found her in the number eight compartment." His eyes went from one to the other of them. He added, decisively, "Yes, sir."

Doc Thorndon was the first to explode. "Her!" he blurted.

Mart Bakr started suddenly to laugh. His chuckle swelled into a roar and the others turned to stare at him in his turn. He was finally able to get out, "April Fool! We all bit again. *April Fool!*"

Spillane looked blank.

The faces of the others relaxed. Even the angular features of Johnny Norsen twisted themselves in a wry grin. He said, "You certainly caught us, Spillane."

The messman looked anxiously from one of the ship's officers to the other. "Yes, sir," he said. "What?"

Johnny Norsen scowled and said, "Run along now, Spillane. It was a good joke. Congratulations."

"Joke, sir? What joke?"

Doc Thorndon had settled back into his chair now. "Oh, come along, Spillane. We—"

A new voice pitched low, and somewhat timid, said from the doorway, "Could I come in, now?"

Johnny Norsen was facing the other way. He didn't turn to look at her for a full minute. Instead, he closed his eyes and muttered in pain, "Oh, *no*. Forty-five men and one woman in a ship that's to be in space for twelve months!"

SHE wasn't beautiful, nor even pretty, as current tastes went—but she had something, very definitely. She was about five-foot-five and probably in her middle twenties. Her attractiveness lay in a certain *eagerness*, a brightness, an interest in what was going on about her, no matter what it might be. Yes, she had something, very definitely. It was hard to put your finger on it.

Right now, she was attired in a simple sports dress, wrinkled and somewhat soiled from her period in hiding among the supplies in compartment eight. Her eyes went nervously from one to the other of them and she self consciously brushed her clothes, avoiding her breasts and hips, as though not wishing to bring her sex to their attention.

Johnny Norsen blurted, "Holy Jumping *Wodo* Miss! Do you know where you are?"

She looked down at the steel deck, toeing in like a little girl who'd been caught at something naughty. Her voice was very low, "Yes, sir," she whispered.

"Oh, you do, eh?" Norsen rasped.

Mart Bakr spoke for the first time since the apparition had appeared. "Don't pick on her, Norsen," he said truculently. "Can't you see the poor kid's scared?"

The first officer spun on him. "Scared?" he said bitterly. "We're the ones that ought to be scared." He turned back to the girl. "Come on, miss. Let's go see the captain."

Mart Bakr and Dick Roland, the latter's eyes still popping, started to follow into the corridor. Johnny Norsen grunted, "You two had better stay here. This many of us can't crowd into the skipper's quarters." He added, sarcastically, "Besides, it's probably going to be a trifle hot in there."

He made no protest when Doctr Thorndon followed and the three of them, ship's first officer, stowaway, and ship's doctr made a procession down the corridor past a score of open-mouthed crewmembers.

"Oh, brother, a dame on board," a jetman muttered happily.

"Knock it off, Johnson," the first officer snapped in irritation over his shoulder.

They rapped at the Captain's cubbyhole, which doubled as his living quarters and the space cruiser's office. A voice from within growled, "What the *kert* is it?"

Norsen fingered the door release and entered, followed by the two others.

There was a flat silence that Johnny Norsen broke by saying dryly, "A stowaway, sir. The crew found her in the number eight compartment."

Commander Mike Gurloff had been relaxed on his bunk, staring unseeingly at the overhead. Now he spun around and came to an elbow, blinking.

"Holy Jumping *Wodo*!" he blurted.

"Yes, sir," Norsen said. "That's what I said. Probably the first female stowaway on a military craft since the beginning of inter-galactical warfare." He added, as though anyone needed reminding, "A year long cruise—forty-five men and one woman."

Doc Thorndon closed the door behind them. He said, softly, "We're only three days out, Mike." He was the only man aboard who habitually called the burly commander by his first name. "We could turn back."

The skipper brought his feet around to the floor and sat up. He stared at the girl, almost vacantly, then lowered his shaven head into his hands. He was a big man and toughened by the long years in the space service that had seen him rise to the position of the outstanding ship's officer of his generation. He sat there like that for a full five minutes.

Finally he took a deep breath and brought his eyes up to her. "What is your name, Miss?" Then he cleared his throat and said, more gently, "Don't be afraid. What's your name?"

"It's Kathleen...sir." She added, after swallowing, "They call me Kathy."

He continued to look at her, and she said, nervously, "Kathleen Westley."

"All right, Miss Westley. Now tell us about it." He indicated the swivel chair at the desk, the only chair in the tiny room. "You might as well sit down."

She sat in the chair, knees together and her hands in her lap, and looked less frightened now.

Gurloff said, "Tell us about it."

She swallowed once mare and said, "I don't see why women aren't allowed in the Space Service." There was an edge of defiance in her voice.

Doc Thorndon said softly, "There are various reasons, Miss. Some of them medical, especially in inter-galactical travel."

"Well. I don't see—"

Commander Gurloff said, "It doesn't make much difference right at the moment, does it? What are you doing aboard my ship, Miss Westley?" His face was expressionless, almost as though he was too tired to care.

She tossed her head infinitesimally, and her lower lip protruded. "I...I've always wanted to be a space...well, a *spaceman.*"

Inadvertently, Gurloff's eyes took in her full breast, her rounded hips. He said, wryly, "I'm afraid something went wrong with your ambitions twenty-five or so years ago."

The girl flushed, but her face remained defiant.

Doctr Thorndon said, "To make it short, Miss Westley, do we understand that you stowed away on this vessel to prove that women are quite as suitable for space travel as are men?"

Her mouth tightened stubbornly and she nodded.

Commander Gurloff asked, "And did you know that this vessel was to be in space for a period of over a year, Miss? A year is rather a long time."

Her eyes widened at that. "A...a year?"

Gurloff grunted, suddenly weary of the interview. He said, "Mr. Norsen, take our...our passenger back to the officer's mess. I suppose she's hungry." He thought it over briefly. "She can have the second and third officer's stateroom. One of them can bunk with you, the other in the ship's hospital." His mouth tightened. "See that the lock on the door is in good repair and that she has a key."

The skipper's eyes went back to the girl. He said, "Later—we're going to have lots of time, Miss Westley—later, you can give us any further details about your decision to become a...a spaceman." He motioned with his head and Johnny Norsen took her by the arm to lead her out.

Gurloff said, "Do you mind staying a while, Doctr?"

After the first officer and the girl had left, Doc Thorndon sank into the chair she had vacated. He waited for the other to speak.

Commander Mike Gurloff sank prone on the bed again and his eyes focused on a rivet in the overhead. He said, "Possibly she's the straw."

"The one that broke the camel's back, eh?"

Gurloff said, "Doc, have you wondered why we've been sent out on a cruise less than two weeks after the last one? Out on a cruise that'll take over a year? A *year!* And half of my men on the verge of space cafard after finishing the last trip."

Doctr Thorndon nodded and rubbed the end of his nose with a forefinger. He said, "No. I haven't wondered. I know the reason, Mike. By the way, did *you* know that they sent us off in such a hurry that our supplies of books, games, music wires, video-wires—all of our means of entertainment, in short—were 'accidentally' not replenished? Nothing, that is, except last year's news wires."

Mike Gurloff's eyes came around to him and his lips thinned back over his teeth.

Doc Thorndon nodded again. "The men are reading books that they've already read a dozen times over; playing games they're sick and tired of; seeing video-shows they've already memorized. They'll never get through the full year, Mike. Cafard will have us in less than six months."

The skipper's face went blank again and he stared vacantly at the overhead.

Doc Thorndon said, "They've got you this time, I'm afraid, Mike."

Gurloff bit out stubbornly. "The crew is with me. We're the proudest ship in the fleet. We've got a record that's the envy of the solar system. We'll—"

The doctr shook his head. "I'm afraid you're going to have to turn back, Mike. I can't guarantee this crew's mental health for a period of a year."

Gurloff held a hand up, clenched the fist. "We've *got* to make it!"

He came to his elbow again, faced the other. "I've got them this time, Doc, if we can just make this trip. Don't you see? The filthy *makrons* can't stand outspoken criticism. They hate the popularity I've been accumulating with the public. I've become the spokesman for the opposition, and they've tried to keep me quiet by a series of cruises that seemed impossible to succeed. They've sent the *New Taos* to spots that required a full fleet, and we came back with the information they wanted. They sent us on assignments impossible to achieve, and we achieved them. And each time we won out, we gained that much more of the public's approval."

Doc Thorndon allowed a half smile to touch his mouth. "Sure, "Mike. And each time we returned from a cruise, you made a withering speech against the powers that be, against the present administration. And, each time, they've pulled the same trick; they've sent you out on another long cruise to get you away from Solar System politics. Each time they figured to be rid of you—and this time, Mike. I'm afraid they've won."

"No!"

"Yes."

The skipper glared at him.

Doc Thorndon held his palms up in a hopeless gesture. "If you try to complete the trip, your whole crew will be down with cafard in months. If you return, before completing your assignment they'll have a legitimate excuse for court martialing you." His voice went gentler now. "Personally, Mike, I'd stick it out with you. I'm behind what you stand for. I think every man on the ship is also. But—"

Gurloff said, in sudden enthusiasm, "I'll give them a talk over the inter-communication system. I'll explain the whole thing. Let them know why we've been discriminated against like this. Why we've been sent out repeatedly, without sufficient rest periods between."

Thorndon rubbed the end of his nose again and scowled. "You'll do nothing of the sort, Mike. At first, they'd all be with you. But, as the months went by and as the grief piled up, they'd begin, subconsciously, at first, to see that it was you alone who was bringing such strain upon them. There'd be too much of that strain, finally, Mike. They'd turn on you."

Gurloff slumped back into his bunk and thought about it. "They'll know sooner or later anyway," he growled. "You said that we've got a full year's supply of news wires on board. It won't be long before somebody runs off that one telling about my last speech, just before we left. Then they'll know why the *New Taos* was sent out again so soon. That is, if they don't know already. Maybe somebody heard the talk, or read about it, while they were ashore."

Doc Thorndon grinned. "I doubt if anybody heard it except me. They were all too busy wine, women, and songing, to listen to speeches. And I took care of the wires. I've made arrangements so that the Video-news wires are run off one a day. The cruise will almost be over before they come to that speech of yours." His face soured again. "But the point is, Mike, that we're not going to last that long. Even if this girl…"

He broke off and stared at the other. Finally he said, slowly, "You know, Mike, maybe we're wrong. Maybe she's not the straw that broke the camel's back. Maybe she's a second backbone for the poor beast."

Gurloff scowled over at him. "I don't get you, Doc."

"You will, Mike. You will. Maybe we'll be able to take this next twelve months, after all." The Doctr licked his upper lip, thoughtfully. "I think I'll just go and see Miss…see Kathy, now. I've got some things I want to talk over with her."

THE conversation between Doc Thorndon and Kathy had been a lengthy one, and the officers and crew of the space cruiser *New Taos* would have been surprised at the ship's doctr they thought they knew so well for his gentle kindliness. In fact, it could hardly be described as a conversation at all, since it started as an argument and wound up as a series of commands none too softly spoken.

Doc Thorndon shook his finger at her, not disguising his irritation.

"You just think you can't sing. Let me tell you, you can *sing*. Can and will! Just remember, you've the only feminine voice on board. To a man, a woman's voice sounds better than any masculine one—particularly after a few weeks in space, not to speak of months. *Any* woman's voice."

Kathy had her eyes on the floor and her lower lip was out in what was almost a pout. "I don't see why—"

Thorndon grunted, "You don't have to see why. I'll do the seeing why, and the thinking, Kathy. I've let it go out over the ship that we are to have a...a *show* in about a month. The men are already spending almost full time in preparation. They're making costumes, arranging scenery, composing songs. It's keeping them busy. Busy, understand?" He paused momentarily, realizing that she didn't know just how important that was.

He finished with, "We've made an agreement, Kathy. Now let's stick to it."

She said, stubbornly, "I still say I can't sing, and, what's more, I've never done any acting."

"You've got a month to learn," Doc said sharply.

Kathy twisted in her chair, shrugged her shoulders. "Seems to me," she pouted, "the doctr on this ship is more important than the captain."

His mouth remained expressionless and she didn't know him well enough to see the amusement in his eyes. He said, "Believe me, Kathy, on a ship faced with space cafard, he *is*."

KATHY sat at the small table in the officer's wardroom and eyed the three of them severely. She said, "Johnny, Dick, Martie—I won't have any more of this bickering. Either you'll be nice, or I'm not going to...to put up with it. I'll go in and talk with Commander Gurloff for the next two hours, and then the officer's share of the day will be through."

Mart Bakr flashed an irritated glance at the lanky Johnny Norsen. "It's his fault," he grumbled. "He wants you to himself all the time. I thought it'd be a good idea if we went into the galley and whipped up some taffy or—"

Johnny Norsen was on his feet. "Why you chunky little chow hound. I'll—"

Mart Bakr jumped up to face him, his face livid, "Don't you call me names, you long legged *makron!*"

"*Please!*" Kathy breathed, putting her hands over her ears.

The usually easy going Dick Roland reddened angrily. "Watch your language, Bakr," he snapped.

JAK HEMING, Space Rifleman, 2nd Class, hurried down the corridor and into the crew's mess, bearing his invaluable burden importantly. He looked about the compartment in surprise.

"Where the *kert* is everybody?" he said. Only three others were present.

Taylor was nearest the door. He stuck his head out, looked up and down the passageway outside. "Any braid around?" he asked.

Heming shook his head. "The officers are all up forward. Just gave me the video-news wire for today. Holy *Wodo*. I expected everybody off watch to be waiting here for it."

Taylor said, "We got *two* shows today, Jak. And everybody but us four is watching the second one."

Heming didn't get it. Scowling questioningly at them, he went to the projector and began to insert the wire.

Woodford, 1st Signalman, explained. "Rosen and Johnson are having it out with stun guns down in the tract-torpedo room."

The space rifleman stared. "A fight! You mean that they're having a fight?"

Taylor said, "That's right." He seemed pleased about it. "A fight it is. The screwy *makrons* got into an argument about Kathy and they decided to have it out. The Doc is refereeing the thing. He made 'em turn the stun guns down so they can't hurt each other too much."

"Doc Thorndon?" That was as surprising as the fact that a fight was taking place at all. "That doesn't sound like the Doc; he's the one that usually cools everything off."

"Let's see the wire," Woodford complained. "Now that I think about it, I'm sorry I didn't go down and see the fight. It's just that I can't wait to see whether or not they got this Jackie Black yet." He shook his head in reluctant admiration. "Now, there's a guy for you. Slick as they come, and tough as they come, too."

Taylor added, "They'll get him. Just wait and see. The Solar System Bureau of Investigation gets them all, sooner or later. They'll—"

Heming snapped, "Like kert they will! You just never hear about the guys they *don't* catch, they don't give them no publicity. Ten credits says they haven't caught Black by the time we end this here trip."

Taylor said sourly, "You know gambling isn't allowed in space."

"Put up, or shut up. I say they won't catch Jackie Black by the time we get back."

Taylor flushed angrily. "All right, all right. I'll just take that."

"Let's see the wire and knock off all this argument," somebody else put in.

The news video began to flash and they lapsed into silence.

IN THE brief darkness of the shadow of a space rifle, Mart Bakr whispered hurriedly, urgently, "I could come to your room later, while Dick is on watch and while Johnny Norsen is sleeping. We—"

"Why, Martie," she said scoldingly, but keeping her voice low, "I...I think you're insulting me."

He protested, vehemently as possible in his whisper.

ON WATCH in the control room Petersen said to Ward, "You know, when she first came aboard, that is, when we first caught her, Kathy didn't look so good to me. Nice girl, you know, but not what I'd call pretty. But these last six months with her being the only gal on board—"

Ward said coldly, "Just what do you mean, Petersen?"

The other shrugged. "You know, like that old, old gag they used to tell about the soldiers in New Guinea in the second—or was it the third or fourth?—World War. The one soldier'd say to the other one, 'You know, the longer I'm here the less black they look to me.'"

Ward spun him around and grasped his coverall front. He bit out between his teeth, "Listen, you *makron*, you're talking about *Kathy*, understand! Watch your damned mouth!"

KATHY, Doc Thorndon, Mart Bakr, Johnny Norsen and Dick Roland sat in the officer's wardroom, preparatory to showing that day's news wire. In spite of the importance of this one break in the day's monotony, the eyes of all three of the younger men were on the girl.

Used, by this time, to the attention, Kathy was able to ignore it. She said, "Just who is this Jackie Black that you're always talking about?"

"The last of the Robin Hoods," Doc Thorndon said softly.

"Robin Hoods?" she frowned.

"Bet you five credits it's something he dug up out of one of his old books," Johnny Norsen snorted.

"You'd win then," Doc said. He turned his face to Kathy to explain. "The original Robin Hood was an outlaw who robbed from the rich but gave to the poor—a very long time ago. Since then, every time a bandit makes a practice of being kind to the poor, they've called him a Robin Hood." He added, dry of voice, "Very seldom do they deserve the name."

She was interested. "Oh? Well, does this…what was his name, again…?"

"Jackie Black," Mart Bakr offered. As usual, he was sitting on the edge of his chair, eyes riveted on the girl to the point that should have caused acute embarrassment.

She went on, "Yes, this Jackie Black—that's a silly name, isn't it? Does he deserve the name, Robin Hood?"

Doc Thorndon shrugged, wrinkling up his cheerful face. "I suppose you'd say he does. Probably the principal reason he's eluded the authorities far so long. He has had considerable support from the rank and file citizens."

Johnny Norsen said, "Well, what is it that he got this time? They've got half the police of three planets on his trail and as far as I can understand, all he stole were some papers."

Dick Roland said, "I heard some rumors, just before we left Terra, that the papers were inside dope an a bunch of the bureaucrats—really incriminating. The story is that Jackie Black figures on blackmailing them."

Doc Thorndon grunted. "Doesn't sound like the sort of thing he'd do. Blackmail is a pretty nasty business."

Mart Bakr said, "Well, let's get on with this news wire. Maybe they've caught him by now."

SHE was on her way to the crew's mess but Roland found time to slip a note into her hand, flushing furiously as he did. She winked, infinitesimally, but hurried her way past him.

His heart thumped over twice, then curled up in its corner and glowed heat. Did that wink mean…?

Kathy entered the crew's mess and smiled at the assembled men who were off duty.

"All right," she said cheerfully, "it's your day—or night, whatever it is—who can tell on a space ship? What shall we do this time, boys? Do you want to draw lots to see who plays cards with me?"

One of the spacemen growled, "I don't see why the officers get your company the same amount of time we do. There's five of them and forty of us. It ain't fair."

She looked at him in mock reproach. "Why don't you get up a petition?"

Woodford muttered, "On a space cruiser, on a mission? They'd string us up by the thumbs."

Kathy tossed her head and laughed at him. "You see. You don't really care. My company isn't nearly as important to you as you'd make believe."

Jak Heming scrambled to his feet and faced the rest. "She's right! Why don't we? Why should forty of us have to share her time equally with only five? It's not as though this was an ordinary situation. How often do you have women aboard a space ship? I say, let's all sign a petition. We should have Kathy's company six days out of the week, they, only once."

"Boys, boys," she laughed.

But they continued to mutter among themselves and the sounds of their voices went higher.

THERE was an almost inaudible knock at the door.

"Who's there?" Kathy called.

"It's me."

There was silence for a moment, then, "Just a moment— *me*."

By the time she opened the door, he was glancing fearfully up and down the corridor. He slipped in.

"Why, Johnny."

"*Darling!*" He reached for her but she avoided him as adroitly as possible in the tiny quarters.

"'Why, Johnny Norsen. You know you're not allowed in here. What would Commander Gurloff say? Besides, I thought you were the one who was so sorry to see me on board."

He was hurried, but emphatic. "Look, darling, Kathy. I didn't know then. I…"

Her eyes were mocking.

He held out a hand. "This ring. It was my mother's…I…I want you to wear it." His angular face was very intent and very sincere.

Her eyes widened now. "Why, Johnny—"

"Listen, sweetheart. I know these aren't the circumstances. That nothing could…well, develop here in the ship. But when we return, when we're back on Terra again. I'm going to give up the space service and we can—"

She interrupted him with a finger on his lips. Her eyes were on the floor now so that he couldn't see the glint of amusement, but she said softly, "I'll…I'll keep the ring, Johnny. We can talk about it when…when we're back again. No, you'd better go." She avoided his arms again. "Everybody would be angry if they knew you'd been in here."

After he'd gone, she put the ring in a small drawer—with a dozen others.

THE sick call was almost daily growing in magnitude and Doc Thorndon didn't like it. Not a bit. The cruise still had half way to go. He was amazed that they'd hung on this far, actually, but six months was still too long a period to stretch before them.

He applied various tests to the last of his callers and then flicked a stylus against his teeth in irritation as he considered the findings.

Rosen said, worriedly, "What is it Doc? Not…not cafard, is it, Doc?"

Thorndon looked down at him and laughed gently. "Ever had even a touch of cafard, Rosen?"

"Well, no sir. But I saw a man with it once." Rosen's eyes went nervously about the ship's hospital. The room was about the size of a bedroom of a Pullman of the 20th Century. It had two bunks, one above the other, a tiny folding table, a medicine chest built into the titanium alloy wall, a lavatory.

Doc Thorndon chuckled. "Don't worry. You'll know it when you get space cafard."

Rosen shuddered. "Yes, sir. I know. The fear of black space. The terror of free fall. Complete, berserk hysteria." The little crewman's eyes went empty.

Doc patted him on the shoulder. "Forget about it, Rosen. Haven't you heard? There hasn't been a case of cafard on this ship since I've been ship's doctr." His face tightened subtly. "By the way, what's this I hear about some of you crew members tapping the tract-torpedoes for alcohol and brewing up some jungle juice?"

The crewman was surprised. He hadn't heard about it. But he came to his feet and began shrugging back into his coveralls. He said, warily, "Where'd you hear this, Doc?"

Thorndon laughed cheerfully. "Never mind, and don't worry about it, Rosen. In fact, it wouldn't hurt you to try a little of it. Get your mind off your worries."

Rosen looked at him, shocked. Nothing was more taboo in space than drinking.

"Get on with you," Doc laughed and shooed him from the room.

After the other was gone, the doctr sank down to the side of the bunk and emptied his lungs in a sigh, which touched on despair. *Six more months to go.*

Kathy put her head in the door and said, "Doctr Thorndon?"

He looked up. "Come on in, Kathy. I'm through for the day and I have some suggestions for you."

She entered and closed the door behind her. She leaned back against it and looked at him thoughtfully, and once again he reminded himself that she wasn't attractive—really. It was her aggressive personality, that and her obvious femininity. You seldom saw mammary glands like… He pulled his mind away from that trend of thought. Doc was masculine too, and not *that* old.

"Well, Kathy?" he said wearily.

She said, "I think I've finally figured out just what you're doing."

"You have? Well, I'm not surprised. You're not a very stupid person, Kathy." He didn't look up as he talked. "How many of them have proposed to you this week?"

"Four. Lieutenant Roland, and three more of the crew members."

He snorted, amusedly. "I'll wager you'll have hooked two thirds of them before the cruise is over." The amusement left him. "*If* it's ever over."

She said, very softly, "It's even more than usually important that the ship get back, isn't it?"

He looked up at her, without speaking.

She said, "I've been picking up odds and ends, here and there. I don't know too much about politics, but from what the crew says, and the officers too, for that matter, Commander Mike Gurloff is pretty big potatoes in reform politics back on Terra."

Doc rubbed the end of his nose with a thoughtful forefinger and wondered just how much to tell her.

She said, "It's pretty important that he get back, isn't it?"

Doc Thorndon said slowly, "More than just get back, Kathy. He's got to return with his reputation as strong as ever. He's got to be able to throw into their faces just what tricks the present administration has been pulling on him."

She sank into the one chair the room boasted. "Are we going to make it?"

Doc pursed his lips. Finally he said, "The odds are against it, Kathy."

They sat silently for awhile.

Doc took a deep breath. "By the way, Kathy. I just had Rosen in here, you know, the signalman. He's in the first stages of cafard. He doesn't know it yet, but he is."

Air hissed through her teeth.

He nodded, seriously. "We've got to snap him out of it, but quick. One bad case and it'd spread through this ship like wildfire. Now this is what you'll have to do…"

She listened very carefully and nodded. The two of them looked like a pair of conspirators, leaning toward each other, their faces very serious.

COMMANDER GURLOFF looked up and down the corridor, spotted no one and slipped into the ship's hospital. He closed the door and turned to Doc Thorndon who was lying on the bottom bunk reading.

Doc looked up from his book and said, "Hello, Mike. Have a seat."

Mike Gurloff scowled at him, but lowered himself into the indicated chair.

He said, "Doc, what the *kert* are you trying to do with my ship and crew? The whole command is falling apart."

Doc Thorndon put a finger in his place. "Oh?" he said.

"Yeah, *oh*. Don't act so innocent." Gurloff hesitated, then went into the matter that bothered him in some detail. "Doc," he said, "You've always had a lot of leeway on the *New Taos*. Of course, it's not just the *New Taos*; any ship's doctr on any spacecraft on a long cruise has lots of leeway— as much as he needs to fight off the threat of space cafard.

Maybe you've had a bit more than most, but maybe that's because you've accomplished more than most."

The doctr reminded him softly, "We haven't had a serious case of cafard since I've been aboard, Mike."

In an earlier age, Commander Gurloff would have knocked on wood. Now he shuddered. "All right," he said, "I'll take that. But this time, Doc, I'm afraid you're going too far. What's this about stun gun fights between crewmembers down in the tract-torpedo room? What's this about gambling going on, more or less openly, and the crew being on the verge of mutiny because of Kathy? What's this about Mart Bakr and Dick Roland starting a fistfight in the wardroom the other day? And Rosen going on duty soused to the eyeballs?" His voice became more incisive. "Discipline aboard this ship is falling apart, Doc. And, to my surprise, I seem to find your fine meddlesome finger in every case I note that's adding to this collapse."

The doctr nodded, "That's right," he said agreeably.

"*That's right?*" Gurloff blurted. "What do you mean? I come in here expecting you to have some explanations of your actions and here you merely say it's true, that everything I've accused you of is true."

"It is," the Doctr said mildly.

"That you're inciting the crew to mutiny, that you're encouraging fighting and drink, that—"

"Yes," the Doctr said.

Gurloff blinked at him. Stared for a moment. Then came to his feet. He stood, looking down at the other, the back of his hands on his hips. He was incredulous.

He snapped, "Doctr, you realize that a crew without discipline is incapable of running a ship?"

"Let us say that it's incapable of running a ship indefinitely."

"And you say that you're deliberately encouraging a collapse of half the rules in the service?"

Doc sat up, putting his feet on the deck. He said, very seriously, "Mike, how long have we been out thus far?"

The other scowled. "Somewhat over six months."

"How many cases of space cafard, so far?"

The answer was a growled "None."

"Without books, without games, without any entertainment, for all practical purposes, we're through half of this cruise without one case of mental collapse, and that in spite of the fact that the crew had less than two weeks rest after the last trip."

Mike Gurloff leaned back against the bulkhead and scowled at him. "You mean you're preventing cafard by—"

Doc Thorndon leveled a finger at his skipper. "I'm preventing the complete collapse of this crew by every method I can devise. I can tell you right now, *if* we ever get back to Terra, this crew as a unit, will probably never be fit to take a ship out again. It was you, Mike, who said we had to make the cruise; you said that if you could make it you'd be in a position to upset the corrupt bunch of bureaucrats that are running the space service now.

"All right, Mike Gurloff. I believe in you. I'm trying to get this ship back before it turns into an asylum of howling, raving maniacs. It's taking every dirty deal, every little trick, every bit of double dealing I can think of to keep monotony and boredom, the breeding ground of cafard, from setting in."

"Including using that girl, Kathy, to keep the men in a continual dither?"

"Definitely! She's my best weapon."

Mike Gurloff thrust his hands into his tunic packets and stared, unseeingly, at the medicine chest. He muttered,

"There's one other thing, Doc, that I hadn't thought of before."

"Yes?"

"It's true that the *New Taos* has become the most popular craft in the fleet. Why?"

Doc Thorndon said indignantly, "For good reason! In the past two or three years it's made at least four cruises with outstanding success against the Kradens. Every time the *New Taos* returns from a cruise, it has a victory to report. Why—"

"Every time but this time, Doc," Gurloff said wearily. "And how long does a hero remain in the public eye when he slacks off an his heroism?"

Thorndon frowned.

Gurloff said, "Doc, this time they've sent us off on a year's cruise into empty space. There's nothing in this direction. No enemy, no galaxy that we'll reach. No nothing. When we return—after a full year of being out of the news— we'll have nothing to report." He thought it over for a minute. "I wouldn't be surprised if the powers that be so time it that just about when the *New Taos* berths, some other ship, with a skipper and crew more amenable to the present administration, hits the headlines with some outstanding deed. Just you watch."

He turned on his heel, mumbled a farewell, and left. Mike Gurloff was beginning to show both his age and the accumulated bitterness of years of having his career thwarted.

Doc Thorndon gazed after him, and rubbed the end of his nose with a thoughtful forefinger. "I hadn't thought of that angle," he said out loud.

IT WAS the traditional toast of the officers of a space ship after a successful cruise, held in the ship's wardroom only moments after landing and immediately before opening the hatches.

Commander Mike Gurloff had brought the bottle of Stone Age brandy from his quarters and was filling the glasses. He said, spiritlessly, "Where's Doc Thorndon? If anybody is to be given credit for bringing us through this time, it's him."

"Saw him just a few minutes before landing. He was talking with Kathy," Johnny Norsen said.

"Well, let's get about it, gentlemen," Gurloff growled. He took up his glass and eyed them, one by one, "My last cruise, gentlemen," he said, his mouth a straight line.

They stood there, holding their glasses, their eyes widening.

He said tightly, "Surprised, gentlemen? What could you expect? It's either that or they'd have this craft out into space in another week or so. —And this time, we *wouldn't* come back."

They said nothing. There was nothing to say. Each took down the drink, stiff wristed. Then they set their glasses down on the small table.

Dick Roland flushed noticeably and said, "As a matter of fact, sir, the same goes for me."

All eyes went to the second officer.

"Don't be ridiculous," Mike Gurloff rapped. "Your career has just started."

Dick Roland squared his shoulders and said, "Kathy and I are going to be married and—"

"*What!*" Johnny Norsen blurted, angrily. "Are you trying to make a fool of—"

"Marry *you?*" Mart Bakr yelled. "Kathy and I are engaged. *I'm* the one that's quitting the space service and—"

Johnny Norsen spun on him, then back to Roland. "Is this supposed to be some stupid joke?" he bit out. "Kathy and I are—"

Gurloff was looking from one to the other of them in utter astonishment.

"Boys, boys," a voice from behind them said softly. They turned, each still sputtering his indignation. It was Doc Thorndon.

"In the first place," he said mildly, "polyandry is still illegal on Terra and the latest statistics show that Jackie—that is, Kathy—is engaged to forty-three of this ship's complement of forty-five officers and men."

There were four different ejaculations, but he went on. "And, in the second place, in spite of his capable disguise over the past year, Jackie Black is a very masculine character, and I doubt if he'd be interested in marriage—not to anybody of the male sex."

They were dumb. It was just too much to assimilate.

Doc Thorndon handed an envelope to Commander Gurloff. "Jackie Black thinks you'll be able to use these documents in your next speech, Mike. You didn't bring home your usual victory, perhaps, but you'll draw your usual attention!" He rubbed the end of his nose with a forefinger and grinned, cheerfully. "When he saw what a hornet's nest he'd awakened when he swiped them, he could figure only one way of avoiding the regiments of police on his trail—he stowed away on a craft scheduled to be off in space for a year's time. His disguise as a woman went still further in preventing his identity from being guessed."

Gurloff was thumbing through a sheaf of papers in the envelope. "You mean, that all along he planned to hand these over to someone who would expose—"

Doc shrugged. "I don't know, Mike. Maybe not. But I think that little story about Robin Hood rather appealed to him. Besides, I was rather persuasive, just before he left the ship."

The Doctr turned to go.

"Just a minute," Gurloff snapped, his face dark. "How long have you known the identity of this—this criminal Jackie

Black? Just because these papers are now in our possession doesn't mean we can brush away his existence on my ship for a year. We have a duty to perform. *Where is he?*"

The doctor allowed himself only the faintest of grins. "As to how long I've known...well. I've suspected for some time, really, that our Kathy wasn't quite as feminine as she'd like to have us all think. I—"

Dick Roland, still in a semi-state of shock, blurted, "But...but...Kathy...I thought she was so womanly. So..." he reddened again.

The Doctr cleared his throat. "As a matter of fact, my first clue was based on that very fact. In one of my old books I ran into the slang word, *falsies* and—"

"The kert with all that," Gurloff blurted. "Where is this criminal? Our duty is still to apprehend him."

The Doc said, "I'm afraid that 'Kathy' was the first man off the ship, Mike. Must have been ten minutes ago. Seems to me I saw him leave by way of the torpedo hatch."

Gurloff was weakening, but he grumbled, "Just because he turned these papers over to you doesn't give him the right to escape the punishment that—"

Doc said patiently, "Good grief, Mike, how sadistic are you? After what that poor man's been through the last twelve months with this ship full of Romeo's, you want to punish him *further*."

For an instant there was silence; then Mart Bakr grinned ruefully. "I guess you got a point there, Doc."

Halftripper

Mars was strewn with the human wrecks of halftrippers—terrorized cowards of space travel. But perhaps the saddest, and the most fearful of all was the immortal spacebum called Micheal.

THIS SECTION of New Sante Fe was off my beaten trade I've been on Mars a long time and am more than usually familiar with the various centers where we Terrans do our congregating. However, it'd been years since I'd come through here.

I was sitting in an obscure tavern, called, with commendable restraint, simply Sam's Bar, lapping up Martian brandy and facing the prospect of returning to the spaceport in a few hours with no particular enthusiasm.

I only half-noticed the old man who got up on the stool next to me. Sam came over and asked him what he'd have.

The oldster carefully counted out some coins on the bar and said, "Wine, Sam; a glass of Martian wine."

"You know I don't want your money, Joseph," Sam told him.

The old man answered reproachfully, "The wine would taste that much the less, my friend, if I had not earned it by the sweat of my…"

"Okay," Sam sighed. He poured the wine and rang up the money and went off to wait on someone else.

A halftripper sidled up to me. "How about a drink, spaceman?" he whined. "I'm a graduate of the academy myself, class of '72." He must have noted my United Space Lines uniform.

"Sorry," I said gruffly, keeping my back to him. Any spaceman can tell you that if you talk to a halftripper for long you'll soon be showing symptoms of space cafard yourself. The underlying terror in him; the mind shattering fear of space; the way he stares at you, thinking that you can go home, while he is afraid to risk the trip. There are few of them that can hide their disease.

"I need a shot bad," he whispered urgently. He probably did, too. Few halftrippers are able to secure jobs on the planets of their exile. Most of them become beachcombers of space. Of course, there are some exceptions, especially if they have money and connections.

I shuddered. "Beat it," I grated, hating myself and him.

The fear of space cafard must be somewhat similar to that of seasickness every new sailor had back in ancient days when man sailed the oceans of Terra. He never knew until he made his first voyage if he was going to be susceptible; and, if he turned out to be, it meant the sea wasn't for him.

OF COURSE, space cafard goes tragically further. A new man usually succumbs his first few hours in space, if he is going to get it at all. He probably makes it to the next planet, sometimes not; sometimes he goes incurably mad, right off the bat. But even if he does make it, wild horses could never get him on another rocketship. He becomes a halftripper, marooned on an alien world. Usually, although I have known of several exceptions, if you don't get it on your first trip, it seldom bothers you; you're immune for the rest of your life.

He repeated, "How about it, spaceman?"

Sam began to approach threateningly. He couldn't afford to have halftrippers hang out in his place. For one thing, the shipping lines would soon declare him out of bounds for their crews. You just can't let good men come in contact with obvious victims of space cafard.

The old-timer Sam had called Joseph was distressed. "You know not what you say," he told me gently.

I managed a sneer. "Am I supposed to buy a drink for every spacebum that comes along?"

The halftripper's eyes lit up and he came closer to the old man. "How about it, pop? Could you loan me the price of a nip of woji?"

Joseph's face was compassionate, "I am sorry, brother, I myself have nothing, but I commend you to the generosity of the tavern keeper."

I snorted at that. I could imagine how much generosity the space leper would get from the bartender.

That's where the surprise came. Sam sighed, "Okay, halftripper, what'll it be?"

The spacebum ordered a double woji, got it down quickly, as though he was afraid Sam might change his mind, and then beat it to find a place to have his dreams when the full force of the also-narcotic drink hit him.

I finished my brandy, ordered another, and grinned wryly at the old-timer. "You give me kert for telling him to beat it, but you give Sam the high sign to let him have woji with which to rot out his brains. I'd think I was being the kinder of the two of us…"

"Each man's salvation is within himself," Joseph said softly. "You won't redeem him by attempting to keep him from his weaknesses."

"You talk like a saint but I notice you're sitting here at a bar."

He looked at me penetratingly, and there was vast emptiness behind his eyes. "There is little to enjoy in life," he said softly, "but I have had ample time to investigate all of the supposed pleasures. At one time I drank greatly and kept myself in a state of continual intoxication for a period longer than you could believe. Then I went through a state when I let nothing pass my lips but water. Now I see the mistake of both extremes and can enjoy an occasional glass without feeling the need of swilling it down until intoxication dulls me."

He had me interested now. I said, "You sound as though you've found the way in which to get the greatest satisfaction from everything in life but I notice that you don't appear particularly happy."

He was silent for a long time. Finally he sighed and answered, "Happiness is not to be found in wine, nor in food, nor in beautiful women, nor even in wealth and power. It is from within, what you have done, what you are in the eyes of your fellow man."

He looked as though he was about to say more, but he fell silent, his eyes on something far away, although he seemed to be looking directly into my face. Then a light returned to them and he came back to our conversation. "I am sorry," he said. "For a moment you reminded me of someone I knew long and long ago. But now I must be on my way." He left his drink half-finished on the bar and walked wearily to the door.

Sam took his glass away and wiped the bar reflectively. "Whenever he's here, I can't turn down any halftrippers or other spacebums," he complained. "I tried it once, and the old boy looked so pathetic that I damn near cried myself."

"He seems to be quite a character," I said, only half-interested.

"Sure," Sam said. "Haven't you heard about Joseph? He's immortal."

"What?" I said, startled.

"IMMORTAL. You know, he lives forever." He poured me another brandy and leaned on the bar. His other customers had left and he was obviously in the mood for talking.

"I thought everybody knew about Joseph," he went on. "He was one of the first spacebarons, a real bigshot, controlled the whole of Calypso; him and his brother. They not only personally owned all of the satellite, but even all of the space lines that served it. When it came to law there, he was judge, jury, and owner of the courthouse and jail. Brother, that was one monopoly."

"You mean that old man that was just here?" I said in amazement.

"That's right. Joseph, we call him now. He probably had a longer name then. It was a long time ago.

"Anyway, to get back to the story, one day a space liner radios in that it wants to make an emergency landing on Calypso for medical assistance. They had some virulent disease on board and the passengers and crew were dying like flies.

"Well, this brother of Joseph, Micheal, or something like that his name was, advises Joseph not to give them permission to land. The captain of the liner pleads with him, but Joseph tells him to move on, he doesn't want to take any chances. The ship tried to make the next port, I forget just what it was, but, anyway, to cut it short, they all died. That's what started things churning in Joseph's bailiwick; a full-scale revolution, no less."

"You missed something there," I said. "The people wouldn't have been expected to be so upset. After all, no matter how mistaken, he must have thought he was acting in the interests of everyone on Calypso."

"Yeah," Sam pointed out, "but the thing is that among the passengers was Joseph's own boy, the most popular person on the satellite and the apple of his old man's eye. Nobody had known it, but the kid was playing hookey from his school on Terra and was making a cruise of the Jupiter moons.

"Joseph himself had never been very popular with his people, neither had this younger brother of his, Micheal. Too strict, see. But everybody liked the boy and was looking forward to the day when he'd take over the reins of government. When it came out what happened, they went berserk. They cornered Joseph and Micheal and a dozen or so of their close associates in the palace, which was actually more of a fortress than anything else."

Sam wiped the bar again without need, and said reflectively, "It must've been quite a fight. Not that Joseph himself participated. The boy had been his whole life, and he just moved around like he was in a trance.

"They threw everything at that palace. Every weapon, every device that had been thought up for centuries; but it didn't crack. Finally, the fight was ended by a fleet of cattle cruisers from Terra. Joseph and Micheal and the rest were removed and brought here to Mars. None of them dared to remain on Calypso."

I poured myself another brandy from the bottle that Sam had left on the bar. "You make quite a story of it," I told him, "but you didn't tell me what you'd started to about the immortality."

"Yeah," he said, "that's right. Well, it seems that in the atomic bombardment of the palace something happened that wound up with Joseph and his friends all immortal. Don't ask me what; I don't know and neither did these scientist guys when they tried to figure it out. Of course, it didn't become known for years; not until it became obvious they weren't dying, or even aging. They continued to appear as they had at the time of the fight. I don't mean they couldn't die at all; one by one they dropped away. Two were lost in space; one was blown up in an explosion on Terra; another was burned to death; but the only way they could die was through accident—or suicide. After a few hundred years they were all gone but Joseph, and, of course, he'd gone batty."

I interrupted. "You mean he's insane?"

The bartender grinned. "Crazy as a makron."

I said slowly, "He seemed normal enough to me. Uh…perhaps a bit eccentric."

Sam said, "Brother, he's as far around the corner as you can get. You know what he thinks? He thinks that he's wandering through space, going from planet to planet, trying to find a situation similar to that in which he sent away the person he loved most to his death. He thinks that if he ever finds that similar situation, he'll be able to make the opposite decision from the one he made before and that will redeem him."

I FROWNED. "Where does he get the money for his wandering around the planets?"

"He don't need no money. He's good luck. There's not a captain in the system that would refuse free passage to old Joseph." Sam shrugged his beefy shoulders. "And who am I to say otherwise? That's why I give the bums free drinks when he's around; so does every other bartender."

Two customers had entered and Sam made his way down to them, leaving me alone.

A half tripper scurried through the door and cringed up to me. He whimpered, "How about a drink, spaceman? I…"

I flipped him a coin, "Sure, buddy," I said, repressing my usual nausea at the sight of him. I got down from my stool and made my way out. It was time for me to return to the spaceport and my job.

I suppose that I forgot to tell the cabbie to take me to the administration building entrance—the first time I'd made that mistake in years. I was preoccupied with thoughts of Joseph and the story Sam had told of him. The guards at the main gate must have let us through without question when they saw my United Space Lines uniform. At any rate, when I looked up, it was too late. Not only was I on the landing field and in full view of the concrete take-off aprons, but one gigantic freighter was in the process of blasting off.

All the horror of it flowed over me with a rush. The careful training of years; the work of the doctors who had treated me; all my own self-discipline—were gone. I shook with terrified frenzy. The depths of space! The free fall! The black emptiness! The utter, uncontrollable terror!

I screamed shrilly and the cabbie turned, wide-eyed, to stare at me.

He knew the symptoms. "Space cafard! A halftripper!" he gasped, and spun the cab about to get me to a hospital. He must have realized then that my uniform didn't neces-sarily mean that I worked on the liners themselves, but that I could be an office employee who only on rare occasions went near the ships.

He knew too, that the very sight of a spacecraft blasting off was enough to put me in bed for a week; and that I was uncommonly lucky to have the funds for the hospitalization. Mars was strewn with the human wrecks of halftrippers who hadn't.

As we whirled from the yard, we passed the bent figure of Joseph walking unhurriedly toward a liner which was loading for the Venus run.

My heart cried out, even through my terror, my sickness:

Joseph, Joseph... So you too are still alive; and still seeking forgiveness. I had thought I was the last.

But you are by far the better off of we two, Joseph. For at least you have been free to wander while I have stayed on this one hated spot since all those centuries ago when we fled from Calypso and the wrath of the people who had loved the boy so. As though we hadn't loved him ourselves, Joseph.

Yes, you are the better off, you can seek throughout the stars for forgiveness. Then, too, your mind is forever dulled with your madness, while mine is horribly aware, always, of what we've been through and of the centuries ahead; it is only blurred when the space cafard comes.

Joseph, Joseph... You didn't even recognize your brother Micheal, nor I you, when we met.

Ask Me No Questions!

They knew that the Martians were in the drug business on Earth. They wanted to know why—and strangely, so did the Martians!

THEY'D chosen me to interrogate our Martian prisoner, not because I'd had any more experience than the others, but largely due to my research in 20th Century novels and films. Then too, I suppose, my scorn of cosmetic surgery might have had something to do with it. I've never even had my beard permanently removed and for this occasion I had let it grow several days so that my face would look as brutal as possible.

I'd rehearsed for hours, running over again motion picture films of the mid-20th Century. I had my props at hand and thought I was as ready as I'd ever be.

After the kidnapping—the first such crime in more than two and a half centuries—they'd brought him immediately to the small suburban underground house which we'd used for our base for the past six months. It was a comfortable enough establishment, typical of the neighborhood, but we'd altered one room in preparation for him; barren except for a small table and a battered chair to which he was tied, it looked as much like the den of a gang of thieves as we could make it.

He was allowed to remain there, bound and gagged, and—we were hoping—terrified, for several hours. Then I entered.

I had a cigarette dangling from the side of my mouth. I let the smoke spiral upward from it, and refrained from puffing. For one thing, that's the way they did in the films; for another, I was afraid it would make me deathly ill. Tobacco is used only in some of the most isolated spots of Terra, and only by those who are as yet unacquainted with *dwarr*, or Martian Poppy as it is usually called.

I sat on the edge of the table and looked at him, cold faced, emotionless; trying to appear vicious. Finally, I took the cigarette from my lips and ground out the burning tip in the palm of my left hand. Doctr Gardnr, one of our group, had prepared the palm earlier with resin, but, of course, the Martian didn't know that. His antenna twitched as he saw me extinguish the stub on what seemed bare flesh.

Still not taking my eyes from his face, I reached my hand into my jacket under my left arm and brought forth the revolver. I'd been practicing handling the horrible thing for several days, but I was still clumsy at it; however, it was unlikely that he'd know the difference.

I reached over and pulled the gag from his tiny mouth and stuck the muzzle of the revolver to within inches of his face.

"Know what this is?" I growled.

He shook his head in negation.

THAT WAS something to be thankful for. He'd been kidnapped at random; at least we'd picked one that knew Amer-English even well enough to be familiar with our gestures.

"No," he said, his tone wistful, as is always the case with Martians; invariably they look and speak as though they'd just received news of their mother's death.

"It's a gat," I told him, trying to work an element of the sinister into my voice, "a rod."

His antenna flinched, and his melancholy eyes went a deeper green. "You mean ith a weapon?" he lisped unbelievingly.

I waved the muzzle near his face. "That's right, pal," I said from the side of my mouth. "Pretty hard to come by now, but just as lethal as ever." I gestured with it. "Now this just happens to be a .358 Magnum; one of the deadliest hand-guns the ancients made; great favorite with the boys back in the old days. I picked it up in a museum. Watch!"

I leveled it at the far wall, turning my back to him so he wouldn't be able to see me close my eyes, and pulled the trigger.

In reconstructing the ancient weapon from diagrams in publications of the time, we'd had to make various improvisations. For one thing, we hadn't been able to decide whether or not the pellets, or bullets, the things threw exploded upon contact. We decided they did but that it would be a mistake for us, perhaps an injurious one, to try and copy that feature. Instead, Franz Mect, one of the engineers of our group, volunteered to conceal a small explosive in the wall of the chamber in which we were going to question our prisoner. In this manner, we planned to simulate the effect of the gun, rather than go through the actual experience.

At any rate, the results were gratifying. The revolver jumped in my hand and made a slight noise; Franz, stationed at a peephole, ignited the explosive in the wall; the wall exploded and when the dust cleared there was a hole large enough for a man to walk through.

I turned back to the Martian and nonchalantly returned the revolver to the holster under my arm.

"We mean business, pal," I grunted at him. "Now then, are you going to talk, or do I have to go to work on you?"

"I'm thor I don't know what you mean," he lisped, obviously shaken, but still defiant.

I laughed hoarsely, sneeringly. "Why do you Martians sell *dwarr* here on Terra?"

A deeper fear showed in the wilting of his antenna, and his eyes went green as emerald.

THE VARIOUS Terran governments had already established two or three Space Stations, revolving around our planet at varying distances and had sent several expeditions to Luna at the time of the arrival of the first Martian spacecraft. Had the Martians waited even another two or three years, we would have visited them first, although it's unlikely it would have made much difference.

From the first, intercourse between the two planets was on the friendliest plane. The Martians, somewhat smaller and more delicate than the Terrans in appearance, were approximately equal intellectually; the slightly higher I. Q. enjoyed by the humans being offset by the antiquity of the Martian civilization.

They had been receiving our radio emanations for generations and had painstakingly managed to decipher our means of communication to the point that even their first explorers to land among us were able to speak not one, but several of our languages. That, of course, was before Amer-English had become universal on Terra.

During the first decades of our relationship with the sad eyed, lisping life forms from Mars, we earthlings had profited greatly as a result of their suggestions and assistance in various fields. World government was established, for one thing, and a stable socio-economic system. Various fundamental diseases were wiped out and earth entered a new era of health and prosperity.

Trade between the two planets consisted principally in exchange of techniques, although there was considerable interest in each other's art forms. In fact, the dream art of Mars became exceedingly popular overnight on Terra, and the Martians became quite intrigued with Terran music, especially the more primitive types such as Calypso.

Conflict between the Martians and ourselves was unthought of, especially after the first half century of relations with them. War on Mars itself had been eliminated so many millenniums before that even the historic accounts of their conflicts were lost in antiquity, confused with legend; and with the establishment of the World Government, it became impossible on our own planet. Weapons soon became as illegal and unknown on Terra as they had been for centuries on Mars.

Seemingly, we were set for an indefinite period of peace and friendly relations with the only other planet in the Solar System, which supported intelligent life.

Perhaps that last is misleading. According to the Martians, there was life on Venus, but it was hostile, backward, and living conditions on the planet so impractical for either Terran or Martian, that after one or two half-hearted attempts, we gave up our efforts to communicate with them. Perhaps, we reasoned, in a few thousand years they would have developed on their own to the point where they could take their place with Mars and Earth in a three way relationship as satisfactory as that between the two of us.

It is unknown, exactly, when the Terran use of *dwarr* first began. Introduced on a small scale in the beginning, its use grew only infinitesimally. It was decades before its spread had reached the point where it was investigated—discreetly, of course, since its source was Mars and we had no wish to cast aspersions on our friendly neighbors in the sky.

IT WASN'T a narcotic; not in the ordinary sense of the word. The use of narcotics on Terra had disappeared except for medicinal reasons, long years before. But *dwarr* did have a good many of the effects of the opium poppy of long ago.

It wasn't habit forming, there was no known case of a person becoming addicted, but it did lead to a dream world that was utterly desirable. In the early stages of its use—it was usually taken in beverage form—it wasn't much more effective than tea, or coffee, those mild narcotics of yesteryear. It gave a slight *lift*. As the user continued to indulge, however, the effect became stronger and after a period of years the use of *dwarr* led to a dream world beyond anything accomplished with opium or even hashish.

Dwarr had the ability to select each person's most inner desires and give him realization of them. Were you a would-be poet, your *dwarr* inspired dreams had you writing sonnets that put Shakespeare and Spencer to shame; were you a scientist, *dwarr* had you conquering the problems of the universe. Were you a lover, *dwarr* gave you hours far more beautiful than Mohammed had ever conceived in his paradise for the faithful.

There seemed to be no physical or mental after effects to condemn the Martian Poppy. A *dwarr* drinker could be taken from its use for any period and never feel the worse for it, except, of course, a desire to enjoy its pleasures again as soon as it was possible.

The most thorough investigation showed no injurious effects as a result of the beverage's use, and the government dropped its probe of what some had feared a dangerous narcotic.

Fifty years later, half the population of Terra used *dwarr* and another investigation into its nature took place. There were still no signs that either mental or physical damage was done by its continual use, and eventually the second government investigation was dropped as had been the first.

Our friendly relations with Mars continued; we exchanged scientific developments, we traded our art objects. And they sent us *dwarr* in return for titanium, which was evidently almost unknown on their planet. Several attempts were made to grow the Martian Poppy in Terran soil, but they were unsuccessful; its use continued to depend upon our Martian friends.

The final government investigation into the use of *dwarr* was made approximately one hundred years ago, and was less successful even than previously. Perhaps this was due to the fact that for all practical purposes *all* Terra was now using the beverage. Even those who investigated its use were enamored of it; and the bare news that such an investigation was taking place had been enough to bring waves of protest from all earth. The probe was dropped.

Scientific development lagged, art came to a standstill, ambition was a thing long dead; but the use of *dwarr* continued, increased, expanded.

We were the only ones, our little secret society consisting of perhaps twenty persons in all—what in yesteryear might have been called an underground—who fought the Martian Poppy. Convinced that some sinister purpose was behind its distribution to earthlings, we conducted our study of *dwarr* quietly, determinedly. This kidnapping and interrogation of the Martian trader was the culmination, thus far, of our efforts. From him we must wrest crucial answers, if the fight was to continue.

"I'M THOR I don't know what you mean," the little Martian lisped. I rasped out a laugh, then sneered down at him. I took from a pocket a small clasp knife, another relic from the museums, pressed a button on its side and let the blade flick out only a fraction of an inch from his throat.

"Maybe you need some persuasion," I growled, wondering if I sounded authentic, and wondering how Doctr Gardnr and the rest who I knew were peering through peepholes in the door and walls, were taking it.

The very thought of imposing physical violence upon another, turned my stomach slightly, but I must never let him know this. Everything depended upon his believing his life was in danger.

I let the light flicker on the knife blade. "You're going to talk, Martian," I told him coldly, "or you're going to go through something you never knew still took place here on Terra; something our government's kept secret from you." I laughed bitterly. "Probably ashamed of it."

His antenna twitched and his eyes went from aquamarine to emerald in apprehension. "You...mean...torthur?" he lisped, shocked.

I whetted the blade on the palm of my hand. "Torture is right, pal." I put the point to the base of his thin neck. "Now talk, or else," I grated.

I have never seen such living fear as that reflected in every facial expression, in every twitching movement of the thin framed, wistful appearing little Martian. I was afraid for a moment that his mind would crack under the pressure, and told myself I should have known better than to have gone so far.

There has been no war, no crime, no physical violence on earth for at least two centuries. From earliest childhood, in our schools, in our homes, our books, our means of entertainment, we are taught to abhor violence. But while it has been so on Terra for two centuries, it has been so on Mars for at least twenty.

It was the very shock effect that we were depending upon.

His sad face was rigid with alarm, and his voice tight—it undoubtedly would have been shrill were Martians capable of inflection. I let the blade touch his throat, gently.

"Yeth, *Yeth!*" he lisped. "I'll tell you whatever you wisth to know."

Victory!

I leaned back and considered him, as though I was sorry he hadn't given me the opportunity to work on him with the knife. "Okay, pal," I growled, "Wait'll I call in some of the other boys."

I went to the door and stuck my head out into the hallway. Doctr Garnr was there and Franz Mect and two or three of the others. The rest were about the house or scattered around the neighborhood on watch to warn us in case of emergency. The penalty, if our crime was detected, would be sur-amnesia, the equivalent of death, although, of course, our bodies would continue to live supplied with a new personality to replace that which society had rejected as injurious to the majority.

The others came in and stared as coldly as possible down on the little Martian trader, seated there in his bonds. They attempted to carry on the atmosphere I'd created, but modern cosmetic surgery makes it difficult for a person who has chosen to be made godlike in appearance to look sinister.

I jerked my thumb at the Martian. "He'll talk," I rasped, returning the knife to my pocket. I brought out the revolver again and trained it on his chest.

Doctr Garnr began softly, "In the past, here on Terra, we put our souls, our desires, into many things; into ambition, into investigation of the mysteries of science, into the arts, into love, into good food and good drink, and into a myriad of other things that made life worth the living.

"But what do we have *now?*—Why should we value the work of a master chef when we can eat garbage and afterward take *dwarr* and feast on the food of the gods? Why should we love a beautiful woman when *dwarr* will give us a beauty a thousand times greater. Why should we attempt any ambition, when your Martian Poppy concedes us any desire, any pleasure?"

THE MARTIAN sat, a picture of pathos, his eyes still shining green with fear and his eyes going from the doctor to my revolver and back again.

"Why do you sell *dwarr* to Terrans?" the doctor snapped.

The Martian lisped in fright, "For the titanium we get in exchange for it."

I sneered.

The doctor said softly, "You underestimate us, my friend. We happen to have spent years in this investigation and know titanium is used practically not at all in your industries. You have no need for it, at least not at all in the quantities we have to send you in order to supply Terra with *dwarr.*"

I tightened my finger on the trigger and his antenna flinched.

The doctor held up a hand as though to restrain me momentarily. "We also happen to know," he said, "that the use of *dwarr* is unknown on Mars. You know its effect, you know what it has done to us; and *you don't use it yourselves.* Why, *why, why!* do you Martians sell *dwarr* to earth. Are you attempting to weaken us so that you may take over our planet and possibly colonize it with your own race?"

There was a touch of scorn in the melancholy face of the Martian. He lisped, "We have no desire for your humid and heavily gravitized planet. We who trade here can hardly wait to return to our home world."

"Then why do you sell us *dwarr?*" Franz Meet cut in. "Is it because your own civilization is on the downgrade, and you're jealous of our potential growth to new heights?"

There was contempt in the other's lisping answer. "Our thivilization ith on the decline no more than ith yourth." The green hue of his eyes had lessened, a sign that he was losing his fear of us, becoming defiant.

I growled at him, "The decline on Terra is caused by the Martian Poppy. Why do you sell it to us?"

"We thell you *dwarr* to thecure the titanium," he lisped sadly. "It ith the only thing we theme to have in quantity that you of earth dethire."

Franz Meet snorted, "But you don't use titanium to any extent. What do you do with it?"

The little Martian was silent. His antenna pointed forward slightly, a sign he was being stubborn. Obviously, he'd reached the point where he wanted to go no further.

Doctr Gardnr sensed that we'd touched on the crucial point. "What do you do with the titanium we give you for your *dwarr*?" he said urgently.

AFTER a long moment of silence from the alien trader, I sneered. "You boys better leave again. I'll do a little work on him." I put my hand into my pocket for the penknife. "He cheated me before," I said, licking my lips nervously, "started talking before I even touched him." I pressed the button and the blade flicked out wickedly.

The desperate little Martian's eyes went verdure in color and his antenna sagged in fear, "Thith ith illegal," he lisped rapidly, "don't let him do thith to me."

"Talk," I barked.

The others turned to go. I noted from the side of my eyes that even Franz, who'd known me all my life was staring at me with an edge of uncomfortableness. They hurried for the door as though to be out of the way before I started the actual horror of physical violence.

"Yeth!" the Martian yelped suddenly, "Yeth, I'll tell you!"

Doctr Gardnr turned and said softly, "What do you do with the titanium?"

The Martian drooped, "We thell it to the Venuthians," he lisped sadly. We stood silent for a long moment in incredulity.

Finally Franz Mect cleared his throat and said, "But what do you get from the Venusians for the titanium?"

The frail Martian straightened to the extent possible within his bonds, into his wistful face came a gleam as though of inspiration brought on by something greater, something more important than any of us.

He lisped proudly, "They thell us *maridee. Maridee*, do you hear? Now do you know why no Martian ever uthuth *dwarr*? Now do you know?" His green eyes blazed fanatically, "Who would ever uth *dwarr* wonth he had tathted the playthurths of *MARIDEE!*"

After long minutes, someone said, unbelievingly, "But the Venusians haven't an economy advanced enough to use titanium. What do they do with it?"

The fire had left the little Martian's eyes. He slumped back into his chair again, his face showing puzzlement. "We've often wondered," he lisped sadly.

D. P. from Tomorrow

The little man was very sincere, very... But then, so many of these guys are!

THE PHONE rang and Ed Kerry picked it up and said, "*Daily Star.*"

He listened for a moment and said, "Yeah," and then, "Hold on a minute." He stuck a hand over the mouthpiece and said to the city room at large, "It's one of these drunks settling some bet. He wants to know when Lord Byron died."

Sam, over on the rewrite desk, said, "He died on April 19th, 1824."

Kerry said into the phone, "He died April 19th, 1824," and hung up.

Jake, the city editor, had been leaning back in his swivel chair, his feet up on the desk. He said to Sam, "How do you know?"

Sam shrugged and said, "Just happened to."

Jake said idly, "Offhand, I can't think of any information that makes less difference than when Byron died."

Ed Kerry said, "It's the queerest thing in this business. Some jerk phones in and wants to know what caliber gun it was that killed Lincoln, or maybe how many molecules there are in a drop of water. And what happens? Somebody in the city room always knows the answer. It's the same on every paper I ever worked for."

Jake growled, "You can't tell them to go get lost. These characters that phone into newspapers at the drop of a hat might stumble on the biggest story of the year ten minutes later. You don't want them phoning some other paper because they're sore at you for not telling them who got in the first punch in the Dempsey-Firpo fight."

Kerry said, "Yeah, but what gets me is that when these jerks ask their screwy questions, somehow or other they always get the right answer."

Somebody on rewrite said, "I remember once some drunk phoned in about four o'clock in the morning and wanted to know how tall Jumbo, Barnum's elephant, used to be. The guy who was working next to me says, 'Eleven feet, six inches,' without even looking up from the story he was on."

Jake said, "It's because on a newspaper you got a whole room full of guys with a lot of general knowledge. Remember back in the 1940's or 1950's or whenever it was, they had this 'Information Please' program on the television?"

Sam said, "It was radio back then."

Jake growled, "What difference does it make? Anyway, these guys knew all the answers and there were only maybe three or four of them, mostly newspapermen. In a city room you've got a dozen or more men who've read so much that it starts…"

The phone rang again and, since nobody else stirred, Ed Kerry sighed and picked it up again. He said, "Yeah?" He repeated that a few more times and then, "Hold it, Ted. I'll ask Jake."

He looked over at Jake and said, "It's Ted Ruhling. He's over at Leo's…"

"This is Ted's night off," Jake grunted.

"…He says he's got a refugee over there with a story," Ed Kerry finished. The phone was still squeaking and he put the receiver back to his ear.

"A refugee, yet," Jake snorted. "What's Ted got in mind? He must be sober; when he's drunk he's got more story sense. We've had so many Martian refugee stories…"

"This isn't a Martian," Kerry said. "It's a guy claims he's from another space-time continuum."

Somebody on rewrite said, "That does it. Now I've heard it all."

Jake began to say, "Tell Ted Ruhling to have himself a few more drinks and forget about... No, hold it. Tell him to bring the guy over here and we'll get the story. Maybe it'll be good for a humorous piece; besides, there's nothing going on anyway, we'll get some laughs."

Ed Kerry said into the phone, "It sounds like a real story, Ted. Jake says to rush the guy over here." He hung up.

Sam, over on rewrite, scratched himself reflectively. "I've seen a lot of stories in my thirty years in this racket, and I've seen a lot of stories about refugees. Refugees from Asia, refugees from Europe, refugees from South America and from Texas; even refugees from Luna and Mars. "But I'll be a *makron* if I ever heard of a refugee from another space-time continuum."

Kitty Kildare bustled from her tiny office and hurried breathlessly toward Jake's desk.

Ed Kerry said softly, "Kitty looks like she's got another world beater. Tear down the front page, Jake."

Kitty gushed, "Jake, I really have something for tomorrow's column. Actually, I mean. Jake, this..."

Jake held up a weary hand to stem the tide. "Kitty," he said, "listen. That column is yours; you can put anything in it you want. It's none of my business. For some reason or other, people even read it. Don't ask me why."

Kitty Kildare simpered, "Now, Jake, you're always pulling my leg."

Jake shuddered.

Kitty went on, "But you'll see tomorrow. Actually, I mean." She bustled out of the city room and off to whatever story she had found to cover for her column.

Ed Kerry said wonderingly, "Kitty can get breathless over any story hotter than a basketball score."

Jake said, "What's another space-time continuum? Seems to me I read about it somewhere, or..."

Sam laughed. "Now we know Jake's secret vice. He hides in his room, locks the door, and reads science fiction."

The city editor scowled, "I don't get it."

Sam said, "Another space-time continuum is one of the favorite standbys of these science-fiction writers. You know. The general idea is that there are other, well, call them universes, existing side by side with ours. We aren't the only space-time continuum; we're only one of them."

"One theory is that there are an infinite number of continuums," Ed Kerry put in. "That means that somewhere everything is happening, has happened, and will happen."

Jake growled, "Shut up, Ed. Sam's explanation was getting bad enough, but..."

Sam said, "No, Ed's right. According to one theory, there are an infinite number of alternative universes, some of them almost identical to this one. For instance, in an infinite number of universes, Hitler won the Second World War. In an infinite number of others, Hitler was never born. In still others, he spent his whole life as a paperhanger."

"Wait a minute, now," Jake said. "You mean to tell me that somewhere, in some other space-time whatever-y'call-it..."

"Continuum," Ed Kerry supplied.

"All right. Anyway, everything possible has happened, will happen, and is happening? *Everything*, no matter how unlikely?"

"That's the theory," Sam told him. "Consider, for instance, how improbable this space-time continuum in which we live really is."

Jake snorted, "Holy Wodo. Ted Ruhling has brought in some screwy stories in his time, but a refugee from..."

"Here he comes," somebody whispered.

"Okay, boys," Jake said softly. "The works. Somebody tell Jim to bring his camera."

Ted Ruhling wavered unsteadily toward the city desk, ushering along a little, wistful-looking character dressed in clothes that looked oddly out of style. The stranger's hair was going grey and his small face was much lined; he looked to be about forty.

Ruhling blinked at Jake and said, with considerable dignity, "This story is beyond the call of duty, y'realize, Jake. Oughta getta bonus. Wanta introduce Martin Cantine; refugee from another space-time continuum. Met him by accident in Leo's Bar." He slumped into a chair as though the effort of the introduction had exhausted him.

Jake got up and held out a hand to the little man, "Welcome to...uh, that is, welcome to our universe, Mr. Cantine."

Ed Kerry and Jim the photographer and several others crowded up with, notebook and camera.

"Mr. Cantine," Kerry said excitedly, "what do you think of our space-time continuum's girls?"

"Shut up, Ed," Jake said from the side of his mouth.

But the little fellow answered seriously. "The same as I think of those in my own, of course."

Kerry said, as though disappointed, "You mean there's no difference?"

Martin Cantine found himself a chair, sat down, and said, earnestly, "I see that there must be some misunderstanding here. You gentlemen must realize that the continuum from which I fled was almost exactly like this one. Almost exactly. I note, for instance, that this city has identical buildings and in other ways is precisely like my own, except, of course, for the time element."

"Oh, oh," Sam said. "Here we go. The time element."

"What's different about the time element?" Jake asked cautiously.

The little fellow frowned worriedly. "I hope I can explain it to you. You see, the device which was constructed by my friends to enable us to flee our own period was designed to remove a living person from one space-time continuum and to place him in another. But it must be realized that in transporting ourselves to another *space* we at the same time, of necessity, transport ourselves also to another *time*. In all, we transport ourselves from another space, another time, and another space-time continuum. Actually, of course, the three are really one. Is that clear?"

"No," Ed Kerry said.

"Shut up, Ed," Jake growled. "Go on, Mr. Cantine."

Mr. Cantine was pleased that at least one person was following him.

"Our device was set to remove me only slightly in *space*, and, consequently, only slightly in *time*. If I am correct, my time was about ten years after yours."

Jake closed his eyes for a long moment. Finally he opened them again and said, "Let's have that last again."

"In my space-time continuum," the little man said, "I lived about ten years in your future. In other words, in 2030."

"I get it," Sam said. "Ten years from now our space-time continuum will be like yours when you left—in most respects; that is. What you did was travel backward in time for ten years and to a slightly different continuum."

Ted Ruhling had managed to stay awake thus far. But now that he saw everything was under control he muttered, "Bonus," and slumped forward on the desk at which he was sitting.

Jake looked at him and grunted bitterly.

Ed Kerry said, "Well, let's get the rest of the story. Why did you leave home and come to our fair continuum?"

Martine Cantine frowned. "I thought you realized that I was a refugee. Didn't Mr. Ruhling explain on the phone?"

"Of course," Jake told him. "Now just what were you a refugee from, Mr. Cantine?"

The little man took a deep, dramatic breath. "From Gerald Twombly, the most vicious despot the world has ever seen!"

Ed Kerry choked on that. "Twombly!" he said, trying to hold his laughter. He swallowed hard, then said, very seriously, "How do you spell that?"

"Gerald Twombly, T-W-O-M-B-L-Y," Martin Cantine told him. "And now that you have been warned, you'll be able to defend yourself against this scourge."

"I missed something there," Jake said.

The little refugee explained, "As I pointed out, this continuum is almost exactly like mine. The principal difference is that you are ten years earlier in time; Gerald Twombly is not as yet in power. You have time to fight him, expose his nefarious schemes."

"Twombly," Ed Kerry said, "I *love* that name. Hitler, Mussolini, Caesar, Napoleon—none of them quite have the ring of Twombly."

Jake looked up at the clock on the wall. They were going to have to start work on the bulldog edition. Besides, he was getting tired of this nut. He nodded his head to Bunny Davis, down at the other end of the room, and she surreptitiously took up a phone and called the city hospital.

Ed Kerry was asking, "Just what form will this despotism take?"

Martin Cantine leaned forward earnestly. "The most vicious and bloody the world has ever known. People have forgotten, it has been so long since dictatorship has existed, how ruthless persons in power can become to maintain themselves. We've also forgotten that many of the devices that have been invented in the past one hundred years can be turned to horrible use by a police state. Truth serums, for instance, used ordinarily for psychiatry, but a terrible weapon in the hands of a secret police. Cybernetic-controlled wire and radio tapping devices that can listen to every conversation that takes place over instruments throughout the whole planet and immediately flash a report whenever anything the slightest degree removed from what is permissible is said. Radar..."

Jake yawned. "And just how did you manage to escape this guy...er, Twombly?"

Cantine frowned. "I am not the inventor of the S-T Invertor, but one of several who have been secretly removed to another continuum to escape Twombly's secret police. I am not exactly clear on the workings of the device."

"Shucks," Ed Kerry said. "I was afraid of that. Tell us what you do know about it." He was beginning to give up the pretense of taking notes.

Martine Cantine looked from one to the other, frowning. He was beginning to suspect the truth of the situation, and a red flush was creeping up his neck.

"I am afraid you gentlemen, think I am exaggerating," he said tensely.

"I wouldn't exactly put it that way," Jake told him, stilling another yawn. "But part of it seems..."

The little man came to his feet, his expression tight. "I see," he said. He took a deep breath, then went on slowly, and very sincerely. "Even though you think me a charlatan, I beseech you, for your own sakes and for this continuum's— investigate this Gerald Twombly. You *must*. Or your space-time continuum will..."

Two white-coated interns came through the door and looked about questionably. Jake motioned to them and they advanced.

Jake said, a touch of unwonted kindliness in his gruff voice, "Here are two friends of yours, Mr. Cantine."

The little man looked about him unbelievingly: "But...but...you think I'm insane. You don't realize..." He shook off the hands of the interns, and spun about desperately to confront the city editor again. He began to shout, "But you must...Gerald Twombly! ...You must...!"

They led him out, struggling.

There was an embarrassed silence in the city room. The gag had not been as amusing as they had expected.

"Well, let's get to work," Jake said. "Kerry, you see if you can do up a stick or so on this Cantine. Gag it up a little, but don't go overboard. Jim, did you get a decent shot of the little guy? Those phony clothes he'd had made up for himself might make a..."

Sam, over on rewrite, said, "You know, the funny thing was that his story made a certain amount of sense."

Jake snorted, "Every nut's story makes a *certain* amount of sense. The only trouble is that, when you check it, it doesn't hold up."

"What'd'ya mean, check it?" Sam said argumentatively. "What part of Cantine's story were you able to check?"

Jake growled, "For one thing, this guy Twombly. What a name for a dictator. Anyway, who ever heard of a Gerald Twombly? Did you Kerry...Jim...Bunny...Sam?"

They shook their heads. So did everyone else in the city room.

Jake shrugged. "Okay. There you are. This character says that in ten years Twombly's dictatorship is going to be so rugged that we'll all be wanting to take a powder out of here to another what'd'ya call it?"

"Space-time continuum," Sam said grudgingly.

"Yeah. Well, none of us have ever heard of him. Remember what I said earlier about all the general knowledge you find on a newspaper's staff? Okay, where's somebody that's even heard of this guy?"

"I guess you're right," Sam admitted. "But he seemed to be kind of a nice little duck."

"The nut factories are full of nice little ducks," Jake grunted. He tossed a story over to the rewrite man. "Here, shut up and get to work or you'll be getting as screwy as he is."

Sam grinned and took up a pencil. "Okay, Jake."

Kitty Kildare hustled into the room, brandishing a sheaf of paper. "Jake," she said breathlessly, "wait until you see my column tomorrow. I'll have them dying, *dying*. Actually, I mean."

Jake shuddered. "Okay, what is it this time?"

She closed her eyes and breathed ecstatically, "A wonderful man; actually, I mean. I have the first interview he's *ever* given. He has a new political system he's advocating."

Ed Kerry said sarcastically, "I'll bet his name's Twombly."

Kitty turned and stared at him. "How in the world did you know?" she said.

If you've enjoyed this book, you will not want to miss these terrific titles…

ARMCHAIR SCI-FI, FANTASY, & HORROR DOUBLE NOVELS, $12.95 each

D-21 **EMPIRE OF EVIL** by Robert Arnette
THE SIGN OF THE TIGER by Alan E. Nourse & J. A. Meyer

D-22 **OPERATION SQUARE PEG** by Frank Belknap Long
ENCHANTRESS OF VENUS by Leigh Brackett

D-23 **THE LIFE WATCH** by Lester Del Rey
CREATURES OF THE ABYSS by Murray Leinster

D-24 **BLACK MAGIC HOLIDAY** by Robert Bloch
STAR HUNTER by Andre Norton

D-25 **EMPIRE OF WOMEN** by John Fletcher
ONE OF OUR CITIES IS MISSING by Irving Cox

D-26 **THE WRONG SIDE OF PARADISE** by Raymond F. Jones
THE INVOLUNTARY IMMORTALS by Rog Phillips

D-27 **THE EARTH QUARTER** by Damon Knight
ENVOY TO NEW WORLDS by Keith Laumer

D-28 **SLAVES TO THE METAL HORDE** by Milton Lesser
HUNTERS OUT OF TIME by Joseph E. Kelleam

D-29 **RX JUPITER SAVE US** by Ward Moore
BEWARE THE USURPERS by Geoff St. Reynard

D-30 **SECRET OF THE SERPENT** by Don Wilcox
CRUSADE ACROSS THE VOID by Dwight V. Swain

ARMCHAIR SCIENCE FICTION CLASSICS, $12.95 each

C-7 **THE SHAVER MYSTERY, pt. 1**
by Richard S. Shaver

C-8 **THE SHAVER MYSTERY, pt. 2**
by Richard S. Shaver

C-9 **MURDER IN SPACE** by David V. Reed
by David V. Reed

ARMCHAIR MASTERS OF SCIENCE FICTION SERIES, $16.95 each

M-3 **MASTERS OF SCIENCE FICTION, Vol. Three**
Robert Sheckley

M-4 **MASTERS OF SCIENCE FICTION, Vol. Four**
Mack Reynolds, part one

www.ingramcontent.com/pod-product-compliance
Lightning Source LLC
Chambersburg PA
CBHW050554260626
47157CB00002B/562